Just Tell Me What You Want

Jay Presson Allen

Just Tell Me What You Want

E. P. DUTTON & CO., INC.   NEW YORK   1975

Published simultaneously in Canada by
Clarke, Irwin & Company Limited, Toronto and Vancouver
ISBN: 0-525-13785-8

Library of Congress Cataloging in Publication Data

Allen, Jay Presson, 1922-
    Just tell me what you want.

I. Title.
PZ4.A4265Ju   [PS3551.L3938]   813'.5'4   75-12508

Just Tell Me What You Want

Chapter 1

The normal working procedure was that his early-morning tapes would be picked up first. Then, when the limousine called for Stella at precisely six a.m., she could ride and listen and take notes on which of Max Herschel's latest commands required her personal attention.

In the limousine with Stella this particular February morning was a girl whom Stella had instructed to listen and to learn.

"Honey," Herschel's voice came confidingly off the tape, "somebody down at Morgan Price is trying to rinky-dink me—and it had better not be Mr. Prentice Tilford Farquhar the Third, or his marker's going to be suddenly overdue. You call Farquhar and remind him that Herschel-FAU is an *insurance* company . . . which means a Ph.D. in fraud. Then you remind him I'm also in the *hotel* business . . . so I know all about manager rake-offs and no hustlers in the lobby. Herschel Industries knows as much about no hustlers in the lobby as Morgan Price knows about no Jews in the Club . . ."

Cathy Kronig listened to the tape as intently as Stella.

". . . You tell Farquhar that, Stella. And tell him to pass it on. Casually, of course. Across a backgammon board. Or however they do it at Morgan Price." The voice chuckled, then continued. "Now, listen, honey. I'm taking the Paulson job out of Switzerland. I see red flags all over the Alps . . . the IRS is schussing right along beside us. So put six million into certificates of deposit in a London branch of a South African bank and . . . no, better make it a little more. Make it seven million. Just for fun . . ."

My God, Cathy thought. It was still dark out and she was riding in his limousine listening to his voice making *fun* with seven million dollars. My *God.*

Cathy's thoughts were frequently addressed to a distant midwestern God whose stronghold of Flatcar, Missouri, she had rashly departed at the age of eighteen. And although Cathy had now been in New York over a year, she had yet to discover God's Manhattan division director.

There was something particularly godless about riding through predawn New York in a big black limousine. Going to Mr. Herschel's house. Going to *his* house in *his* limousine driven by *his* liveried black man. There were many words italicized in Cathy's head, and Stella Liberti could read them all.

She had hired Cathy because of her guileless nature and clean good looks. Cathy Kronig more than met the aesthetic requirements of Herschel Industries, but she was not sexy. Another plus.

Stella, an irreproachable virgin of fifty-five, was as fine a professional judge of female flesh as Iceberg Slim. Her specialty was choosing office girls who were decorative but who would not raise the erotic impulses of her employer above a manageable simmer. Cathy was perfect. No risk bringing Cathy to the house.

As Stella listened to the tape, she watched the girl's eager face. Stella grinned. Cathy looked as if she were about to burst into song. About to sing along with Max.

". . . and get me the new yogurt culture that guy from the UN was talking about. Then get a memo off to whatsisname at

[2]

Consumex and tell him I think the deal looks good but it doesn't smell good . . ."

At Fiftieth and Park, the car turned east and headed toward Beekman Place. Max's voice continued. "If I leverage it through FAU, nobody knows nothing. But for that I'd want sixty-seven percent, nonnegotiable. So if whatsisname's board can't see it that way, he shouldn't waste my time on the telephone. Let Lehman Brothers handle it. But if you get any backtalk, don't worry about it, honey. It's not worth dropping everything. Don't worry."

There was a momentary silence.

Stella sniffed. "For future reference, Cathy, when Mr. Herschel says don't worry, that means *duck*. He's been stockpiling shit and he's getting read to dump, and furthermore . . ." She stopped short as the voice resumed.

"Remind me to call Bones before she leaves for the office."

Again silence. Stella and Cathy waited. Then the softly compelling voice spoke once more. "Good-bye for now, sweetheart. I'm going to put on my pants."

Stella turned the tape off and gathered up her purse and gloves. The car was approaching a double townhouse commanding one of the precious Beekman corners. "Now Cathy," she continued, "there's no need to be nervous. The routine's exactly the same here as at the office. You make the call, then give Mr. Herschel the signal to pick up. You've seen Ruth and Janet do it hundreds of times."

"My God. I just never can get used to a brilliant man like Mr. Herschel, that he can't use a punch phone."

"Well, he can't. He can't work the buttons. He likes old-fashioned telephones on separate lines, and he can afford anything he likes."

It was precisely 6:25 when the car stopped at the front door.

Ignoring Ben's exquisitely slow pantomime of his chauffeur's role, Stella yanked open the car door for herself. "Stay here, Ben. Wait and see if there's anything else to go to the office. If not, then just deliver the tapes. You don't have to be back here till nine-forty-five."

[3]

She walked toward the door of the house, getting out the keys as she briefed Cathy. "We'll both leave here and go to the office when Mr. Berger comes . . ." She unlocked the door and conducted Cathy into the foyer.

Cathy gasped. "Oh, wow! Isn't it beautiful!"

To Stella it was something more than a beautiful hall. Thirty years ago she had decided that, to a girl from the grim, gray streets of Little Italy, there might well be spiritual nourishment in silvery blue seventeenth-century Chinese wallpaper.

She herded Cathy into the elevator and punched five. As the machine clanged and creaked upward, Stella advised Cathy. "Now if you need to go to the little-girls' room, please do it right away, dear. It's almost six-thirty, which is eleven-thirty in London, and twelve-thirty in Paris and Geneva, so you won't have another chance until around ten New York time. Which is eleven in the Bahamas. Do you have to go or not? Don't take chances."

Cathy shook her head.

"Because I don't want to look over at you in the middle of the calls and see you with a squirmy look on your face. If you've got to go, dear, go now."

The elevator shuddered to a stop; Stella opened the grill and stepped into a dimly lit room. Moving directly to an expanse of curtains behind a sofa, she parted them, then began turning on lamps.

Cathy's gaze traveled hungrily around the room. This was Max Herschel's sitting room. Right off *his* own bedroom. Where *he* was, right this minute. *Himself.* And she was in *his* own private sitting room. Practically a *billionaire's* sitting room. Still, she felt a twinge of disappointment. The room did look expensive, but then it was sort of filled with junk too. She wondered if the picture on the far wall was supposed to be a joke. It was an ugly, naked, redheaded woman constructed of patched and stuffed satin and felt, reclining on a hip and elbow. Between her legs was a terrible abundance of dense, red, three-dimensional pubic hair that looked like yarn.

Cathy blinked. Hanging from the compelling red nest was one long, white string. Tampax?

Stella, tracing the direction of the girl's stare, saw what Cathy

[4]

saw. Giving a little hiss, she strode to the picture and plucked the string from the lady's privates.

"Honest to God! Mr. Berger's eighty-one years old!" Stella flicked the string into a wastebasket, then admonished Cathy. "Cathy, this is not an office. It is Mr. Herschel's private sitting room. Generally, if he wanted to stick a white string in that lady, I'd say it's his room and his picture. But not today with old Mr. Berger coming. Now watch yourself in here. Those vases there, for instance, are Sung Period. Eleventh century. And that one," Stella pointed to a large creamy vase standing in splendid isolation on a pedestal, "is Mr. Herschel's *Gulbenkian.* Stay away from it. If you broke *anything,* you could phone and file and turn the Rolodex for the next fifty years and never pay for it."

She paused to let the warning sink in. "Just so you know." She indicated the desk on which stood eight standard 1960-style black phones. "*His.*"

Then she pointed to a table well removed from the desk, which bore eight more phones. "Yours. And the can is through there . . ."

By now Cathy was determined not to go before she got back to the office. *That* would prove to them. "I don't have to go, Miss Liberti," she insisted. "Honestly."

She watched as Stella removed her glasses and put them in her purse, exchanging them for the contact lenses on which, Cathy knew, Mr. Herschel insisted. None of the females in Mr. Herschel's office wore glasses. *Mr. Herschel* did not wear glasses.

As Stella inserted the bits of convex plastic beneath her eyelids, her face assumed a contentedly martyred look. I mortify my flesh with plastic, she thought. I genuflect to wallpaper. I am Italian. I have a religious nature.

For twenty-nine years Herschel Industries had been Stella's altar and Max her Host, and the passionate dedication of her life had brought rewards peculiarly akin to those of a nursing nun's. She was blessed with the certain knowledge of her own unflinching nature, the daily exercise of power in someone else's name, the discipline of her flesh, which, like that of certain female religious, had remained preternaturally youthful.

On their twenty-fifth aniversary together, Max had offered

Stella a facelift. She had declined. And she felt now, at fifty-five, that she looked better than she had at forty. She was still slender, her skin was fine, and her gray hair was softly becoming. Stella Liberti was an intelligent, warm, and attractive woman, but she had never married. Her life was consumed by Max Herschel's demonic intensity. That intensity had even divorced her from her family. She saw her sisters and brothers and their offspring infrequently. They were not fascinating.

She regretted nothing.

The contacts in place, Stella squeezed back the tears and caught the worried look Cathy was directing at Max Herschel's bedroom door.

"What is it, Cathy?"

"Miss Liberti . . . what if I do something wrong this morning? What will Mr. Herschel say? *Do?*"

"It is not what Mr. Herschel will do, Cathy. It is what *I* will do. Don't worry about Mr. Herschel. You are working for *me*. I chose you for the job because I knew you could do it. There is absolutely nothing whatever to be frightened of. If Mr. Herschel gets out of hand, I discipline him."

"My God. *Mr. Herschel?* How?"

"Work to rules. No interpretation. Follow orders literally. He says get me Joe Kram when he means Joe Brill. Who he always mixes up because they're both bald. And I know he doesn't mean Joe Kram because he hasn't had any dealings with Joe Kram for three years since Kram bucked him on a merger Max wanted. But he *says* Joe Kram, so I get him Joe Kram. Who is in Nepal. And Max has to scream across the Himalayas for fifteen minutes to Joe Kram about a deal he is trying to put over on Joe Brill. That's what I mean by working to rules. I don't have to do it very often."

"My God."

"It's almost six-forty-five. From now on, no talking and no trips to the little-girls' room. You had every chance."

Cathy sat resolutely at her desk.

Stella settled herself near Herchel's desk, breathed deeply and waited for her day, her life, to begin.

The bedroom door opened on cue, and Maximilian Herschel

swung into the room, darting his eyes from Stella to Cathy with the eerily quick fix of a predaceous bird. He was in high feather today, Stella thought.

At 6:45 in the morning, after four hours' sleep, Max Herschel's color was good, his aspect frisky. His face wore the cheery look of an habitual winner. His heavy, fleshy nose, so sensitive to the scent of money and women, was, in Stella's judgment, riding today at about the right angle for business. So far, so good.

At 6:45, Max was impeccably turned out in a conservative, London-tailored, three-piece suit, white shirt, gold cufflinks, and navy and white geometric print tie. He had dressed for the appointment with Berger, Stella realized. Another plus.

The jacket to Herschel's suit finessed the width and power of his shoulders, and the vest lay smugly over a flat, disciplined stomach. The trousers, however, did not disguise his short, aggressively muscled legs. Because the trousers were slung over his arm.

He tossed the pants to Stella as he sat down at the desk.

"Fix the fucking zipper. And there are more tapes too, by the bed."

Stella instructed Cathy to go into the bedroom, fetch the new tapes, and add them to the collection. "Move," Stella ordered, and Cathy did, so rapidly that the only impression she got as she whipped in and out of Max Herschel's bedroom was that it seemed unexceptional. Like Mr. Herschel himself.

To Cathy, Max Herschel looked quite unexceptional, which always surprised her. Very trim and pretty young for his age, sure, but why shouldn't he be when he played tennis nearly every single day, and had his own saunas and airplanes and ate all that yogurt? *Still.* Except for his sort of scary black eyes, Mr. Herschel was just average. Average height, average grayish hair, average everything. He was just an *old man* who, when you thought about it, looked a lot like Mr. Martinson at the drugstore in Flatcar. So why, when she looked at Mr. Herschel, did her eyes glaze over and my *God,* her nipples poke out like this?

Defensively, she hunched her shoulders so that her breasts could not assert themselves against her blouse. And she would *not* blush when he spoke to her.

"Good morning, Cathy."

[7]

"Good morning, Mr. Her—"

"Where's Ruth? Or Janet?" Max demanded of Stella.

Stella had spread Max's trousers across her lap and was gently maneuvering the zipper back onto its tracks. "Ruth has a virus. She's running a fever. Janet's taking over for her at the office."

"What kind of fever? How high?"

"One hundred one and a half."

"She taking antibiotics?"

"Aureomycin."

"Who's her doctor? Some intern she's banging to save money? Cathy, call Dr. Rossman and tell him I'd appreciate it if he could make a house call. I'll send a car any time. Then call Ruth and tell her when Rossman's coming. So she doesn't have the intern hanging around with his dong out. And warn her she mustn't ever take antibiotics without yogurt. Her horny little intern probably hasn't taken that course yet. Then call Hammacher Schlemmer and order a yogurt-maker. A driver will pick it up at the store and deliver it to her."

Stella sighed and restrained Cathy, who was already spinning her Rolodex. "Not yet, Cathy. It's not even seven. Dr. Rossman and Hammacher Schlemmer don't come in before nine. I expect Mr. Herschel will want to get started on the overseas calls first."

Max shot Stella an accusative look. "I've already made half of them myself."

"You got the calls through yourself?"

"You can't haul your ass over here till the middle of the day. What do you expect me to do? I did all the Swiss calls."

Stella knew Max was lying. For some reason, he didn't want to talk to anybody in Switzerland today. She played along. "Made all those calls yourself? Good for you."

Max tried to shoulder through. "Either I'm going to have to take on the overseas calls myself or find somebody willing and able to get in here at a reasonable hour."

Stella nodded sympathetically. "I'll try to help you find somebody."

Making no ground with Stella, Max turned his attention to Cathy. "Place the calls in this order. Ten minutes apart . . ."

Stella interposed. "Fifteen minutes for London calls. The British have gone down for the third time and they still won't work their hands and feet."

Max always appreciated a burn at the British. Abruptly, he was again all grins and good humor. He beamed at Stella. "If you say so, kid. Now, Cathy, first I want Sir Brian Schlesinger, London. Then Billy Baumgart. You'll have to track him down. Try the London office of Consumex to start. Then get me anybody who can speak English at—" Max pulled a scrap of paper from his jacket pocket and squinted at it. "—at 82-74-93 in Paris. Then I want to speak to Prince Karathi. He's not in Geneva today. He's at Claridge's or at the Kempenski in Berlin . . ."

He broke off and queried Stella. "Karathi's people are some kind of Arab, aren't they? I figured he ought to be able to get that vase out of Syria."

"No, they're not Arabs. They're Indian, and I don't see him doing any illegal schlepping for you. He's not your man for Syria."

Max scowled challengingly at Stella. "Then who is? Goddam it. If my affairs were handled by Morgan Price, I wouldn't have to run around one foot on the curb, one in the gutter . . ."

Stella shook her head in grudging admiration. "With your money, at your age, and you're still trying to move up in the world. Morgan Price! You've had a hard-on for Morgan Price ever since I've known you. That's a thirty-year unrequited yen. You're a very romantic man, Max." She smiled at him. "You should see your face right now. You look like a locked-out lover."

Cathy risked a glance at Mr. Herschel. Miss Liberti was right. Mr. Herschel looked broody.

Max was plaintive. "It's their finesse, Stella. The finesse of those mothers. Bull markets, bear markets, no markets . . . but never a shock-wave at Morgan Price." Wistfully: "Third-market runners in diapers . . . all automatically Maidstone or Piping Rock. No Jew accounts. No Greek accounts. No matter *who* we marry. Right? You got to have the right religion for blue chips. Ah, well. Screw 'em."

Stella pointed an accusing finger at him. "You know what the

Investment Banking House of Morgan Price is to you, Max? Morgan Price is to you the quintessential shikseh."

He pitched her a piece of hard candy from a celadon bowl on his desk. "Have a honey drop." Without looking at Cathy, he pitched another piece in her direction. Then he took one himself and sucked greedily. "An investment banker—any investment banker, sweetheart—is not the quintessential anything. He's just a percenter who bends down to pick up the money. *Way* down. So don't ever give up your subway seat to a banker." He chomped ruthlessly into the candy, which crumbled so satisfactorily between his molars that he relented slightly. "Sure, I'd like to infiltrate Morgan Price. Try going to Lehman Brothers or Kuhn, Loeb about a stolen T'ang dynasty bowl buried by a communist gonif on the fly through Aleppo."

Stella slung Max's pants at him. "Here. I wish you could get it through your head that you can't pull down on zippers like you're yanking for your life on a parachute line. Gently, Max. Gently."

Max stepped into the pants and zipped them with vengeance.

"It's all very well, sweetheart, to go gently when you're pulling up. But things can get urgent when you're pulling down." His eyes flicked toward the pink-faced Cathy. "Nice blouse, Cathy. Good fit. Now, honey, before we start on the overseas stuff, get me Bones."

"That's Miss Burton, Cathy," Stella instructed. "288-3751."

Cathy dialed the number with awe. On her third day with Herschel Industries, the other girls in the office had informed her that the expensive-looking little blond who had swept through the office was Miss Burton. Who belonged to Mr. Herschel.

The call connected, and Miss Burton's phone began to ring. Once, three times, seven times.

"Miss Burton doesn't answer, Mr. Herschel."

"Let it ring. She's there. She's just browned off about something." He smiled to himself. Bones' nerve always broke before the twentieth ring. "She never puts the silence button on at this hour. She hasn't got the balls."

He was bragging, Stella thought, showing off for Cathy. She lowered her eyes before Max could catch the look she had inadvertently shot him. Stella knew Bones better than Max did, and recently Stella had been reading signals which Max, speeding blithely along, was choosing to ignore.

In Stella's opinion, Max was getting careless. In Stella's opinion, underestimating the lady's balls was dangerously careless. In her mind's eye, Stella could see the telephone beside Bones' bed. Reflectively, she began to count. *Ten. Eleven . . . twelve . . . thirteen . . .* The housekeeper, Stella knew, did not come in until after Bones left for the office, and Amelia, the live-in, was a young Portuguese who had no English and was forbidden to answer the phone. *Fifteen . . . sixteen . . .*

Chapter 2

Bones was coordinating her exercise to the rhythm of the ringing phone.

Ring. Inhale, suck in the stomach, raise the legs . . . tooo the chest. Hold. Ring. Exale, lower the legs. *Hang.* And . . . ring. Inhale, suck in the stomach, raise the legs . . . tooo the chest. Hold. Ring. Exhale, screw you, Max. *Hang.* And . . . ring . . .

Bones did not know why she was angry; she only knew that if she was, she had a right to be.

She managed three more knees-to-chest before the ringing finally got on her nerves.

She let go the exercise ladder and dropped to the floor.

"*All right.* I'll speak with Mr. Herschel."

Bones waited for Max to get his phone girl's signal, pick up the wrong phone, and cross a couple of lines before he finally made the connection.

"Bones? Are you there, sweetheart? . . . Hold it a second, the goddam wires . . . there. Hello, sweetheart. How'd you sleep?"

"Asleep at ten, up at six."

"Lucky, kid. I was in bed at twelve and up like a lark at two."

Bones let his little joke lie there.

"Bones? What's the matter, honey? Something bothering you?"

"No, I'm fine. I'm going to fire Warner."

She listened for Max's already solicitous voice to turn liquid with paternal warmth. "Why, darling? Is he giving you trouble? What's he up to? Isn't he doing his job?"

Because she still could not locate the source of her anger at Max, she tried to sound reasonable.

"He's doing his job. He's also trying to do my job."

"He's ambitious. He's got energy. You don't penalize a guy for that, honey."

"He's crowding me, Max. I was out of the office two days and he brought in a third casting director and a new researcher."

"Why were you out of the office?" Max asked.

Ah, she thought. To lay it on him now, or later? *Lay it on him now.*

"Last week, Max. When you were in London."

"What happened? You come down with a cold? Did you call Rossman?"

"No, I called Benechek."

"Benechek?"

"I didn't come down with a cold. I came up with an abortion."

Bones began to count silently in measured beats . . . one . . . two . . . three . . . four . . .

"You should have told me."

Five . . . six . . . sev . . .

". . . that you weren't feeling well."

Just under seven. Not too bad. Not in the twelve-to-fifteen range like the golden days, but not four-minus like last time.

"I said you should have told me."

Ah, the real thing now. The enveloping authentic cashmere-warmth of his total attention.

"Max, I tell you that I'm not feeling well, and you say, 'I'll get Stella to make an appointment.' I can make my own appointments."

[13]

She hung up.

On the other end, Max listened briefly to the buzz of the disconnected line, then began to improvise. "Is that a fact? . . . Well, that's just great, sweetheart. I'm glad to hear it . . . Look, Bones, I've got a couple of things to take care of. I'll call you back . . . Bye, honey."

He hung up, and turned accusingly to Stella.

"Bones had the flu. Why didn't anybody tell me? Now look—an idea I had last night. I want you to call the Beverly Hills police and see if you can negotiate a flat monthly rate on my speeding tickets." Max ignored Stella's snort. "Also, there's a Severini going at Parke-Bernet today. It's a piece of junk, but she likes it, and it's her birthday next week. Leave a bid."

"How much?"

"More than the *previous* bid, Stella. Just buy the goddam thing."

"Okay. What else?"

"I want to know what the stall is on that Canadian land. Can those Canucks deliver or not? If they need dummy buyers, then get them dummy buyers, but I want ownership by the end of the month or Herschel Industries is crossing its legs. Tell them that. Tell them to spend a little money in Ottawa. Tell Derek to . . . no, don't tell Derek anything." He hesitated, sighed. "Don't tell *anybody* anything. I'll take care of the schmeer myself. Tell Protestants to spend a little money and that's exactly what they do. Spend a *little*. So the job doesn't get done plus you're out your investment."

The elevator cables began to squawk. Cathy shifted her eyes inquiringly in that direction.

Max snapped his fingers at her. "You listening to this, you little Wasp? If you're going to offer somebody a bribe, make it a nice fat one. Remember that, Cathy. You don't bribe, you don't ride. Don't ever be a piker with a bribe."

"I won't, sir. Shall I start the overseas calls now, Mr. Herschel?"

Max regarded the girl's earnest young face and tried not to laugh. Aside from her hair, which was a boring color, she was a cute kid. Forget it. Fishing from the office pool wasn't worth a battle with Stella.

The elevator door opened and a great Irish wolfhound leaped hugely, hairily, into the room, sideswiping Cathy and sliding on the rug before hurling himself against Max, the adored object of his gigantic affection. Max laughed and tried to wrestle free of the beast. He shoved a fistful of honey drops into the monstrous mouth and yanked futilely on the straining animal's collar.

"Sid! You Irish idiot. Get down! Down! Jock!" Max shouted to the man who had come up in the elevator with the dog. "Get him off me! Down! Goddammit, that's enough now! Get him down, Jock!"

As Jock Kelly rescued Max from the hound, he took in Max's three-piece suit. "No game this morning, pal?"

"Maybe later, Jock. Have to see how the work rolls. Get rid of Sid and take a seat."

Cathy thought Jock Kelly was the most beautiful man she had ever seen. A few years ago, when he was playing at Forest Hills and Wimbledon, she had cut out his pictures from papers and magazines. Now he was paid to play tennis only with Mr. Herschel. When you thought about it, Mr. Herschel *owned* Jock Kelly. It was a scary idea.

Jock dragged the love-besotted Sid back to the elevator, shoved him into it, pushed the down button, and closed the grill and then the door against the big black nose. To the last, Sid never took his mournful eyes off Max. The Caliban of a creature somehow managed, Stella thought, to look like just another betrayed ingenue.

Cathy pulled her eyes off Jock and addressed Max.

"Shall I start the overseas calls, sir?"

Max shook his head at Cathy. In losing Sid, Max had also lost his struggle against anxiety from which the dog's antics had briefly diverted him.

"Hold it a minute, honey. There's something I forgot to tell Miss Burton. I'll make the call myself."

While he dialed, Stella, who suspected that Bones had hung up on Max, looked studiously at her notebook.

Jock, who despised Max's duty calls to his women, draped his splendidly long body over a comfortable chair and pulled a copy of *Sports Illustrated* out of his jacket.

[15]

Cathy lowered her eyes to the Rolodex but did not turn it.

Acutely conscious of the silence, Max willed Bones to answer her phone. To his relief, she picked up almost immediately.

"Sweetheart, if you fire Warner, you'll have to pay up his contract in full. Very expensive. Now about the other. Is it okay?"

Bones answered matter-of-factly. "Yes. I just did fifteen knees-to-chest on the ladder. Forget it. And I *am* going to fire Warner. Today."

"Sweetheart, I think you're being emotional. Over Warner. You're probably a little shaky from the flu. Know what I mean? You're not thinking straight. If you get rid of Warner, who'll you get to replace him? If you turn him loose, somebody else will hire him. Never forget the old Pedernales saying, sweetheart. 'It's better to have the sonofabitch inside the tent peeing out than outside peeing in.' Look, darling, I'm sorry I wasn't around last week. Come on upstairs today and have lunch with me. Okay?"

Bones did not respond. She eyed the exercise ladder and decided she would do ten more knees-to-chest.

"Sweetheart? Are you there? Listen, honey. I brought you a little present from London. And I'll order something good to eat from home. Okay, sweetheart? One o'clock?"

She ran her hand over the tight muscles of her naked stomach. Maybe even fifteen more.

"Honey? Bones? You're going to like what I've got for you. I was on Bond Street . . . just walking by Cartier's. I was going to save it for an occasion, but I'd rather give it to you now. So I'll see you at the office at one. I've got to hang up now, honey. I've got Paris on another phone. Bye."

Bones stood by the telephone and visualized Max in his sitting room with Stella and the phone girl. There would be a moment of silence; then the girl would say, "Are you ready for Paris?" And Max would say, "Hold Paris." Then he would turn to Stella and tell her to call Tom Dooley at Cartier's. "I need something quick . . . for Bones . . . something in the ten thousand range . . ."

Bones walked back to the ladder and lifted her arms, reaching for the highest rung she could grasp. I *need* these muscles, you prick.

Her scenario was accurate, as far as it went.

When Stella asked Max what price range, he did say ten thousand. But then his eyes suddenly moistened, and he blew his nose punishingly. One of his contact lenses became dislodged.

"Goddam dust all over the desk! Why doesn't anybody in the goddam house ever think about *me!* I'm allergic to *dust!* I pay a staff here big enough to run the Waldorf and they can't keep one goddam desk dusted!" He wiped his eyes.

Max's tears. Stella sighed inwardly.

Sad movies, stories detailing the vicissitudes of plucky little kids, Bones' abortions, all brought on gentle showers. Connie Herschel, the Herschel daughters, even Stella herself, all of Max's women were weakened in their dealings with him by the plea-bargaining of Max's easy gangster tears. Only Bones resisted them.

Max blew his nose again, then sighed. "Oh shit. You better tell Dooley to go a little heavier . . . up to twenty thousand. I'll take the Paris call now."

While he fussed with the phones, he alerted Stella. "I want a daube sent to the office for lunch. Tell the cook to use Beck's recipe. And when I'm with Bones, I don't want any calls or interruptions. Nothing between one and two."

He blew his nose a third time. "Shit. You better make it two-thirty."

The poor devil, thought Stella. He still loves her. Or whatever he calls it.

My God, thought Cathy. He must *adore* her.

Jock was disgusted. Why did the old man let them all pussywhip him like that?

Bones lay in the marble tub and indulged in a pleasure that never failed her. The splendor of her bathroom. She rejoiced in its expanse of creamy marble, in the great, austere antique English mirrors, the Georgian cut-glass bowl filled with soap, the baskets of white azaleas, the stacks of coroneted Houk towels by the bidet. Embroidered coronets of the Duchy of Beuchtold.

When the twelve dozen Beuchtold towels came up at Christie's last summer and she had the flash of drying her tail on those coronets, she bought them. They had proved a steady source of satisfaction. Get it how you can, she thought, sliding down in the water.

If she skipped her third cup of tea, she could spend five extra minutes in the tub and make the office by 8:10, thereby preceding Warner, who had taken first to coming in at 8:30 and now, more recently, at 8:15.

To indulge in another intensely satisfying exercise, Bones opted for five more minutes in the tub, running mental filmclips of Before.

A scrawny little girl with her mother. The mother wears green eyeshadow. Mother and child are coming out the employees' exit of Woolworth's. They walk past a group of men clotted up close to the curb for the purpose of tobacco spitting. And old Mr. Mawson, who shaves only twice a month, glares at the mother. The mother's palm is wet. Then Mr. Mawson says, "Boys, never marry no woman what won't pick cotton."

It was at that moment and on that spot, outside the Gum Springs, North Carolina, branch of Woolworth's Five and Ten, that Bones' life had taken its most decisive turn. It was then she decided there was even less to men and marriage than sorry circumstances had already given her to suppose.

Bones began to look forward to lunch with Max. She would twist his tail. After lunch she would fire Warner.

Max's timing was off. He had missed three of his overseas calls and had failed to get satisfaction from two others. He slammed down the receiver and snapped at Cathy. "Hold the goddam calls."

Before Max could turn his frustration against Jock, Jock moved. Quickly reaching in his pocket, he took out a dark plastic bottle, pitched it to Max.

"I told you I could get them. But they're strictly experimental, pal."

Stella watched Max open the bottle, shake out two pills, and pop them. She frowned. "What are those?"

"Thousand-unit Vitamin E's." Max spoke around the dry swallow.

"Who told you to take that much Vitamin E? That's four times the dose Rossman has you on."

"I need it," Max snapped.

"Who says?"

"My date last night."

Max turned back to Jock and was struck once again by how much he paid the tennis player for all these hours of sitting on his butt. Say they managed an hour a day, five days a week, on the court, which they never did, plus two to three hours Saturday and Sunday. That was nine, ten hours a week, maximum, for which he paid Jock a thousand bucks. Every hour he spent with Jock on the court cost him one hundred and eleven dollars and change. But that hundred and eleven escalated to well over a thousand if you listed the courts at Bedford under Jock's column. Which Max was tempted to do because no member of the Herschel family had spent a night in the Bedford house for three years, not since the time Connie had found that kid's Compacto and thrown herself down the stairs. So there the damn place sat, forty-odd rooms and nobody in them but the Swedish caretakers. Max hung onto the property solely because of the grass tennis court. On most Saturdays and Sundays, Max and Jock would helicopter in and out to Bedford because the drive was a bore and Max didn't like to stay overnight in the house. It gave him the willies.

Max was not pacified by the Vitamin E. He cast a flinty glance at his athlete. He knew he wouldn't be able to play at all today, but if he let the clown off, Jock would go over to the club and hustle a couple of sets and pocket a profit. On Herschel time. Let him sit.

Jock's presence always stirred in Max a faint anxiety about his own health. He turned to Stella. "And while we're on the subject, where are those books I ordered?"

"*Getting Older and Staying Younger* is out of print. I had to put Research on it. Ben's picking it up this morning."

Max frowned. "What about the others? I ordered three books. What about *The Heart Doctor's Heart Book?*"

"The one you're really waiting for is *Sex Can Save Your Heart and Life*," Stella teased. "In the last ten years you've ordered every book on the subject that's been published. They all say the same thing."

"Not the charts. The charts vary. The odds keep changing." He shifted his shoulders impatiently.

Stella sighed. "Max, you'll outlive me and Jock and probably even little Cathy."

"It's not just a question of outliving you. The problem is doing it con brio."

Stella laughed. "If there's one thing I don't worry about, it's your brio. You've got to be the only sixty-two-year-old man in the Western world who can't get it down."

Infinitely soothed, Max cheerfully shifted gears back to business. "I've got 752,066 common shares in Artists International. That's nine percent, right?"

"Right."

"And Smitty's got the other nine. So as long as nobody catches us in the men's room together and hollers 'Sweetheart!' our eighteen percent controls the vote . . ."

Stella doodled without looking up. "So what are you trying to tell me? I can add."

Max leaned back and regarded the ceiling. "Well, it's painful. You know that? Berger, I mean. The poor old devil to have to come around begging me not to vote his putz grandson out of the studio. You know, when he called, he asked if he could come to the *office* to see me!" Max shook his head. "Not '. . . have lunch, Max,' or '. . . shoot a few holes of golf next weekend . . .' No. He *asked* to come to my *office*."

Stella was unmoved. "You've been waiting thirty years for Seymour Berger to ask to come to your office. Next to crawling in bed with Morgan Price . . ."

"What do you know? You're a woman. No sentiment. No heart."

"Who do you think you're kidding. *Me? Seymour Berger?* You think Seymour Berger doesn't know you began collecting porcelain just to be able to grab something away from him? 'Pay anything! *Anything*, Stella!' I remember those auctions. 'I don't care what it costs, Stella. No limit! Just don't let Berger get it!'"

"Well, but that was then. Now he's eighty-one years old with this grandson God knows who Seymour blackmailed to get the boy the job. Can you imagine being eighty years old and out hustling for a fag grandson?"

Jock Kelly lowered his magazine. "Michael Berger of Artists International? He's a fruit-ma-toot?"

Max nodded.

Kelly protested. "Berger's a pretty good club player. I saw him once in a pro-celebrity tournament at Palm Springs. The guy's got a very smooth backhand. He didn't hit the ball like any fruit-ma-toot."

Max laughed. "He's a fruit-ma-toot with a very smooth back-hand. What do you think, fags can't play tennis? Tell you the truth, Jocko, when I first saw you I figured . . ."

Jock gave a furious snort and returned to *Sports Illustrated.*

Max grinned and went back to Stella. "Poor old Berger. An *old man.* All he wants is to save the name. Do you realize what it costs him to come to me for that?"

"His two flagship theatres. Because you want the ground they sit on. That's what it'll cost him."

"But I couldn't do it to him in the office, Stella. 'Come to the house,' I told him. 'I'll be there at nine,' he said. *Nine!* Coming around with his hat in his hand at *nine.* 'Make it ten, Seymour. Mornings, I work at home. Don't rush your breakfast on my ac-count. Don't come till you're ready.'"

Max sighed. "It's the end of an era, you know that? In New York real estate, Seymour Berger was the biggest. And the tough-est. There was a time he wouldn't give me a job bribing fire in-spectors. Now he has to come crawling to me to keep his name from disgrace . . ."

Max sighed contentedly. "Christ, when I bought up United Vending, you know I didn't give a thought to all that Artists In-ternational stock they held?"

Stella kept her face straight.

"I haven't touched theatrical stock for twenty-five years," Max continued. "You invest in that business, it shows a spectacular dis-respect for money."

"Nevertheless."

Max couldn't restrain the whoop any longer.

"Yeah. Nevertheless! You know, I always thought I'd have to

get those sites from Seymour's estate." He shook his head. "But I'm going to be *nice* to him. I'm not going to rub his nose in it."

"Be adorable. As only you can."

"Goddam coffee!" Max sprang to his feet and quick-stepped for the bathroom, addressing Cathy over his shoulder. "Listen, honey, I better talk to my wife."

As he slammed the bathroom door, Stella called after him. "Easy on that zipper!"

Cathy looked quizzically at Stella. "Where is Mrs. Herschel?"

"Area Code 203-263-4894. The Connecticut Neurological Clinic. He'll want to speak with Dr. Coleson first."

Cathy started to dial. "Is Mrs. Herschel seriously sick?"

"Mrs. Herschel is having a breakdown." Stella decided to give Cathy an honest briefing. "She's been having it for over twenty years. For your information, Cathy, Mrs. Herschel's father was General Tor Sunderson, *the* General Tor Sunderson, and her mother was a Parkins heiress. All of which has not, dear, made for true happiness. Okay? Got that? All clear?"

Cathy ducked her head and busied her hands.

Max came from the john zipping himself with ceremonious deliberation for Stella's benefit. The Coleson call was ready. He managed to pick up the right phone on his first try.

"Hello, Doctor. All right if I speak with my wife this morning?"

He laughed. "No, Dr. Coleson. I keep about the same hours you people do—up before five to see what I can make go wrong by seven . . . Yes, I'd appreciate that. How's she doing? Is the new drug effective? . . . Well, I'm glad to hear that—and I'd like to speak with you again after I talk with Connie. Okay?"

Cathy, with no calls to occupy her, could not help overhearing. Jock buried his face in an article about the despised Billie Jean King. Better even Billie Jean than Connie. Jock had heard all the Connie talks he could stomach. Christ, how did Max put up with it?

Only Stella was overtly attentive to Max's conversation with Connie. Max himself was regally unconcerned with his audience.

"Hello, darling. How are you? . . . What are you going to do today? . . . Meringues? You're making real meringues? Gee, that's great. How many eggs you use? . . . Save the recipe for when you come home, sweetheart. And speaking of coming home, I thought you'd want to come down for Baby's and Stan's anniversary. It's number five, sweetheart. Remember? This month. On the twelfth. I thought we ought to throw a party. Get them down from the Massachusetts woods, invite all their old crowd, fly Jill and Pat in from California, hire a band, dress up . . ." Max stopped talking and listened.

He listened patiently, not interrupting, not contradicting. His concerned expression never altered.

At last he said, "Connie, honey, of course we need you. We all need you . . . what the hell would it mean without *you*? . . . Now Connie, don't cry. There's no reason on earth to cry. You're gonna make *meringues*, right? Look, sweetheart, you'd only have to be away from the clinic a couple of days. It's for Baby and Stan. Let's celebrate they're together and happy. Don't you think we owe them a party? I do."

Again he listened. And now the silence in the room was terrible. Then, once more, he cajoled. "What do you mean, *nothing?* What about Baby? And Jill? Listen, your daughter's going to be the first lady of California . . . Jill *counts* on you, sweetheart. *I* count on you. That's nothing? Now look, darling, you go wash your pretty face and tell Dr. Coleson you're coming home the eleventh and twelfth. You can go straight back on the thirteenth. Okay? Now you just put Dr. Coleson on, sweetheart. I'll see you the eleventh."

He waited impassively. "Hello again, Doctor. Connie's anxious to come home for our daughter's anniversary party on the twelfth. So do whatever needs doing. Pick out a nice nurse to travel with her. I'll send a plane. I want her here for two days . . ."

He listened briefly. Very briefly. "Don't give me that crap, Coleson. She's not fragile. She's just a lady with a hobby. The only purpose of which is to hand me a hard time. Which it does. So you just get her ass out of Hartford on the eleventh. She can come back the thirteenth, but on the eleventh I want her in New York . . . No, Dr. Coleson, *I* pay the bills, I also make the donations to the foundation and sponsor the out-patient facilities.

And listen, Coleson, send two dozen meringues down with her. I want everything I'm paying for. Now I know you're a busy man, Doctor. We'll talk another time. Good-bye."

There was a long pause after Max hung up. Then Stella asked, "Still going to California on Thursday?"

He looked at Stella, his face set against her.

"No. I'm going tonight. And I don't want the Gulfstream. I'll fly United. Both ways."

Stella's expression went stony. "United?"

Defiantly. "United."

"Oh for God's sake, Max . . ."

"Not your department, Stella."

"The hell it's not. Who has to make out the checks and line up the schools and . . ."

"You want a raise?"

"I'll take less money for less work. Less *dumb work* . . ."

"Just stick to your own business, Stella."

"You are my business."

"Then you're getting a short count. Buy some clothes, take up yoga. Do anything, but butt out of my private business."

Stella sighed deeply. "Some business."

Max turned coldly from her. "I'll finish my overseas calls now, Cathy. And I mean *now*," he snapped. "So shake it."

Chapter 3

Jock was furious. "You mean we're not playing today *at all?*"

"Jock, you sat there and listened to me talk for twenty minutes about Berger coming up here. A very important meeting. I have no way of knowing how long it will take. Then I've got a lunch date with Bones. You were *listening.*" Max knew full well that Jock never listened to any talk that did not feature Jock Kelly center-court.

Kelly was physically magnificent, narcissistic, temperamental, stupid, and much too lazy to sustain the rigors of year-round tournament competition. When Max had bought Jock, he had hoped that maybe he was getting a little vigorish on the side for Connie. Connie's one slip in thirty-two years of marriage had been long ago in Spain with a Basque jai-alai player. The affair had given Max hope that he might assuage his own guilt by cultivating athletes for Connie. But the jai-alai player was an aberration never to be repeated. Connie was not interested in Jock nor he in her. Connie was not his type. She was not a tennis fan. What aroused Jock was the sight of a female tennis fan crazed with lust for Jock Kelly. Her visible ardor was for him the human equivalent of the female chimpanzee's swollen and inflamed rump.

Jock was a loss where Connie was concerned, but by the time Max had plumbed Jock's shallows, he himself was hooked on the athlete's starlet vanity and consummate teasability. Max wouldn't have traded him now for a softball team of Gabors. In the hierarchy of Max's affection and pride, Jock more than held his own with Sid.

Max relented. "Take the whole day, Jock. Go on to the club and hustle something up for yourself. I won't even hit you for a percentage."

Stella advised Jock that Ben was taking her and Cathy to the office and could easily drop him off at the club. As she and Cathy and Jock waited for the elevator, Seymour Berger was announced over the intercom. He was fifteen minutes early. Max ordered Teddy, his Korean houseboy, to send Mr. Berger right up.

"Now all of you stay here and say hello to him. He'll be thrilled to meet you, Jock. And he'll want to give you a big hello, Stella. Christ, he's so nervous, he came *fifteen minutes* early. Poor old bastard. Now everybody make a fuss over him . . ."

Max's minions were standing in a receiving line near the elevator, waiting, when Max, in a split-second decision, suddenly sprinted across the room and wrestled the lady with the red pubic wool off the wall. The startled trio at the elevator watched Max stagger to his bedroom with the heavily framed picture, then reappear moments later with an inoffensive Utrillo landscape of the same approximate size. He hastily hung the Utrillo in the lady's place as the elevator hummed, then made the threatening, throat-clearing noise it uttered prior to all ascents. Seymour Berger's arrival was imminent. Max gave the Utrillo an approving glance and turned back toward the elevator.

Stella finally spoke. "Max, I already took out the Tampax string."

Max gave her an offended frown. "What Tampax string?"

"The Tampax string you had stuck up that picture."

Max clapped a hand across Stella's mouth, silencing her. "For chrissake!" he hissed. "Will you shut up about Tampax! He'll hear you from the elevator!"

Max, one hand on Stella's mouth, reached out the other to the elevator door in anticipation of Berger's arrival.

The only sound in the room was the squeak of the cables, and not until the elevator finally clanged to a stop did Max release Stella. He flung open the door in welcome.

"Seymour . . . Seymour! It's a treat to have you here! Come in. Come in."

Tall and slender, his blue eyes sparkling, the handsome old man smiled his Head-of-the-Tribe smile at Max, and for the first time Max acknowledged to himself that his thirty-year battle with Berger must have sprung in part from his resentment of Berger's great physical elegance.

Ceremoniously, Max introduced Jock to Berger as "a great, great champion. I know how many times you must have seen him play at Forest Hills, Wimbledon . . ." Jock was gracious. Berger, who had never attended a tennis match in his life, was bewildered, but gracious in return. He then exchanged a dignified greeting with Stella. Lastly, Max presented Cathy, who gave Berger a lovely smile. Berger gave Cathy a lovely smile. The formalities ended. Stella, Cathy, and Jock were free to go.

None of them spoke in the elevator going down. Stella contemplated how grateful she was not to be there when the old man was humbled . . . Frankly, she was just as glad she'd never had children, the things you had to do. That to bail out his grandson, Seymour Berger, at eighty-one, should have to come cap-in-hand to a man who stuck Tampax up pictures . . . who would hold the old man up like daylight robbery . . .

Cathy hadn't wanted to leave. Mr. Berger had impressed her. She would have loved to stay on with him and Mr. Herschel. It would have been interesting and educational to see how Mr. Herschel was going to do whatever it was he intended doing to Seymour Berger. With a little shudder, Cathy realized that what she wanted more than anything else in the world was to be around Mr. Herschel *all the time*. What did that mean? She suddenly felt warm and damp between her legs. My God! A blush that began around her hips rose like thermometer mercury, tinting her neck and face a bright pink. The need for oxygen caused a sharp intake of breath.

Jock, who was not thinking anything much, looked down at her, and Cathy, feeling his stare, bravely raised her lust-glazed eyes to meet his.

The sight of Cathy's sex-swollen face jolted Jock to attention. Jesus. The kid wanted it right here in the elevator! He served her a triumphant six-love, six-love flash of teeth.

"What's your name? Cathy?"

She nodded dumbly, barely able to focus on him, but relieved to have her disordered thoughts diverted from Max Herschel.

"Like tennis, Cathy?"

Again she nodded, then managed to choke out, "I was on the team at school."

Jock smiled a lazy, knowing grin. He gave her right bicep a light squeeze.

"Well, Cathy. What do you know about that? You know what I bet? I bet you've got one sweet little stroke!"

Alone with Seymour, Max surveyed his victim with relish. How erect the old man was, how alert. His voice was crisp and his eyes shone with health.

"Well, Seymour, would you like some coffee? Cake? A little fruit? Have a little fruit."

"Max, at my age, you go for a little fruit like you'd go for a hoop against the Knicks. Fresh fruit is fibrous, Max, I get my fruit out of a jar of Gerber's."

Max was shocked. "You eat *baby* food?"

Seymour nodded serenely. "Very good. I eat a lot of their banana-apricot mix. With a little tapioca in. Very tasty. And no fibers." He was amused at Max's expression.

"Over sixty, you help yourself to the fruitbowl, you help yourself to tsuris of the colon, believe you me. A slow death. For the consultation, no charge."

Max felt a clinch in his bowels. He was over sixty and a fruit freak. Which Seymour probably knew. Berger was trying to wrong-foot him with his lousy fibers. Max relaxed and smiled. He'd take care of his own fucking colon.

"Ever read up on those peasants in Southern Russia live to a hundred and twenty? Yogurt. That's the answer, Seymour. Yogurt."

Seymour nodded amiably. "Nothing wrong with yogurt. Yogurt and *no fruit*."

Max managed a little chuckle and got down to business. "Tell me, what can I do for you, Seymour? You name it, it's yours."

"Well, Max . . ." Berger broke off, looked around. "I see you've got it up here in a work room."

Max threw him an inquiring glance.

Berger smiled his sharp, old-world smile.

"The Gulbenkian Ch'ai. Up here in a work room. I admire that, Max."

"Oh, the Ch'ai vase. Well, you know I had it downstairs for a while, but then I started wanting it where I spend the most time in the house. This room is where I spend the most time."

"I admire you've got it here. Shows you really care."

"Sure I care." Stung by Berger's implied doubt, he blurted out, " 'Blue as the sky after rain . . . Seen through the rifts in the clouds.' "

Then, instantly furious at himself for having relinquished something private, he pointed a finger at Berger. "I'll tell you something, Seymour. I first began collecting just to give you a pain in the ass."

"Oh, I know that. If I'd been collecting buffalo turds, that's what you'd have started collecting, buffalo turds. Sure."

"You know something I don't know, Seymour? There's a rising market in buffalo turds?"

Berger smiled again. "But the thing is, you've got a fine collection now, Max. Very valuable. Very select. A first-class collection. Almost as good as mine. I want to talk to you about that, Max."

"About my collection?"

Berger revealed that he had recently been approached by the Cleveland Museum and asked to donate his own collection.

"For my lifetime, they wouldn't move a thing. Everything in its place. Each and every piece. But the tax break, for Marsha's sake, it happens now." The old man's nod implied what he did not say, that Marsha should be spared the simultaneous loss of her husband and any portion of his estate.

"And, you know as well as me, the Cleveland Museum has got as good in porcelain as the Metropolitan. It's a testimony to my collection they want it. An honor."

Seymour had given it serious thought. He was willing to give. If Max would give. Their collections complemented each other, and if the Cleveland Museum got his, it ought to have Max's too.

Max listened carefully.

Berger said, "Everything stays exactly where it is during our lifetimes. You want your best Ch'ai piece in this room, it stays in this room. But you get the tax benefit now."

Max looked at his favorite vase and objected. "But Seymour, when I look at that piece, I like to think, sweetheart, you're *mine*. I don't want to look at it and think, sweetheart, you're the Cleveland Museum's." Max shook his head adamantly. "No, Seymour. I don't want to." He gave Berger a searching look. "I can't believe that's what you came about."

Seymour Berger nodded. "I was asked to ask you, and I asked you. I'll tell you the truth, Max. I don't want to give mine either. If I'd really thought that you would have given yours, I wouldn't have asked."

Max relaxed. "Have some tea. Tea couldn't hurt." He pressed down on the intercom but nothing happened. He punched it once more, and it began to hum shrilly. He yelled into it. There was no response. He punched it again. It stopped humming, and he could not make it hum again. He picked up the box and thumped it down heavily on the desk.

Defeated, he confronted Seymour Berger and confessed. "Japanese. You know I've never come out better than even on any deal with the Japs?"

Berger was sympathetic. "I hear they're very tough."

"*Very* tough, Seymour. Herschel Industries pulled out of Japan three years ago. They didn't keep anything of mine, but I didn't take home anything from them. I figure I lucked out. Sorry about the tea."

Seymour Berger said that he didn't really want tea.

Max asked if Seymour had an intercom system in his own house.

"Machines don't give that service with a smile, Max. I need to communicate, I've got Marsha, God willing she outlasts me."

"Give Marsha my love." Sourly, Max reflected that if he had married a nice Jewish girl like Marsha Berger, he would not need a goddam army of elusive servants and all this Japanese junk you couldn't communicate through.

Max almost found himself wishing he *had* married a nice Jewish girl like Marsha Berger. Why the hell was Connie always accusing him of being anti-Semitic? Fuck Seymour and that old cow, Marsha.

"So, what did you really come about, Seymour? How can I help you?"

"Well, Max, let's be direct. Modesty is for the ladies. We should talk out direct. Max, you're a big man. A very big man. You've got a lot of power. You've made a lot of money. You're still making a lot of money. What are you worth? Don't tell me. Pushing half a billion. Right?"

Max's look was self-effacing, not denying, not confirming. Seymour smiled. "A very big man. *But.*"

But???!!!

"*But.* You're getting on. What are you, Max? Sixty-two? Right? I looked it up. Sixty-two. That's getting on. Not like me, of course, and you can thank God for that. I'm eighty-one since May and what can I say? I've got an emotional colon but otherwise very healthy."

Max warmed at the mention of Seymour's moody colon. Maybe it was even true. "You *look* good, Seymour."

Seymour nodded, satisfied with his lot. "Yes, considering everything, very healthy."

"I'm glad to hear it. And I'm glad to see it. And I'm glad I'm in a position to do something *for* you, Seymour."

"That's right, Max. We're not boys anymore—not fire-eaters like days gone by. We're grown-up men, Max. Men with positions in the community. And responsibilities to it. Men with the power to do something for the community."

[31]

"What community?"

"The New York community."

Cautiously: "I grew up in Chicago."

Calmly: "For close to forty years, you're a New Yorker, Max."

"I guess you could say I live in New York."

"That's right. New York. It's our city. We've taken a lot out of this city, and now it's time we put something back."

Even more cautiously: "What should I put back?"

Seymour's commanding patriarchal eyes lasered into Max.

"The Mt. Gilead Maximilian Herschel Memorial Wing for Special Diseases."

Max was stunned into silence. Berger just sat there, smiling benignly, as if he had offered Max a ninety-day free option on Columbus Circle.

"*Special* diseases? What kind of *special* diseases?"

"Max, you wouldn't believe, they're finding new diseases every week. I know you, Max. You think a low cholesterol is going to keep you safe out of heaven. But that's narrow, Max. Very narrow. And I'm not talking about what happens from cigarettes and pollution. God forbid." Sadly, Berger shook his head. "It's not enough from what diseases we already know, but they're finding new ones every day. Terrible things, Max. Mother Nature is a cunt, Max. In the *bad* sense of the word. They've got such new diseases . . ."

"You really came up here to see me about new diseases? New *diseases?*"

"A hospital *wing* for new diseases. The *Maximilian Herschel* Memorial Wing."

"What's the tab?"

Seymour shrugged. "It would be *your* wing, Max."

Max gazed mournfully at the Utrillo. Dull picture. Dull painter. He decided he hated Utrillo. "Well." He sighed. "Well, that's interesting, Seymour. I'll certainly think about it. The wing."

"The *Maximilian Herschel* Memorial Wing."

Max decided to swing. "I hear your grandson's got some trouble out on the coast. They'll try to dump him, you think? What's going to happen? What will you do?"

[32]

Seymour blinked serenely. "Let him sink. Like a stone. He's a terrible disappointment, that boy. Not a family man, you know what I mean."

Max punched hard. "He's made five faggy movies in a row."

Seymour nodded. "'Pictures for the new audience,' he says. 'But Mikie,' I tell him, 'there just aren't that many homosexuals. It's simple mathematics.' The boy can't add." Seymour fluttered his hand in a gesture of regret. "He'll have to go."

"Go?" Max was shocked at the old man's cool. "But what if they vote him out? Aren't you going to try to save him? Save your name?"

Seymour shook his head. "*My* name's good. What could I save the boy? I could buy him two years maybe, and then have to do it again all over. He's a dead loss. A terrible disappointment to Marsha. Marsha never knew another lady with a fag grandson. She's a bewildered woman."

His sigh was heavy, but he rose lightly to his feet. "Well, Max, I thank you for seeing me. Think about the wing. The *Maximilian Herschel* Wing. Let me know."

The old man walked slowly over to the great Ch'ai vase on its pedestal. The vase that was the heart of Max's collection. His famous Gulbenkian Ch'ai. Seymour stood reverently before it, his intense blue eyes filled with longing. "You know how much I wanted it. If you ever decide to sell . . ."

"Only to you, Seymour. Not that I ever would, but if I did, only to you."

Herding Seymour toward the elevator, Max regretted he'd never been able to get along with his own father. If he had, he might have picked up some of the old guy's manual dexterity. Learned to use his hands a little. Then he'd have been able to rig the elevator to drop like a block of cement to the goddam basement with Seymour Berger in it.

"It's been a great honor, Seymour. Thanks for coming."

When Seymour bestowed a final smile of benediction on Max, Max noted the caps on Seymour's teeth. Ten thousand dollars. Minimum. Eighty-one years old and caps. Which meant the stubs were still there. The old sonofabitch had even kept his teeth. Why had he ever thought Berger was going to let go of his theatre sites?

"A real honor, Seymour. And you know I mean that."

"Thank you, Max. We always understand each other. That's relaxing. Which gets more important as the years roll on."

Brittle as a Butterfinger. Old bones. Just a little fiddle with the cable. How would you go about fritzing an elevator cable? God knows. He'd have had to get Stella to call the Otis people and make an appointment. He sighed.

"I'll think about the wing, Seymour. Because it's *you* who asked. I promise I'll think about it. Very, very seriously."

"You've become a big man, Max. I always said you would."

Prick. What you always said was I would wind up in the slammer. And what could you do to help put me there.

Max smiled warmly. "My best to Marsha. Tell her I said you're a lucky man."

"Thank you, Max. And remember me to the charming Connie."

"Good-bye, Seymour. We'll shoot a few holes one of these weekends . . . The boy downstairs will see you to your car . . ."

Max pushed the button for Berger and shut the gate with finality.

At last the elevator was moving down. Max stood before its door, glaring at nothing and snapping his fingers. He made half-a-dozen small, irritable snaps, followed by one big popper, then he whirled about and trotted off to his bedroom. He came out dragging the naked lady, and, rapidly deposing the Utrillo, positioned the redhead back on her turf.

What the hell was Stella going on about Tampax? Did that little bitch last night do something nasty to his picture when he wasn't looking? What was the kid's name? Lettie . . . Lottie . . . Lennie? *Brucie!* That was it! Brucie something. What was her number? Where'd he get her? Hell. He'd never remember. Wait. Norman. He got her from Norman. Norman kept numbers. Max picked up a piece of paper from his desk and made a note to himself to call Norman.

Last night was none too clear. The kid had been slightly buck-toothed and, because he didn't want to worry about orthodonture, he'd turned on. She was also a giggler, but maybe she was giggling because she knew something he didn't. Namely that she had, so to speak, drawn a mustache.

He chuckled. He was beginning to feel better already. By the time he left the house, he was whistling merrily and swinging his arms.

Chapter 4

The thought of Brucie did not sustain Max all the way to the office. She did not even sustain him past Third Avenue. Between Third and Lexington, Max's thoughts returned, broodingly, to Seymour. He stared out from the cozy depths of his limousine, trying to take some comfort from the sight of pedestrians, wooly, red-nosed, and miserable in the February wind.

Shit. It wasn't as if he needed the goddam sites. He just wanted them. He wanted them because the air above them was valuable, because of their potential for . . . Max knew he was rationalizing. The truth was that he wanted the sites because thirty years ago when he *had* needed them, he could not get them. Berger had teased Max with them, and then when Max reached out, had slapped his wrist. Over the years Max had come to regard the sites as something pretty. Something nice to have. Something pretty and nice that *Berger* had.

So what? When times got tough enough, Max knew he would win.

The center of the storm was Max's natural habitat, providing him with a unique perspective and a great ride. From his serene seat in the hurricane's eye, he welcomed the inflations, the recessions, even the wars. He flourished in climates which other men regarded as adverse and cruel.

Max had made one of his most spectacular coups during World War II. He had purchased, for what amounted to pocket-lint, a number of Philippine-based companies, which were, at the time Max bought out their astonished and grateful refugee proprietors, firmly in Japanese possession. He had figured, hell, suppose the Japs win? With luck, Max Herschel ends his days clipping hedges for some Jap businessman colonizing Santa Barbara. But if the U.S. wins, then Max Herschel owns some very nice set-ups on islands with cheap labor and a fairly stable economy. Max had taken over title to the companies for what he described gleefully as six bucks and change from a ten. He had initially invested six hundred thousand borrowed dollars and had come out, before it was over, with close to a hundred million.

Max may have profited by the war, but he had also done his bit. Early in 1943, when he perceived that Washington would not be handing out E-for-Effort awards to real-estate manipulators, he had quickly grabbed up a small California engineering outfit and inflated it to a sizable factory for the manufacture of pilot-training units. This patriotic gesture eventually won him nine E's and proved to Max's personal satisfaction that he had helped win the war.

Max was proud of that first California company. It had not only supplied the armed forces with a valuable product, it had also been the first company of its size to solicit the services of across-the-board social rejects. He was still pleased to point out that he, Max Herschel, had brought employment and a place in the sun to thousands of blacks, 4-F's, cripples, retardates, and women. He had trained them and paid them good wages. His E's certified that Max had acted patriotically. That he had even mended rents in the social fabric.

Why then, Max had always wistfully wondered, had his California operation so enraged his father-in-law, General Tor Sunderson, America's Attila in the Pacific? Enraged him to the point that, after the war, he had packed in his general's stars and gone after a highly influential job in Washington, from which position of strength Sunderson had launched his war against Max's West Coast operations? Christ, it wasn't as if Max had been shipping wet gunpowder to the General's troops.

Max had captured Connie Sunderson in the spring of '41.

That his lovely blond daughter had married Max Herschel was hateful to the General, even disgusting. But Pearl Harbor had distracted him, and he had remained content to limit the domestic war, the war over Connie, to conventional weaponry. It wasn't until much later, after V-J day, that the General had reached for the ultimate button.

Without comprehending what had escalated the hostilities, Max fought back gamely, and that confrontation had been the *real* war of his youth, an occasion of high romance. Although he had never understood the action, he had gloried in it.

The secret lay in a phenomenon alien to Max, the nature of personal identity. He was American, sure, and Jewish, maybe. It was difficult for him to go beyond that without getting claustrophobic. But General Tor Sunderson's sense of self was unyielding, and it was inextricably rooted in a region. That region was not, however, Minnesota, the place of his birth; it was California. It was to California that the General had so passionately converted, California, the home of four generations of Parkinses and the sacred source of his wife's millions. The protection of the Parkinses' coastal holdings against the Asiatic hordes became obsessional. General Sunderson fought the Pacific war with a savagery startling even to the enemy, to say nothing of his troops and to his own commanding officer, General Douglas MacArthur himself. When that great soldier had been called upon to decorate Sunderson with the Medal of Honor, he had pinned the ribbon on Sunderson's broad chest, looked into Sunderson's fierce Viking face, his ice-lake eyes and, recalling the report of one grisly detail in a Sunderson clean-up action, had felt a shuddery little thrill of awe. Sunderson was not, MacArthur considered later, very intelligent. But he was a splendid-looking fellow. And he was most impressively *terrible*.

When the war against Japan was over, Sunderson turned his talents against the enemy at home. Maximilian Herschel had not only abducted and married his daughter, he had spread himself into the General's holy California and had reached loathsomely on into the Pacific, leeching dollars from the very ground on which Sunderson had caused so much blood to be shed for the noble cause.

The General turned guerrilla. He stripped off his uniform and went to Washington to apply his ferocity to Max's destruction. And for a while he had, indeed, given Max serious difficulty. Until Max, with an instinct for the uses of power far surpassing any soldier's, had simply hired his own army. He chose a former staff general of flamboyant personality, whose joyful disregard of opposition was mythic. In less than two months, Max's own maniacally murderous general had outflanked and run over Sunderson like a tank tamping a golfcart into a sand trap. Connie's father had subsequently retired to La Jolla, not precisely broken, but embittered enough to spend the remainder of his life with lawyers and trust officers, devising a will which assured him that even when he was gone, Max would never forget his enemy.

Not that Max's memory for points ever needed jogging. He kept accurate scores, and the books were never closed. They were still not closed on his long-dead father-in-law. They were not closed on any man who had ever really crossed him. And they sure as hell, Max thought now, were not yet closed on Seymour.

Chapter 5

Bones raced through the morning's correspondence with Mark. No, Roberta Jeunesse could not have a leave of absence from *Lost Generations*. Her contract was ironclad, and it was not the policy of Burton Productions to release contract players for other shows, even for the second female lead in a feature film directed by Gil Weisinger. "Sorry, Roberta, but I'm probably doing you a favor. Weisinger does not stop the world for women."

Bones picked up a manuscript, pitched it to Mark. "Send this back with the form rejection." She then picked up a second manuscript and slid it easily across the desk toward him. "But this one is interesting. Make a date for Andy to meet the writer and see if he has any other ideas and how fast he writes. If Andy thinks he has possibilities, tell Warner to sign him up for six shows, at minimum, then have somebody find him an agent. Now. The market is going very soft on Nick all over the Bible Belt. We had seven cancellations after the transvestite panel. Call a sales-staff meeting on Nick's show for three this afternoon. And tell Warner I want to see him between two-thirty and three."

Burton Productions had only two shows on network time, but with those shows the company was batting one thousand. *Lost Generations* was the second most successful soap on the ratings, and Nick Hoffman hosted an evening talk show that had maintained top position for three seasons.

Burton Productions' space on the thirty-fifth floor of the Herschel Building was sunny and pleasant. Bones' own office was comfortable. It had a mass of thriving plants and two abstract paintings. The effect was tailored to Bones' intention—that in this office, she herself should be the most decorative object.

"Mark, why didn't we get Steven Routledge for Nick?"

"Routledge was very snotty, Miss Burton. He wouldn't even come in to be interviewed for the interview."

"Why?"

"He does not '*do* television.' Can you imagine! Very snotty. I was shocked. I mean, one novel not even on the list? And *poetry*?"

Bones remembered with great clarity the photograph of Routledge on the novel's jacket. Routledge was young. He had style. He was gorgeous.

"He has an interesting background. I'd like to use him."

"Well, Routledge certainly gave Mr. Magill the finger. I think he'd be very hostile to Nick. And you know how Nick lets people like that run over him."

Bones smiled at Mark's misplaced maternal instincts. "Don't worry about Nick. Make a note for me to try to get at him from another angle. Is there anything else?"

Mark, who had spent three blissfully masochistic years as Bones' secretary, peered shyly through the lush tangle of lashes which fringed his great, aquamarine eyes.

"Welll . . ."

Bones waited patiently for him to speak. The protracted "welll" meant that Mark had a complaint to register against someone. He required about a dozen rapid blinks before he would be able to get it out. First he blinked, then he modestly let his lids drop. Bones knew that Mark appreciated the devastating effect his eyes had on others, but as his nature was exceedingly gentle, he tried not to take advantage. Mark used the terrible magic of his eyes with great discretion, which amused and touched Bones. She was fond of him.

"So? What's the problem?" she asked.

"Welll," he repeated, reluctantly, his lids still lowered.

"What is it?"

"I don't like to have to say anything . . . but Mr. Magill."

"What about him?"

"Welll . . . I don't know, exactly. He's been asking me to help him out sometimes . . . just little things, but why should he need *me?* He has two secretaries of his own. And I've got enough on my . . ."

"Mark, you tell Warner that you belong to me. Right down to your toenail parings. Tell him you *save* them for me. Tell him that."

Blinking frantically, Mark giggled and hid his mouth behind his hand. "Oh, I couldn't!"

"Yes, you could. Because from now on I *want* you to save your toenail parings for me. Bring them in every Thursday. In a matchbox." Her tone was only semihumorous. "You do belong to me. Now scat."

After Mark had gone, she sat staring through the plants. Was Warner trying to maneuver her into a confrontation? He was the best executive vice-president in New York television. She couldn't possibly find a replacement of his quality. She forced herself to stop that line of thought, to consider, instead, whether she overreacted to Warner, and if so, why? Was he too good? Was he better than she? Did he know it? Did *she* know it?

What difference did it make? Burton Productions was hers; she met the payroll. These were her offices, her employees, her hallways, her Mr. Coffee. *Hers.*

She wouldn't fire Warner. Not yet, anyway. She sighed and pushed the intercom. "Millie, I'm going directly to the *Lost Generations* rehearsal after my date with Warner. Then set me up a meeting with Mr. Carlyle at NET. After four. Make it four-twenty."

She stood up, stretched, and went into the bathroom to repair her face before going up to Max on the thirty-sixth floor.

She looked curiously at that face, the gentle, patrician, gray-eyed face that seemed to have slipped over her head and taken possession one night during her fourteenth year. Over sixteen years later, she still wasn't used to it. She always thought of it as Bonita's face.

She had been baptized Bonita, but no one had ever called her that except the church people during her mother's brief but wildly passionate fling with a Pentecostal preacher. The church people and the school principal who'd summoned her to his office with painful regularity to deplore her "attitude."

"Why does such a bright girl, a straight-A student, laugh out loud in assembly whenever 'America, the Beautiful' is sung? Answer me that, Bonita."

Bones had tried to answer honestly. "It's just one line, Mr. Miles . . . 'Across the fruited plains . . .'"

Genuinely baffled, Mr. Miles looked at the doll-like girl, who both attracted and repelled him. He attempted to keep his voice judicial, detached. "'Across the fruited plains'? What's funny about that, Bonita? 'Across the fruited plains . . .'? That's a beautiful phrase. I don't see anything funny in it. Explain the humor to me."

"I can't, Mr. Miles. Either you think it's funny or you don't, I guess. To me it's funny." She had tried to smile, but could not. She was angry and close to tears.

"I don't like your attitude, Bonita. I don't like it one little bit. And neither do a lot of other people around this school."

Bonita sensed the sexual frustration in his voice. She was aware that Mr. Miles was restraining a shameful urge to slap her. She also knew that he never would. She smiled.

"Get back to class, young lady."

A lot of people still did not like Bones' attitude, but now, it was they who got summoned to the office.

Thirty-one next week. What about that?

Not for a moment did Bones associate her birthday with the amorphous anger she had been feeling against Max. The anger grew, in truth, from fear. Because of all the lessons Max had taught her, the most compelling was to fear age.

Bones inspected Bonita's pearl-perfect reflection. She considered using some blusher but decided against it. She would wear the pale face upstairs to Max. Max. He was asking for it. The mirror imaged the sly smile that came unbidden to Bones' sweet mouth. It was a smile that invariably appeared whenever she thought of the extraordinary weapon she had forged against Max. Because the Nick Hoffman Show was a weekly shape-up for Bones. All she had to do was crook a finger at the procession of writers and artists, the actors, at the politicians and dialecticians who paraded, all ego and ambition, through the show. That parade provided Bones with whatever description of lover the occasion demanded. Every size and shape and variety of Max-tease, to give her points in their game, points to help Bones' struggle against her opponent's greater skills.

Choosing a lover whenever Max provoked her, Bones took comfort from Max's unadmitted but certain knowledge of the other man's existence. Patiently, Bones tolerated the lovers' presence in her bed until she had attained her goal—to stay somewhere near the center of Max's sexual focus. For whatever pleasure Bones took in sex, she took only from Max. What satisfaction she sought for her sexual self, she sought from him. Other men had sexual reality only in that they could arouse Max to reaffirm his ferocious sense of property. They alerted him to reclaim what was his. To assure her again of the great security which rested in being a base component of Herschel Industries.

Routledge? She splashed cologne on her wrists and filed him away. Sooner rather than later, she guessed. Because if she were brooding about her age, then so was Max. Dispassionately, Bones appraised the face in the mirror. Then abruptly, she turned and left.

All right. Upstairs. To see what Cartier's had come up with on such short notice.

Max had put his name on the Herschel Building in 1949, and his quarters had been decorated to satisfy needs that no longer obtained, hungers that no longer raged. Only the Oriental porcelain had any current value for him. He no longer cared about and seldom even noticed the correct, eighteenth-century English furniture, the Hunt and Rowlandson prints in the outer rooms, the fine Stubbs and Sawrey-Gilpins in his own office, the leather buckets, tobacco jars, surveying instruments, the dark mahogany and gleaming brass. On the rare occasions when he did take notice, the decor amused him. All of it was, in a way, the detritus of the war between Max and his father-in-law. General Sunderson had never actually invaded Max's territory, but when Max crashed through the General's barricades and stormed that warrior's turf, Max had the heavy cultural guns of Adam and Chippendale, of Isfahan and Ghirdes behind him.

By now, these old weapons were no more interesting to him than was Connie, the original casus belli. Max valued both his office and his wife only to the degree that they stimulated memories of the General. His war with Sunderson had been so consuming, so exquisitely satisfying, that for the time it lasted, it had totally blinded Max to the terrible tedium of life behind the lines with the General's daughter.

In the early years, Max's fantasy had been that when he eventually crushed the General, that fallen hero would be brought to Max's office for the final humbling, the negotiation of peace terms. *Max's* peace terms. In anticipation of this historic occasion, Max had bought, in 1949, a pair of vice-regal chairs, hugely clawed and balled and scaled to a mighty, military seat.

It was in one of those chairs, across from Max, that Bones now perched, her shoulders straight, her spine a good ten inches from the chair's elaborately carved mahogony back, her toes barely touching the floor. It always pleased Max to place Bones on these chairs and to observe the childish figure playing queen.

Bones' eyes were lowered as she listened to Max talk about his meeting with Berger. An appreciative smile bracketed her sweet mouth, to which she conducted almost none of the daube. She's not eating to annoy me, Max guessed.

"Don't you like the daube, sweetheart?"

"It's lovely, Max. I'm just not hungry. Go on. Finish about Berger."

"All I can think of is all those poor bastards with new diseases dying like flies all over the Maximilian Herschel wing."

Bones asked, "Will you give it?"

"Why not? Who knows? Not everybody goes with a coronary."

"Oh, anybody worth his salt goes with a coronary," Bones needled him.

He took the dart without flinching. "Right." He gestured magnanimously with his fork. "But what about middle-management? They've got to die too. This is still a democracy."

Bones smiled. "Well anyway, you won't be getting the theatre sites, will you?"

"Not while he's alive, I won't." Glacing at her untouched plate, Max defensively helped himself to more of the daube. "Eighty-one and still has his own teeth," he muttered.

"Will you vote Michael Berger out now?"

Max nodded mournfully. "It's more merciful to put him out now. While he's still young enough to find an honest trade. I owe it to his grandfather."

Bones laughed, but Max stayed serious.

"No, sweetheart. I mean it. It's bad for the company and bad for the boy. Even without him, it's a schlock outfit, that company. A meshuggeneh business generally. And this particular case is carrying over a hundred million in bank loans with interest lapping up the black ink like it was grand cru. I've told you before, sweetheart. I'll tell you again. If you want to make money, don't get too close to your product. Too involved personally. It always happens in that business. People lose track it's a business."

"So what are you going to do?"

"I've got nine percent and I've run Smitty's stake up to the same amount. We'll take over the board. Then I'll offer a tender and Smitty will hitchhike. The stockholders will fall all over to grab the offer. And that's it."

"Then what? What will you do with the studio?"

"Get out the old push-cart. Peddle the assets and hang onto the real estate. The studio's in a location I can get zoned light industrial. Which clears the householders out of the neighborhood. We pick up what they vacate at a realistic price. But we don't go industrial, we build instead another Co-op City. The householders who moved out, move back in. They just pay a little more. Or maybe I'll put up a really great hotel and complex. That might be fun again."

"What about the studio people? The employees?"

"Every man for himself, said the elephant as he danced among the chickens."

Bones pushed the daube around her plate, seized with a very different appetite.

"Keep it, Max."

"What?"

"The studio. Give it a chance. Put me in. Let me have it."

"Have *what?*"

"The studio. Shove me down their throats. Not as titular head, but with a heavy bat and swinging room. You can do it if you want to. Let me have a chance at it."

Max chewed carefully.

The studio? What the hell was she talking about? Was she trying to pull his leg? The studio? He shot a glance at her wide gray eyes, which were cool, clear, and limpid with chutzpah. She was serious? Christ. All women were crazy one way or another . . . poor little mutts . . . Connie was a goddam Edison for inventing ingeniously unworkable forms of suicide, and now this one thought she was Louis B. Mayer. It would be pathetic if it wasn't funny. Shit, it wasn't even funny, because he had to live with them. The only trouble with cunt, Max brooded, is that women have got all of it.

He drew on his vast memory of sexual maneuvers, his field marshal's experience in the pacification of women. Reaching across the table, Max took Bones' small hand in his.

"Honey, why won't you ever believe me about that place? You think I don't know what I'm talking about? Hollywood's a locker room. No women. It's a sick place."

"What kind of argument is that? We're talking about a business, not a neurotic condition."

"The neurotic condition is the business. Believe me."

"I'm not afraid of a town, Max. Please. I *want* it."

[47]

He swiftly abandoned one path and hared off up another.

"What about me, sweetheart? I want *you*. And I live in New York."

"You move around." Her tone was arctic. When a woman's temperature went down, Max's soared. He knew his forehead was damp. Almost fourteen years and she could still make him sweat bullets. Easy now. Watch out she doesn't go off in your hands . . .

"Well, Bones, anything I can give you . . . you can have."

There was a long, wary recess as they sat, eyeing each other. Bones' gaze was searching and guarded while Max's was open, conciliatory. At last Bones permitted her falsely generous mouth to curve upward at the corners, dimpling and slightly trembling. "Thank you, darling." Her lids lowered submissively.

He stared fascinated at those luminous lids, little white flags that lowered to acknowledge his power.

His power to *give her what she wanted*.

"Thank you, darling." That was very good. Sweet, humble, womanly. He had to give her credit. She was the greatest female impersonator he'd ever seen.

"Bones. Sweetheart. *Don't*."

The eyelids rose and Max looked into the steely gray barrel of a moonshiner's gun. Oh shit.

Make her laugh.

"What do you want me to do, Bones? Go down on my knees? You know I've got calcium deposits." He tried again. "Sweetheart, listen to me. Now listen. You think I don't know Hollywood? Jesus, half the wheels out there are my ex–band boys. I've told you how when I first had the hotel and I used to bring in the bands to work for scale because I'd hustle wire time for them . . . I was the only hotel owner that ever glommed time directly following the news . . . so I had my pick of the bands . . . they begged to work for me . . ." Max cupped his mouth with his hands and crooned ". . . and now, ladies and gentlemen of the radio audience, it's my pleasure to bring, for your listening pleasure, the great band of the great Sammy Snow, coked to the gills and emanating from the Indigo Room of the Hotel . . ."

"You've told me."

"So what do you want to mix it up with all those creeps? You're too good for those people."

"Max," she sighed. "Don't give me that shit."

"Okay. Okay. You won't listen to what's right for you, how about what's right for me? I don't want to be without you. I've invested a lot of years in you. I *won't* do without you. And I couldn't stand what would happen to you out there. They'd cut you off at the knees. For no reason at all except you're a smart broad. You know what happens to smart broads out there? They can't get laid."

For the first time, Bones smiled. "Oh, I expect I could get laid. Somehow."

"Five will get you fifty. *Stars* can't get laid! No female over eighteen gets laid! It's in the city charter!" He warmed to his argument. "They're zoned against it! I swear!"

"Oh, come on, Max . . ."

He persisted: "No, no, I swear! I swear to God! Middle age out there, it starts at twenty-four. I'm *telling* you."

"Herschel paradise," Bones submitted.

"Sweetheart, listen to me. You want to know what running a studio is really like?"

"Why don't you tell me again?"

He would not be put off. "Checking out big items like did your top star get a negative Pap smear. And how do you keep a picture on schedule when the director's freaked and shot the same scene eight days running. And always worried, *always* worried about the goddam banks."

Bones appeared to be studying her wine goblet, but Max was confident she was listening to him.

"Honey, years ago somebody sent me a book: *How to Marry a Millionaire*, it was called . . . they bought the title for a movie, I think, anyway, the first paragraph I still remember. It said how this girl was born in L.A. and turned out to be a real looker. She went to Hollywood High. She said something like '. . . and by the time I was fifteen I was going out with actors. Then I found out actors were all nervous about agents. So I started going out with agents. Then I found out agents were all nervous about casting directors so I tried casting directors. *Them?* Nervous about studio heads. I got me a studio head. And *he* was nervous. Nervous about the banks, which were all back east. So I decided to go east and be nervous at the source.'"

Bones frowned faintly at the goblet. "What happened to the girl who wrote the book? Did she marry a millionaire?"

"I don't know. What's the difference? She wasn't a romantic, she must of wound up okay. Like you, sweetheart, if you keep on the track. Pursue the art of the possible, sweetheart. And for you, so much is possible. You're a smart, gorgeous, disciplined lady . . ."

He reached into his pocket and pulled out a leather case from Cartier's. "Here. The thing I got for you in London."

Bones evaded his eyes as she opened the box and took out the coral and diamond pin. She sighed. "It's beautiful. I love coral."

"I know. When I saw it in the window, I said, that's for Bones."

By the time she finally looked up, her eyes were not as clear as they had been. She straightened her shoulders and pulled him down, kissing him softly on the mouth. "Oh, Max . . . you get guiltier and guiltier . . ." She fiddled with the pin, then murmured, "If I'm so disciplined . . . why do you think I do it?"

"What? What do you do, darling?"

"Let you knock me up every couple of years."

Max counter-punched with rough, desperate humor. "Because that little bush between your legs is mountain scrub, sweetheart. Hillbilly country. Your instincts keep telling you to pop out a parade of mental defectives. Bad blood, Bones. You gotta fight it, kiddo."

"Thanks for the pin." She stood up. "And I won't bother you anymore about the studio."

Max repressed a sigh of relief. "I'll find a bracelet to match the pin . . ." Then the hook: "And, honey, there's not really time to talk about it now, but . . . what do you think about starting up a new magazine? Something fresh. Special interest publications are making it. The field's wide open. Might be something you could really run with. Think about it, okay?"

"Okay." She paused, then continued softly. "And I'm not going to fire Warner. You're right about him."

Max beamed. "I adore you." He gently lifted her hand and kissed it. "Sweetheart, if I let you go out there . . . I *know* what I'm doing, honey. Trust me. In six months they'd have you walking on your ankles."

She stared away from him.

"I'm the guy who levels with you, sweetheart. Remember? Anytime you don't hear it from me straight, you can hit me with your purse. Believe me, sweetheart. Try to believe me."

"All right. I'll try to believe you. Are you going to California this week?"

"Tonight. Back Thursday."

"Stay over and I'll come out for the weekend."

"Honey, I'd rather come back. Five days out there, I'm a basket case. Maybe we'll go up to Boston and visit Baby this weekend. You'd like that, wouldn't you?"

"Sure." She reached up and brushed Max's cheek with cool, dry lips.

"I've got to run. See you Thursday."

"Thursday. We'll have dinner. Maybe I'll cook . . ." He followed her to the door and opened it. "You really like the pin?"

She nodded. "I really like it."

Standing only a few feet from the door, Cathy Kronig caught a glimpse of the pin and heard Bones' offhand response. She could discern no warmth in Bones' words, only the flat admission that she found the pin acceptable. *Boy!*

Cathy had invented enough work to keep her in Max's outer office until Bones' departure. Normally, Bones would have noticed a pretty girl hanging around. She was hypersensitive to the women who worked close to Max, keeping close track of their backgrounds, their relative abilities, and their potential for causing her trouble. Normally, she would have had a word for all and possibly even cast out a couple of lures, complimenting one or the other of them on a sweater, a haircut. But today, distracted and anxious to escape Max's aura, **she** smiled vaguely and passed quickly through.

All the girls knew Bones was wearing a new piece of jewelry, and four pairs of eyes hungered for a look. Only Cathy was more interested in the woman than in the trophy, and when Bones walked past her, Cathy scrutinized her. Cathy saw what she had seen before, a pale lunar beauty and a diminutive but highly charged figure which left in its wake the musky scent of money. Cathy faced the facts. Miss Burton was in a different league. Miss Burton was beyond envy. No wonder Mr. Herschel adored her.

What had Mr. Herschel meant this morning when he said Miss Burton didn't have the balls to put on the silence button? Cathy, walking slowly back to her own shared desk, speculated on what kind of balls Miss Burton lacked.

When Cathy pictured the word "balls," she saw nice, white, fresh-from-the-can tennis balls. Which led her instantly to thoughts of Jock Kelly. Which was terribly confusing because how could she have been so *horribly* affected—in *that* way—by Mr. Herschel and then have the feelings get all mixed up like they did with Jock Kelly in that elevator?

Later, when in spite of everything, she had gone out with Jock, she had let him take off her blouse and fool around. Because the main thing she felt about him was that he was *safe*. Well, maybe not safe, but *safer*. Safer *than*.

Cathy Kronig was only inexperienced. She was not stupid.

Inside his own office, Max called his personal lawyer, Bernie Seiden. Bernie was a wildman who screamed louder and easier than any man Max had ever known. When Max felt jittery, he always called Bernie. The attorney's raging unreason made Max, by comparison, feel in cool control.

"Hello, Bernie. Max. What do you think about we go back to the first plan?" Max teased solemnly. "You know, leave the Paulson job in Switzerland. Why should we run scared in Zurich just because . . ."

"Fuck Zurich!" howled Bernie. "Fuck Switzerland! You and I know they sold out to Washington! You want every fucking dollar you spend to pass through some fucking IRS man . . . fucking . . ."

Max leaned back and listened, calmed.

Downstairs at Burton Productions, five minutes before her

appointment with Warner, Bones called an office at La Guardia.

"Hello, Bart. This is Miss Burton . . . I thought I'd check directly with you instead of bothering Mr. Herschel. I've got an enormous package to send to California and I don't want to burden him unless he's taking the Gulfstream. You know how he is. He'd drag an elephant onto a commercial flight if he thought I wanted one shipped . . . Oh, he's not taking the plane? Good thing I called you. I'll just send my package air freight. Thanks, Bart. Good-bye."

She slowly replaced the telephone in its cradle and felt fury rising in her like lava. The intensity of the anger surprised her. She breathed deeply, willing her neck and shoulder muscles to relax.

All right, Max. *All right.*

She flipped the intercom. "Get me Steven Routledge's agent's number . . . No, don't try her, just get me the number. Then call the publisher's and find out where Routledge stays in New York. Now, send Warner in."

As Warner leaned eagerly toward her, Bones considered that one of the things she didn't like about him was his hair. It was red and wiry and looked as if he bent rather than brushed it into place. He had always reminded her of something she could not quite identify. Today she would concentrate until she got it.

Sitting eagerly forward with his head cocked intelligently to one side, listening to her very punctuation, racing ahead, bouncing back . . . an *Airedale*. That was it. She repressed a grimace. Time to throw him his bone. Get it over.

"Warner, I just wanted to tell you personally how impressed I am with the new casting girl. She's first-rate. Where did you find her?"

Warner's bright auburn eyes sparkled at her.

"She was stashed away in Comco's New York office. I've had my eye on all their shows for the last year. Always impeccably cast, but no casting credits. So I went sniffing around . . ."

Precisely, Bones thought, seized by the image of Warner with his nose pushing right up the backside of Comco. She listened as he continued his recital of his raid on the rival producing company.

"All I had to do was offer her a little lustful appreciation," Warner smirked.

For the thousandth time, Warner searched Bones' perfect little face for the slightest sign that she reacted to him as a man. Nothing. He knew instinctively that she hated him, but that fantastic face never betrayed her.

Funny, he thought. There she sat, beautiful as mountain mist. Smart, which he liked. And she hated his guts, which usually got him off. But the only time he ever wanted her was after she'd been upstairs with the old man.

It occurred to Warner that power might be as potent an aphrodisiac for a man as for a woman. So was he sitting here horny for Bones herself, or for Bones-the-old-boy's-proxy? Warner Magill did not have much humor, but the notion of his lusting after Max Herschel made him grin.

Bones' suddenly raised eyebrows made him realize that he had not been following her speech, which did not matter because it was just a lot of bullshit about how much she appreciated him. Her surprise, he knew, was in response to his grin. He endeavored to turn the grin into an open invitation.

Fucking creep, she thought. Nevertheless. She tossed him a grin of her own, then ran the sword through his heart. "I'm only going to stop by the *Generations* rehearsals for a minute. I have an important meeting at NET."

The NET dramatic series was Bones' special project. She had no intention of sharing any detail of it with Warner. She acknowledged that more than half her impulse to sack him stemmed from her possessive feeling about the NET programs. She sighed inwardly. If she were not going to dump him, she would be compelled to fence him off.

She let Warner help her on with her coat. The question was, how to fritz Warner? Light some small brush fires at *Generations?* Keep him busy leading the bucket brigade? Stupid. *Generations* was a steady show which brought in a lot of money. Getting

Warner out of her hair at NET was not a good enough reason to risk roughing up *Generations*.

What was she so itchy about? *Generations* was *her* show. So why this nagging anxiety to keep Warner out of her way? What would Max do? The hell with it. She would go back to mopping up tables at Schrafft's before she'd ask him. But she just might take Stella to lunch next week for a quiet chat.

As they left her office, Warner offered to take over the *Generations* errand and leave her free to concentrate on NET.

"You're too busy, Warner. I put far too much on you as it is. I know I do."

In the outer office, Mark handed Bones a memo which listed Steven Routledge's telephone number and a Park Avenue address. "Big Spender. When in New York, stays with Bernard Jess Routledge, a cousin."

Bones looked up at Mark and gave his arm a tender little touch. "Remember. Thursday. In a matchbox."

Chapter 6

Many years ago, when Max made his first transcontinental flight, the trip took thirteen hours. The plane was a bi-motor Douglas with two single rows of passenger seats, seven to a row, divided by the aisle. The airport was a field in Teterboro, New Jersey.

There was great glamour attached to the flight, and Max, thrilled, had eagerly searched for his own name among the privileged on the passenger list tacked to a wall outside the terminal building.

"Seat Number Eleven, Maximilian Herschel." Who was in Seat Number Twelve? . . . B. B. Bondy? Never heard of him. Number Ten? . . . Jonathan Hambro. Never heard of him . . . Then his eye caught the jackpot name. "Seat Number Seven, Mr. John Hay Whitney." *Jock Whitney!* Such proximity to the Real Thing dazzled Max. Whitneys, Vanderbilts, Astors. Then he read the next line. "Seat Number Six, Mr. Whitney's Feet."

A short time later, from seat number eleven, Max watched Whitney's entrance. Jock Whitney was accompanied by a flunky bearing a long, leather-padded board, a stadium blanket, and a substantial pillow. Whitney's man swiveled seat number six so that it faced number seven, then arranged the board so that it bridged the space between the two chairs. Once the board was in place, Whitney sat down and stretched his legs luxuriously along the improvised chaise, as his attendant solicitously arranged the blanket around his lap and legs and feet. Lastly, the flunky carefully placed the pillow behind Whitney's head and hung a Mark Cross book bag within Whitney's easy reach.

Jock Whitney's feet had haunted Max for over thirty years. In fact, they had become for him the symbol of life's incalculable potential. Even the sauna in his own Gulfstream could not compete with the Romanov splendor accorded John Hay Whitney's feet those many years ago in Teterboro, New Jersey. Stella might think Max's nutshell ambition was Morgan Price, but Max knew it was really John Hay Whitney's feet.

Tonight, Max sat in the window seat of United's Flight 15. Like Whitney, Max now bought two seats when he took a commercial flight, but the extra space was not for feet. Max liked to keep the aisle seat empty so that the stewardesses were obliged to bend closely toward him, proferring, along with the drinks, mixed nuts, and inedible meals, their own infinitely appetizing young persons, their sweet solicitude. Max was touched by the girls' innocent pride in their dreadful profession. He knew they worked sweatshop hours and were so poorly paid that they generally lived five and six to a high-rise apartment. In flight, they had to eat standing up, out of the passengers' sight, and no matter how many hands grabbed at their bottoms, or brushed against their breasts, they remained, thanks to the iron training of stew-school, unflinching and good-humored. They are our geisha, Max acknowledged with tender gratitude.

Maximilian Herschel's heart went out to all poor young girls. It seemed grossly unfair to him that such charming creatures demanded and received so little. It delighted him to lavish pretty things on them, and when they attempted to repay him with squeals and hugs and puppyish wrigglings, he was both amused and moved.

In flight Max never touched the stewardesses, but was always gallant and outspokenly appreciative of their services. He was funny. He made them laugh. Later, when their duties intensified and they grew rushed and harried, he showed concern. He never watched the in-flight movies, or listened to the canned concerts. Max watched United's stewardesses and listened to their chatter.

By the time the plane landed in Los Angeles, he would have singled out the most promising stew aboard. He would have engaged her in conversation, researching where she lived and with whom, what level of education she had attained, or, when he was lucky, aspired to. He would have made a close guess at her IQ, at her suggestibility, and the degree to which her ambition extended beyond United Airlines. He would have gauged her spirit-docility ratio, then if she had indicated the faintest flicker of ambition or humor, he would walk off the plane with her.

And United Airlines was screwed again.

The dinner at La Cote Basque had not gone well. Routledge was clever and he was handsome, but he was a shit.

Bones had finally been provoked enough to state her case sharply. "Have you considered, Mr. Routledge, that it's a trifle dated to despise TV?"

"The fact that I do not wish to *appear* on television, Miss Burton, does not mean that I despise it. Actually . . ."—he flashed her a bright, perjurous smile—". . . actually, I love TV. I never miss *Let's Make a Deal*."

Bones' experience with Routledge's brand of snobbery was limited. Her life was manned by Max's world of high but hybrid achievers and those gangs of quasi-eminents who competed for the limelight of the Hoffman show. She was uncertain how to proceed with Routledge, and the only satisfaction she got from the meal was when a small glob of pudding missed his mouth and had clung eggy and unsightly, to his chin.

It was the fugitive pudding which softened her. Although she mistrusted the impulse that triggered the invitation, she had suggested they move on to her apartment for coffee and brandy.

Now, settled into separate corners of the limousine, they rode in wary silence to East End Avenue.

In the gloom of the car, she covertly catalogued his features. The light brown cap of softly curling hair was cut ruthlessly back from his high forehead and brought no relief to the sharp angles of his face. The eyes were green, deep set. Myopic? The nose, narrow, arrogant. A touch too long? The mouth a little thin, but saved from cold austerity, as was the face itself, by unpredictable smiles that exposed dazzling, rich-boy's teeth. Routledge's looks would be a real pain in the ass to Max.

Inside the pale gray silk walls of Bones' apartment, Steven paused, bemused. The place, a lot better than he had expected, had been furnished by a serenely confident hand.

He had endured the evening with this artificial and irritating young woman for the sake of the meal, which was splendid, and for her diphthongs, which were not. Her speech was as phony as her manners, both undiluted Hollywood British. But, he was interested to see, in her home she had framed herself to uncommon advantage. The apartment was filled with quietly beautiful things. Its owner had not taken refuge in color or fashion.

In the foyer's age-clouded glass, Bones caught Steven's gaze and saw in it the first stirrings of interest.

He addressed her silvery reflection. "Duplex?"

"Yes. Much too large. But it was a bargain."

"What do you call a bargain?"

"Three hundred thousand."

Steven let out a hoot of laughter.

Bones asked, "What amuses you? My apartment or me?"

"Where did you go to school?"

"Wellesley."

"How did a little cracker like you get to Wellesley?"

"On a Maximilian Herschel scholarship."

"Maximilian Herschel?"

"You don't know who he is?"

"One of those names that come to mind when you read about sinister forces in our society."

"Sinister? Max would be flattered."

"'Max'? You call your scholarship fund 'Max'?"

"He encourages these little intimacies." She took his coat and led him into the living room.

Steven tried to recall how Jessen, his friend at Boston University, had described Stan Munshin's famous father-in-law. Something like "The hookers' HEW."

"Actually," Steven informed Bones, "I've met Mr. Herschel's daughter and son-in-law. We have a mutual friend at BU who took me to dinner at their place one time."

"To Baby and Stan's?" An unmistakable tremor of uncertainty registered in Bones' voice.

Steven had felt hustled all evening by this little lady, and he was not inclined to let her off free. "According to my friend"— Steven chose a blunt instrument—"the old man keeps a stable of whores."

Bones smiled. "That's right. I'm one of them."

"Does he do this well by all of you?"

"No. I'm exceptional." She held out a silver cigarette box. "I've been with Max since I was eighteen. I'm top girl. He sent me to school and paid for this apartment and most of the things in it. He set me up in Burton Productions. *But.* I work very hard and very successfully and earn upward of a quarter of a million a year. Of my *own.*"

"Then you are not only exceptional," Steven conceded. "You are extraordinary."

Feeling a strong impulse to put space between them, he took a few steps toward a large painting across the room. "Is that a Carrà?"

"Yes."

Bones sat down and waited patiently as Steven embarked on a silent inspection of the drawing room and library. When he returned and sat down opposite her, he said, "I count eleven Italian Futurists."

"Do you admire them?"

"Not really."

"Nor do I. I feel about the Futurists the way you do about give-away shows. Do you know what I mean?"

"They make you feel better about yourself?"

"Something like that. Max despises them."

Bones stood up and walked across the room to the Marinetti. Regarding it with contemptuous affection, she pronounced, "As you probably know, Carrà and Marinetti were disciples of Bergson and Nietzsche, theoretical anarchists. Carrà and Boccioni, Russolo, then, later, of course, Severini and Balla, were all attacking the tyranny of tradition . . ." She smiled slyly. ". . . the Establishment Nude, as it were. Italians never seem to hit the political bullseye, do they?"

Steven's expression applauded her little aria. "Well, now. Your academic career must have given great satisfaction to your benefactor."

"I was summa cum laude. 'Satisfactory' enough to my 'benefactor' so that he sent me on for a master's in art history. The Institute of Fine Arts at New York University. I did my thesis on Oriental porcelain, 'Sung, a History of Surmise.'"

"There's not a piece of Oriental junk in the joint."

"No, that junk is all over at *his* joint. And at my gallery."

"What gallery?"

"My gallery on Madison."

"You're the Burton Gallery?"

"That's me." Bones turned. "I promised you coffee." Motioning him to come along, she left the room. Steven followed her through the dining room and butler's pantry, and on into the kitchen.

As she prepared the coffee, Steven examined the stunning array of electrical devices with which the kitchen was equipped.

"Miss Burton, I jes' love your kitchen."

"Do you? Max is the cook. Not me."

"A pasta machine, two microwave ovens, a trash-masher, a twelve-speed blender . . . I never even heard of a blender with more than eight speeds."

"You jes' hate my kitchen."

"Absolutely not. How could a man who loves *Let's Make a Deal* hate this kitchen?"

He carried the tray back to the library, and explained the difference between old-rich kitchens and new-rich kitchens. "That is to say, *more recently* rich kitchens," he temporized. "Old-rich kitchens run heavily toward eleemosynary green . . . worn linoleum. Exposed pipes."

Bones handed him coffee. "No shit?"

Steven leaned back and allowed his very real curiosity to show. "Since you were eighteen. How old are you now?"

Bones was surprised to hear herself say, "Thirty-one next week." She could not remember telling anyone the truth about her age since the Tucson, Arizona sheriff had caught and frightened her into admitting she was only twelve.

"How old are you?" Bones asked Steven.

"Twenty-nine." he answered. "Thirty-one minus eighteen . . . you've been with Herschel almost fourteen years."

"That's right."

"So what happens when some odd cock like me comes scratching around? By, I believe—but correct me if I'm wrong—invitation?"

"You mean what does Max do if he finds out I'm fooling around? The answer is nothing. He ignores it. The odd cock."

He sipped thoughtfully at his coffee.

"Does the idea of Max bother you?" she asked.

"His presence is palpable."

"Only figuratively. Right now, Max is in southern California, screwing the ears off some United stewardess. Trying to get her back in school." She smiled magnanimously. "Max Herschel is one of our nation's most tireless workers in the field of higher education."

"You're absolutely sure she's with United?"

"Max made a take-over pass once at United and got rebuffed; ever since, he's confined his raids to that one line. The trouble is he really doesn't have the time to devote to it. This is his first foray in months."

"How many has he got now? In school, I mean."

Bones shrugged. "I don't keep track anymore. There are two I know about . . . A little brunette named Betsy Pennypacker who's a sophomore at Santa Cruz. She's been giving Max trouble . . . dropping the two courses he's interested in . . ."

Steven laughed but Bones continued gravely.

"The other one is an acting major at Carnegie Tech, named Annamarie Venturi. Annamarie's having a lot of expensive dental work done because when Max had her nose bobbed, it made her upper lip too prominent. Once the teeth are realigned, they think her chin will be strong enough to compensate for the lip. It's all quite painful, and Annamarie has been very irritable lately, especially when she misses out on romantic leads because of the braces. Max has been steering pretty clear of the Tech campus."

Steven sighed happily. "Unreal. Unreal."

"If your novelist's curiosity is titillated, you can sit by the tub while I soak, and I'll tell you more. I'm exhausted."

"Will your tub accommodate two?"

But in the bath, she did not, as she had promised, tell him about Max's girls. She did not speak at all as she closed her eyes and sank, into the hot foamy water.

She soaked quietly, never opening her eyes or speaking. For a while Steven studied her closed face, then at last, he began to talk. Bones listened to his voice, measured, mock-solemn. His turn of phrase was faintly formal, and he spoke in natural paragraphs. Steven told her about growing up a diplomat's son and attending schools in Brussels and Brazil and Cairo.

"While you were making it on school holidays with a notorious financier, Miss Burton . . . how are you called? Familiarly?"

"Bones."

He eyed the tips of her breasts rising above the bubbly water, her rounded arms extended over either side of the room-centered tub, the gentle curving line of her neck and shoulders. "*Bones?*" he queried.

"My mother named me Bonita. Probably got it off a can of tuna. Then again, maybe not. She wasn't what you'd call a great reader. Anyway, I've always been called Bones. I prefer it."

"I see. Well, Bones, as I was about to say, while you were bedding down with Maximilian Herschel over the hols, I was under the impression that in the main, sex was confined to the lower social orders. I was still a virgin at nineteen." He went on to describe how, at that point, his retardation had been noticed by a self-effacing Bostonian aunt. Her husband, Steven's Uncle Stewart, was commodore of the Quequod Yacht Club, and a household tyrant of considerable talent.

"He made daily inspections . . . hell, he still does . . . of all domestic wood and metal surfaces, regularly up-and-downgrading both Aunt Cora and her staff. All according to patina."

Bones was acutely conscious of Steven's long legs under the suds. She had drawn her own knees slightly up to avoid contact with them. Now as Steven talked, he was absently punctuating with one of his feet, gently whipping the water and occasionally touching Bones' left hip. Keep your goddam toes off my hip, she thought, irritated at the movement but reluctant to interrupt the saga of Aunt Cora.

"All those surfaces." The image seemed to amuse him.

"What about them?" she inquired.

"Well, since surfaces are Uncle Stewart's specialty, Aunt Cora is always careful to give him precisely the one he wants in a wife. Mild, dutiful, *custodial* . . ." Steven smiled. "She's never been caught."

Although Bones was ahead of the story, she wanted the details. "Caught?" she asked.

"At it. She always had the Yankee good sense to limit her lovers, not numerically, God knows, but socially. For over thirty years she has resolutely screwed beneath her station." Again his foot tapped against her hip.

She inched away. "Go on."

"Well, she was forty that summer. I had just turned twenty. I must have been pathetic. It was . . . in the beginning anyway . . . simple kindness on her part." He paused, narrowed his eyes thoughtfully, then continued. "I spent the most exciting summer of my life in that staid Quequod beach house . . . in the narrow, white, and altogether seemly bed of my Aunt Cora. My new book is about her."

"Your real aunt? Not just your uncle's wife?"

"My mother's sister. Her middle sister."

"And you mean you're writing a book about how you slept with your aunt?" Bones was aghast. Not at the incest but at the betrayal. She frowned and put a hand under the water to stop, finally, the movement of his foot. "You wrote about *that?*"

"No one will recognize her."

"But, good God. *She* will. If I were some kid's aunt and I took him to bed and he wrote a book about it . . . I mean, Jesus! It's her life!"

"But it's my life, too."

Bones shot Steven a look of such monumental misgiving that it made him laugh.

"Anyway," he continued, "why should a little mountain girl like you bridle at incest? Weren't you raped by your father before you were twelve?"

"No. I was abandoned by my father when I was eight months old," she answered indifferently. "He told my mother he was going to hitchhike to Durham where they were supposed to be hiring at the cigarette factories. And that was it. After he took off, Mama worked at Woolie's during the day and hustled a little at roadhouses at night. I went to school and made good grades and sucked up to rich kids who had electricity in their houses and TV sets. And when I was twelve, I lit out for Los Angeles to become a Mouseketeer."

"I don't know what you're talking about. What's a Mouseketeer?"

"You don't know what a Mouseketeer is?"

"No."

"Oh, of course you didn't grow up in the States. In the late fifties every little hick kid in the country wanted to be a Mouseketeer. On TV . . ."

She sang the Mouseketeer song with plaintive sweetness, holding the final note on "M-O-U-S-E-E."

"I had it all figured out. I was very blond, which was good, and just the right size to introduce myself directly after Cubby. 'I'm Darlene! . . . I'm Cubby! . . . I'm Bonita!'"

"Did you make it?"

"I got as far as Tucson, Arizona. There was a missing-child bulletin out on me, and the cops picked me up. I was dumbstruck that Mama had the sense to get out a bulletin."

Bones slid down lower in the water, seeking more warmth.

"Anyway," her chin now resting on foam, she peered across at Steven and continued, "they bussed me back to Gum Springs, and that's where I stayed, brooding and biding my time till I was sixteen. Then I took off again, but by then I was too old to be a Mouseketeer, so I decided to be a great Broadway actress instead. Mama had a new boy friend and I was cramping her style, so she didn't try to stop me when I left for New York. We wrote to each other a couple of times a year, and I used to send her junk for Christmas, and she'd send me shelled pecans in a Maxwell House coffee can. But I never saw her again."

"Is she still living?"

"No." Bones stood up, ornamented here and there with little beads of bubbles. "I'm getting cold—" She stopped short. He had scooped a handful of foam off the top of the water and laid it gently, experimentally over her little patch of amber hair.

"Summer ermine," he observed, pleased with the effect.

Before she could brush the foam off, he caught her hand, leaned forward, and from a near distance, blew the bubbles away.

A tiny frown soldiered between her brows. "I went to Wellesley with a girl named Bubbles. All the guys in the village used to whistle the song at her. It made her furious."

As he watched her drying off, he considered that she seemed unwilling to either initiate or respond to sensuality. Her body was one softly gracious ellipse, but she preferred to be called "Bones." An image came to him of those Japanese toy flowers that blossom so graciously in a bowl of water. But Bones had disobligingly folded herself up. When he had made a playful, provocative gesture, she had responded with the off-putting recital about Bubbles.

Steven, only half-dry, threw his towel down on the floor and followed her into the bedroom, wondering why he was here and what it would take.

She was more astonished by her tears than by her body's treachery. That it had so unexpectedly, so abjectly surrendered to this stranger was alarming enough, but that she had wept, had watered his chest and face with a flood of tears, frightened her. She had long supposed herself safely immune to any sexual turbulence other than that which Max provided.

When Steven turned on the light and got up to search his jacket for cigarettes, she had stared at him with an unstable mix of distrust and appetite. Watching the stranger, arrogant and possibly unsafe, return to her bed, Bones felt dazed, disoriented. He lay down and put an arm under her head.

"By the way, did you ever become a great Broadway star? You wouldn't be George C. Scott or anybody like that?"

She rolled her head away from him, turned her mouth against his arm, taking his flesh between her teeth, not biting, just holding on; she shook her head gently.

"So?" he insisted. "A sixteen-year-old mountain girl, hopes blighted, alone and penniless in the big city. What happened? Don't leave me hanging."

Bones pushed her tongue hard against his smooth, salty skin, then pulled her head back. "Nothing much happened. I was a waitress at the Seventy-Ninth-Street Schrafft's—"

"Schrafft's uses child labor?"

"Oh, I'd had a couple of waitress jobs in other places first, learned what lies to tell. Anyway, after Schrafft's, I modeled junior dresses." Her mouth curled down. "For a very senior manufacturer . . ."

"Not nice?"

"Not nice. But I was able to go to night school and get a diploma . . ." There was a long pause. "Then . . . I met Max."

Steven waited for her to go on, but she lay still in his arms, until he tightened his hold. Her entire body shivered as she burrowed for space not so much against, as under, him. Even then, she didn't speak, nor did Steven, but he kissed the top of her head, then touched her face, both to caress her and to see if she were crying again. She was not.

At last, she asked, "Would you like to see my jewelry?"

He turned her face up to his and gave her a gentle kiss. "Not particularly . . ."

"Yes, you would." She wriggled out of his grasp and slipped off the bed.

When she came back she was carrying a large crocodile-and-gold-fitted jewelry case.

"Christ. It's just like your kitchen."

"It was made for me in Florence. It cost twenty-seven hundred dollars, four years ago. Probably be about five thousand now."

[67]

"Sweet Jesus."

"What do old-rich jewelry cases cost?"

"Nothing. They're inherited. Mark Cross and Vuitton," he sniffed, "flourish as a result of the middle classes moving up." She was thrilled by his snobbery. "My mother," he went on, "kept her jewelry in a Crisco can."

Bones carefully considered this, then said, "I think it's pretentious to be rich and keep your jewelry in a Crisco can."

"My mother wasn't rich. Even in my grandmother's time there wasn't much left. Nana kept her jewelry in her husband's socks."

"If they weren't rich, what about the jewelry? Wasn't it any good?"

"There were some quite nice pieces, but it was all family stuff. It wouldn't have occurred to mother to sell." He paused. "Of course, when it finally came down to me and my sister, I sold my share. The jewelry was about all there was left to inherit, and I spent most of what I got to pay for my farm."

"Maybe I'll leave my jewelry to a struggling young poet," Bones smiled.

"Leave it to your children."

"I'll never have any children."

Bones opened the case a crack, peered in, then, snaking her hand in, she withdrew something. Instead of revealing it to Steven, she kept her hand closed tightly around the object as she began her story.

"The day I met Max . . . I was walking from Seventh Avenue over to Lord and Taylor's . . . lunch hour . . . I suddenly remembered I wanted to buy a birthday present for a guy I knew, so I detoured up toward Forty-Sixth to Abercrombie's . . ." She grinned. "My friend was kind of a jock. He was a theatrical lawyer who represented all sorts of glamorous people. I think he even worked once for Marilyn Monroe. But the only time I ever saw him get excited about a celebrity was once in a taxi, he screamed—I mean actually *screamed*—'Look! Look there! There's YAT Tittle!' He was shaking, he was so excited."

Steven asked, "Who's YAT Tittle?"

His ignorance of YAT Tittle, even of the Mousketeers, seemed to Bones somehow wonderful. She thought about his innocence of the Mickey Mouse Show, and of the New York Giants. She felt her heart make an infinitesimal shift. "YAT Tittle was a great pro football player."

He prompted her. "So you went to Abercrombie's. And that's where you met Herschel?"

"Yes. Just as I got there, this enormous black limousine pulled up and two men got out and went into the store in front of me. Max had been on the cover of *Time* magazine a couple of weeks earlier, and I recognized him instantly, so I fell back to follow and stare. *Time* had called Herschel Industries the sexiest conglomerate in the country . . ." She quoted, " 'Max Herschel seldom relinquishes a property. "Few of my companies are public," he says, "I am the Industries. Max Herschel personally. I like short decision lines." ' "

Bones absently tapped on the jewel case. "Later, I got a copy of that issue and memorized the article on Max. I still remember every word of it. Fourteen years later."

She glanced at the fist that held her pickings from the jewel case, then continued. "So. I followed Max into the store and into the elevator and got out on the same floor. In the elevator he looked at me once and smiled, but he never stopped talking to the man he was with. The other man was the one who had wanted to come to Abercrombie's. Max was just there because he was selling the man on a deal . . . he might just as well have been in his own office. He never even glanced at anything in the store. I followed them to the fishing department. The man told the clerk that he wanted to pick out some trout lures . . . flies . . . you know?"

Steven nodded.

"I can't be sure what you know or don't know. After YAT Tittle . . ." She reached out with her clenched fist and gave him a tap on the wrist. *Exotic*, she thought. She smiled to herself. He is exotic. "Anyway, the other man was very serious about the trout lures, picking over the trays as if he were choosing diamonds, and all the while Max selling him and selling him. I stood at the counter beside them, where Max could see me. But he just kept on talking and talking, selling and selling . . . if you'd ever heard him when he's really pitching . . ." She shook her head. "Then another clerk came up and asked me if I needed assistance . . ."

Clearly, Bones was enjoying the memory. Steven urged her on. "What did you do?"

"I said I wanted to buy some trout things, too, and I pointed to the trays, so the clerk got one out and I picked out a model I thought was pretty and asked if there was another one like it. He found another and I had a pair. I held them up to my earlobes and let them dangle like earrings. Then I turned around to Max and interrupted him. I said, 'Sir, I'm so sorry to interrupt, but I need some help . . . there just aren't any mirrors here . . .' I tossed my head and dangled the little hooks at Max. I said, 'What do *you* think? Are these cute?' 'Very cute,' he said. 'What are you going to set them in? Gold?' I took down one hand and looked at the lure and at the little steel hook in it. 'No, silver to match the hook.' And I giggled at him. 'Anyway, I couldn't afford gold.'"

"So what happened then? Did he bite?"

"Oh, yes. I was going to go on to the ground floor and be there waiting when they came down, but he followed me to the elevator. He excused himself from the man, walked over to me and said, 'Go get in the car. I'll be right down.' I batted my eyelashes at him and said, 'What car? I don't know what you mean.' And he said, 'The car you watched me get out of.' And he laughed at me. 'You think I don't know when I'm being tailed?' I didn't answer back. I just did what he said. I got in the car and sure enough, in no time he came out of the store. Alone. And got in the car with me." She shrugged as if to say "and that was that." Smiling, she added, "It wasn't even his car. It was the other man's. Max just commandeered it."

Steven reached out and touched her ear. "That's a very romantic story."

"Oh sure. It's been love in a cottage ever since." She opened her fist and extended her palm to show him an earring. Dangling from the fine dark emerald to which it was attached was a shimmering, articulated body of minute jewel stones, exquisitely designed to resemble the bright-hued feathers of a trout lure. On the underside, when Bones turned the earring over, was a diamond-tipped hook.

Steven put out a finger and tested the tip of the hook.

"Pretty hard to resist," he admitted.

"Oh, I didn't resist. I thought here I was a little old kid from Gum Springs, North Carolina, and I'd sure enough hooked the biggest fish in the sea. What I didn't know then, of course, was that he was a dedicated child molester. *Time* hadn't mentioned that."

"You're kidding."

"He likes young girls."

"How young?"

"He's not a fool. He settles for seventeen." After a moment she added, "Of course, when he mixes business with pleasure— like United—he stretches the point. He'll go as high as twenty-two or -three."

"There's a theory current among psychologists," Steven said, "that children are quite often the sexual aggressors . . . that they are consciously provocative. Did you ever hear that?"

Bones smiled. "I haven't heard about the theory, but I know a lot about the practice."

Steven smiled. "He's not a young man. He has a wife. He has you. Still, you say, he persists in this vigorous dedication to the education and welfare of dollies. What's it all in aid of? There are simpler ways of getting laid."

"He doesn't like the simpler ways."

"What does he like?"

"Well . . . of course he likes the illusion that he's helping. Rather than *paying*. You know?"

Steven nodded.

"But what it really is . . ." She shrugged. ". . . he wants to stay young. In a way . . . with the girls . . . In a way he's back in school."

Bones told Steven how delighted Max was when he found out she didn't care what she studied.

"I just wanted an education. Any kind of education. I wanted to be successful."

[71]

Steven smiled. "Successful?"

"Independent."

Max had decided Bones would study Art History. After she got a degree, he would set her up in a gallery. She would help him with his collection or could go on to become a curator in a top museum, whatever she wanted. "I could have exactly what I wanted," she said and fell silent.

"And that's what you got?"

"*Exactly*," she answered, pleased to give him such a forceful affirmative. "That's the way Max works. He finds out what people want and he gives it to them."

"Then they owe him."

She shook her head. "Don't try to make it sound like the Godfather. When somebody goes a big distance to help you, you're genuinely grateful. You want to please him, give him what *he* needs." She shrugged. "Max doesn't hold a gun on you. If you don't want to honor the bargain, what's he going to do?" She smiled. "I wanted an education. I got it. What could he do if I took my Phi Beta Kappa key and skipped? Have me brainwashed?"

"You said you wanted to be independent."

"I *am* independent."

"Really?"

"I live precisely as I choose."

"What happens in business—to people he does business with —if *they* don't honor the bargain?"

"He takes his losses and moves on."

"Really?"

"Yes, *really*. Max does a lot of business. With a lot of people. If somebody doesn't pull for him, he just cuts them loose. That's all. And I'll tell you something else . . ." She smiled. "Max is very tough. He negotiates like a terrier negotiates with a rat. But he's not mean. He's not a hater. He doesn't go in for revenge. Over the years, I've heard a lot of people say a lot of terrible things about Max, but I've never heard him bad-mouth anybody. Not ever."

The hawk, Steven thought, is not an ill-natured bird. If the hawk could speak, it would not bad-mouth the sparrow. "Max sounds like a great guy," Steven smiled. "A real prince." He gave a nod at the case. "Let's see the crown jewels."

She opened the jewelry case, and he appraised the bracelets and pins and rings. "Very nice," he admitted.

She reclaimed the case, chose a bracelet, and put it on. She followed with a second bracelet and a double strand of pearls. Then she picked out a sapphire pin and the new coral and diamond piece and stuck them both into a pillow. Finally, she clipped on a pair of enamel and ruby earrings.

"My little family. Max gives me something beautiful every time I get knocked up." The toad words were out.

"Knocked up by Max?"

"Of course by Max."

"Really knocked up or pretend knocked up?"

Steven thought it interesting that she appeared to be honestly taken aback. Her mouth dropped open slightly at the suggestion that she might have tricked Max by claiming to be pregnant when she was not.

"What for? To get jewelry?" she demanded.

He nodded.

"You don't understand. I don't have to do anything like that. Max will give me whatever I want. For that matter, I could buy my own jewelry. I'm rich."

Steven smiled.

"I mean I've got enough money."

"Enough for what?"

"To do whatever I want to do."

"Do you have enough money to leave Herschel?"

"But I don't want to leave him."

"Okay. So go on. Tell me how rich you are. I love hearing about money."

"Everybody does. They say they don't, but they do."

"Have you got a million?" he needled.

"Yes."

"Then Mr. Herschel is generous indeed."

"Mr. Herschel is generous. But *I* made the million."

"How? It's the intimate financial details that fascinate me."

"Go to hell."

"I'm serious. Tell me how it's done. How can I become a millionaire before I'm thirty? What's the first step? I mean aside from fucking Max Herschel."

"Well," she took the side of reason, "you've got to fuck *somebody*."

"Okay. I accept that. What's the second step?"

"Start small and smart and work your way up."

"How small? Like a little gallery on Madison Avenue that displays in its chaste window the single, simple museum piece? Small like that?"

"When I opened the gallery, those display pieces were strictly on consignment. I was glad to take fifteen percent of the sale, which, according to any reasonable tenet of merchandising, made me a thirty-five percent loser on the transaction. But that window-dressing brought in buyers. Consigners are collectors. They dump one and pick up two more."

When she paused, Steven prodded.

"How much capital did it take?"

"Max and I opened the gallery on an equal-partnership basis."

Steven pried until she revealed that Max had put up five thousand dollars for fifty shares of stock and had given her fifty shares free. "Because I was the mule. Then he loaned the gallery money for inventory and put in pieces he wanted to cull from his own collection. I got him good prices and took no commission. I worked like a coolie for over three years, and I plowed every possible penny of profit back into inventory."

"Which is now worth what?"

"Over a million. I could liquidate or sell at any time and come out with a minimum of half a million for me and the same for Max."

"That's really a very sweet story. Not at all what I was expecting. Now tell me about Burton Productions. How and why did you make the great leap backwards, from fine arts to the Nick Hoffman Show?"

"I wanted something that was completely mine. Max was always butting in at the gallery . . ."

[74]

"Doesn't he butt in on the TV shows? He financed that set-up too, didn't he?"

"No. We both put up capital. Max only holds half the stock, because TV production is dicey . . . highly profitable when you're riding the waves, but with a rocky bottom if you spill. You can get shafted in a hundred ways—sued, shouldered out, swallowed up. But with Max Herschel for a partner we'd be pretty indigestible. If I ever need or want the shares, he'll turn them over to me."

"And he never interferes?"

"No. *I* built that company. It is *mine*. The stock is worth about a million and a quarter . . . possibly more."

"Half in hand and the other half payable on demand."

"That's right."

"Then there's this apartment . . ."

She was amused by his unabashed curiosity. "I told you. Three hundred thousand. And furnishings. All mine."

"What about the twelve-speed blender? That too?"

"That too."

"Outright?"

"Outright."

Steven considered all this for a long moment. "In that case, if there are no major political or religious differences and you like Vermont . . . what's the date today?"

"The third."

"Well, then, moving calmly, deliberately, I expect by the thirteenth, I'll propose marriage. I think I've found the one to fuck."

"Marry me for my blender?"

"One should always take blenders into the soberest consideration when choosing a mate. And I very much like the idea of marrying a lady who has made it on her own. The odds are good that if things go bust, she could do it again."

"But it's my blender," Bones insisted. "Shouldn't you be just a trifle worried about emasculation?"

"Put down by a failed Mouseketeer? Never!"

She laughed and swatted at him. "I didn't fail! I just never got a break!"

[75]

Steven flipped her over on her stomach, effectively muzzling her face. He lay across her, holding her down and kissing the back of her neck. She laughed into the pillow.

"Bones, dear?"

"I'm smothering!"

He turned her head to one side so she could breathe.

"Bones, what happens if I decide I might just possibly want to see you again? I mean when the old boy's back in residence."

"He doesn't reside *here*. Besides, I don't hide anything from Max . . ."

He allowed her to roll over on her back again.

She looked up at the ceiling. "He knows I've had lovers. He doesn't care."

"Are you sure about that?"

"It *annoys* him. But as long as it doesn't last long and I'm reasonably discreet . . ."

Steven edged away from her slightly and propped his head on an elbow.

" 'Reasonably discreet' . . . what does that mean? Cinq à sept? Dining in darkest Yorkville? Keeping it from the servants?"

She turned and looked at him. "Haven't you ever had an affair with a married woman? I mean besides your aunt?"

"Just the odd bounce. No real affairs."

They lay quietly for a moment, then Steven said, "Come up to Vermont this weekend. See my farm."

"I told Max I'd go to Boston with him to visit Baby."

Steven pulled the coral pin from the pillow and held it out to her.

"I count six pieces. I take that to mean six abortions, which would seem to indicate either masochism or malice. Which is it?"

"Max says that it's just a hillbilly instinct for indiscriminate breeding. Bad blood, he says. I think he's probably right."

"I think he's probably wrong. And knows it. What's surprising is that you don't. Or claim you don't."

"What do you think it is? From the vast experience of your twenty-nine years?"

"I think you love him, and want more of him than he's willing to give and that you get yourself knocked up for attention . . . and revenge."

"I don't love Max."

"Then why . . ." He held out the coral pin. "*This?*" One by one, he touched the other five pieces of jewelry. "And this . . . and this . . . and this . . ."

She shrugged away from him.

"Why do you collect pictures you don't like, pick up men you don't want?"

Eyes and mouth challenged his last question.

He proceeded remorselessly. "You brought me up here because you're going to be thirty-one and Herschel is in California tonight with a girl ten years younger than you are. But most of all, why do you speak so dispassionately about a man who has filled your life for thirteen years? If you were really that dispassionate, you wouldn't need to talk about him, certainly not to someone you've chosen to beat him over the head with."

Her heart leapt up into her throat and stuck there. She tried to swallow it back down but couldn't.

"If you think the anxiety doesn't show through the facade . . ."

Hurriedly, she rolled off the bed, walked into the bathroom and shut the door; standing irresolutely on the cool tile, she waited to see if she were going to throw up.

Suddenly the door opened and Steven came in. Bones whirled on him.

"Get out! Don't come in my bathroom!"

"Why not? Up to something interesting?"

Of the two of them, Bones was the more shocked when she swung, fast and hard, landing a blow just below his left ear. It was heavy enough to knock him briefly off balance.

Her mouth opened in dread that he would hit her back, but Steven only studied the light fixtures over her shoulder for a protracted moment, then turned and walked from the room.

Relieved, but still shaken, Bones watched him go to his clothes, sit down, and reach for a shoe. When he began maneuvering his bare foot into it, her fright turned to embarrassment, and she approached him.

[77]

"Listen . . . I didn't mean to do that. I . . . didn't even know I was going to . . ."

As soon as he had one shoe securely on, he stood up. In two strides, the still naked, one-shoed man was upon her. Grabbing her by the shoulders, he turned her around and administered a hefty kick, dead on target, with the foot he had so thoughtfully shod.

Bones was lifted, literally, off her feet, and came to land an impressive distance away. From Steven, there was neither oath nor imprecation. From Bones, neither plea nor cry, even when the deed was done.

Sprawled on the floor, she lay dead-still, her eyes taking in the intricate needlepoint pattern of the rug. Close up, it wasn't so pretty. She methodically checked off as unharmed all bones and muscles, then considered the state of her emotions. She had been decked, kayoed, whatever, but strangely, her overriding emotion was one of triumph. She reran the clip of Steven rocking back when she hit *him*. She ran it again, slow-motion.

And Bones determined somehow to keep him.

She apologized. "I hope I didn't hurt your foot."

He scooped her up, put her back on the bed, and lay down beside her, flipping off his shoe with the big toe of his other foot.

Bones explained, "I don't like anybody to come into my bathroom uninvited. I really don't like it."

"I thought you were going to be sick . . . your skin went all clammy . . ."

"I've never talked to anybody about Max before. I mean really talked about him . . . and me . . . things like the jewelry . . ."

"Not even to your girl friends?"

"I've never had girl friends."

"Never?"

She thought carefully.

"I guess Baby's a friend. I mean, we're *friendly*. But I've never talked to her like this . . . about Max. How could I?" Bones had opened, for Steven, a window into a life so elaborately empty that Steven was shaken. He felt a powerful rush of pity, and in one swift trip he was shuttled to the suburbs of love.

Silently, he accepted the fact that he was settling into the neighborhood for more than an overnight visit. He put his hands on her breasts, hid his face between them, then whispered, "Why me?"

"I don't know." Her body's response to him was inexplicable. Once more, the helpless feeling, the liquid, slippery sensation began pulling her under as her nipples hardened under his touch. She strained to watch his head move from between her breasts down the length of her body, but her vision blurred.

"I don't know!" she lied.

Chapter 7

Stew-wise, the trip out had been a loss, which meant that Max would have to fly back a day early. In case he got lucky on the return flight, he wanted Wednesday night with his prize before the Thursday with Bones. Flying back a day early meant doubling up the work with Dolores.

Dolores was a young Chicano woman on whom Max counted for the smooth coordination of his Los Angeles managements. Dolores had relentlessly shouldered and kneed her way into the job. Using street-fighter's tactics, openly contemptuous of the enfeebling niceness of her Anglo competition, Dolores was Max's dog-walker. She kept top management in all five California-based companies leashed to Max's exact specifications.

Dolores' own loner instincts moved in symbiotic rhythm with her employer's. She knew that Max, in his way, was an artist, an emotional and turbulent man compelled to leave his signature on whatever he touched. But he was also a ruthless top-dog, marking off his territorial boundaries, peeing on every post, staking his claim on more and more ground, which he would subsequently control by outrunning, outbarking, and outbiting any challenger who might come sniffing around.

Max and Dolores worked at the Beverly Hills hotel where Max stayed when he was in southern California. He rarely spent a night at the bigger and more efficient hotel which Herschel Industries owned, because he did not like putting his person within easy access of management. He steered clear of the officers of his various enterprises on the sound principle that the warm currents of personality could fog up the cooler climate of numbers. Without direct access to Max, his companies' managements stayed loose and relatively helpless. The way Max liked them. On many trips, Max did not even visit his main office, and with one exception, he kept completely clear of the plants and outstations.

In the half-day that Dolores and Max had been working at the hotel, they had cut back the payroll at Lenscode and reviewed alternatives to DuPont supplies for Herschel's Flextone Girdles and Flihi Tennis Balls. They had had a good laugh over the SEC prospectus of a chain of funeral homes aspiring to greater glory, but when Max had finished laughing, he had said, "I'll take 'em."

Dolores made a note to start the investigation that preceded each of Max's acquisitions. If Max were going to buy funeral homes, he would want to know down to the pint how much formaldehyde got pumped into the stiffs during any fiscal year.

"Come on, Dolores. Back to the pits. I hear there's three city blocks very wobbly in San Bernardino. North Street between Pedro and Cassin Avenue. Buy us a banker in the neighborhood, and get the area appraised at our price . . ."

The time went quickly and smoothly When he finished with Dolores, he patted her brown, blunt-fingered hand. "What a kid. Too bad you're a spic and I'm already married."

As soon as Dolores had gathered up her papers and gone back to the office, Max headed for the laboratory to visit the gerbils.

The laboratory, which produced organic vitamins and a cough syrup which was popular with Hispano-Americans, was located in a grubby cinder-block building in San Fernando Valley. The laboratory was owned by Smith Processing National, a small, debt-ridden family company mismanaged from New York by an old Union League New Yorker named T. Tilford Smith, Smitty to his friends. Smith was an uncle on the mother's side of Prentice Tilford Farquhar the Third, at Morgan Price.

Max Herschel owned T. Tilford Smith and had a lien on his nephew.

Max had originally bought into Smith because of the gerbils.

The head chemist of Smith Processing National was named McCready. He was a man with a dream. For a number of years, feebly financed by Smith Processing, McCready had stubbornly persisted in experimenting with procaine, and the result was a lab full of seven-year-old gerbils. Seven years for a gerbil was the equivalent of about one hundred and fifty for a man.

Dolores had discovered this intriguing western division of Smith Processing. She had met McCready, a bachelor and a Rosicrucian, at a luau in Van Nuys. He had talked about his work to Dolores, and Dolores had talked about his work to Max.

The project would possibly take years more of McCready's dedicated skills; no big investment of money would change the picture. Only time. There had been no need for Max to take over Smith Processing National in all its boring and unprofitable entirety. Instead, he had become a friend and patron of T. Tilford Smith. It had been Max and Smitty now for several years. Max kept Smith Processing solvent with occasional transfers of personal funds. He was never identified on the company's papers as a creditor. It was not until he eventually decided to put Smitty to some other more practical and immediate use, that he even accepted stock in Smith Processing. Max accepted the stock only to transfer it to a nonprofit organization which he named the Tilford Fund. He turned over the chairmanship to T. Tilford Smith.

The Fund was a charitable one, with only vaguely defined beneficiaries, set up to promote action in the field of geriatrics. To Smitty this meant generally lending a helping hand to elderly distressed gentlewomen; to Max it meant a finer life style for the gerbils. But there was little friction between Max and Smitty over outgoing funds, which were not all that substantial. Max was more interested in funneling funds *in.*

Principally, Max had been diverting money into the Tilford Fund for the purpose of picking up the temptingly devalued stock of Artists International. By now, he had secured, in the Fund's name, almost nine percent of the film company's common stock, a percentage equal to that which Max had so fortuitously come across when he bought United Vending.

Max reveled in all his business ventures. One-night stands or long romances, all had his interest and ready affection. But he had favorites. At this moment, there were two, both tied, if somewhat loosely, to T. Tilford Smith.

Max had what amounted to a passion for the gerbils. And he had been looking forward with positive lust to attaching Seymour Berger's theatre sites. Max had not given up on Seymour. Seymour was, after all, Max had reminded himself, eighty-one. He could eat like Baby Leroy and still die tomorrow. Then the sites might go to the fruit grandson. So it would not hurt for Max to control Artists International since, anyway, he had already accumulated enough stock. Timing was everything. Say he grabbed the studio and say he got lucky and Seymour kicked off within a reasonable length of time. *Then* he'd have access to those theatre sites. So he would go right ahead as planned. With Smitty.

He set out to see McCready and the gerbils. After that, he thought, with a lessening of enthusiasm for the day's progress, he would head for Pasadena, and his martyrdom at the Langdons'.

Doing seventy-five in the wrong lane, Max drove the long miles to Pasadena.

He loved his elder daughter, Jill, but she was not really his type, and an evening spent with her husband, Pat, had to compare unfavorably with a long stretch in the state pen. Still, dinner with the Langdons was overdue, and since Max had nothing to show from the United flight, he was free for the evening, plus Pat was coming up for re-election and would need cueing.

Jill, who had a big Sunderson streak in her, had formulated a battle plan for making her husband President of the United States before he was forty-five. One more term in the California senate, then governor, then United States senator, then President while Jill was still a size-six knockout. But Jill's plans for her husband were one thing. Max's were another.

Max had no intention of getting Pat the presidency. He was not even bankrolling that amiable schlemiel into the United States Senate. Governor of California, yes. What could it hurt California? But *that was it*. Jill would have to cut her coat to fit the cloth provided by Max.

Pulling up in front of the house, Max vowed that not once in the whole damn evening would he allow himself to review the estimates of what it cost per annum to domicile the Langdons in this Moorish mansion with its fifteen acres of perfumed gardens, and its armed guard installed at a minareted outpost to insure the safety of the future First Family.

Inside, in the glowing presence of his daughter and her family, Max reflected that there was no place on earth where he felt so *brunette* as at the Langdons'. Jill had inherited her mother's buttery-blond beauty and, with forthright narcissism, had chosen a mate to match. Pat Langdon was off the same palette, fair-haired, with blue Catalina-on-a-Clear-Day eyes. And the four Langdon children were in the same limited but dazzling color range. Conformation complemented color. No lowering brow, no errant nose, no prognathous jaw blighted the topography of the Langdon maps.

At the dinner table, Pat rambled on about California politics, Jill kept a close eye on the service, and Max brooded about his futile flight on United. Only occasionally would he surface from his depression to make a sociable effort.

But he did remember to tell the Langdons about the party for Baby and Stan. He got their RSVP on the spot.

"Divine to come to a big do at home again!" Jill declared. "But Daddy, if you're going to throw a real party . . . not that they'll appreciate it, you know . . . but if you are . . . for Pete's *sake* see that Baby has something decent to wear."

For Pete's *sake*.

Max's jaw muscles clinched. Jill's strongest expletives were little Presbyterian churchmouse droppings . . . " drat," "fiddle," "sugar!" Words that made Max feel dark and hairy and . . . Minskish.

Max grieved that Jill shared Connie's lack of linguistic integrity. He remembered the terrible shame he had felt, when, in the first year of their marriage, Connie had begun affecting junk Yiddish —"dreck," "bubee," "tush." He had cringed every time Connie referred to her own tight little arrangement as her tush. In time, Max made clear to her that she was born and would die without a tush. In her terrible innocence, Connie had thought it was she who was going to be assimilated.

Max counseled himself to stop thinking about Connie and try, instead, to enjoy the food. At least Jill set a good table. Suppose he had to drag all the way out here to spend these bullshit Langdon evenings but in a dump like Baby's.

After dessert, Jill smiled her superwife smile and excused herself, leaving Max and Pat to brandy and male-bonding.

Max got right down to business.

"What's up, Pat? What can I do for you?"

Pat had everything under control, he told Max. He just needed a little advice. Advice about a land development deal on which he had been approached. There would be federal funds available . . .

"Jump in."

An infusion of federal funds was always an invitation to massive theft. An irresistible bid to suck 'em and chuck 'em. Max looked thoughtfully at this golden goy son-in-law and tried to find another way to phrase it.

"Pat, if you analyze the stable value of the components—land plus the US Mint—you can understand why that type of development recommends itself to the creative investor. It's in profit from the time you get a senator's nod."

"Do you really think so, Dad?"

Max was stuck for a Wasp way to explain it. He had no choice but to give it to Pat straight.

"Say you want to build Co-op City. You meet the requirements for development, and Washington gives you ninety percent. Then with the cooperation of concerned and friendly appraisers, you convert that ninety percent to one-hundred-and-ten. Say the true cost of the building is one hundred million. But you reappraise the costs to one hundred and twenty million. Ninety percent of which is one hundred and eight million, which you get from the government . . ."

Pat's face had taken on the strained look of a boy losing the struggle with his times-nine table. Max pushed on anyway.

"Now remember your real cost is one hundred million. Put that in the reality column. The bloat cost is the hundred-twenty million. That's your bullshit column. It's the bullshit column you borrow on—the bloat price—so you get a hundred and eight million, which leaves you eight million in profit before you turn the first shovel."

Max paused. "Do you understand? You've got eight million guaranteed. For your own pocket."

Pat frowned earnestly. "I don't understand exactly where the eight million came from."

After considering several answers, Max settled on: "From your investment, Pat."

Pat fidgeted. "But that's just fantastic, Dad! A *guarantee* of eight million? Why doesn't *everybody* do it?"

Dryly: "Everybody does."

Max knew Pat would never pull it off. He would find some way to get screwed out of the deal. Or the strong possibility existed that somebody was trying to use Pat or set him up. Max resolved to put Dolores onto it and at least protect the dumb cluck.

Pat had moved from the subject of land development to its natural consequence, voters. He now spoke of the last demographic break-down on the voting population of the southern district . . .

Pat talked, and Max nodded and uh-huhed and began to wonder if it was going to be no dice on United going back east. Maybe he should trace down that Brucie kid when he got home. He didn't really like to go to Norman twice for the same girl. Not for any specific reason. Norman was okay, but why hand him an edge? On the other hand, so what?

It was at this minor block in his digestive drift that Max picked up on the word "zoning."

"What was that about zoning, Pat?"

"I was only relating it to highway routing. You know California, Dad. New highway construction is vital if we're going to meet the basic transport needs of this state, but routing's a perennial hot potato . . ."

Langdon drew an essentially simple outline of a projected freeway and its surveys and the block of organized voter resistance willfully opposing the desperate demands of growth, not to mention the informed and professional expertise of their elected officials.

In four easy questions, Max elicited the locations of the disputed route and its alternative, and the probable outcome of the Highway Commission's decision.

"You understand, sir, that all this is still closed-committee information. God help our poor budget if anything leaked out to speculators."

Max darted Pat a suspicious look. When confronted with seriously slow wits, Max invariably reacted with suspicion. He always thought his leg was being pulled. Now, he had to remind himself that this was *Pat* speaking.

"The Commission is having to fight a bunch of antifreeway kooks tooth and nail. The usual. But of course, we've got an alternative route we've secretly agreed on. It's not as direct, not"—Pat could not repress a look of self-satisfaction as he delivered his next line—"as clean a cut through the geography. As it were. But we'll take it if they force us."

If the actions of the citizens-at-arms continued, Pat told Max, and they came up with serious legal assistance, then the Commission would pursue the alternate route. Pat deplored these emotional, wildcat citizens' groups.

"The men on the Commission . . . those are *knowledgeable* men. And one ragtag outfit of protesters can really throw a spanner in the works. The way the media plays into their hands. It's damn disheartening. I can tell you, sir."

Max kept his demeanor solemn as he advised his son-in-law, the next governor but one.

"A pain in the ass, sure, Pat. But let somebody else fight them. They may be kooks, but they're voters. So don't you come down hard on either side. At least not anywhere you can get quoted."

As he imparted this ABC wisdom, Max was already deciding how much he would have to siphon into the antifreeway brigade and over how long a period to insure its slow but eventual victory. Thereby giving Herschel Industries the time and opportunity to pick up key parcels along the alternative route.

He was thrilled by the simplicity, the symmetry of the equation. The voters of California were going to lose a lot of money to Max Herschel. Still, he would use it not only to give them a new governor, but also to guarantee personally a greater good, namely that Pat Langdon's career would be safely contained within the state's boundaries. Pat's services would be visited exclusively upon the voters of California, who, if they were dumb enough to vote him into *any* office, deserved to bear the costs.

It hadn't been such a lousy evening after all, Max thought, driving cheerfully back to Beverly Hills. He was well fed, relaxed, and content to go to bed alone. Working out the details of getting money into the freeway fight would lull him to sleep more effectively than a Seconal. Before retiring, he'd call Bones to remind her about Thursday and tell her he missed her. He really did. He couldn't wait to tell her about his strategy for funding old Pat into the governor's mansion. She'd love it. But not through the hotel switchboard. You never knew.

Max strode through the hotel lobby to the pay phones and placed the call to Bones. There was no answer. Two-thirty in New York. Two-thirty and no answer?

Disappointed and suddenly lonely, Max placed a call to Betsy Pennypacker in Santa Cruz. He hadn't seen Betsy in a couple of months. Their last meeting had left him snapping his fingers with impatience. Betsy had dropped two courses without consulting him, and had argued that auditing something she could really get behind was better than getting credit for something she *couldn't* get behind.

Then why the hell hadn't she started out with subjects she could get behind?

Listening to Betsy's whining incoherences, Max had had trouble remembering her as she was when he took her off United. He had assured himself she couldn't have been anything like *this*, and he had considered an expression he'd heard one of Connie's doctors use. "The lure of regression." The obliging, malleable, soft-spoken, neat little lady he'd found in a stewardess's uniform had regressed into an argumentative adolescent in jeans and ponchos, who didn't shave her legs and had dropped Concepts in Architecture I and Modern Ethical Theories, the only two courses Max was interested in. And she hadn't seemed to be doing much work in the others.

Sensing lost ground, Betsy had attempted to divert Max in bed. But too late.

"What's the *matter* with you?" she had whimpered. "I can't seem to get your *attention!*"

Now, in Beverly Hills, Max listened to the phone ringing in Santa Cruz. He let it ring ten or twelve times before he hung up, angry. It was twelve o'clock on a school night. Where the hell was she? Max stormed out of the phone booth, snapping his fingers. He marched decisively to the desk and demanded a limousine to drive him to the airport, where he chartered a plane to Santa Cruz, and ordered a car to meet the plane.

By the time they touched down, it was well after two. Max told the pilot to wait, then jumped in the car and gave Betsy's address.

He rapped loudly, demandingly on Betsy's door, only to stare, astonished, when the girl, befuddled with sleep, opened the door against the chain lock and blinked at him.

"Max? Why, Max! What's the matter?"

She was too dopey to open the door, and he was too shocked at finding himself in this place, where he had no wish to be, to demand entrance.

"Where were you? I called you at twelve."

"I was here . . ."

"I let it ring twenty times." He exaggerated, glaring, at her slack face, her fuzzy eyes. "What are you *taking?*" he demanded.

"My *exams!*" she replied indignantly. "I'm *taking* my exams! I haven't been out all day. I was asleep. Exhausted. I'm *studying*. And I'm so hassled that something's gone wrong with all my

[89]

tendons! My wrists? Max, you can't imagine the crap they expect us to . . . what are you still standing out there for? Come in . . ."

She released the chain and flung open the door to reveal a wrinkled brushed-nylon gown from which Max recoiled. Worse yet, Betsy's hair was doing that thing Max had only lately noticed hair doing. It kinked from the roots for about twelve inches then went mysteriously straight. He hated it. When Max had got Betsy Pennypacker from United, she'd had brisk, reddish brown curls circling a heart-shaped face and complementing her amber eyes. She had been very *neat*.

The face was still much the same, although now that he thought about it, there seemed to be more eyebrow. She made him think of some little woods animal growing winter fur. In *California?* The face smiled a hazy invitation at him.

He took a step back.

"Just in the neighborhood, sweetheart. I can't come in. I'll call you tomorrow from New York, you can tell me what you need. Get back to sleep. Good luck, honey . . ." Uncomprehending, Betsy stared at Max as he trotted away from her down the hall, calling back over his shoulder, "Good luck on the exams!"

It was after four by the time he got back to the hotel. What a shitty evening. He was booked on the ten a.m. flight, but he could make an earlier one if he didn't take a pill. He started to put in a call to Bones, then decided against it. She would want to know what he was doing up at four a.m. and Max, guilty about the other girls only when they didn't pan out, was convinced that Bones could read disappointment in his voice at those times. The bitch had been out all night herself, he thought. He wouldn't give her an early a.m. satisfaction.

But he lay awake thinking about her. The scene in his office yesterday worried him. Why the hell did she keep doing it? What more could he give her? How else could he help? And what about that bid for the studio? Jesus. He hadn't expected that one. He had to hand her. She was always good for a surprise. He smiled in the dark. She had balls, the beautiful little bitch, shaking those fishhooks at him. The memory gave sharp pleasure and equally sharp pain. Why did they have to grow up? Why the hell couldn't they stay . . . what they were? The stab of pain blurred. Christ, maybe he would be able to grab a couple of hours sleep after all. His wake-up call was for seven, and he'd be exhausted on the trip home. Suppose he found something worth the effort and didn't have the energy? Just before he grayed out, he told himself firmly that he'd *have* the energy. He'd always had the energy. And he always would.

Chapter 8

On Thursday night, Max cooked, and Bones, relegated to the level of her competence, fixed the salad and set the table.

"Light the candles, sweetheart . . ."

He garnished the duck and put it on the warmer.

"Sure the soup is cold enough?"

"It's perfect," Bones assured him.

"Then let's eat."

Bones knew Max had not found a girl on either flight. If he had, he wouldn't have demanded so detailed an accounting of her time or betrayed such lingering irritation at not having been able to get her on the phone. If he had nailed a new one, his pleasure in the freeway scam wouldn't have been diminished by his not being able to contact her at once and share the fun.

"Next time I'll use more apple in the soup."

"It's perfect."

"Nothing's perfect. So you had dinner with a poet?"

"And novelist. He's written a good book. A little special, but interesting. He's talented."

"Aren't they all?" Max offered, then changed the subject. "We're going to throw a great party. Stella's sent out invitations to about a hundred, I think. She got Duchin's orchestra. And for band breaks she tracked down a bunch of black kids I saw downtown a while back. Call themselves Martin Luther and the Diet of Worms." He grinned. "You know what that means?"

"Yes," she said.

"Oh. I had to ask." He left his soup unfinished and began carving and serving the duck. "We've got one little problem with the party. Everything taken care of except for this one little item. Nobody remembered to invite Baby and Stan. We're short the guests of honor." He laughed. "So what I thought, sweetheart, you and I should go up there Friday. Spend some time with the kids. See if we can talk them into coming to their party. I already called and they said they'd love to have us. So I told them we'd get there in time for dinner."

Bones bit sharply into the crisp duck skin and made small sounds of approval. "Lovely," she complimented him, then, "Max, you weren't very definite about the weekend. I made a date."

"For Friday?"

"For the whole weekend."

He waited.

"I'm going up to Vermont."

"What's in Vermont?"

"Well, actually, not very much, I'm afraid. But I promised to go in a weak moment."

"What weakened you?"

She smiled. "The poet. He did his number so lyrically . . . I'm afraid I'm in for a boring couple of days, but I did say I'd go up."

Max didn't allow himself so much as a frown. The bitch could go right up the fucking North Pole! The duck was too fat. The sauce was too thick. He gave the meat a punishing stab with his fork before he looked up at Bones with false serenity.

"Well, that's too bad, sweetheart. I should have been more definite. We'll miss you. How long since you've seen Baby?"

"Ages. She never seems to come to New York anymore."

"She's just two hundred and thirty-four miles from New York by car and only one-ninety-one by air, but she buys her clothes in Boston. Looks like a dyke lumberjack most of the time. How about picking her out something gorgeous for the party?" He grinned. "Something that will shut Jill up."

Bones nodded. "Chiffon. Stavropolous."

Suddenly, the weight of Max's unstated knowledge fell upon them, heavy and silent as a snowslide. Bones continued eating, making every effort to enjoy Max's meal, while he shuffled the salad around with his fork, sniffed the dressing suspiciously. He risked a bite, then pushed the plate away.

The poet's picture must be on the back cover of his "interesting" book. He'd get a copy tomorrow. Why the hell did she want to spoil his weekend with Baby? Why did she pull this stuff when he was around? He never begrudged her a little action. He was more than fair with her. Why couldn't she be fair with him? Why must she always pick a time when they could be together? When he needed her? He'd known she was a bitch the moment he set eyes on her. He knew it in the store elevator . . . even before she went into her fishing act. Well, then, what did he expect? Rage knotted his stomach. Fuck her.

Exactly. That was precisely what he wanted. To fuck her. He leaned back, giving her the benefit of his undivided attention.

She was going to be thirty-one this coming Wednesday, but in the candlelight she might have been twenty-three or -four. The mouth was full and tender, the skin flawless, the neck delicate and vulnerable. Only the eyes, when they met his in awesome challenge, were flinty. No, the little lady was not soft and not young. Even so, sometimes, he still wanted her. Really wanted her. Not too often. But *now*.

He stood up. "Let's go to bed."

The woman in Bones' head would have liked to tender regrets, to make some insultingly obvious, rejecting response, but mind and body were at cross-purposes. Her mind issued angry commands, which the body obstinately opposed. Tonight, the ambivalence was complicated by the novelty of a new, threatening standard by which to test Max. The possibility that she might find him second best pinned her down like a veteran rapist. She was frightened, frightened that he would wipe Steven out, even more frightened that he wouldn't.

She stood up without speaking, and walked slowly from the room, undressing en route. Just outside the dining-room door, moving past the Lord Nelson mirror, she pulled off her blouse. She yanked it over her head without unbuttoning it, knowing that Max would wince at the strain put on the fabric.

I am walking past his mirror, taking off his blouse. Carelessly. She dropped the blouse. Let Max pick it up. She kicked off her shoes. On his Axminster. She didn't much like the Axminster. She had wanted a Brussels. She unfastened the ebony-and-diamond Deco bracelet and let it clatter on the parquet floor.

Bones did not have to watch to know that as Max scooped up the bracelet behind her, he automatically checked both it and the floor for possible damage, while still keeping an assessor's eye on her.

Were there marks on the flesh? Bruises? Flaws on the fine white skin? New ounces on the hips? An ominous hint of dimpling on the back of the thighs? Was his possession in perfect order? Was the upkeep top-dollar? As she stripped herself for him, she thought about his post-coital habit of feeling her lightly everywhere—nose, ears, neck, all points south, ticking off the parts, obsessively checking the books on his investment, always on the watch for the signs of wear which presaged devaluation in the stock.

Bones had never objected to Max's cataloguing her assets. She enjoyed his pride of possession and was interested and amused by his infinite capacity for take-over.

For all that, Max was a lavishly generous lover, by both instinct and policy. What he principally sought was gratitude, the dividends of which often transcended the bed.

"Thank you, darling . . ." she had whispered once, in final exhaustion. "God . . . thank you, Max . . ."

He had lifted his face from between her limply open legs. "Common courtesy, sweetheart. Common courtesy."

She would have laughed with him had she been able.

Tonight, as he performed his rota of sexual largesse, Max had no reason to suppose that Bones' little body had set itself against him. Feeling him move inside her like an expert mechanic working over an old-model car, her center closed against him. She refused the gift which before Steven, only he had offered her. What Max's hands, mouth, weight, and finally, ah, finally, his own real and urgent passion had always accomplished before, they now failed to do.

In the second before he lost himself, he caught her little smile of containment, and his eyes widened as he pumped into her with helpless resentment. She watched his face until at last he lowered himself onto his elbows and returned her questioning look.

Knowing the answer, he asked the question anyway: "Are you all right, sweetheart?"

"I'm fine," she responded in the voice she used for cheerful good-mornings to the doorman. "Just fine."

The feeling of power rushed through her like a shot of speed and almost made her cry out, as Max's practiced manipulation of her sex had not.

Mentally trembling, Bones perceived the mousehole escape . . . that from this moment, she could be free. Max had given her everything she needed, all she would ever get from him. Nor could he hurt her. There was no way he could hurt her. Ever. With the sudden delivery of this notion, her mind contracted again, pushed down hard, and the dark twin was born. *She* could hurt *Max*.

He withdrew from her, rolled away, turned the bedside lamp up higher, and looked at her curiously.

"So tell me more about the poet."

When she came out of the bathroom, she took her time choosing a nightgown with long sleeves and a modest, high-yoked neck. She pulled it over her head. Max waited patiently as she sat down at her dressing table and began pulling a brush through the uncoiled rope of her heavy blond hair. Finally, she answered. "I'll tell you more after the weekend."

"Fair enough," he responded reasonably. "You're restless. What the hell. I'm sixty-two years old, what can I expect?"

She looked at him, stretched out on her bed with his hands under his head; his powerful, heavily muscled shoulders crushed the ruffled pillows, defeating them. Bones had a flash of all her pillows, permanently flattened, refusing ever to rise and risk another punishing round with Max.

"Sixty-two, sweetheart. Sixty-two isn't such a great year."

She would not challenge the outrageous sham of his suggestion . . . her passionate youth rebelling against his elderly, failing powers . . . the black humor of his petitioning for her pity and discretion. She admired his shameless use of any weapon, from precision bombing to a custard pie in the puss, whatever would work, whatever was handy.

He tried again. "Do what you want, Bones. Just don't rub my nose in it."

She reacted to this bogus plea with quiet seriousness. "I wouldn't, Max. You know that."

No easy mark, Max sat up straighter. "Don't try to rinky-dink me, kid. I have a feeling you're foolin'."

She gazed at him, secret and unspeaking.

"Have I done something worse than usual? Or are you still working the studio pitch?"

"You haven't done anything worse than usual," she smiled. "And I know that if you don't want me to go to California, I won't be going." She shrugged. "I wouldn't fight you over that."

"What *are* you going to fight me over?"

She considered alternatives carefully, chose the truth. "I'm not going to fight you."

He looked nowhere but at her, and stoically, she bore up under his gaze.

At last, he got up from the bed and put on his pants, came over to where she sat, and gave her a light, affectionate kiss. "I don't ever want to lose you, Bones."

Bones leaned against him, her blood pounding, not from fright, but from excitement, the sweet and sour taste of betrayal in her mouth.

Chapter 9

". . . following Harvard, Mr. Routledge pursued Arabic studies at Oxford. . . . In 1970 his second volume of poetry, *Constellations of Fools,* was awarded the Dunning Prize.

". . . *Windrift* is the story of Alenghi, an upper-class Arab, educated and living in the West, culturally and emotionally estranged from his origins and himself. What happens to Alenghi in New York during the six days of the Israeli War is in devastating parallel to the agonizing. . . ."

Max was not interested in what happened to Alenghi during the six days of the Israeli War. He was interested in Steven Routledge. He studied the back-cover picture, which showed Routledge standing on a bleak hill in front of a windmill, hands jammed for warmth into the pockets of a battered and patched old ski jacket, pale eyes narrowed against a stinging wind. He looked cold, shabby, piss-poor, and insufferably superior.

"High hat and no drawers," Max pronounced.

He pitched the book at Stella.

"Read this tonight. *Yourself*. And get a rundown on the writer."

"What kind of a rundown?"

"I want to know how many fillings he's got in his teeth and what enemies he made in nursery school."

Stella did not have to be told that the target was connected to Bones. She examined the picture. "Looks as if he can take care of himself."

Max snorted and snapped his fingers.

"Airbrush out the windmill and that phony patched-up costume and you've gotta know he steps out of the shower to pee."

Stella grinned. "Then what are you scared of?"

"I'm not scared, honey," he sighed. "I'm just a perfectionist." He began sifting through the morning's correspondence, and Stella started from the room.

His voice didn't halt her until she was almost through the door.

"No calls, Stella."

He didn't look up as Stella nodded and quietly closed the door behind her.

As soon as she had gone, he pushed the correspondence aside and leaned back in his chair, seeking consolation in the long curve of the Tz'u Chou bowl in the window. He considered the flawless synthesis of its beef-blood color and its size, the dream logic of its components. If it were a tone darker, it would need to be correspondingly larger.

Then he thought about Bones and her perfect, miniature body. He considered the hateful possibility that as she aged, she might eventually look dwarfed . . . meagre. A spinner's cute, he mused, and there's something *sudden* about someone that little . . . the possibility of unanticipated dangers.

It was too late for cute. Bones was grown up and, aesthetically, her attitudes called for more size.

What he really felt, was cheated.

He sighed and turned back to his work, began dictating onto tape a memo to Smitty. "Let's get together, Smitty, and work out our act for the take-over . . ."

He stopped speaking, unable to wrench his mind off the picture of Steven Routledge. The punk was a peacock . . . had himself photographed with the camera shooting up at him. Made him look eight feet tall. Max gave an irritable hitch to his shoulders and forced himself to return to the memo. "We want to be ready for all that geschrei after the stockholders' meeting . . . know what I mean? . . ."

Bones stared up at the windmill as it turned with absurd giraffe dignity into the shifting wind.

"You mean the only electricity you have comes from the wind-mill?"

"It gives me all I need. I don't have a garbage disposal. I have a compost heap."

"What's that?"

"What's a *compost heap?* Are you joking?" Steven looked down at the alien little figure. For an hour she had sturdily paced his ledgy, hardscrabble acres in her ratcatcher boots from Bergdorf's and her hip-length sable coat. He was aware that her wardrobe was assembled to affirm the fashion principles of *Town and Country.* Dashing but not daring, theatrical but correct.

The careful composition of all her costumes seemed weirdly out of period. She was as exquisite and artificial as a thirties movie. But then, he remembered, she had been fashioned to satisfy the aesthetics of an old man. That at thirty she was as archaic as pink champagne and midnight sailings pierced Steven with tenderness. He put an arm around her sabled shoulder and pulled her along with him.

"A compost heap is not exactly a heap. It's more of a pit. Into which you throw your best garbage. Also leaf mold and lime and manure. Then you let it cook and turn it over occasionally. And when it's done, it will fertilize anything. So don't stand too close. One good whiff and you could find yourself knocked up with not as much as a rhinestone to show for it."

Since her early girlhood, Bones' principle of action toward all things rural had been to turn her back and hit the road. Bones had never experienced anything like Steven's farm. It was a real farm, even a poor one. Its hundred and fifty stony acres had stubbornly resisted generations of cultivation, and current attempts to subdue it were meeting with only marginal success. Yet the land was as strangely splendid as the house constructed out of its elements.

Golden-gray stone, frugally trimmed with wood weathered to tarnished silver, the house was as austere as its owner, Bones thought. Their styles consistent.

The interior of the house was virtually bare of architectural ornament, but the windows sat deep in the stone, and the small panes of glass were old and dotted with micaceous tears. The windowsills accommodated here a small vase of field flowers, there a primitive tool of unknowable utility. Books weighed down old clippings, letters, and lists.

Among one of these careless, schoolroomy piles, Bones had discovered a Klimt color-wash of a high-chinned, dark-eyed young woman. She had picked up the drawing, examined it closely. "Do you realize," she accused Steven, "that this is a *Klimt?*"

"Yes, of my grandmother."

"But it's a *Klimt!* There are stains on it! Why isn't it framed?"

"Well, I only came across it a couple of years ago. It was stuck in an old scrapbook," Steven explained. "I suppose no one liked it enough to frame it."

"*I* like it. *I'll* have it framed. Before it's ruined or lost!" Bones held the paper away from Steven as if she suspected he might use it to light the fire.

Steven smiled at her battle stance. "Would you like to keep it?"

"Your grandmother's picture? But it's quite valuable," she protested.

He shrugged. "If you like it, then I'd like for you to have it."

Much later, after they had made love for the last time and Steven was sleeping with his long limbs organized about her in complex patterns of possession, she lay awake and wondered at him and his life. He had no money, yet he casually offered her a drawing of his grandmother worth several thousand dollars. He lived in a meanly furnished house without rugs or curtains or—she grinned ruefully in the dark—trash-mashers.

Except for a profligate array of photographs framed in tarnished old Aspray silver, there were no pictures and only one graphic, a Calder still acclaiming McGovern for President, which hung in the kitchen. Yet this empty house, all wood and stone and rough plaster, was, mysteriously, the loveliest house she had ever seen. It seemed an extension of Steven himself, clean, cold, spare, challenging her tastes to stretch for new definitions.

Steven, working alone, had restored the house, building on the remains of an abandoned derelict structure. He had spent three years restoring the house and writing the book.

"I sanded the last floor and wrote 'fini' the same week. Then I drove down to New York and went on a three-week party. I hadn't seen or talked to anybody but Farmer Schmirski for almost eight months."

She regarded him curiously. "What about girls?"

"I had a nice one for the first year. But she got lonely. She went back to Philadelphia and married a divorced stockbroker with five kids."

"Did you love her?"

"Certainly."

"Do you still?"

"No."

He changed the subject. He told her that his acres were worked by Mr. Schmirski, who owned the neighboring farm. At harvest time, Steven worked along with Schmirski.

"I trade him the grain crop for produce. Except for luxuries like coffee and sugar, I'm almost self-sustaining. When I bought the farm I paid as much cash as I could. My mortgage is very low. So are Vermont property taxes. And at least once a week I make a list of all the things I don't need. You know what they say, 'You're only as rich as the number of things you can live without.'"

Bones smiled. "I didn't know they said that."

Steven was determined, he told Bones, to keep his scale of living so low that he would never again have to take a job teaching American Lit. courses to pridefully illiterate college freshmen.

The farm's electric power came from the windmill, and there was no telephone. For the rare emergency, Steven used his neighbor's phone. The only big domestic luxury he allowed himself was a portable TV on which he watched late movies and game shows. "I like all those ladies leaping up and down and jiggling their tits and screaming when they win clipped lamb coats and Samsonite luggage."

He gave her a cup of coffee, and asked her if there was anything on television she wanted to see. "*Let's Make a Deal* is on in an hour," he suggested.

She shook her head, sipped, and made a face at the coffee.

"What *is* this? It's ghastly."

He apologized. "It's probably the pot. I found it at the dump."

She set the cup down on the nearest table. He apologized again.

"Sorry. Do you die without coffee?"

She shook her head. "I don't die without coffee. I *sleep* without coffee."

He put his hand on the back of her neck and turned her face up. "No threats."

She didn't sleep, as it turned out, until almost dawn. She lay peacefully through the night hours, without any wish to extricate herself from his long legs and arms. The touch of his body so tranquilized her that only two or three times through the night did her mind assemble sequential thoughts.

For a moment or two she thought about her clothes and what she could wear the next day that would not make her look like a store mannequin. It had been fourteen years since she had owned anything suitable for this farm.

For fourteen years Max had encouraged her every extravagance, and it pleased him when, to save time and energy, Bones had begun using a personal shopper to select the best numbers from each season's lines and bring them, with accessories, to her apartment. By the time Burton Productions was in its second season, Bones had not been in a shop for over three years, and had not ridden in any public conveyance, except elevators, for even longer.

When Max had first given her a driver of her own, Bones had protested that she could take cabs or drive herself.

"Don't be dumb, sweetheart. Get it through your bean that there's a natural division of labor in this world. Your job is outmaneuvering the networks, not New York traffic. Let a driver drive. And while he's doing his job, you do yours. Read the trades, dictate . . . even do a little arithmetic, it wouldn't kill you." He patted her cheek. "Do your arithmetic right, it'll pay for the driver."

His hand traveled to her breast.

"You want to be a producer, sweetheart, get up early. Be the best. You can do it."

Max sold a very special brand of snake-oil. It was labeled Infinite Possibilities.

But somewhere during the long Vermont night, Max faded from her mind. She hardly even thought about herself and Steven; feelings, not people, were the actors in her trance. She was happy.

Baby had spent a lot of Herschel money remodeling and enlarging an old carriage house off Beacon Street, and in it she placed the several good antiques which Max had pressed on her. That much accomplished, Stan took over, filling the house with the best bargains he could find in functional furniture. Then he covered the walls with his own massive collection of quite worthless pictures.

When the place was ready, the Munshins had turned it into a kind of halfway house for strays and stars. If Baby knew Max was coming, she would empty the house of all but family because she wanted him to herself. But whenever Max showed up unexpectedly, he would find distinguished bolters from Iron Curtain countries, artistically inclined junkies whom Baby was casually rehabilitating, an occasional fugitive from the Somerset Club, delinquent children, compatriot psychologists, and almost always an eclectic selection of the Munshins' students.

There was an equally eclectic and frequently changing cast of dogs, cats, and hamsters, and for two dodgy years, there had been a raccoon called Birdman, a naturally nocturnal creature whose fearful aberration was crawling cozily into bed to take midnight naps with uninitiated guests and household help. The staff was always minimal, the turnover rapid. When guests pitched in, hot meals were available. Cleaning was a sometime thing, and the antiques democratically suffered the same abuse as the less valuable furnishings. This very evening Max had spotted the remains of a Mounds Bar melting into the precious patina of a valuable serpentine commode, a piece he had proudly presented to the young couple at the time of their marriage. He made a mental note to point out the desecration to Jeffrey, the only member of the family he considered housebroken.

Jeffrey was an eleven-year-old Arab orphan whom Baby had picked up off the streets of Marrakesh the spring she first became pregnant. The boy, then about eight, had followed her and Stan around the town for several days, trying to sell them everything from dull and decent postcards, stolen from the Marrakesh Holiday Inn, to his own services as high diplomatic courier. Baby eventually impounded him like the stray he was. She needed, she declared, an older brother for her baby, and this young street entrepreneur would do just fine. First babies suffered from too much parental attention and anxiety, she explained to Max. Look at Jill if he could bring himself. And furthermore, she intended to go back to work after the baby was born, and she didn't trust nurses when no one was around to tattle on them. Tattling would be one of Jeffrey's principal duties.

She had scrubbed and outfitted the boy, VIP'ed him through Immigration, and named him Jeffrey. After no one.

The first time Max met Jeffrey, Baby, six months pregnant, her aplomb as enormous as her belly, had pushed the swarthy, wide-eyed little desert rat toward Max. "This is your new grandson. His name is Jeffrey."

Max and Jeffrey sized each other up, as instinctively wary as two fast guns eyeballing one another in a Dodge City saloon. Across centuries and continents, against all cross-cultural odds, recognition between conspecifics took place, and, without a word, the two made common bond.

That first night, Jeffrey had slipped silently into Max's room. In his smooth, tourist-touting English, he informed Max that he, himself, "never smoked no more hash," but he'd found where he could get some if "the Father" wished. Max asked where, and the little hustler said "Crambridge." A shy, dimpling smile, and then softly, "In Crambridge are many pleasing things, sir. Many girls

Crambridge." One glance at the wicked old eyes in the ingenuous young face told Max that Jeffrey had read him like a rap sheet.

Max didn't protest or patronize.

"I'll give you a tip, kid. The nooky hanging out on street corners in Cambridge is likely to be all clapped out."

The idiom didn't faze Jeffrey. He nodded solemnly, graciously accepting the advice. "Hash?"

In the spirit of research, Max gave the little nomad twenty-five dollars, and Jeffrey, all business, slipped out. He came back late, after the house was asleep, and again entered Max's room. He and Max sampled the drug. It was top quality. Max thanked the boy gravely and said he would take the hash as a gift to a friend, since he had smoked only to test the quality of the drug and to seal his friendship with Jeffrey. He advised the child on this country's extremely punitive laws regarding the sale of the cannabis weed, then asked Jeffrey what profit he had made on the night's exchange.

"Only two dollar, sir," was the unhesitating lie.

Max figured it had to be, at a minimum, three times that, so he negotiated a deal. For every week that Jeffrey stayed out of the clutches of the law, he, Max, would put the princely sum of ten dollars in an envelope and mail it to the boy. For this weekly investment he expected nothing more than that Jeffrey stay clear of the tempting Crambridge Casbah and be a watchful friend to Baby. Max and Jeffrey shook hands, and the deal was consummated with an advance of ten dollars.

When Baby's little girl was born, Baby and Stan had, to Max's distress, named her Rebecca. The name was a bit too Old Testament for Max's taste. Max never referred to his grandchild by any name other than New Baby, and as Jeffrey followed Max's lead with unflagging persistence, the name stuck. New Baby she was. Jeffrey took over as bodyguard, companion, spy, nurse-vigilator. He watched over the infant like a Berber guarding the waterhole.

Jeffrey earned his keep. He even, when Max explained the problem and pointed out the danger spots, attempted to police the antiques.

This was as much control as Max was able to exercise in the

Munshin household. Max knew he was always welcomed, even cherished, in the Boston ménage, but he had no authority there. Stan Munshin had taken a girl passionately attached to her father and turned her into a woman passionately attached to her husband. This was accomplished with a sleight-of-hand that Max never caught. One minute Baby had been his, and the next, Stan's.

Baby had been Max's darling. She had been a dark, fat dumpling of a little girl whose short legs moved with the speed of a roadrunner's in her eagerness to do Max's bidding.

"Baby's *fast!*" Max used to marvel, "Baby hauls ass faster than any three-year-old I ever set eyes on!" he would brag.

Baby was, in fact, very much like Max himself.

When Max had stood behind the nursery glass for his first view of his new child, he had instantly recognized the baby by its big Herschel head set squarely on broad Herschel shoulders. When he first heard its peremptory, demanding yell, so much louder than the cries of the other infants, Max had felt a wild elation. It was not unlike the exhilaration which had whipped through him when he had pulled off his first million-dollar deal and knew he wasn't going to get caught. This time Max felt that he had pulled one off on General Sunderson.

Twenty-seven years later, standing once again outside a hospital nursery, looking at Baby's child, Max had spotted the same Herschel features and felt the same thrill. This time, he had pulled one off on Stan Munshin.

When Baby was little, she had been a miniature version of Max. She was dark and quick and gifted with Max's own supranatural energy. When she was older and talking like a typewriter, she would begin most sentences with the imperative: "Listen!" "Look!" "Hurry!" "Come *on!*"

She would yell *"Come on!"* at Jill, who from the age of four was filled with a sense of what was and what was not seemly feminine demeanor. The older girl would walk at a meticulous pace behind the dashing, heedless Baby.

Baby not only had Max's speed, she had his wits. Baby could add, subtract, and divide in her head. Baby could do long division in her head. In school, she got all A's except in Home Room. She was the only girl in the memory of the Brearley staff to fail Home Room. Baby could not, would not, sit still. Nor silent.

Baby despised her older sister. Jill had not got into Brearley. She had attended Miss Hewitt's classes. Jill loved Miss Hewitt's. As she had loved wearing white gloves and going to dancing class at the Pierre. Baby had attended only one of these sessions in social deportment, during the course of which she kicked three sets of male shins and made an eight-year-old gallant from Buckley cry. She never went back. She never *looked* back. Baby did not want to go to dancing class with eight-year-old boys. She wanted to go to the office with Max. She also wanted to go out in the evenings with him. She wanted to get in the shower with Daddy and into bed with Daddy. Baby thought her mother was dopey. Baby was delighted whenever Connie "went away."

Max had treated Baby exactly as he treated any female who pleased him, with his own blend of seductive teasing, short shots of mesmerizing attention, and droughts of indifference which he tried to ameliorate with material largesse. At the age of eighteen, Baby had never once been in love. She took top honors in school and lived for those unpredictable moments when Max would turn his attention to her, take her with him on a trip, buy her clothes, tell her outrageous stories—all true—about his business. Or enroll her in another beauty course.

Baby was not pretty. She was dumpy. Her black hair kinked like a pot scrubber, and her nose was too big. But her skin was beautiful and her brows arched temperamentally above eyes dangerously black and quick like her father's. She had Max's splendidly white square teeth. And always, anywhere, in any gathering, she was the *healthiest*-looking person in the room. Baby had sex appeal, but she did not know it. She did not send out signals to any man but Max.

When Stan rescued her, Baby was foundering helplessly in the current of Max's sexual seas.

Max passed through the Munshins' entrance hall, noting the nasty gob of candy on the serpentine chest but without giving a glance to the hundreds of pictures that covered the walls. The pictures had absolutely no value. They were photographs, cartoons cut out of magazines, framed postcards, insignificant drawings by artists of no particular talent.

The mass of pictures had, from his first sight of them, bewildered and offended Max. Stan's collection was not beautiful or bizarre or even erotic. Max did not know what the hell the collection was supposed to be, and he damned sure wasn't going to ask. Stan, who kept what Max did not recognize as a cordon sanitaire of semitic chauvinism around himself and Baby, would probably tell him they all related somehow to the Diaspora or some shit like that. Max was fond of his son-in-law and impressed with the young man's brilliance, but sometimes Stan acted like a professional Jew, and that got on Max's nerves. Bad. What was the sense of naming a little baby with a big nose Rebecca, for chrissake? Max took it as a personal affront.

If he had ever stopped and carefully examined Stan's "art" collection, Max would have seen that it was unified and illuminated by a subtle sting of mordant humor. The collection was the clue to Stan, but Max never picked up on it. Stan had one of the world's straightest faces. Max bought the straight face and lost the game.

"Hello, Max," Stan pulled himself up from a reading chair— an ugly chair, in Max's opinion—and came to greet his father-in-law. Stan was very fond of Max, but he was even fonder of Baby, so he kept Max on a chain collar. And though Stan puzzled Max and constantly pissed him off, Max liked him. He wished the kid would fix himself up. Get some shirts that fit, wear contacts, do *something*.

Stan was only five feet six. An inch shorter than Baby. And he was skinny. He weighed one hundred and twenty-seven pounds, while Baby never got below a hundred and forty-five. Stan had a big head with a regular aurora borealis of curly red hair. He had a long, elaborate nose, white skin, and freckles. He wore thick-lensed glasses over weak green eyes. He was generally dressed in obstreperously colored corduroys.

Over the years, Max had given Stan thousands and thousands of dollars' worth of clothes. First, he had said, "Go down and get what you want, Stan. Charge 'em to me. My pleasure. *Indulge me, kid.*" But Stan never seemed to get around to shopping. Then Max took to picking clothes out *for* Stan and sending them to Boston. He would always receive a charming letter of thanks, but he never saw one goddam rag he ever sent on the boy's back. Used them for dusting, Max fretted. Except nothing in this dormitory was ever dusted.

Tonight, Stan was wearing corduroy pants two sizes too big and a mean shade of green. A red-and-black plaid wool hunting shirt—Jesus!—and moccasins that had never been new, much less good. Max averted his eyes before they were exposed to the socks.

"How are you, son? You're looking great. Where are the ladies?"

Stan put an affectionate arm around Max and led him to a sofa. Before Max could sit, Stan had to sweep the cushions free of a pile of newspapers, toys, half-eaten dog biscuits . . . a chewed-up prune? Max again averted his eyes.

"Baby ran out to get some whipping cream and New Baby's having a bath." Stan announced. "In honor." He explained that Max's visit occasioned the breaking of New Baby's three-week-old boycott of the tub.

"Are you telling me that kid hasn't been bathed in *three weeks?*"

"Well, she's not accustomed to being bathed. She's accustomed to bathing herself. But three weeks ago she learned to spell out a word . . ."

This news excited Max. Three-and-a-half and already *reading!* "What was the word?"

"Exxon."

"Exxon?"

"It's an easy word. Anyway, when she got it, she was so excited she didn't want to take a bath that night, she wanted to 'read.'" Stan explained. "Then it seemed she wanted to 'read' every night. After the fifth or sixth night, everybody got into the act and she and Baby went ten rounds. But she didn't bathe. Finally, Jeffrey took over and told her, okay, New Baby, you *can't* bathe. And you can't 'read' either. He locked away all her books."

"Her books?"

"You know, Levi-Strauss and *Touch-the-Bunny*," Stan grinned. "Anyway, she marched downstairs and got a copy of *Newsweek* and took it back to bed with her. She's been working on *Newsweek* ever since. The au pair finally threw in the towel last week. We just got a new girl, but we wouldn't have held on to her if you hadn't shown up. New Baby announced to Jeffrey about half an hour ago that she was going to do a bath for her Grandad."

The story both pleased and annoyed Max, as did everything in this unruly but obviously happy home. He couldn't understand the formula.

At that moment, Baby came hurtling into the house, calling out, running in to Max and throwing herself into his arms. He smelled the healthy smell of her and his heart swelled with love. On another level, he couldn't help noticing that she was wearing a duplicate of Stan's shirt that was too small and made her look fatter than she was.

"Where's Bones?" Baby demanded. "Upstairs?"

"She couldn't come."

"Oh shit!" Baby had been looking forward to seeing Bones, but did not stop to dwell on the disappointment. She had to whip the cream and get it mixed with the egg whites.

"Before the damn mess collapses on me," she called over her shoulder on her dash to the kitchen.

As Baby disappeared, Jeffrey came downstairs to greet Max and to show off the sweet-smelling New Baby. Max took her on his lap and asked about her "reading." She smirked with pride and told him that Exxon had two x's but that most words didn't because Exxon was a made-up word by a bad company that had too many everythings.

Max shot a look at Stan's mild face. Supposed to be a goddam psychologist, not some kind of pinko spouting Nader at three-year-old babies, for chrissa—Max sighed and returned his attention to the child.

He asked New Baby with great seriousness what she would charge to let him kiss the back of her neck. She wanted to know what "charge" was. Max gave her a succinct lesson in sexual economics, and they settled on fifty cents for the back of the neck and a dollar for the tip of the nose and another dollar for the belly-button. Worth a dollar, Max declared, even through the flannel pajamas.

New Baby giggled happily while Max got his three kisses. Then she collected the two one-dollar bills and two quarters in her fat little fist, looking to Jeffrey to be sure she was not getting a short count. Then she said Max had had enough kisses; she wanted to "read."

Aware that she would be banished as soon as the grown-ups sat down to dinner, New Baby preferred to make an impressive exit on her own terms. She sought Jeffrey's hand. She knew that since she had taken a bath and pleased him, Jeffrey would read to her for a long time this evening. She gave Max a free hug, then kissed her Daddy before, accompanied by Jeffrey, she marched off to the kitchen to kiss her mother good night. Jeffrey grinned back at Max, who made a circle with his thumb and forefinger. Max would take care of the kid later.

Over Baby's dinner, Max talked about the party. And about Connie and how anxious she was to come, how eager she was to see them, to be with them. It was going to be a great party. Max hadn't thrown a big one in over a year, and he was as excited as a child.

Baby proudly urged Max to take more of the sole dieppoise, on which she had risked her all. Max hesitated, almost turned it down. He had not been hungry since the evening with Bones, but because Baby had cooked this elaborate dinner for him, he put another helping on his plate.

Stan's gently myopic expression never changed. During Max's moment of hesitation over the fish, Stan had mentally advised Max that if he didn't go all the way for Baby, as she had for him, then he, Stan, was going to name the next child Isadore. To be called, from the moment of conception, Izzy.

"So what happened to Bones? Why didn't she come? You didn't tell me."

"She went up to Vermont. She's got a boy friend."

Baby never missed a stroke with her fork. "Really? Serious enough to make her fink out on *our* weekend?"

"Ever read anything by a guy named Routledge? Steven Rout-ledge?"

It was Stan who answered. "Wrote some poetry. Only so-so, I thought. But a guy in the English department at school says he's talented. He brought Routledge here for dinner once."

Max was momentarily taken aback. That was more solid evidence of Steven's actual existence than he cared to face at the moment. He asked for no further information. Instead, he offered some. "He's a novelist now."

There was a brief silence before Max threw in more details.

"She's spending the weekend up in Vermont with him." He gave a savage little grin. "Seems he's got this windmill-type farm up there. Lives there. Eats granola, for all I know."

Stan noticed that after Baby laughed at the granola line, Max's appetite seemed to pick up. He was cleaning his plate.

"That doesn't sound exactly Bones' style . . ." Baby hesitated, but like her father, she was strong for instant gratification. She wanted to know, so she asked.

"Did she just come straight out and tell you? That she was going off with this guy?"

"She never needs to tell me. I always know," he answered flatly.

Baby had never realized that Bones had lovers or that Max knew.

He saw the expression on her face, "Honey, Bones and I have been together for fourteen years. I'm away a lot."

Baby understood what Max meant by "away." She had known about her father's girls since her own eleventh year. Her early jealousy had been a bitter, raging thing, which she had learned to live with. Not like Connie, passively accepting the role of the sexually inept woman, but by fighting for him, demanding his attention and love, heroically trying to battle those armies of females she never actually got her sights on.

Bones was the first one of them to assume the outlines of flesh and blood . . . to reveal herself to Baby as a realistically *wound-able* enemy.

Baby had found out about Bones when she was a Smith senior

[113]

and Bones, a year older but academically two years behind, was a sophomore at Wellesley. Baby had hoarded her knowledge and spent every minute she could spare ferreting out information about the other schoolgirl.

She had asked Max for money which she claimed to need for a friend's abortion. The girl was desperate, Baby lied, and had to have a thousand dollars. Max never questioned the demand, so Baby got the cash to hire a private detective who found out enough about Bones to give Baby a feeling of power. Armed with Bones' photograph and a considerable amount of background knowledge, Baby bided her time. Baby wanted drama. She had waited for two years. She had waited for Bones' graduation, and when that June arrived at last, Baby flew back from Paris, where she had been doing a year at the Sorbonne, and drove up to Wellesley.

It was a beautiful day. In the school chapel, Baby took an aisle seat well forward where Max, dutifully in attendance on Bones, couldn't help but see Baby as well. When she was sure Max had spotted her, Baby had given him a big smile, then turned back to the commencement speaker. Sweat, you old bastard, Baby thought. Just wait. Baby had bought a present for Bones.

Baby sat through the ceremonies, keyed-up and anxious, but pleased with the scene she was playing out.

The recessional was struck on the organ; the girls marched out in their long white dresses carrying their virginal bouquets. Baby joined her father in the aisle, following along with the rest of the crowd. She held his arm lightly, but didn't speak. Neither did Max.

Bones stood quite alone outside waiting for Max, looking beautiful but also very small and vulnerable. Baby had no pity, only a thrill of conviction that here was no real rival. She could easily devour this pale little person. The three confronted each other. Max gave Bones a chaste kiss, introduced Baby.

"Bones, this is Baby. You've heard me talk about her. This is Bonita Burton, Baby."

Until that moment, Bones had been coldly certain that Max had shown up for her graduation with another of his girls. Now, abashed, she stared at Baby. Baby showed her strong white Herschel teeth.

"Congratulations, Miss Burton. I know how pleased Daddy must be with your performance. But I wanted you to have a vote of confidence from someone else in the family." She thrust her prettily wrapped offering into Bones' reluctant hand and smiled encouragement. "Open it. Please." As Bones' fingers obediently began working off the ribbon and paper, both she and Max stared fixedly at them as if they were a new hot novelty in the anatomy market.

When the fingers had, on their own, managed to get the package unwrapped, fine old leather, rich with age and oil, appeared. Baby's gift was a book which Bones made no effort to explore beyond its beautiful antique binding. She was, quite literally, terrified.

Baby reached out and gently pushed the book—and the hands attached to it—upward. "I wanted to give you something appropriate. It's a first edition."

Finally, Bones opened the book's cover and looked at the title page: *Fanny Hill, Memoirs of a Woman of Pleasure.*

Max took the book from Bones' hand and read the title, but before he could protest, Bones spoke.

"Miss Herschel, it's you Max loves. He only fucks me."

Bones touched Max's arm consolingly and walked away.

He stood silent, watching Baby's scarlet face, her black eyes hot with tears. He leaned over, kissed her cheek, "You ought to think about growing up a little, Baby." He left his daughter and went after Bones.

The following week, Baby turned up at Bones' New York apartment. The impulse which propelled her there being if you can't lick 'em, join 'em. And before she left, they had formed the cautious bond two women occasionally make to strengthen and ratify their separate positions in the life of one treasured man. From that shaky beginning, Bones and Baby came eventually to like and admire each other. For Bones, Baby was the only other female with whom she had ever shared anything resembling friendship. Baby's attraction for Bones was her physical and temperamental likeness to Max. It was, on the other hand, this same likeness which made genuine intimacy impossible.

Baby was so like Max, so demanding and unpredictable, that Bones self-protectively denied both father and daughter any real purchase on her emotions.

For Baby, the relationship with Bones became a conduit to her father's other life, the one from which she had been so long excluded.

During that time, Baby restlessly moved from one job to another, working first as publicist and social shill for a French couture house, then in the New York offices of Robert Kennedy, next shooting off to finance and fuss around a new graphics gallery with two penniless homosexual friends. What she really wanted, all the time, was to be with Bones and Max.

Baby met Stan at a party in the Village.

Bored and ready to leave, Stan had spotted Baby as soon as she came in, and had at once shuffled across the room toward the incredibly healthy-looking girl. He had fallen in love with her in something under seven minutes, but it had taken him seven months to pry her fingers, one at a time, off Max's life.

Stan removed Baby to Boston and did for her precisely what Max had done for Bones and others; he screwed her and put her back in school. It was an arrangement of supreme satisfaction to Baby.

While Stan was, in his person and in his modus operandi, nothing at all like Max, he had power. He had been a prodigy, graduating from Harvard at seventeen. He was a tenured professor in psycholinguistics at Boston University by the time he was twenty-four.

At thirty-two, he was at the top of his profession. He published steadily and had only to reach out for any financial grant available to his field. Stan needed nothing from Max and took nothing, with the exception of those mountains of Botany and cashmere which he accepted graciously, held for a while, then parceled out among his shabbier friends on the teaching staff.

Not only did Stan take nothing from Max, he reversed roles on his father-in-law. It was Stan who did the giving. He openly and overtly enveloped Max in his affection, was endlessly kind and

considerate of Connie, and showed, in the face of countless re-
buffs, a steady, unwavering loyalty to the Langdons. If something should ever happen to the Langdons, Stan would, Max
knew, unhesitatingly take in the Langdon children and give them
as much love as he gave to New Baby.

Stan's love and Baby's happiness put Max in Stan's debt, and
the debtor's role was not one in which Max was comfortable.

Max stayed the night in Boston, and the next day, went to the
university with Baby to be shown the graphs and conclusions
drawn from her current project, a study of the verbal/cultural
cross-pollenization of the city's South End, Back Bay, and ghetto
jargons.

That evening Max took the Munshins and a small but noisy
party of their friends out to dinner. As always, when he came
here, Max saw how happy Baby was with Stan, how final the
remove. Stan not only had Baby, but New Baby too, and Jeffrey.
It did not seem fair.

When Max left Boston after dinner, he was more than a little
depressed.

Chapter 10

Bart had taxied the plane into its La Guardia hangar before Max woke up.

He was delighted with himself. He had dozed off ten minutes out of Boston and slept right through the landing in New York. He was an hour up on his night's sleep. How about that? He peeled off a couple of bills and stuck them in Bart's shirt pocket.

"You fly a great flophouse, Bart. Magic Fingers." But on Beekman Place, in his pajamas and in his own bed, he was wide awake and restless. He dialed Bones, got no answer, and slammed down the receiver.

Then, with a start, he remembered that the Artists International stockholders' meeting was coming up on Tuesday . . . Wednesday? . . . no, Tuesday. And he had not talked to Smitty since . . . how long? Certainly over a week. Two weeks? Had

Smitty answered his memo about the meeting? Max could not remember. He grabbed the phone to ring Stella.

Stella blinked at the luminous dial of her bedside clock as she picked up the remorseless phone and spoke firmly into it.

"It's twenty-five past one, Max. I've been asleep two hours."

"Then you're two hours ahead of the game. Listen, Stella. Did I get a letter or memo or phone message from Smitty last week? About the stockholders' meeting? In answer to *my* memo?"

"No."

"What do you mean *no?*"

"No you did not get a letter or memo or phone message from Smitty last week. About the stockholders' meeting. In answer to *your* memo."

"Why not?"

"How do I know why not?"

"When I don't get an answer to a memo, it's your goddam business to find out why not!"

He banged down the phone, and then looked up Smitty's home number and dialed. There was no answer, which was ridiculous, because Smitty was sixty-five and acted seventy-five. Because he lived with his ugly old wife in Scarsdale, and when his phone rang at one-thirty in the morning, he should be there to answer it. Max slapped at the disconnect button several times then dialed the number again. There was still no answer.

Max called his lawyer.

"Bernie? Max."

Bernie screamed. It was the middle of the fucking night. *He* didn't know anything about Smitty. Why the fuck should *he* know anything about Smitty? *He* was a lawyer, not a private eye. Max wanted to put surveillance on that suck-off Smith, Max should hire an Intertel spook. Why the fuck should *he* know why Smitty didn't answer his fucking phone in fucking Scarsdale?

Max listened with a loving ear. Every time Bernie sounded as if he was beginning to run down, Max would conduct him back up to full decibel, and by the time the lawyer's voice began to hoarsen, Max was even feeling sleepy.

"Don't worry about it, Bernie. Smitty probably just turned off his bedroom phone. Probably sleeping like a baby."

The picture of Smitty sleeping like a baby with his phone turned off set Bernie into a three-alarm effort. His voice shrilled obscenities.

Max rested the telephone receiver on his pillow, switched off the light, and lay back. With his head near enough to the receiver to catch the melody of Bernie's night music, Max drifted into sleep.

Most of Monday was spent trying to track Smitty down. His office said that he had gone fishing. Fishing in Mexico. Mazatlán. No, there was no way at all of reaching Mr. Smith. He was on a boat. No, it had no ship-to-shore. It was just a local fishing boat. No, they couldn't say where Mrs. Smith was. She was not in Scarsdale, but she was not in Mazatlán, either. Definitely not in either place. But, yes, Mr. Smith would certainly be back for the Artists International stockholders' meeting on Tuesday. It was on his calendar. Definitely on his calendar. No, he had said nothing about proxies. Actually, the secretary volunteered, she no longer handled the Tilford Fund business. All of the Tilford Fund business was now taken care of by another girl, a girl named Molly. But Molly only came in once a week. Would Mr. Herschel like her telephone number?

Indeed Mr. Herschel would.

There was no answer at Molly's.

Max had a flash of a bikini-clad Molly on the fishing boat in Mexico, but he dismissed it. *Smitty?* Not a chance.

By midnight Monday, Max had still not made contact with Smitty. That meant he would have to attend the goddam meeting himself. Max's shares had been voted early through United Vending. The shares registered with the Tilford Fund would be voted at the meeting by Smitty himself, acting as agent for the Fund.

As Max dressed on Tuesday morning, he cursed Smitty with every button, bow, and zipper. He wondered darkly if all the time he had been keeping his eyes on those gerbils, he should have been keeping them on Smitty. Max still could not believe that his own cosmic capacity for suspicion had let him down. It had to be nothing more than some crappy mix-up. Still, he felt instinctively he had better go to the meeting.

Stockholders' meetings. At his age. Max had known since he was eighteen that stockholders were sheep and their annual meetings were ritual pantomimes staged by the Men With the Shears. He seldom attended the rites for any purpose other than fun.

The fun was provided by that sport among stockholders, the active dissident. Max had his favorites among the dissidents, generally women who held small amounts of stock in many companies and who made careers of harassing managements.

Most recently, Max had become the ardent fan of a superstar dissident named Mrs. Cornwallis-Blount, a good-looking blond who spoke with a burlesque Nazi accent and wore hot-pants even in January. Mrs. Cornwallis-Blount was an irrepressible paranoic who devoted her unnatural energies to plaguing automotive and entertainment stock boards. She made identical charges against both groups. Fiduciary malfeasance and rape of the environment.

The automotive people were always outraged at being accused of fiddling the books; the entertainment organizations were indignant at being defamed as polluters.

Max was continuously astonished at the essential innocence of stockholders' denunciations. Stockholders seemed, to Max, pathetically lacking in criminal imagination.

Today Max knew he would watch rather than listen to Mrs. Cornwallis-Blount. Her charges were just goofy, but her showmanship was worth the ticket. The lady invariably claimed an aisle seat so that she could grab a hand mike from the management minions who roamed the aisles, electronically equipped to amplify the bleating of the sheep. Mrs. Cornwallis-Blount would seize one of these microphones and prance up and down the aisle with it, punctuating her harangues with a maximum of body English. She waved her arms and bottom, ducked and bobbed, and showed a lot of rhythm. Max admired the ruthlessness with which she glommed onto a mike. She was a pro. A regular Joey Adams.

Riding downtown to the meeting, Max was hoping that Mrs.

Cornwallis-Blount would show. He hoped *somebody* would show. What the hell could that old fool Smitty be up to? Was he actually trying to cross up Herschel Industries?

Lunatic and unlikely.

It made no sense. Smitty was only sixty-five. If he crossed up Herschel Industries, he still had maybe twenty years to live and suffer pitiless Herschel vengeance. So it made no sense. No sense. Was maybe Smitty turning prematurely senile? Max made a mental note to insist Smitty get a thorough going-over from Dr. Rossman. Max himself would check out Smitty's diet. Get him a yogurt-maker. It was stupid to do close business with somebody who didn't watch his health.

By the time Ben turned the limousine into Broad Street, Max had convinced himself that Smitty had suffered a series of those sneaky mini-strokes, so tiny they were difficult to detect singly, but which in multiple led to memory loss, careless dress, disinterest in sex. *Senility.* For eight long blocks Max had brooded blackly, then cheered up as deeper diagnosis made him conclude he had probably caught the condition in time. The damage to Smitty's brain might be reversible, to a degree, if Max moved in fast.

"Stay put, Ben. I don't know how long I'll be."

The meeting had already been called to order when Max slipped in, sat far in the back, and scanned the heads for Smitty's distinguished white locks. He gave an uninterested once-over to the men on the dais. Pelzman was chairing.

". . . A certified list of the stockholders of the Corporation as of said record date has been compiled by the Corporation's transfer agent, register and transfer company . . ."

And there was young Berger in from Hollywood. Christ, he was handsome. Max grudgingly admitted that the Berger genes threw off a line of spectacularly handsome men. Still, handsome as the boy was, he did not look like a fruit. Jock was right. But who did look like a fruit anymore? The old kind of fruit had gone all out of style. Now they wore big hairy mustaches. Michael Berger had a mustache. A mustache and a Harvard Business School suit. And a self-confident expression. Max did not like that expression. He began to check out the crowd.

". . . has been designated as Inspector of Election of this meeting. The Inspector of Election has been asked to make a list of all the stock represented here either in person or by proxy and to compare this list with the transfer agent's certified list. Also, I would like at this time to express the officer's appreciation and confidence . . ."

"No convidensse in noddink! *In noddink!*"

Max's eyes jumped to the left aisle. Ah. Mrs. Cornwallis-Blount!

"Vy doss der shairman expecdt der convidensse of der people herein ven doublecrossdt on effry page from der Annual Report? And ledt me ask vy iss dis company pudding der annual repordt . . ."

"If the lady will confine her comments to the period following the opening of the . . ."

"Der lady convines nodding! Noddink! Vy iss dis company pudding der annual repordt mit silfer paper backinks? Non-biodegradable . . . silfer backinks!"

Max saw with passing interest that Mrs. Cornwallis-Blount's neat little bottom was encased in purple velveteen shorts that just barely covered the defining crease between her leg and buttock.

But where was Smitty? There were only fifty-five or sixty people in the auditorium, and Smitty was definitely not among them. Where the hell was he? With those goddam votes bought and paid for by Max Herschel . . .

And then Max spotted Seymour Berger's lawyer. He closed his eyes and swiftly ran down the list of all stockholders owning shares amounting to as much as one percent. Next, he did all stockholders of any size who had ever voted the proxies of other stockholders to the amount of two percent or over. Berger was not on either list. Nor was his lawyer. And where was Smitty? Max heard Pelzman's voice rise above Mrs. Cornwallis-Blount's.

". . . so you will *sit down* and give us a chance to proceed. The answer *is*, because we want that picture to play in broad release. If we couldn't go this fiscal year with our very best shot for it, we would prefer to hold back and go with what we are confident will be a real blockbuster . . ."

"Blockbuster bullshidt!"

"Madame!"

"Shame!"

"Mr. Chairman! I protest! Must that same lunatic female always . . ."

"Lunadic bullshidt!"

"Throw her out!"

"Bullshidt! Bullshidt! Bullshidt!"

There was no way Max could account for Berger's lawyer's being at this meeting, and no way that he could account for Smitty's *not* being here. Two unaccountables.

Max sat in frozen concentration. Calling around for Smitty was ridiculous. If the sonofabitch was laying low, he sure as hell wasn't coming to any phone. There was no *time!* In another twenty minutes—maybe half an hour if Mrs. Cornwallis-Blount kept up the good work—the hold-out shares would be voted. If Smitty didn't vote, Max's nine percent would not carry the board. If Smitty's shares were being voted by Berger's lawyer (he couldn't believe it, but look at the odds!), Max would not carry the board. In either event, Max would not carry the board. What he had to do was somehow track down that senile doublecrosser Smitty and mash the votes out of him. Max had to *make* time!

Pelzman's voice was shaking with indignation.

". . . refuse to posture ourselves defensively on *that* account, Madame. Now please be good enough to sit down, or I will call for security!"

"Ha! You tink I vill permit to be touched mineself by your lousy SS!"

Mrs. Cornwallis-Blount hunched into a fighting crouch and swung the hand mike in a ninety-degree arc, tangling the mike's trailing cord around the neck of a hapless stockholder sitting in the row behind her. While all eyes were glued to this action-shot, Max slipped from the room. As he dashed for a pay phone he heard Pelzman shouting: "No violence, gentlemen! No violence! Although I assure *you*, Madame, I will indeed instruct these men to carry you out of the hall if you do not . . ."

Mrs. Cornwallis-Blount: "Ya? Ya? Come on, boys! Giff us a show, boys! Get up vit der shairman undt all show us your legz!

Ya! Finally ve maybe get somedink for our money! Show us your legs! Ya!"

Max dialed Stella, and when she was on the line, he whispered urgently into the phone.

"Don't talk. Just listen. I want you to get out to a pay phone. *Quick.* Call the first precinct. Report that a bomb has been planted in the auditorium of the Overland Trust Bank at 6 Broad Street. Hundreds of people are about to lose their lives . . . Shut up and listen! I'm going to hang up and I want to hear the goddam bombsquad geschreiing this way within three minutes or you're fired! Now get to a pay phone! Move!"

He hung up and made a run for the front door. Once inside the car, he yelled at Ben.

"Seven-oh-nine Madison Avenue and don't stop for anything on the way. And I mean anything. Lights, cops, or little old ladies! Now *move!*"

Max got out in front of Smitty's building, leaving Ben to deal with two howling patrol cars that screeched up behind the limousine. Without even looking, Max knew the cops would have their guns drawn. As he ran to the elevator and laid a twenty on the operator to go straight up to the fourteenth, no stops, he wondered, if worse came to worse out there on Madison, how much he would have to settle on Ben's widow.

It had not worked, of course.

The meeting had been disrupted by the bombsquad. A full fifty minutes were lost, or gained, however you looked at it. Everybody had an exciting time. Unshakably convinced that the terror-tactics were Mrs. Cornwallis-Blount's, Pelzman had preferred charges against her. But aside from that, it was trick and no treat. The stock in the name of the Tilford Fund, designated the week before in favor of management, had effectively secured the existing board's support of Berger's grandson.

Somehow, Berger had weaseled out the link between Max and the Tilford Fund and had got to Smitty. Although Max knew he'd never prove it, he was dead certain that the Molly who tended once a week to the Tilford Fund had found her way there via Seymour. Max's flash of Molly in a bikini had been more than projection. Flashes of that nature were the stuff of his genius.

What Max *could* prove was that in the few short months that Molly had given herself to the Tilford Fund and to its chairman, the mischief had been accomplished. Poor Smitty mistook his sputtery little flame for a towering conflagration from which he, the Phoenix, was rising once again. And as the fuel to keep the fire ablaze, he chose silver futures.

Smitty had gambled big on silver futures. Caught in a bad margin squeeze, he had been desperate and terrified to confess his folly to Max.

Smitty had gained considerable advantages through his association with Max, and it should have been clear to the meanest intelligence that crossing Max would send Smitty's fortunes into an irreversible decline.

But Smitty had crossed Max, for in his first panic and shame, he had allowed his new friend, Seymour Berger, to bail him out. Then, suddenly, the new debt was more urgent than the old. And Smitty had somehow fastened onto the notion that Berger would protect him from Max.

Max did not have to confront Seymour to see that fine brow lower sadly at the contemplation of a gentleman like Tilford Smith imagining that he needed protection from a gentleman like Maximilian Herschel.

Max knew that Seymour had, for the present, saved his grandson's position. Which had always been his intention. Once again, Seymour had outmaneuvered Max.

"For a piece of tail! Who told you you could still handle tail, you schlepper!" Max's roars filled the room. Smitty sobbed into his handkerchief while Max, his legs spread, his fists on his hips, yelled at him. "You shitty little swindler! You gonif! Why didn't you just sneak off and drop it all at Aqueduct? Or flush it down the crapper? You slow-track, split-the-pot goy schmuck! You cost me my studio! I'm gonna break your goddam back! You felon! You know what I'm gonna do, Smitty? I'm gonna take a couple of days off and work out a foolproof frame and when you're inside Danbury looking out, I'm gonna send you cookies!"

Smitty blew his nose into the twelve-dollar square of ivory silk, but made no effort to restrain the flood of frightened tears.

"Max! I'll do anything! Anything. I'll go down on my knees to you. Is that what you want? Do you want me to go down on my knees?"

Max stared into Smitty's runny, red, old man's eyes. He considered the offer for a long moment, then shrugged.

"Suit yourself, Smitty."

Smitty was unable to discern what Max wanted. Was it possible? Did Max *really* want him to go down on his knees? *Literally?* Max just stood there, waiting. Definitely waiting for something.

Smitty sniffled, shielding his eyes from the possibly fatal radiation of Max's anger. Seconds passed in terrible, throbbing silence before Smitty's back bent and he dropped down slowly, creaking in the hips, onto first one pin-striped knee and then the other. Slowly, slowly, he straightened his back and raised his fine white head. From a supplicant's position, the handsome old man looked pitifully up at the terrifying Max.

"Is this what you want, Max? Is this how you want to see me?" he whimpered. "Will this help? Getting down on my knees to you? Will it help?"

Max cocked his head.

"I'll tell you the truth, Smitty . . ." Max said indifferently to the kneeling man. "It vouldn't help, it vouldn't hoit."

Smitty was still on the floor as Max marched to the door. Before he closed it between them forever, Max turned and yelled back over his shoulder.

"And you're on your own with the yogurt too, you dumb putz!"

Later, Max wondered why he had been so angry. He hadn't *really* wanted that crappy studio. He had meant it when he told Bones a studio was a burden and a pain in the ass. He didn't even *really* want the real estate it sat on. All he had wanted from the Artists International shares was to leverage old Berger out of his theatre sites. And he had given up on getting those during Berger's lifetime, which was clearly nowhere near over. No matter what Max told himself.

It was nonsense getting so mad; the odds were wrong. Why get so crazy pissed-off at being snookered by an old hat-in-hander like Smitty? Smitty was nothing. It was Berger who had rinky-dinked him. And when he stopped to think about it, Max couldn't help being tickled. Old Berger was cute. The meeting at Max's house, making Max believe he would dump his own grandson, diverting Max's mind with special diseases. Cute. Very cute.

The only thing was, now Max would *have* to go after the studio. He couldn't throw in his hand to Berger like that. With Berger so lively, so feisty, Max had to play. He'd have to go after the studio seriously. Not just for jokes. Shit. Because now it would take a couple of years and a lot of concentration. It made him tired just to think about it. Shit. Oh, well. One good thing, he could tell Bones that for the time being there was no studio to take over. He could tell her that with a clear conscience. She wouldn't be able to hang one on him over *that*.

Max decided he'd call Seymour and congratulate him. If he were going to go after the goddam studio, he might as well start now. He'd lead off with a nice call to Seymour. He sighed, then straightened his shoulders and dialed.

". . . I'm glad you can take it like that, Max. You're a big man. A big man."

Max's geniality was not altogether feigned. He sincerely admired Berger's coup, and said so.

Over the phone, Berger's voice was chipper. "I'll tell you what I'm going to do, Max, because you deserve to know. You still hold a lot of stock and you're entitled. I made a bargain with the boy. He stays on, but takes a little discreet guidance, you know what I mean. *Loving* guidance. All in his best interests. Marsha and I are going to move out to the Coast for a while. And I'm going to exercise veto power on any project over a million. You know what I mean? And this is just between you and me. I don't want to break the boy's spirit. But I want to see him make nice general-release pictures. Clean up the image, I tell him, and you'll clean up at the box office. Bring families back to movie houses where they belong."

Max laughed until he wept as he recounted all this to Bones. He told her about old Berger moving to Hollywood and clapping a chastity belt on the fruit. An eighty-one-year-old man was going to pass on all of Michael Berger's pictures, and all those whores at Artists International were going to scrub off the lip-gloss and pull on blue serge bloomers.

"Can you see it, sweetheart? Marsha and Seymour moved into one of Zsa-Zsa Gabor's old pads in Bel Air, soaking their corns in the Jacuzzi and up all night mixing scripts?"

Max wiped his eyes, sighed contentedly, and abruptly changed the subject.

"So how was Vermont? No snakebite?"

"No snakebite."

Max let it drop. It was Bones' birthday. He wouldn't needle her. She had accepted the Severini with a big smile, taken down one of her lousy Ballas and hung the lousy Severini in its place. Max sighed. What the hell? If she enjoyed screwing herself . . .

"What's on your calender for the rest of the week, sweetheart? I've got Pittsburgh and a trip to D.C. on a little IRS tangle. Out-side of that I'm pretty clear. The party for Baby's shaping up no trouble. What would you like to do? Anything worth a look in the galleries? I'll order some movies. What do you want to see?"

Bones got up from the sofa and poured herself another cup of coffee. They had dined on trays in her library because Bones had wanted to see the current NET series at nine.

"I've got a lot of work to catch up on," she said. "My week's jammed." Again, Max let it drop.

"Well that's the way it gets sometimes." He strolled to the television set and switched it to Channel 13, then settled down next to Bones on the sofa.

"Don't let me forget to give you the list for the place cards. If I don't call you in the morning, call me."

"Okay."

Max took off Bones' shoes and pulled her up comfortably against him. He wanted to feel good about Bones tonight, to appreciate and warm to her. As they watched the show, Max held Bones' hand, occasionally taking it up to rub against his mouth, running the tip of his tongue around the smooth half-shells of her nails.

Bones kept her eyes serenely fixed on the television screen.

With Bones' small warm body close to him, her fingers passive and trusting against his teeth, Max was seized with an old familiar satisfaction. The potter's pride. He had made a cool and clever lady out of an ignorant little redneck. He gave the palm of her hand a big kiss.

"Gotcha," he grinned.

"Shhhhhhhhh."

He slid a hand beneath her skirt and up between her thighs. Bones did not react; her attention was unblinkingly focused on the pallid television drama.

You're some little ice-ass, Max thought, not without admiration. Then from dark depths within him, a peculiar phrase surfaced. "Protective custody". . . that's all it is, protective custody. All it is? All *what* is? His heart suddenly slammed against his ribs. Jesus! What had brought that on? To divert himself, he began to use the hand between her legs. Long moments passed before she slowly turned her head toward him, her mouth open and vulnerable. But the look she gave Max, before she slid down for him and closed her eyes, was not a look of love.

Chapter 11

"Connie and me, Baby, Stan, Jill, Pat, Buzz and Laura Drink-water, Gregor and Howard Minton, you and Andy. Just the twelve."

Bones, the phone cradled in her neck, jotted down the names as he gave them to her.

Max liked Bones to make his place cards. He admired her fine, precise printing and had supplied her with every variety and tip-width of draftsman's pen. She had even mastered an italic hand for him. For a long while, all his guests' names had been rendered in the type of Vergil, until the evening Max had caught a sly smile of derision on Connie's face as they sat down to a dinner he was giving for a British cabinet minister and his titled wife.

Max had lain awake that night, tormented by a strong feeling of dissatisfaction that buzzed as hatefully around his head as a fly that wouldn't light. It was almost three before he was able to swat it. Then he sat up, turned on the bedside lamp, and looked at Connie. She lay flat on her back, pillowless, her fine-drawn face relaxed, her arms composed in easy curves outside the covers, with sheet, blanket, blanket cover, all pulled neat and wrinkleless across her chest. That Connie could sleep like an enchanted princess never ceased to outrage Max. A drop of brandy, a quarter-grain of Seconal, Ovaltine—anything—and a woman who was too hysterical to run a house, choose her own clothes, travel alone, ride elevators, meet strangers, you-name-it . . . one tap and she was sacked out for eight hours, *without a pillow* even. While all he had to do to insure himself three solid hours of intense mental agitation was to lie down and turn off the light.

Awake, Connie was a woman atremble and atwitch; allergic, a victim of rashes, hives, nervous nosebleeds, protracted bouts of hiccoughs; a woman who frequently swallowed food the wrong way; who was always bruised from crashing into table edges and door jambs, who sprained, scratched, burned, cut, and generally abused whatever part of herself she attempted to utilize; a woman in whose feeble grasp nothing was secure, who dropped, spilled, misplaced, lost.

All of the tranquility and confidence that eluded Connie's days, however, graced her nights. Connie Herschel yielded to sleep as to a natural element, and Max couldn't stand to watch her in it. That night he looked at the serene and innocent face of his sleeping wife and superimposed on it the expression he had intercepted at the dinner table. He reached over and gave her shoulder a demanding shake. In her sleep, Connie mumbled a pitiful little protest, but Max kept shaking until Connie's eyes opened and she looked up at him in alarm.

"What were you smirking at tonight? What was the matter with the place cards?"

Connie stared at him, not as if he were demented, but as if he had every right, at three a.m., to an explanation of her expression seven hours earlier.

"I'm sorry, Max."

"Sorry what? I asked you what was wrong with the place cards?"

Connie struggled to find a way to say it gracefully, in a way that wouldn't make Max any more agitated, or worse, more patient. Her left arch bent in a terrible cramp. She gave a little cry.

"What's the matter? You're not awake enough for anything to be the matter."

"My foot . . . a cramp . . . oh . . ."

"Put it flat on the floor. How many times do I have to tell you?"

Connie crashed over on the other side and attempted to push her leg out of the bed. Awake, she faced, as always, a hostile and treacherous environment. The bedcovers, only moments before as quiescent as a shroud, were now transmogrified into a Portault Laocoön, twisting angrily about her legs and holding her thrashing body half-on, half-off the bed. Max bounded up and ran around to her side. He extracted her legs, sat her up on the edge of the bed, and firmly placed both her feet on the floor. Even as he acted, he noted, with satisfaction, that his wife's feet were still pretty and unmarked. He could see which one was cramped, and he pressed down hard on the arch with the palm of his hand. As the foot flattened against the cramp, Connie gave a little moan of relief.

Max sat down on the rug and began to massage the foot.

"You were trying to dump yourself out on your head, for chrissake."

Connie held back tears.

"You're helpless. You know that?"

She nodded.

He kneaded her arch with his blunt, powerful fingers.

"But you've still got good feet."

She blinked nervously at him. He sighed.

"What the hell would you do, Connie, if I popped off? Tell me that?"

Dumbly, she shook her head.

Connie often fantasized, secretly, guiltily, what she would do without Max. She would take over the business and quadruple the holdings in the first quarter. Or lots of other things.

There would be another war, Max would be killed in the first bombing. Connie, driven into refuge with thousands of other women and children somewhere south of Pennsylvania, proved herself General Sunderson's daughter. Swiftly, smoothly, she organized the victims into cadres of implacable resistance. Years later, when she finally returned, triumphant, to the ruins the men had left, she searched out the place where Max was buried. She had him dug up from the common grave where his bones mingled anonymously with those of a hundred other forgotten men (but Max's were distinguished by forensic dentistry). She had him cremated into clean and sexless ash.

"That ought to do it. You're okay now, aren't you?"

Connie nodded. She whispered. "Thank you, dear."

Max stood up and decided that while he was on his feet he might as well piss. He went into the bathroom and relieved himself, then drank a glass of water and caught sight of his reflection in a brutal magnifying mirror. He put down the water, turned on a brighter light, and stuck his face up close to the mirror, staring balefully at his swollen image. The dark, heavy-featured face was crumpled and creased; the eye lids hung in draper's folds. Christ, even his earlobes were pendulous. Every night, gravity won another battle. Max put four fingers of each hand on either side of his temples just below the line of his eyes and gently lifted, tightening the skin. He took a step back to observe the effect.

Why the hell shouldn't he? Thousands of men were doing it. His body was strong, his mind young, his energies abundant . . . why the hell did he have to go around with some old man's sour apple face? Not a real *lift* . . . just a couple of tucks . . . He leaned in closer to the mirror, challenging it. Balls. If you're going to do it, do it. Why take a rap for *attempted* rape? Pull it up from the *knees,* if you're going to do it. He backed off. I'll think about it, he promised his reflection, then turned out the light and marched back into the bedroom to confront Connie

"What was the matter with the place cards?"

Futilely, she turned her face away from the light. "Oh, Max, it's three o'clock . . ."

"So before it gets any later tell me what was the matter with the place cards."

He sat on the edge of the bed like a crib-side, pinning her in. He turned her face toward him. She picked nervously at the hem of the linen sheet, as she quietly told him that the italic printing on the cards seemed a little . . .

"A little what?"

"Just . . . a little labored, maybe . . ."

Max had subsequently instructed Bones to forget the italic effect.

Bones considered the list Max had just given her for Baby's party and asked him if he had mentioned the celebration to Andy by any chance.

"Why should I? Andy's your department, sweetheart."

Over the wire, Bones felt rather than heard Max switch to alert. "Don't you want to bring Andy?"

Bones had a vision of Max, all his antennae up like the flailing arms of Park Avenue matrons trying to flag cabs in the rain.

"Actually . . ."

Max hated that word. When they started the sentence with "actually," you knew they were going for your balls.

"Actually," Bones said, "I've asked Steven Routledge. He knows Baby and Stan." She paused. "I knew you wouldn't mind. And I'd like for you to meet him."

"Sure, sweetheart. Bring whoever you want. Surprise me."

The other surprise arrived with Connie, who did not come down from Hartford until the afternoon of the party. She was not accompanied by a nurse. She was accompanied by Dr. Coleson. She looked pale, drawn, and sedated, and made no effort to explain Dr. Coleson's presence. Her dry lips merely brushed Max's cheek, whispered how tired she was, requested a room on the second floor if Max didn't mind, and asked him to see that Dr. Coleson be put close by in case she needed him.

With a glassy, apologetic smile, she followed Teddy upstairs, leaving Max to sort out Coleson.

"How about a drink before you go up? You didn't use the plane, I hear. You drive or what?"

"I drove Connie down myself. Yes, I'd like a drink. Very much."

Coleson was a squared-off, solid man in his mid forties, with a fine head of sandy, graying hair and a substantial but neat mustache. He wore well-cut tweeds and palely tinted glasses with metal frames. His manner was gentle but deliberate, his speech slow and thoughtful. "I drove Connie down." No question about it. You knew that *he* had driven her down. That he had *driven* her down. "Yes, I'd like a drink." He *would* like a drink. He would *like* a drink. *Yes.* He *would really like a drink.*

Max's heart sank as he gave Coleson a hearty, "Good for you," and charged off toward the library, hearing with prescient dread Coleson's evenly spaced footsteps behind him on the darkly gleaming parquet.

The drink that Dr. Coleson liked was a small tot of bourbon in a large amount of water. On this occasion, Max, who seldom drank much of anything, reversed those proportions for himself.

"Very kind of you to bring Connie down, Doctor."

"Connie is a lovely woman. A lovely woman."

Max interpreted the answer literally. Dr. Coleson had been kind enough to drive Connie to New York because she was a *lovely woman.* Not because he had to come anyway, not because he was worried about her and afraid to turn her loose without his attendance, not because she had begged, bribed, blackmailed. Because she was a *lovely woman.*

Okay. Connie was a lovely woman, but for some reason the statement alerted Max's suspicion. Shit. He was in for it; whatever it was, he'd face later.

"Yes, she is. Really lovely. Well, we'll have a good talk this evening . . . or tomorrow . . ."

"I will be taking Connie back early tomorrow. As soon as she feels like traveling. I'm needed at the hospital."

"Then we'll talk tonight. Once the party gets going . . ."

Max rang for Teddy and asked him to check Mrs. Murray about a room for Dr. Coleson on the second floor, near Mrs. Herschel. Teddy assured Max that Mrs. Murray had seen to it and that he had already taken Dr. Coleson's bag up to the blue room.

"Dinner's at eight, Doctor. Just the family and a few kids. By the way, did anybody remember the meringues?"

Coleson nodded equably. "I did, Mr. Herschel. Two dozen. They're packed in my bag. I will give them to the boy."

Max laughed and Coleson smiled evenly, pleasantly, then followed Teddy out.

Max stopped laughing. Those meringues could cost him.

Then it occurred to him that Coleson would make thirteen at dinner. He briefly considered calling Bones and asking her not to bring Omar Khayyám, but decided it might provide her with a satisfaction he was in no mood to hand out. Instead, he picked up the phone and dialed Stella.

"Stella, Connie came home with her doctor and I need a woman for dinner. Send somebody over."

Stella knew that by "somebody" Max meant under twenty-five, good-looking, acceptable to Connie, and not obviously threatening to Bones.

"It's four p.m., Max."

"We've got a hundred people coming for the dance and supper. Don't tell me you can't shake some fox loose for dinner. And if you bomb out on the guest list, then send over one of the kids from the office . . ." He paused, then continued with more enthusiasm. "Send Ruth. Get her a dress."

"I'll see what I can do, Max."

Stella hung up. She was not going to spend an hour on that list, trolling for an extra woman. She'd send one of the office girls, but she wouldn't, on principle, send the one Max requested. As she mentally fingered down the payroll, she recalled that Cathy Kronig had been seeing that idiot Kelly for the last two weeks. Stella didn't like Kelly, but Kelly was invited to the dance and was giving himself airs. It would be one in his eye if Cathy attended the family dinner and was waiting to extend a gracious welcome to him when he showed up with the proles. She pushed the intercom and buzzed Cathy.

On Beekman Place, Max hung up and leaned back, knowing Stella would never send the girl he'd asked for. Asking for Ruth gave him about a sixty-seven percent chance of getting that Cathy. That little Sunday-school piece. Stella liked Cathy. Plus she didn't like Kelly. If Max was aware Kelly was seeing the girl, Stella absolutely knew it.

Kelly had told him that Cathy was a tennis player, which probably meant he was getting in. Which annoyed Max. He paid Kelly good money, but the perks of the job did not extend to Max's office girls, especially nice little things like Cathy. Kelly would mop up the court with her.

The more Max thought about it, the more indignant he became. He'd have to take time out tonight to fritz Kelly. Plus the shit Bones was trying to hand him, plus the good gray doctor and whatever nuttiness Connie was up to. What the hell was going on? It was like a rebellion of lab mice. Max laughed and decided to go up to the sauna.

Stella pushed through the doors into Bendel's and headed purposefully through that establishment's ground-floor garden of delights. On both sides of Cathy, ahead . . . now behind . . . were plants, heavenly smells, boutiques of jewelry, stockings, purses, what? *What?* in the middle of the aisle! Oh, God. *God,* what was . . . ? And shoes . . .

Trailing along behind Stella, Cathy knew that on her own she could not afford to buy a pair of pantyhose in this place.

"Cathy . . . *move.*" Stella prodded the girl into the elevator.

Stella consulted the elevator's floor directory. "Savvy," she muttered. Cathy's eyes moved up the listing. "Savvy" was the fourth floor. Did that mean budget?

When they left the elevator, Stella immediately engaged the attention of a saleswoman, and told her what she wanted. Stella and the saleswoman did not solicit Cathy's own wishes or opinions.

They selected six dresses which Cathy modeled for them. Stella did not dither. She quickly settled on a mauve chiffon.

"I'd like to see it with silver shoes and purse," the saleswoman submitted and Stella nodded. She pointed out a long, smoke-colored cape on a passing model.

"What about that?"

The saleswoman said, "Oh I'm afraid that's from the *second* floor, madam. Pure cashmere. Nine hundred."

Stella told Cathy to try it on. Then, as the girl stood dumbly

[138]

before her in the wrap, holding her breath, Stella eyed the total effect. It was soft, pretty, and not sexy.

"We'll take it."

My God! thought Cathy, being herded ahead of Stella toward the store's exit. Two-fifty for a dress from the *budget* department! Ninety for the sandals, seventy-five for the purse, nine hundred for the cape. Thirteen hundred dollars and something plus tax! In her entire life Cathy had owned only one dress that cost over a hundred dollars. She had bought it for sixty-five dollars from a friend who had only worn it twice.

Back in the limousine, Cathy warmed herself with thoughts of the cashmere cape which she wished she could wear all evening. Cathy loved the cape. It had cost nine hundred dollars. But she was not sure of the dress. She had never had anything like it. It was so plain.

Stella read her mind. "The dress is perfect, Cathy. You'll be okay tonight. Just be yourself. Talk to everybody." She smiled reassuringly. "That means smile and let them all talk to you. And, Cathy . . ."

Cathy listened earnestly.

"You're the Herschels' guest tonight. Not Jock's. Okay?"

Cathy blushed and nodded.

Chapter 12

Cathy sat at the Herschels' dinner party in the mauve chiffon. Her dress was as pretty as anybody else's except for the gown worn by Mr. Herschel's blond daughter from California. Cathy thought Jill's dress was just fantastic.

Cathy sat between Steven Routledge, who had come with Miss Burton, and a plump, shiny young man named Howard who was married to the exotic, green-eyed brunette named Gregor. Cathy couldn't imagine how a girl got to be named Gregor. It made her extraordinary. But Mr. Herschel had welcomed Cathy as effusively as he had welcomed Gregor or the other girl, Laura Something, who wasn't so striking, but who was lively, talkative, and obviously an old favorite of Mr. Herschel's. She and Baby had gone to school together at a place called Brearley.

"Oh, Baby was a shocker in kindergarten!" Laura Drinkwater said. "The teacher had a routine . . . we would all draw pictures of whatever interested us most, as many pictures as we wanted, then we would dictate the stories of the pictures to Miss . . . what was her name, Baby? Our kindergarten teacher? Miller?"

"Catherine dePeyster Miles," Baby answered.

"That's right. Miss Miles. Wow, was she tough! Baby used to draw endless pictures of a woman, always the *same* woman, getting killed in the most lurid ways. Then Baby would dictate to Miss Miles. And Miss Miles would write what Baby said, making captions under Baby's pictures. 'Miss Miles getting mashed under the school bus.' 'Miss Miles getting flushed down the school toilet.' 'Miss Miles dead in the sewer along with the ugh.' My own favorite was 'Miss Miles getting all her freckles punctured and poked out with a sharp stick.' The figure wielding the stick was a splendid self-portrait of Baby!" Laura called again to Baby. "Do you still sketch, darling?"

Baby smiled. "A great talent too soon burned out. Right there in Miss Miles' classroom, I think."

Laura laughed. "Everybody but Baby was scared to death of Miss Miles. We thought Baby was the most thrilling girl in kindergarten."

Everyone laughed but Mrs. Herschel, who smiled wanly, and Dr. Coleson, who looked with great interest from Max to Baby and back. Cathy didn't know who to watch, Mrs. Herschel or the two daughters or *Miss Burton*. Mrs. Herschel was beautiful for her age and so was the blond daughter . . . from where? California? What was interesting was that Miss Burton looked a lot like Mrs. Herschel and that daughter, except smaller and younger. Mr. Herschel must really go for blonds. Cathy felt a stab of hatred for her own brown hair. Maybe she should try a few streaks. Her skin was fair enough. She wondered how much it would cost to get it done right.

"I'm sorry . . ." Startled, she apologized to Steven Routledge. "I didn't catch . . ." Who was this Mr. Routledge? He was terribly good-looking, she thought, but kind of stuck-up.

"I just asked you what you do for Herschel Industries."

"Oh. Well, I'm kind of new. I'm just one of the girls under Miss Liberti. Sometimes I get to do the telephones."

"*Do* the telephones?"

"Mr. Herschel doesn't use punch phones. You see, he has a very personal system of phoning. Mr. Herschel does everything his own way."

Two places away, Max was aware that while Steven was listening to Cathy, his eyes never left Bones, who was seated directly across the oval table from him. Seeing Steven and Bones focus on each other in such flagrant violation of his own seignory caused Max to experience an actual thrill of outrage.

Taking swift advantage of a change of courses, Max decided to improve his position. He stood up.

All eyes looked toward him expectantly.

"I'm going to ask the gentlemen to rise and pick up their wine glasses . . ."

Expecting a toast, the other six men obligingly rose, glasses in hand.

"Now, with the left hand, pick up your napkins . . ."

There was a flurry of damask, then Max made a clockwise gesture. "Every man move two places around . . . Buzz, you go take Stan's place . . . Dr. Coleson, that puts you where Pat is now . . ." Max pushed his own chair back and claimed Coleson's former seat on Bones' left.

The new arrangement now placed Bones squarely between Max and Steven. Connie got Coleson to console her. That would be okay for this round, Max figured.

He then quickly checked out Cathy, who was now sandwiched between Stan and Pat, where she could come to no harm. He shot her a wink, at which she gulped and pinkened.

Stan caught the exchange as he sat down beside the girl, relieved to escape Connie, who was stoned, and the siren Gregor, who had been giving him heavy-lidded looks over the quenelles. Man, he didn't envy old Howard.

Before he addressed himself to Cathy, Stan sent one last look in the direction of Max and Steven and Bones. He understood Max's imperative, but *still*. He was pissed off for Baby. Why couldn't the old bastard have stayed put beside her for the duration of dinner? Still . . . if you've got hot grease popping all over the stove . . .

Max was smiling across Bones to Steven, giving him the full wattage. "After dinner when we can get a little privacy, I'd like to talk to you about your book . . . your novel."

Bones, who knew that Max had not read a novel in at least twenty years, lowered her eyes and smiled faintly. Catching the look, Max determined that his little chat with Steven would be very private indeed.

"Now your first book. Your first poems. *A Jolly Muster at Smithfield*. Is that right?"

Steven nodded, surprised and amused that Max was able to produce this esoteric detail from his curriculum vitae. Only a hundred copies had been privately printed while he was still at Harvard.

"What does the title mean?" Max asked.

"Oh, it's very pretentious . . ." Steven disavowed it. "I was only nineteen."

"You're apologizing for writing a book when you were nineteen?"

"Not for writing it . . . just for letting my aunt have it published."

That aunt? Bones wondered.

"So what does it mean? All I know from Smithfield is hams. What's a 'jolly muster'?"

"Well, to make a not very interesting story overlong . . . Late in the reign of Henry VIII, when the Reformation was swinging right along, all objects of religious veneration were ordered removed from the churches, to be destroyed or burned at Smithfield. Bishop Latimer sent along a statue of the Virgin. He said, and I quote, 'She, with her old sister of Walsingham, her younger sister of Ipswich, and their two other sisters of Doncaster and Penrice would make a jolly muster at Smithfield.'"

Blank incomprehension. A moment of heavy silence in which Bones made no attempt to rescue either man. Finally Max spoke, "I don't get the ham connection."

Max's bewilderment was so wistful that Steven hastened to relieve it.

"That's a rather feeble joke, I'm afraid, Mr. Herschel . . ."

"Max," said Max.

[143]

"Max. Well, as I said before, the book was the work of a very young man quite reasonably embarrassed at playing the glittering undergraduate at a lady's expense. What the title really means is that here is a small collection of poems—verses, really—fashioned by man, but possibly inspired by something beyond man. Sacred? Or fit only for the flames?"

Steven was painfully conscious of sounding like a pedantic jackass. His nerve began to falter. "The—uh—well, let's just say, I mean, the chances were—are—that they're only fit for the flames —the verses—and if flames it's to be, then that's all right too. May they make . . ." he finished lamely, ". . . a 'jolly muster' . . ."

What the hell was Routledge talking about? Max's mind fell all over itself trying to piece together a sensible response.

Bones ate with the steady, spurious self-containment of a child determined not to be drawn into adult confusion.

Steven felt a blushing urge to redeem himself, which brought on a twitch of rebellion, but he resumed mulishly. "Latimer was, of course, subsequently burned at the stake himself—" Steven tried a chuckle. "—a possible parallel the author acknowledged but hoped to avoid."

Max struggled through the maze. "The author?"

"Myself. The flames being a metaphor for—" there had to be some way to make a joke out of this! "—for the critical basting . . ." Even without seeing the trapped look in Max's eyes, Steven knew there was no exit. He shrugged. "I told you it was pretentious."

Valiantly, Max tried again. "Was Latimer a writer?"

The overweening goodwill of his host once again stimulated Steven to press on. "Only incidentally. He was a famous ecclesiastic . . . I think I mentioned . . . Bishop of Worcester. Actually . . ."

Max's mind seized on the word "actually" and responded with instinctive hostility. "*Actually*, I don't get it." He regretted the statement before it was out of his mouth. Steven's thin features went even sharper. "I mean, I thought you said they burned this *writer?*"

Steven felt a vein throbbing in his left temple. "I was referring to myself. " Suddenly, he was quite willing to see Max suffer along with him. He proceeded remorselessly. "Latimer was the man who sent his statue of the Virgin to be burned. Ironically, he later met the same fate. When Mary acceded after her brother's death, she sent Latimer and Ridley and Cranmer to the stake, which was the occasion for the most famous statement of the Reformation period. 'Play the man, Mister Ridley. Today we . . .' "

Christ, was there no stopping it? Max's one overwhelming impulse was to extricate both of them from the worst goy conversation he had ever been mixed up in. Max trusted that Steven was as horrified with this confrontation as he was, but the boy didn't seem to be able to stop himself. If Max didn't put the lid on this, Routledge was going to wind up furious with him, which was not the idea at all. Max forced his mind to the task. Desperately, he leapt into the ring.

"Reformation. Yeah. I got it now. But all I know about the Reformation was they weren't after the Jews."

"No, they weren't. It made for a nice change."

Relieved, Max laughed at what he chose to interpret as evidence of goodwill, and at Max's laugh, Steven's anger evaporated. He slumped in his chair. Only now did Bones finally look up and smile.

Max and Steven got through the rest of the dinner with utmost caution and exquisite politesse.

Afterwards, when the dancing began, Max could not help appreciating that Steven and Bones moved together with the happy precision of playing dolphins. It was beautiful to watch and it made Max a little sick.

However, first things first. He'd dance his obligatory dances, then a couple for pleasure . . . where was Cathy?

He'd take care of Coleson later.

Max opened the humidor and noted with interest how carefully Coleson examined and chose a cigar. The humidor contained twenty or so identical Upmann Number Ones, all from the same box and the same leaf, of uniform size, texture, and smell. Nevertheless, Coleson peered at each one through his spectacles, as if their lenses gave him microscopic vision. It was Coleson's pleasure to *choose* a cigar, despite the fact that no real choice had been offered.

Coleson's reaction, Max intuited, was that of a man whose options for decision were infrequent.

Looking at Coleson's beautifully groomed hands, at the long, tapering fingers holding the special cigar, Max felt a tingle of trifling affection for Connie's doctor. Smiling a kindly smile, he waited.

Coleson settled back on Max's sofa, which, he realized as he sank alarmingly into its voluptuous embrace, was not a piece of *business* furniture. He knew instantly that he must decide between abandoning himself to a submissive position in the sofa's downy depths or struggling out and moving to a chair from which he could confront Herschel on a dignified, egalitarian level. Either way, he had lost face.

It was in this microsecond of uncertainty that Coleson caught sight of the patchwork lady's flaming pubic wool. The picture hung near an open casement window, and a breeze had set the long tendrils of wool in delicate, feathery motion. Coleson stared at the picture and Max stared at Coleson. When Max's glance shifted to the picture, Coleson seized the moment to pull himself up out of the sofa and stroll over to examine the picture. He turned back to Max with a faintly superior expression.

"Interesting. No matter how contemptuously an artist attempts to treat the Maja convention, the erotic impact is always reinforced."

Max had never considered that the man who made the redhead was "contemptuous of the Maja convention," which he assumed to be a nude in the pose of Goya's Duchess. Well, yeah. Maybe. He could see that, but he did not find the picture erotic. He had bought it because the lady made him laugh. He said as much to Coleson.

"Precisely," Coleson nodded sagely. "You are *laughing at the woman*. Although she is passive, defenseless, *horizontal* . . ."

"Yeah?" Max was not interested. Still maybe he could learn something. "Tell me, what would you say about a girl—a woman—who stuck a white string in there . . ." Max pointed. "You know. Like a Tampax?"

"I'd say she was masochistic."

Max made a face and turned up his palms. "Well, Doctor, you know how they are."

Coleson did not respond. Instead he chose a straight-back chair and moved it closer to Max. He sat down, crossed his legs, puffed evenly on his cigar, and regarded Max with a master's kindly gaze.

Max acknowledged the gambit.

"I guess you know how we *all* are. I mean that's how you earn a buck. Right?"

"I think you're trying to say that I hold an advantage. As one of your wife's doctors, I know a great deal more about you than you do about me."

"Not necessarily."

Did Herschel's enigmatic answer mean that Connie had already broken down and spoken to him? Or that Herschel had got wind of something earlier and had him investigated? Nonsense. Penny-ante paranoia. He was letting Herschel psych him. Coleson forced himself to appear serene.

"You feel that Connie lies about you? About your marriage?"

Max made a church and steeple with his fingers, and waggled a benediction. "No, no. Not at all. Connie's not a liar . . ." he granted generously. "She just tells a different truth."

"Ah." Coleson allowed his eyes a tiny twinkle. "But it is Connie's truth with which we must concern ourselves."

Max judged that he had devoted the necessary time to opening moves.

"I'll sum it up, Dr. Coleson. My wife is an unhappy woman who is not crazy, but who for reasons best known to herself and a series of psychiatrists chooses to live mainly in institutions. Whenever she comes out and attempts to spend any amount of time with me, she becomes overtly self-destructive. Now. The implications of this are as obvious to me as they are to you."

"I'm sure they are, Mr. Herschel. And *Connie* understands . . ."

Although the tone of Max's recital had been objective, even humorous, Coleson made his response sympathetic and soothing.

Coleson began his spiel. Red flags. Max prepared himself, got ready for the note he knew was coming.

". . . Connie understands all too painfully," Coleson announced. "She quite correctly interprets her self-destructive impulses as acts of aggression against you." He stopped, waited for Max's response.

"I know she understands. And I understand. We both understand. We've been through this a dozen times with a dozen different doctors, but nothing changes."

"Of course nothing changes."

Ah, Max thought. There it was, the woodnote wild. Max answered, in perfect harmony.

"What you're saying, Doctor, is that because I *won't* change, she *can't* change. And that given the choice between living with me or in hospitals, Connie elects to spend her life in places like the Neurological Center . . ." Max paused just long enough for Coleson to prepare his first carefully worded retort. As his lips shaped themselves for the opening consonant of the initial word, Max pounced.

"*But.* It *needn't* be that way. Not if I have the best interests of my wife and of myself at heart. Because the situation must be almost as destructive to me as it is to Connie. What Connie needs, craves, is not only the supportive atmosphere of a hospital, but also the love of a man trained to understand and make every allowance for her behavioral problems. A figure of authority, which she, as a profoundly neurotic woman in her fifties, is unable to turn away from completely. But this man should also be judiciously permissive, approving, nonthreatening. In other words, a doctor. A doctor like you."

Earlier Coleson had wondered why Max had selected a cigar but neglected to smoke it. Now he saw that Herschel had been holding back until he could use the Upmann to punctuate this discourse. As he began speaking, Max had absently rolled the cigar between his fingers. Not until he got to "a doctor like you" did he elect to amputate.

He severed a substantial piece from the cigar's end, then pierced the cigar deeply, finally clamping it hard between strong square teeth and lighting it. Spellbound, Coleson watched; unconsciously he crossed his legs.

And he listened. Max's casual use of psychiatric jargon barely skirted the knobby knees of satire. The words were delivered in a voice pontifical with sincerity. The bastard was not only invading Coleson's territory, he was fouling it.

"As long as Connie is tied to me—and I to her—our lives will never transcend the distressing circumstances in which we have lived for so long," Max intoned. "Nor am I to blame myself for this ugly and destructive pattern. It was established for Connie by her father, and she has assigned his role to me. I play the part of the unloving, neglectful male parent. She imprisons us together, with me as jailer and herself as exploited slave. She relates to me with overt subservience and covert rebellion. Her physical breakdowns, her hysteria, the self-inflicted injuries, are indirect attempts at communication. She wants to be free of me. And in all fairness to myself, this climate between us is ruthlessly stunting my own psychic growth." Max took a deep, satisfying pull on his cigar.

"Now. A different man, with different needs, might make the adjustment necessary for coping with such a wife. But I am not the man, and I cannot and will not make those adjustments. *So.* Wouldn't the wisest move be to sever this double-bind and release both myself and my wife? Shouldn't I rejoice that she has found a man and a situation which will free me of both the burden and the guilt? Allow the lady to go off into the sunset, holding the hand of the doctor, perhaps, but saying my name like a prayer?"

Max, puffing expansively, eyed Coleson with compassion.

"*But.* There are two problems with this switch, Doctor. One, of course, is money."

"Money?"

Max nodded. "Money. Connie would want her doctor, her *husband*, to have his own clinic. She couldn't be hustled in, and maybe *out*, of institutions where her husband was just another guy on the payroll. And I don't know, of course, how a clinic's management would view an employee whose wife was there on a quasi-nut basis. In any event, I'm sure we agree that it wouldn't do for Connie. She has never in her adult life, if you want to call it that, had to account for money."

Max rose, walked a few paces to a cellaret.

"At a rough estimate, I would say that maintaining Connie in the cotton wool to which she is accustomed, costs close to a million a year. That, of course, includes incidentals like private railroad cars and chartered yachts. Since she's not really crazy, she can't be expected to spend all her time in hospitals, and when she's out, it's only natural she likes to get around in comfort and privacy." Max returned to Coleson, handed him a snifter of brandy.

"Connie becomes highly anxious if she thinks she's going to have her little outings cut short, so the yachts and cars are chartered for a minimum of three months. *Just in case,* although she never uses them for more than a week at a time, unless I go on a boat with her. On *boats* she likes me. She's happy with me on boats. A perfectly controlled environment, I guess. But I can't stand being on boats more than a week, so that's that. As to other aspects of travel, well, you understand that Connie is too shy to stay in hotels. She hasn't stayed in one for over fifteen years. A house has to be leased and staffed for her wherever she wants to go. It all adds up."

Throughout Max's talk about Connie's extravagance, Coleson had been appreciatively sniffing the extraordinary aroma of Max's brandy. Now he tried a small sip. It was superb. It warmed him. It emboldened him to make a direct inquiry.

"But Connie is a rich woman. Why shouldn't she have what she is accustomed to?"

Max regarded Coleson with hostly concern. "The brandy, all right?" Coleson nodded.

Max, reassured, returned to the subject of Connie's finances.

"You mean why shouldn't she pay for those things with her own money? Because she can't. When Connie's mother killed herself, she left her entire estate to General Sunderson. Now Sunderson would have locked the money up in trust in any event, but when Connie married me, he threw away the key." Max grinned. "You've got to understand that to General Sunderson it was like his daughter had married a combination of Sammy Glick and the International Jewish Communist Conspiracy. The Parkins millions—" Max puffed belittlingly on the cigar. "—all *six* of them, will never fall into my greedy hands." He laughed. "Funny how few millions look like a fortune when the money's a couple of generations removed from sweat. People always talk about the Parkins fortune, for chrissake. A lousy *six*." He paused again, aiming at Coleson a look of hostly solicitude.

"Is this boring you?"

"Not at all. Anything you'd like to tell me . . ."

"You never know. Some people don't like to hear details about money . . ."

Coleson wondered who those people were. "I'm interested in whatever concerns Connie."

Max nodded. "Naturally. Well, as I said, the General fixed it so I could never get near the money. He even put the nix on my kids. The old man set up a trust agreement under which not only the principal, but the income from the principal, is held inviolate for the grandchildren. Except for five hundred dollars a month to Connie and each of the girls. That's supposed to keep them off welfare when I eventually abandon them or go to the pen. Now, these quarter-blood Herschels will inherit to the extent of one-half the trust's *income*, to be divided equally among them, whatever their number, when they reach their collective majority." Coleson, well into his portion of brandy, noticed that Max had not touched his. Another nasty trick? Like that business with the cigar? he wondered. Max's voice droned on.

"They will inherit, that is, if they are attending the Episcopal church as dues-paying members and have proved themselves to be in all other respects worthy in the eyes of the Trustee. The Trustee is another military man. And if this Trustee should trip on his sword, a *third* military man will be appointed. If the whole military establishment gets wiped out, then there's still God and the Probate Court Lower Case which will appoint a substitute Trustee of the same general class, education, and persuasion as his predecessors, who will be able to 'divine the intention of the original Trustee and guarantee the continuity of intent.'"

Max spoke with such obvious relish that Coleson could see what great satisfaction the General's spiteful will afforded him.

By tying up the money, the General had, in effect, delivered his daughter totally into Max's hands. And Max, challenged, had gone on to make God knows how many times the amount of money Connie would have inherited.

What had caused Max such glee, however, was not his antique triumph over the General, but the clause in the will designating the Episcopal faith as the only one and true. It was delightful to Max because he knew that Sunderson's parents had been first-generation Swedish Lutheran emigrants, to whom the liturgical pomp of an Episcopal service would have been as unspeakable as the link with Zion was to their ambitious son.

Max, his brandy still untouched, puffed triumphantly on his cigar.

"So," Coleson said, resolutely keeping any note of disappointment from his voice, "for any practical purpose, Connie has no money of her own."

"Didn't she tell you?" Max asked solicitously.

"We've never talke 1 about money. Not really."

"Never talked about money?" Max smiled. "Then you've never talked about life or death or politics or sex. 'Not really.'"

Coleson grasped the nettle. "Is the trust irrevocable?"

"Believe you me!" Max laughed and regarded the inch-long ash of his own Upmann with satisfaction. Without warning, it disintegrated and fell all over his chest and lap. Automatically he started to brush the ash off his dinner jacket. Not until after the first smear did he remember Churchill had never brushed away *his* ash. Churchill, Max had heard, would sit imperturbable under layers of ash, like a survivor of Pompeii. There was no burying Churchill. Max stared at the streaks on his jacket, torn between the compulsion to clean off the powdery mess, and the impulse to show Connie's quack that there was no burying *Max*. He chose, with considerable psychic discomfort, to let the ash lie where it had fallen, and tried to forget it by puffing up another one.

Coleson sensed Max's conflict, but did not understand what had motivated it. His distrust of Max was so pervasive that both Herschel's good humor and the loss of it were equally threatening. Was he dropping ash all over himself as an insult? Symbolically fouling himself as a gesture of contempt for Coleson? *Nonsense*. Don't *project* . . .

"Of course," Max continued after a deep draw on the cigar, "of course, no trust is eternal. The terms are kaput twenty-one years after the death of the last descendant who was alive at the time the trust went into effect. That means twenty-one years after our two daughters die, because they had both been born before the General's death. So twenty-one years after the last girl dies, the principal is released from trust. That's a federal law called Gray's Rule Against Perpetuity." Max beamed at the concept of Gray's Rule. Something about it so pleased him that he took his first sip of brandy.

"So. Say that Baby, who's almost thirty and the youngest, dies at the age of seventy-five. That will be, in the year of General Sunderson's Episcopalian Lord, 2021. Then. Add the twenty-one years required by law and you're up to the year 2042. In 2042, the trust expires and the hungry heirs, having survived for two generations on a diet of communion wafers, dash off to the bank to collect." Max chuckled. "Except for one thing. General Sunderson willed that when the trust expires, the entire principal is to go to the United States Military Academy at West Point for the establishment and everlasting maintenance of a new Episcopal chapel."

Max had abandoned his brandy after the one sip. But he sucked passionately on the cigar. He sucked and smiled. Smiled and sucked. He admired the General's forcefulness and ingenuity in carrying out the dictates of his bigotry.

"So you see, Doctor, Connie is not a rich woman. She is, in effect, a poor woman who costs a rich man a lot of dough. Whatever she needs or wants comes from me. From lipstick to uh—" Max pointed his cigar at Coleson. "—highly specialized medical attention. I'm the bank."

Coleson picked his way carefully. "Perhaps . . . perhaps she would . . ." He paused, scrutinizing the geography of Max's face for landmines. "Let's suppose for the sake of . . . not argument, certainly, but for the sake of . . . speculation . . ."

Max cut him off. "That if she married you and I set you up in a clinic, that you could take care of her in a way that would be okay for her and cost me less than my current outlay per annum?" He did not wait for Coleson's reply. "You remember I said there were two problems? Money's only one. The other problem is me."

Coleson's own cigar had gone out. He laid it down.

"You? In what way do you consider yourself a problem, Mr. Herschel?"

"We talked earlier about Connie's truth. Now let's talk about mine. My truth is that while I'm sorry Connie's not happy with me, I don't believe she'd be a helluva lot happier without me. Also she's very, very spoiled. I've given her everything, and it's been my pleasure. It still is. I *like* to charter yachts for my wife. She tells you I don't love her. She tells herself I don't love her. I don't know what to say to that. I *care about* her and I want to take care *of* her. In my book, that's love. And I'm proud of Connie. Every now and then, when I . . . let's say . . . urge her, she pulls herself together for a state appearance, like tonight. She's a beautiful lady, and I'm proud of her. Proud I'm her husband.

"Of course, since you know 'Connie's truth'—and this is one point where our truths jibe—you know I like women. Plural. As plural as I can manage. Which means that from time to time I'm bound to hit one that's a pistol. Tempting. Now as long as I've got my wife of thirty-five years, who I have no intention of shaking loose from, then everybody stays cool and the demands don't get out of line. I'm being very honest with you."

Max got up and strode back to the cellaret for the brandy bottle. He moved in on Coleson and refilled his glass. "Great stuff, isn't it? It was given to me by Guy de Rothschild." Coleson was unable to repress the look of greed that flashed in his eyes. Max did not miss it. He resumed.

"Connie has never been much of a mother. I couldn't expect her to be because she never had one herself to learn from. But since she's the way she is, the girls only knew *they* had a mother when I pushed all their heads together and said 'this is your

[154]

mother,' 'these are your kids,' and ordered them all to act accordingly. It's not much, but it's better than nothing. The proof is that both girls are married and mothers themselves and not too bad at it. Now that there are grandchildren, I think it's important for them to see their grandmother from time to time. When they see Connie, they see a real lady, who's pretty and gentle and generous. But there's nobody going to guarantee them they see that lady except me. Left on her own, Connie would *mean* to see them, she would *intend* to, but she wouldn't quite make it. So it's my job to see that she does. And it's not one I'm going to pass off on you because, one, I don't want to, and two, I don't believe you could deliver anyway. You can't guarantee me anything past the first step, which is, if I'll divorce her and make a substantial settlement, you'll marry her. I fail to see what I'm getting for my money. You're asking to be subsidized for taking away a woman I don't want to lose. The answer is no. To everything."

Max stubbed out his cigar. "So here's the deal. Connie won't be going back to Connecticut with you. She'll stay here, or if she's too upset, she can check into Payne-Whitney for a couple of weeks until she decides where she does want to go. You'll have her stuff sent down. I'll see that this little fishing expedition shouldn't cost you. You tell your boss you did everything possible to prevent Connie running away, and I'll back up your story. In fact, I'll take the rap for her leaving. Just so you don't bother Connie tonight, and you pull out quietly in the morning without seeing her. I don't want her set off." Max apologized. "I know you're disappointed, but look at it this way. You could have wound up with no money, bad professional publicity, *and* Connie . . ."

Max reached for the humidor, reached in and recklessly pulled out a fistful of cigars. He reached across to Coleson and thrust the cigars into the doctor's pocket. "Here. I like to see a man who appreciates a good cigar. Look, Doctor . . . you've only seen Connie in a relatively stable condition." He hesitated, then pushed on. "She's . . . she can become . . . under stress—*normal* stress . . . pretty . . . dependent. For instance . . ." His smile was sad, paternal, acceptant. "Sometimes she won't go to the bath-room without me. To—uh—take care of her . . . and, you know . . . flush."

Coleson knew without doubt that Max was lying. Coleson had studied Connie's records carefully and conferred with her former doctors. He was familiar with the etiology and symptomology of her disease, if it could be called that. He knew the outer limits of her behavioral aberrations. No one had ever had to . . . *tend* Connie in the bathroom. Or flush. Max Herschel was a sonofa-bitch and a liar, but Coleson was dazzled by the lie. Its imagery was so devastating that he and Herschel both knew he would never look at Connie again without the vision of Max gently leading the infantile Connie to a toilet and *tending* her.

The game was up, but Coleson was reluctant to let the other man think it was the final cruel attack that had bested him.

. "Mr. Herschel . . . do you realize, Mr. Herschel, that at no point in this conversation, that at *no point* did you seem in any doubt . . . that you never *asked* me about Connie? Or myself? Or what the situation between us might be? How were you able to assume that . . ."

"Coleson," Max leaned forward and patted the doctor con-solingly on the knee, "you're not Connie's first doctor."

"Well, of course I'm not Connie's first doctor. The poor woman has . . ."

"I mean I've had other offers to finance clinics."

Coleson's knee shrank from Herschel's hand.

Max rose. "Sorry you had to make the trip down for nothing. I'll be glad to send you back in the plane. Have your car driven up. Oh, and say! Thanks for the meringues. I ate a couple. They're great."

Max watched the elevator door close on Coleson's bemused face, then grabbed his untouched brandy snifter and poured its contents back into the bottle. Max had picked up a dozen cases of the brandy at a London auction. It was in fact superb, and there was no sense wasting it. Personally, he hated the stuff but it always came in handy. It was good local anaesthesia for opera-tions like tonight. He closed up the cellaret, walked back to the sofa, and lay down, his arms behind his neck. He eyed the red-head on the far wall and thought about Coleson and Connie.

It took Max less than a minute to conclude that Coleson might go away feeling he had retained some possible nuisance value. Max acknowledged the possibility and decided that it could be most effectively canceled by investing in Coleson's future. If possible, he would buy Coleson a little interest in the Neurological Center, which would be deductible.

But he wouldn't spring unless the doctor found true love. Maybe a nurse? Max knew that a romantic guy like Eric Coleson would not have to look hard. Or long. He smiled. He would encourage Coleson to find a nice Jewish nurse. Max always liked to see nice Jewish girls marry doctors. Doctors were wasted on shiksehs who were not raised to show that special respect. Nice Jewish girls should be guaranteed all the doctors. Better also for the doctors. Everybody, as far as possible, should get what was best for them.

His mind made up and confidence at full tide, Max bounded to his feet and headed back to the party. He was ready for Steven.

Max rode straight to the basement, where he was sure to find Sid cowering from the party. Sure enough, Sid lay trembling near the familiar, comforting hum of the furnace. Max got a hand on Sid's collar and dragged the beast with him to the elevator. Sid did not want to go and barked a protest which Max ignored. He shoved Sid into the elevator with him and slammed the door.

Upstairs, after Sid was leashed and tied to the front door, Max went in search of Steven, whom he found at the edge of the dance floor, talking with Stan. Max saw without surprise that, although Steven was talking to Stan, his attention was fixed on Bones, who was dancing with Pat Langdon.

Steven, watching Bones' blond head, calculated the high percentage of blond females on the dance floor. Herschel knew what he liked.

Max approached the two young men and gave his son-in-law a fond clap on the shoulder.

"Your wife looks beautiful tonight. Why aren't you dancing with her?"

"Well, Max, she told me to get lost. She said she wanted to lean on your tennis player." Good-naturedly, Stan pointed out the couple.

Max saw Baby pressed up against Jock Kelly, as close as a mousse in a mold. Stan smiled at Max's suddenly downturned mouth.

"It's okay, Max. She just doesn't want to waste the new dress on a short Jew."

Max glanced at Steven to see what he thought of this. Apparently, he didn't think anything at all. For all their differences, Stan and Steven seemed easy together.

"What's the script? What were you two plotting?"

Max never disappointed Stan. Two young men, standing by a dance floor rather than moving in on the nearest female victims, were perceived to be *plotting*. Plotting what? Moving in on the nearest female victims?

"No plot, Max. Just book talk."

Max noted Cathy among the dancers, floating demurely in the mauve chiffon he had paid for. He liked the way she looked. Very ladylike. Very nice. He shook his head sadly at the two young men. "I throw a sensational party, two bands you shouldn't hear yourself think, champagne flowing like cream soda, fifty beautiful broads, fifty, and you kids stand off here chewing over the library?"

He looked out over the dancers and spotted Connie, somnolently following Dr. Coleson's stolid lead.

"Stan, do me a favor, will you? Go cut in on Connie. She's not getting any laughs out of the baby-sitter." Then he addressed Steven. "I'm going to walk one of the dogs. Want to come with me? Get a breath of air?"

Steven understood he was being summoned by the headmaster. Nodding agreeably, he set off with Max.

Locked in the athletic embrace of Pat Langdon, Bones watched Steven and Max leave together, helpless to prevent their pairing off.

Outside the house, Sid continued to sulk, forcing Max to drag him along the sidewalk on his haunches. Then, with no warning whatever, the hound rose to his feet and took off into the night, dragging Max on a wild, goalless gallop, leaving Steven to lope along last. They must have looked, he imagined, like figures in a badly shot home movie, alternately stopping and flapping through the same few frames, over and over, then going out of control and falling out of the picture.

What most interested Steven was Max's good-natured incompetence with his enormous pet, his utter lack of concern at cutting a dignified or even sane figure. Their madly erratic progress made conversation impossible until suddenly the dog, in an idiot impulse of affection, turned back on Max and butted him in the stomach, pushed him up against a wall to lick his face with a great lolling tongue. Max shoved and swore until Steven wrested the animal off him.

"Goddam Irish," Max laughed. "Wonder this country survived them."

Steven took the leash from Max and doubled it twice around his own right hand. He gave the dog a powerful jerk and advised it firmly to heel. Sid gave Steven a silly, astonished look, then with his hound's version of a sheepish grin, heeled.

Now that the farcical chase had been transformed into a civilized stroll, Max walked contentedly along at Steven's side.

"Look, that conversation at dinner, I guess it was pretty obvious I never read a book of poetry in my life. 'Casey at the Bat,' a couple of dirty limericks, and I've shot my wad."

"Don't apologize, Mr. Herschel . . ."

"Max."

Steven was vaguely embarrassed, but he tried. "Max." He brought Sid more sternly to heel. "No one reads contemporary poetry but contemporary poets."

"You don't have to be nice that I'm illiterate. Anyway, it's not the poetry I want to talk about. I want to talk about your novel. Hell, it's not only I don't read poetry, I don't read many novels either. But I read yours. I thought it was wonderful. Fucking wonderful." A faint smile. "It made me cry. Tell you the truth, I cry easy," Max confessed. "But not usually over books."

Steven was shocked at how badly he wanted to believe Max,

and, aware that he was flushing with pleasure, felt grateful for the dark.

"Well . . ." Steven struggled for words.

Max helped him. "I guess plenty of jerks tell writers and artists what I'm going to tell you, but with me it's the truth. If I could do anything in the world, be anything . . . I'd be a writer."

Steven doubted it. "Would you? Why?"

"Well, everybody thinks they've got something to say, of course. But it's not that. It's . . . *power*."

Max had spoken the one word that could have suspended Steven's disbelief. In spite of himself, he listened.

"To get at the emotions of thousands of people and rip into them, move them, that's power. What you do is—to *me*—a goddam miracle." Max broke off and shrugged. He had, Steven understood, offered him—diffidently, shyly—a mantle of cultural divinity. Steven could warm himself with it or let it drop. Max had simply made the offer.

Steven attempted to postpone the option. "Writing is . . . well, it's easier to say what it isn't. It *isn't* anything mysterious. Mostly it's just hard work and self-discipline."

Max made a derisive sound. "Yeah? *I* work hard and *I* discipline myself. Why can't I write?"

"Maybe you can."

"I can't."

"Well," Steven smiled, "I can't make millions of dollars."

Max looked at him, incredulous. "What do you mean? Of course you can. *Anybody* can make money. Anybody. Look around you."

"I'll tell you what, Mr. Herschel—"

"Max."

"All right. Max. I'll give you a few good tips on the writing game. One, verbs. That's the big secret. Strong verbs."

"Strong verbs."

"And easy on the adjectives. When in doubt, *no* adjectives."

"No adjectives. Got it."

"Now you give me a tip on how to make millions."

"Start with something you know about. Like books. But you can't just give birth and then throw the kid out in the snow. You've got to give it a loving, nurturing environment. Give it a Jewish mother."

"Are you talking about publishers?"

"I'm talking about the whole megillah. Publishers, publicists, market analysts, movie studios . . ."

"Writers are seldom in a position to dictate how and where . . ."

"Don't buy that crap. It's your baby. Possession is nine points of the law. Make them come to you. You've got the product."

"But they're the ones who decide whether they *want* the product."

"*Nobody* knows what they want. They have to be told." He smiled. "Get any movie bids for your book?"

"Nothing to speak of. One independent producer . . . a fellow named Raskin—Jules Raskin . . . ever hear of him?"

Max shook his head.

"Neither had I. Anyway, he kept taking me to lunch and telling me how he was going to handle the 'property.' He seemed to think Richard Bradford would walk into the Pacific if he didn't get to play Alenghi . . ." Steven laughed. "I'd say, 'But Richard Bradford is blond and blue-eyed.' And Raskin would shake his head and say, 'What's *with* you, sweetums?' "

"Sweetums?"

"Mr. Raskin liked me," Steven replied, straight-faced. " 'You never heard of wigs, sweetums?' he'd say. 'Of *Clairol* for chrissake? You don't know they got different-colored contacts give you any color eyes you want? You think Bradford's not creaming to play Grunette? How many big box-office stayers they ever had was *blond?* Name me *four.* You've got your Nelson Eddys and your Alan Ladds and your Van Johnsons. *Then* what have you got?' "

Max laughed. "You've got your Jules Raskins. I don't know him, but I *know* him. So what happened?"

"He could never get up the option money."

"See? You threw the baby to the wolves and there wasn't even a wolf out there you could respect. Right? Look, what do I know about movies?" He shrugged. "Nothing. I've seen a lot of them, I know a few people in the business. So what's my opinion worth? Popcorn. But I think there's a movie in that book."

"I thought so, too."

"There. You see? You're the author. You have the instinct. You probably know just how to do it . . . where to take the story, the characters . . . You know what I'd like to do, Steven? With your permission, naturally. What I'd like to do is show it to a couple of people I know. People in the business whose judgment you've got to respect. Not just fans, like me."

Max sighed heavily. "I just got screwed on a deal with a studio where I could have swung a lot of weight. Which is too bad, because right now Max Herschel is a dirty word in that quarter. A damn shame . . ." Max stared moodily into the night. "The guy there . . . production head of Artists International . . . he would have gone for your book . . . the Arab angle would really get to him . . . he'd go for *you*, too . . ."

Max sighed again, clearly regretting that his own failure at Artists International should unfairly weigh against the promotion of Steven's film career.

"But I know other guys. Not placed so nice for fast action, but pros, knowledgeable. If you give me the word, I'd like to send copies of your book to them."

Steven felt like the farmer's daughter being offered a weekend in Atlantic City. He knew what it meant, but he'd never *been* to Atlantic City. He smiled. At himself and at his seducer.

"And what can I do for you . . . Max?"

"You've got connections in the Middle East. You can help me get a very valuable vase out of Syria. Illegal."

The promptness of the reply and the open acknowledgment of the quid pro quo did more to disarm Steven than anything Max had said or done all evening.

Steven reached out in the dark, found his cigarettes, shook one out of the pack, and lighted it.

"What you never told me was how . . ." He wanted the exact word. ". . . how *disarming* he is. He's pretty goddam disarming."

Bones, lying apart on her own side of the bed, said nothing.

"I mean he let that dumb dog drag him all over the street." Steven laughed "He was as good-natured about that chase as a village idiot. Then when he makes what sounds like some sort of bribe—maybe it is, maybe it isn't—but whatever it is, he's like a kid. He offers you his best aggie, then tells you fast and straight out what he wants in exchange." Steven proffered Bones a drag of his cigarette. She shook her head. "The extraordinary thing is . . . I think he liked the book. I mean *really* liked it."

Bones closed her eyes. Max had homed in on Steven's ego like a tomcat clearing a backyard fence to pussyland. The tension she had felt all evening exploded behind her lids in a thousand angry little jets of pain. She turned toward Steven. "Put your hand on me."

He rather absently obliged.

"How did Max start? What did he come from?"

Bones repressed a moan of impatience. She knew that she would be nursing Steven through a siege of Max fever.

"Chicago, Lace-curtain Jewish," she began. "When he was a kid he had a newspaper route for the *Examiner* and they started up a promotional scheme to sell cheap accident insurance through their newsboys. Fifty-cents-a-month premiums. The kids would deliver papers and collect the fifty cents from their customers. When Max had sold all his regulars, he branched out, started canvassing office buildings all over Chicago. He made some kind of incredible record for selling low-premium insurance. He was only thirteen and he was outselling grown men with full-time jobs working for regular insurance companies."

She worried her head deeper into her pillow.

"Go on. Then what?"

"Max says that after his twelfth birthday, he never took a dime from his father. By the time he was seventeen, he was in business for himself, using his brothers for fronts till he was of age. He went from insurance to hotels. He bought his first hotel when he was twenty."

"What about his family? What did his father do?"

"Repaired watches for Marshall Field. Max says the old man tried other jobs from time to time but he never made a go of anything. He was in the watch-repair room at Marshall Field off and on for over forty years and he never even became top repairman."

She did not tell Steven what Max had once said to her about his father. "He was a failure. Failed in everything. It was *Death of a Salesman*. But he was a sweet guy. A very sweet guy. Good to his family. Very decent. I hated him."

"How many children in the family?" Steven asked.

"Two older brothers and a sister, who died young. Both the brothers worked for Max. One is retired now and lives in Florida. The other one became a Canadian citizen so all Max's holdings there wouldn't make the Canadians nervous. Max owns half the damned country. Most of it in the brother's name. The brother doesn't *do* anything. Max just bought his name. It's . . ." She grinned. "Trevor. Derek Trevor."

"*Derek Trevor?*"

"Max wanted something nice and English that would fit in Toronto."

"I wish I didn't believe you." He laughed.

Steven lay back, thinking about Max and Derek.

"What was Derek's name before it was Derek?"

"Morris."

"It's crazy, you know. When you hear or read about men like Herschel"—across Steven's narrow Routledge face a faint look of scorn was traced—"you despise them. They represent everything you instinctively reject. But then you meet one of the bastards"—Steven's ancestral face, the face of witch-burners and hanging judges, softened—"and he sets out to charm you, and even when you can see the moves coming, anticipate the flattery . . . all of it so patently obvious . . ." Steven shook his head in amused admission of defeat. "You find yourself rolling over on your back, all four paws in the air, begging for the belly-rub." He laughed and stubbed out his cigarette. "So much for moral superiority."

Steven gathered Bones up against him. "But the extraordinary thing is," Steven repeated, "I think he liked the book. I mean *really* liked it." He felt the breath that seeped from her. "Do you think he honestly intends to get some movie people to read it?"

"Yes," she answered truthfully. "He probably does. But that doesn't mean," she warned, "that anything will actually come of it."

"Still," Steven declared, "it's a generous thing for him to do . . . under the circumstances."

Max's power, Bones knew, lay not in his ability to make people believe him, but to make them *want* to believe him. She felt terribly tired.

Max put the letter from Coleson on Connie's breakfast tray and instructed Mrs. Murray to stay in the bedroom until Connie had read the letter, then come directly out.

He waited in the hall.

When Mrs. Murray emerged from Connie's room, she nodded at him. He went in.

Connie lay in bed, the untouched tray beside her, the opened letter on the floor. Little twin tears rested on her smooth cheeks. She was hiccoughing regularly but gently. Everything was precisely as Max had expected.

"Good morning, sweetheart." He sat down in the small velour chair beside her bed, unconsciously assuming the pose of a consulting physician. "I missed breakfast with Dr. Coleson. He had to get back to Hartford, Teddy said."

A faint gagging sound from Connie.

Max patted her hand.

"Nice you brought him down. I think he had a good time at the party."

Slowly, Connie turned her face toward Max. She opened eyes wide and sparkling with the tears of her small, futile rage.

"I hate you, Max. I hate your guts."

He sighed. "I know you do, Connie. I know you do." He turned his head from side to side, as if trying to shake out some consolation for her.

"I'd hate you, too, sweetheart. If I could."

Laughter erupted from Connie like vomit. For the short time it lasted, Max was close to being unnerved, but it stopped as abruptly as it had begun, cut off by a giant, head-jerking hiccough.

"I can't stay in this house, Max! I need a doctor. I want a doctor!"

Max relaxed. He was back on familiar ground.

Chapter 13

Steven was showering, and Bones was on the exercise ladder when Max called. Bones had not seen him in the four days since the party. Connie had rejected Payne-Whitney, so Max had flown her to one of her old clinics in California and then, since he was in the neighborhood, had stayed on for two days with Dolores. He had called Bones every night. He always called every night when he was out of town, although when they were both in New York, a week could pass without word from him.

And every night Steven had listened to the conversations with Max.

"You never say you love him."

She smiled. "I don't."

"Or that you miss him."

"I don't."

"Or that you're lonely and wish he'd hurry home."

"I don't miss him and I don't care whether or not he comes home," she insisted.

"But when he does, you'll go to bed with him."

Her silence gave affirmation. But still he pressed.

"Won't you?"

"What does it matter? Are you jealous?"

"I don't think so."

"Then what?" Bones wanted to know.

"It's sad."

"*Sad?* What's sad?" she demanded.

"I guess it's sad that you don't love him. Or think you don't."

"What the fuck does it take to prove to you I don't love Max Herschel!" she blazed.

"More than a few nights in the sack with me. I mean, you've spent fourteen years in bed with him and you insist *that* proves nothing."

"What do you want me to do? I don't know what you want!"

"Nor do I."

They glared at one another but were fearful of unleashing real anger. When Bones spoke again, her voice was calm.

"You want me to leave him."

"Yes, I do. But I don't see how I can ask." He smiled thinly. "I don't think you're all that eager to settle down in Vermont."

She was surprised, and she showed it. He laughed.

"You see? If you leave Max, what exactly do you leave him for? You don't hate him. You don't want to get away from him. Be truthful. Give up everything he represents for an occasional weekend in New England? It doesn't make sense. You can have that and Max too. Why hurt him?"

"What do you care if I hurt Max?"

"Because whether you admit it or not, you owe him something. And because I like him. He doesn't deserve to get sand in his face just because you feel like kicking."

Every fiber in Bones yearned to tell Steven that the man he was protecting would blow him a kiss as he signaled the firing squad. She knew that whatever was between her and Steven would be tentative and uneasy until Steven understood Max better. She also knew that the enlightenment could not come from her.

And so they quarreled, but without spirit. Pride on both sides demanded a quarrel, but neither of them wanted to widen the natural distance between them. They were, rather, searching for bridges, shortcuts, connections. And they were uneasy because they found so few.

Bones was aware how badly Steven wanted to get back to Vermont. He spent his New York days scratchily vagrant. He sometimes saw his cousin Jess and his editor, Jerry Tester, but both of them kept office hours, Jess on Wall Street and Jerry at Darby Press.

"Are those two the only friends you have in New York?" she wondered.

"What do you want me to do? Ring up old war buddies? Go to alumni dinners?"

Bones dropped it. Writers, she knew from experience, swung radically between periods of reclusive withdrawal and binges of socializing. She did not press the subject of New York friends. She was more than pleased to have Steven to herself.

During Bones' working day, Steven caught up on movies and did desultory research at the Forty-Second Street Library. The rest of the time he spent stalking restlessly around Bones' apartment, taking frames off pictures to examine the canvases, then slapping them back together. One of her Carràs, he advised her, was a fake. She knew it was not. They quarreled. But carefully.

They always ate alone in the apartment, though occasionally they would have drinks first with Jerry or Jess Routledge and one or another of Jess' many girls. Bones liked Jess, although he didn't resemble Steven in any way. Jess was an enormous young man, over six foot four, full of high spirits and indiscriminate good will. He was hearty with Steven, and he treated Bones as if she were one of his own pack of handsome; healthy girls. These girls' lives seemed to consist of traveling great distances to use their muscles. They talked earnestly about "the absolute *primo* scuba spot," which was, Bones gathered, at Cozumel off the Yucatan Peninsula. One girl had nearly bought it at Cozumel when her J-valve clogged. Another girl tried to instruct Bones in the harrowing details of hang-gliding. Orange County was "primo" for hang-gliding.

The girl who bored Bones least was a bouncy little brunette whose short, strong legs reminded Bones of Max's. The girl talked with jolly malice about one of their friends, a girl named Lolly with whom she and Jess hunted at Far Hills.

"Too cheap to keep her own horses. She's always on some borrowed beast. Lolly'll be a paraplegic before she's thirty," Jess' girl declared cheerfully. "I've never known a rider of any class who is so insanely insistent on being overmounted."

"Overmounted." Bones treasured the word. If not the hours spent with the sporting crowd.

Nor did Bones savor the times with Jerry. He was scrawny, ill-groomed, contentious on principle. He did not, Bones knew, do well with girls. He was like dozens of young men Bones met in her work, clever, articulate, *cross* rather than angry. He did not engage her interest. She was always relieved to escape with Steven back to the apartment, where they would eat whatever Mrs. Patterson had prepared for dinner. Afterwards they would almost trip over themselves in the rush to bed.

Bones did not want Steven to leave. But she could not find the arguments to keep him with her. She was thirty-one years old and had no experience whatever in accommodating her hours or her ways to a young man. Steven had been with her in New York for seven days, two days before the party, the day of the party, and four days after the party. It seemed like a lifetime. Both of them longed and feared to end it.

"This is ridiculous," Steven finally declared. "I'm really leaving tomorrow. I can't just go on hanging around here. I've got to get back to work. Come up to Vermont on the weekend."

"I *can't*. I haven't had a session with Andy in . . ."

"You could come if you *wanted* to," he accused.

"And you could stay here if you wanted to. The apartment's empty all day. The extra bedroom could be turned into an office in about twenty minutes . . ."

"I live in Vermont."

"I live in New York."

"This is childish."

"Agreed."

"I'm going tomorrow morning."

"No, not in the morning! Not till I come home!"

The rising panic in her voice surprised them both. He kissed her.

"Okay, we'll have dinner tomorrow night. What do you say that before I go we have one dinner without Mrs. Patterson?"

"If we have dinner . . . without Mrs. Patterson . . ." Bones smiled, "couldn't you spend the night? You don't want to travel on a full stomach. Just one more night?"

They agreed that if Steven spent that one additional night, Bones would make no further fuss about his leaving.

It was on the morning before their last evening that Max called. He asked her how she was, pronounced California a drag, and suggested dinner.

"You got anything on for tonight?"

Her pause was scarcely discernible. "I'm having dinner with Steven."

"I thought he lived in Vermont."

"He's going back tomorrow."

"I'd like to see him again. How about we all have dinner together?"

"Well, actually . . ."

Actually. Max braced.

"Actually, I'd planned to give him dinner here."

He waited two seconds for the invitation, which did not come, then shouldered through. "I'll cook."

Bones speedily weighed the options. Having Steven to herself for the entire evening as against finally exposing Max to Steven and then *really* having Steven to herself.

"Oh, would you, Max? That would be wonderful. What shall I have Mrs. Patterson order?"

When Steven came out of the shower, she told him that Max was joining them for dinner and asked him if he minded. "He wanted to cook dinner for you," she told him.

She expected and allowed for the twinge of bitterness when Steven's face lit up.

The beignets de crabe had been splendid, the flan perfection. Max had been consistently tactful, charming, warmly hospitable.

Hospitable, Bones marvelled, in her apartment. To her lover. Worse, Max had found ground on which he and Steven could safely meet, detouring the shifting sands surrounding the person of Bones. It was to the congenial landscape of the Middle East that Max guided Steven.

"I try to tell this story to anybody who doesn't know that part of the world they look at me like I'm hookah-happy . . ." Max beamed, pleased with his alliteration. "But you know the place. You'll believe it." Max poured Steven more brandy, then settled back comfortably and went on talking. "I was doing a little business out there one time . . . this hot-shot sheik invited me for a meal. Silk tents and Nubian slaves—you never saw such rugs we were sitting on. There were about twelve of us. The sheik's people and me and a couple of Swiss bankers and three krauts. Anyway, about twelve. And behind each of us stood a black slave wearing long robes and a jeweled belt. And hanging from the belts were hand grenades. *Plus* every one of those spades held a sub-machine gun. Twelve spades with twelve sub-machine guns. But now wait. Here's the good part. The hand grenades and the sub-machine guns were all *gold-plated. Gold-plated*. I *swear*. I swear to God!"

Steven laughed.

Bones was not convinced. "Gold-plated? Where on earth would you get a sub-machine gun gold-plated?"

As one, the men turned patronizing eyes on her. "Purdy's," they chorused.

That Steven would have known a custom gun shop in London to be the inevitable source of gold-plated munitions, Bones accepted. What she could not accept was Max's expertise and the natural bonding of the two men against her.

She manufactured a humble little smile. "Stupid of me. I should have known."

"Why should you have known that, toots?" Max asked. "You got other kinds of weapons."

Steven smiled.

Bones was hotly aware that Steven did not smile *at* Max's cheap chauvinism, but *with* it.

"Max . . ." Bones turned and leaned forward in such a way that she blocked Max's view of Steven, ". . . Max, I've been wanting to ask you something. In Steven's book . . . I wondered what you thought about the scene on Long Island. Where Alenghi first hears that the war has broken out? Did it bother you that he wasn't with Carol when he heard the news?"

Bones felt Steven tense behind her. Max looked quizzical, hesitated. "Because *I* thought they should have been together. It would have made it even harder for him. How did you feel about it?"

"Rephrase the question," Max demanded.

"I just asked if it bothered you that Carol wasn't with Alenghi on Long Island."

The bitch was trying to set him up. Max peered around Bones, made a rueful face at Steven.

"I read it in one sitting, kid. I don't recall the specific scene."

Steven considered telling Max that there was no such scene. He did not know whether Bones was trying to embarrass Max or himself or both of them.

Finally, he answered Max. "It's not important. It's just a scene . . . a situation that men and women are apt to feel differently about," then Steven quickly changed the subject.

It was not yet ten when Max got up and made his apologies, saying he had to meet a man. He seemed content to leave Bones with Steven.

To Bones, whose cheek he gave a chaste good-night kiss, Max said that he'd forgotten to tell her about the stockholders' meeting and would call her tomorrow at the office. She walked him to the door, where he turned to face her, took her hand and kissed the tips of her fingers. He nibbled thoughtfully on two of them as he searched her remote eyes, then gave a sharp little nip to the fingers and released them.

"You shouldn't be such a bad girl. It isn't necessary." He patted her cheek. "Good night, sweetheart. I adore you."

She stood in the door and watched him step into the elevator. He smiled a last good-bye and blew her a kiss.

As she closed the door and returned to Steven, Bones' heart pounded with anxiety.

"Like to explain?" he offered.

"He hasn't read a book in twenty years."

"What I need to know is are you pissed off because he likes me, or because I like him?"

"He doesn't like you, darling. He hasn't read your book, and he doesn't like you."

"Then why would he go into such an elaborate act about loving the book? It's stupid. He's not stupid."

"No. He just doesn't read. He wants you to like him and trust him, and he knows precisely where to bore in."

"Why didn't you tell me after the party? Why wait till now to pull such a cunty scene?"

"But I hoped against hope."

"For what?"

"That he couldn't nail you."

"Nobody's nailed me, Bones. Not you and not Big Daddy."

"Oh, Big Daddy nailed you all right. Bullseye. Right between the 'e' and the 'go.' 'He liked the book, Bones. I mean *really* liked it.' What the hell do you care whether or not Max likes your book? He doesn't know one infinitesimal fuck about writing. Good, bad, indifferent. He couldn't care less. He's just trying to soften you up, make you look like a jerk. To me."

Steven regarded the toe of his shoe for a long moment, then rose from his chair.

"Well," he submitted, "I daresay he pulled it off." He shoved his fists deep into his pockets. "Thanks for dinner."

"Thank Max."

"I'll write him a nice note. Thank him for everything."

He was in the hall before she cried out. "You don't owe him anything! *I* don't owe him anything!"

Steven's pocketed hands trembled in anger.

"I have to go."

"Don't."

"This isn't my game."

"Don't go."

"I'm not playing, Bones." As he took the last few steps toward the door, she cried out, "What do you want me do to? Hang onto your goddam knees?"

It was almost two when Steven sat up in bed and turned on the lamp. Bones, who had been pretending to herself, as well as to him, that she was asleep, reached for him.

"Don't go!"

"I'm just looking for cigarettes."

"Oh." She exhaled. "Steven . . . I forgot something . . ." It was she who got out of bed. "I'll get it. And I'll find you some cigarettes."

When she came back, she tossed him cigarettes and a lighter, and when he had managed a couple of drags, she handed him the wrapped package she had been holding behind her back.

"Present."

It was the Klimt drawing of his grandmother, matted and framed. Steven looked up from the picture to Bones.

"You see?" she pled. "You see how lovely it is?"

Her anxiety about the picture seemed to Steven, for reasons he could not clearly define, terribly sad.

"Yes, it is."

She sat down on the bed beside him and looked at the picture.

"I can't understand . . ." She hesitated, searching for the words. ". . . a famous artist did a drawing of your own *grandmother* . . . and you gave it away." Bones reclaimed the picture, held it against her chest. "Didn't you like her?"

"I loved her. But I have lots of pictures of her and lots of good memories. I don't *need* the drawing. And you seemed to have . . . a feeling for it."

It was she who needed an idealized drawing of a proud and beautiful mother figure. He pulled her down, kissed her.

She whispered. "Don't go, Steven. Stay here. Stay with me."

Through the night and into the morning they argued cases.

No, it was not that Steven objected to living in her apartment on her money. The money was neither here nor there. It was simply that he worked better at the farm. He wanted to finish his book. He wanted her there with him. He wanted her away from Max. She should have a child sooner rather than later.

She was not at *all* sure she wanted a child. Later *or* sooner.

Oh, but *he* was sure she did.

Nevertheless. She couldn't possibly leave the shows in the middle of the season. They had eleven weeks to go. She had serious commitments and responsibilities. It would take time. Why couldn't they commute between New York and Vermont? Anyway, she did not want to *marry*.

"If you don't marry, Bones, you'll never get away from him."

"I'm already *away* from him."

"No, you're not. You're attached at the hip. It'll take surgery to separate you."

She pointed out that since he equated marriage with surgery, it was no wonder she faced the prospect with misgivings.

Not misgivings, he argued. Funk. She was terrified to take the one step which would cut her off from Max.

"I'm *not* afraid of leaving Max. I *want* to leave Max. It's *marriage* . . ."

"No it isn't. It's 'don't let go the hand of nurse, for fear of getting something worse.'"

"And you're the something worse?"

"Apparently."

Her faint smile was distant and impersonal.

"Steven . . . when I met Max . . . I was on call."

He did not seem to understand. "On call for what?"

"Tricks. Sex."

"Oh."

"That time has no relevance for me. None at all. But it might for you," Bones advised him.

"You said you were barely eighteen when you met Max . . . how long . . ."

"You mean how *many*? I can tell you exactly. When I met Max I was saving everything I made . . . outside modeling . . . to go to school. I had made seventeen hundred dollars at fifty bucks a pop before I moved to the East Side and doubled the tab to a hundred. When I quit, I had twenty-one hundred. Simple division. You don't need a pocket calculator."

Steven stared at her curiously. "I would have thought . . ."

"What?"

"That you could have managed school. Some other way."

"I tried. I worked and went nights for over a year. To finish high school. But I wanted to go to a good college and I wanted to go full time. I wanted to go to a college . . ." she sighed, "with . . . oh, you know . . . a campus."

"How did you get started?"

"Hooking? An older girl, a model for a very fancy designer, recruited me. It wasn't difficult—recruiting me, I mean. I didn't feel *a thing*. I *never* felt a thing." She held his eyes, attempting to instruct him in a vital lesson. "And I didn't really mind it. I was completely frigid. A big asset, I expect. Almost all of the men were nice. No one ever tried to abuse me. Some of them even gave me more money than I asked for, and when they did I saved the fee and spent the extra for clothes and perfume. Capital investment." She paused briefly, then summed up what she had been trying to make him understand. "In the same situation, I would do exactly the same thing again. Max understands that."

For the first time since she began the confession, Steven's expression lightened. "Is that in the nature of a challenge?"

"I don't know. Maybe."

They eventually agreed that Steven would return to Vermont and meet Bones in Boston for the weekend. He would take her to visit the Routledge graveyard in Dedham, a preliminary ritual, Steven insisted, before meeting his family.

"Including Aunt Cora?"

"Especially Aunt Cora."

There was a trace of hysteria in her giggle. "I don't think I can stand this!"

"Sure you can." He echoed Bones' words back to her. "You won't feel a *thing*."

Bones spent the three days preceding the trip in a state of icy-calm panic and the three nights in feverish serenity.

[177]

She felt altogether odd, out of touch, disconnected from the commonplaces of her life. Without warning, familiar, everyday things would turn against her, assuming foreign and unknown estates. On Tuesday night, walking through the hall to her dining room, she caught the reflection of the Nelson mirror out of the corner of her eye. As she turned toward it, she was bewildered to see her image in a strange, oddly framed glass. "It's the Nelson mirror, you ass," she told herself firmly, and walked on. It happened a dozen times in a dozen ways.

Early Wednesday morning Max telephoned her at home.

"Hello, sweetheart."

"Who is it?"

"Who is *what?*"

"Oh. Hello, Max."

She was disoriented, floating. She would have been wildly happy if she had known how to be.

Chapter 14

Mary Routledge
Died, 6th December, 1759, aged 44
She pass'd through life,
under a heavy pressure
of long affliction,
Piously sustained in the supporting
prospect of a better state.

Mary was the thirteenth or fourteenth—Bones had lost count—
female Routledge who had looked to death as a distinct im-
provement over life.

"There's rather a lot of 'long affliction' here for my taste," she
suggested to Steven.

"It isn't the affliction that counts. It's the spirit in which it is
borne. Here . . ." He read aloud another epitaph.

"With what unwearied patience
and resignation she lived.
With what integrity
and cheerfulness she died."

"How old was she?"

"Thirty-four. She died in 1699, so let's see, that would make her my great-great—oh well, five or six greats ought to do it—grandmum."

Bones stood before the grave of the girl, reading the lines to herself. Steven walked a few steps to a marble bench that curved around a yew tree and motioned the faintly frowning, silent Bones to join him.

"What are you brooding about?" he asked.

"My mother. She was only thirty-seven when she died. She got her head shot off by one of her dumb hillbilly lovers. Jealous, juiced-up, and armed with a squirrel gun."

She sat down on the bench. "I was in my last year at Wellesley. I didn't want to go to the funeral. I knew it would be ugly and mean. Some cousins who despised her had taken over. But Max forced me to go. He went with me. He just charged in and gave everybody orders, and made the funeral . . . all right. He even got a lawyer for the stupid sonofabitch who killed her—a poor slob of a farmer with ten scratch acres and a family he could barely feed. Max went to see him in jail, and he told Max that Mama had been the only 'beautiful' thing in his whole life."

Steven put his arm around her and gestured toward the outer reaches of the Routledge enclosure. "We'll go somewhere along there, you and I. I hope you appreciate you're in the very nick of time. After the nine Routledges of my generation, there will be no more room for wives. There won't even be room for all of the children. My Uncle Arthur has already had the slaves dug up and put outside the enclosure . . ."

"Slaves? In Massachusetts?"

"There were Routledge slaves up through 1748. Anyway, Uncle Arthur had them all dug up and bought a very nice plot for them—sort of a Routledge annex—outside the sacred grove, alas. But even with the slaves gone, Uncle Arthur says all of us over six feet are going to have to be buried with our knees bent." He poked a finger at her. "How tall are you? Five one, two? Uncle Arthur will be delighted with you."

Bones regarded him with an expression which he correctly read as a mixture of fascination and horror.

He touched her face.

"What I thought, darling, was that all this . . ." He gestured to the Routledge graves. "I thought this and Uncle Arthur . . . not to mention Aunt Cora . . . might weigh in the balance against the account of your seventeenth year."

She continued to stare at him for a long moment.

He stood up. "Come on. Let's go. I told Aunt Cora we'd be there by three."

With careful dignity, Jeffrey carried the tea tray to the library for Baby.

"Thanks, Jeffrey. Bones and I want to talk. So keep New Baby out. Okay?" Jeffrey's obsidian eyes flickered over Bones' face, normally so pale and cool, now flushed with barely contained excitement. Jeffrey wondered what the women wanted to talk about.

"Only three cookies, Baby," he warned, then closed the door softly behind him.

Baby chomped on a cookie and eyed Bones.

"What are you up to? You're *pink*," she accused.

"I'm thinking about getting married."

Baby's tea splashed on the upholstery. She sponged awkwardly at the stain with New Baby's rag doll, her compelling Herschel eyes locked on Bones' face.

When no comment seemed to be forthcoming, Bones continued. "What I came up here for . . . I came to meet Steven's family." Suddenly Bones was giggling and the hand that held the teacup shook. She put the cup down before there was further spillage. Baby had never seen Bones' nerves so exposed. Baby was outraged for her father, but Bones' shaken aplomb gave her pause.

"What's his family like, as if I didn't know?" she asked.

Bones tried to make Baby smile. "They leave twelve and one-half percent tips. To the penny."

"Bones . . . after *Daddy?*"

"You know the first woman Steven ever slept with? His aunt. His mother's own sister. And when I met her yesterday . . . here was this nice mousey little lady . . . just so *nice*. Steven claims she's had dozens and dozens of lovers . . . besides *him*. And she looks as if she breaks the ice in her basin every morning to wash, then goes to prayer and porridge, and spends the entire day in good works. Do you know what I mean?"

Baby snorted. "Pure Back Bay Wasp. They look like that, and get away with murder."

Bones opened her purse and pulled out a small object wrapped in tissue paper. She undid it and lifted out a diamond pendant on a chain. The diamond was blue-white, fine, three carats.

"She said she wanted to give me a nice stone . . . that perhaps Steven would want to have it set in a ring for me. An engagement ring." Bones' eyes met Baby's. "She said she knew all girls wanted a nice ring. Even if they were too sweet and modest ever to say so."

Max's eyes glittered challengingly out of Baby's face. "Why didn't you tell her how many 'nice' rings you've already got?" The eyes jumped to Bones' hands, which clutched at one another in her lap. Bones felt herself flush.

"I'm in love, Baby."

Baby sniffed. "Enjoy."

"Are you *trying* to sound exactly like Max?" Bones demanded.

"So what about Max?"

"I'm in love with Steven. I'm in love for the first time in my life."

"Oh garbage! You're thirty years old. You've been with my *Daddy* for thirteen years."

"I'm thirty-one and I've been with your 'Daddy' fourteen years. But I didn't love him fourteen years ago and I don't love him now."

"I don't believe you."

For some unfathomable reason Bones had thought Baby would be glad for her. She tried again. "Baby, what I loved . . . I loved the action."

"Then you loved Daddy. Because that's what he is. The action." She measured Bones for an enemy, but stopped short. Bones was her friend, a friend who, in Baby's judgment, was falling into bad trouble. "If you're really serious about running out on Daddy," she warned, "my guess is that you'll get plenty." Baby popped a whole cookie into her mouth, and crunched energetically. "Plenty of what you claim to love. *Action.* It's gonna hit the fan, chum."

Bones shrugged. "No, it's not. Max will be hurt, but not much and not for long."

"Is that what you think?"

"Oh, he'll rave around with a meat axe for a couple of days, but then he'll settle down. When it gets to the bottom line, Max is always reasonable."

Baby was dumbfounded that Bones could have been with Max so long and understood him so little. To Baby, the most obvious thing about her father was his sublime disregard for reason. It wasn't the sales that began when the customer said no. It was the war. The *fun.*

"Bones, you're not going to just *spring* it on him?"

"He knows I'm sleeping with Steven."

"That's not what I mean."

"Well, Baby, I'm not going to draw him a map so he can head me off at the pass."

Baby felt an urge to yawn and realized how shallowly she had been breathing. Her palms were wet. She leaned forward and tapped a warning finger on Bones' knee.

"Darling, I think you're making a terrible mistake. *Terrible.*"

Bones was attempting to rein her rising indignation. "You married a man you love. A young man. Who loves you. You've got . . . children. Why is it such a mistake for me?"

"But it's not the same. You're used to . . . so much."

Now Bones was dumbfounded. She knew that Baby, having always had everything, attached little importance to the goods and materials deriving from Max's favor. Then she grasped what Baby meant.

"You mean Max? Baby, I never *had* Max. He had me, but I never had him. You know that, Baby."

Baby spoke softly. "I didn't mean *just* Max. I meant what he gives you." She searched for the word. "Latitude."

Bones mustered up a smile. "Yes. He does give me latitude."

"And I don't mean only in sex," Baby argued Max's case. "I mean in *everything*. He helps you to do everything you want but still leaves you with breathing space. He understands you, and he does love you, Bones."

"He doesn't love me. I told you that the first time we met. Why can't you get it through your head? What he's got with me is . . . a deal. That's all. A deal."

"Well, what does Daddy get out of the deal?"

"You tell me. I've never known."

Baby was now popping cookies as fast as she could swallow them. Bones picked up the plate and moved it out of reach. "I thought you were on a diet."

"Sure, I take a No-Cal with my Danish."

Silence fell between them, then Baby twisted her shoulders in Max's impatient, angry shrug.

"Oh shit, Bones. I certainly hope you change your mind before you split your britches with Daddy."

Bones shook her head. "I don't think so."

Baby had a shivery premonition that she was losing Bones forever. She thrust out an impulsive hand. "I think it's lousy, but I'm your friend."

There did not seem to be anything more for either of them to say. Estranged, embarrassed, the two women looked away from each other.

Bones stood up.

"Steven's waiting for me."

She looked at Baby and realized with a pang of tenderness and distrust how extraordinarily she resembled her father.

Through an upstairs window, Jeffrey viewed Bones' departure. Jeffrey had made a dash from the hall door behind which he had eavesdropped before Baby and Bones crossed the living room to the hall door. His face burned with rage and shame as he watched Bones' small, neat figure get into a car.

Jeffrey had always accorded Bones the respect due any of Max's possessions. That one of those possessions would willingly detach itelf from Max produced in Jeffrey a kind of culture shock that Boston and the Big Mac had never effected.

That evening at dinner with Baby and Stan, he sat quietly, listening. Baby was highly agitated. She was also worried. Worried, more about Bones, it seemed to Jeffrey, than about Max. To the boy, Stan's opinion was shocking and inexplicable.

"He asked for it," Stan said. "Sooner or later, some guy was bound to pick her off."

Pick her off? Jeffrey barely breathed.

"Max set himself up." Stan continued eating. "But what's going to kill him is that the guy turns out to be a snot like Routledge."

"I thought you liked Routledge," Baby said.

"I like snots."

Baby herself refused to see anything in Steven beyond the vulgar attractions of looks and youth.

"I mean how in hell could she compare him to *Daddy?* She doesn't seem to have a clue to how much Daddy's given her. She thinks she's done it all herself. She doesn't realize how incredibly spoiled she is. She's going to be like somebody yanked out of an iron lung." Baby put down her fork. "Oh, shit." Tears welled up in her eyes. "It's *lousy*. And it's going to kill Daddy. What can I *do*, Stan?"

"Nothing. And nothing's going to kill Max. So you stay out of it. Understand? I don't want you calling him or getting mixed up in this in any way. Is that clear? There's no law to stop Routledge taking her away from Max if he can."

When Jeffrey softly asked to be excused, they paid no more attention to him than they had throughout the meal. He made an unobtrusive escape.

So. Max's woman had been stolen. She was not simply, womanlike, running away with every expectation of being pursued and reclaimed. She was being stolen. And the law protected the thief. The terrible injustice caused Jeffrey's knuckles to whiten. He despised Stan for his passive acceptance of this raid against the Father's property.

For the first time since coming to America, Jeffrey wept. He wept for Max's lost honor, for the cool indifference of the son-in-law, for the daughter's misplaced sympathy with the whore. When he had finished weeping, Jeffrey went to the bathroom and washed his face. Then, moving stealthily to the telephone in Stan's upstairs study, he dialed Max's home number.

Chapter 15

Bones walked briskly into Max's outer office, almost colliding with one of the girls. The one who had been at Baby's party. What was she called?

The girl gave Bones a breathless hello.

At the last second, Bones dredged up the name.

"Hello, Cathy. You looked beautiful the other night. That color was very becoming." She smiled and passed on.

But Miss Burton, Cathy thought, didn't look as well today as she usually did. She wondered exactly how old Miss Burton was. Jock said over thirty, but he was dumb about women and kind of mean. Jock was not turning out to be Cathy's idea of a *man*, but he might be right about Miss Burton. She looked kind of *drawn.*

Bones stopped at Stella's desk, and smiled uncertainly.

I *knew* it! thought Stella. Something's up. Something rotten. Max had started the morning distracted and explosive. When she had asked him what was the matter, he had narrowed his eyes at her and snarled, "Don't you know? Aren't you in on it?" When she had asked, "In on what?" he had brusquely told her to shut up and mind her own business. Stella had told him that any time he wanted to get somebody else to mind *his* goddam business for him, he could just say the word. Then she had marched to the bathroom and locked the door. She stood there seething for a few minutes before she took a bottle of aspirin out of the medicine chest and swallowed two. Then she sat down and waited until Max began pounding on the door, yelling that he was sorry.

From there, the morning had proceeded in uneasy fits and starts until almost noon when they left for the office. Once there, Max had shut himself off and refused to take calls.

"Stella . . ."

"Hi, honey . . ." Stella said. "He's expecting you."

"Stella . . . it might get a little hairy in there today."

"What's the sonofabitch up to now?"

Bones shook her head. "Just stand by. Okay?"

"Okay."

Bones did something very unusual. She touched Stella fleetingly on the shoulder, than dropped her hand and moved toward Max's office door.

Stella reached in her desk drawer and brought out another bottle of aspirin. She would take two more. *Now.*

Bones, closing Max's door behind her, could hear Bernie's voice storming over the phone before Max spoke.

"No, no, now listen, Bernie. Just listen to me . . . Will you listen? . . . Look, the IRS wants my money so bad, they can sue and we'll appeal right up to the ghost of Cardozo. In the meantime that money's working for me, not them. So tell 'em to blow it out the Lincoln Memorial. Bye-bye, now, I've got an appointment."

Max hung up, leaned back in his chair, and smiled amiably at Bones. "Bernie wants to refrigerate the beef by us putting on our hats and flying down to Washington to punch the Secretary of the Treasury in the nose."

Bones smiled at Max's pleasure in this bulletin. Max had probably been teasing his lawyer.

Bones sat down. Max swiveled in his chair and handed her a heavy manila folder. "I couldn't find you for two days. Where've you been?" He did not wait for an answer. "Remember that magazine thing I mentioned to you? I had Research go into it. Here's what they've come up with. Take it home and look it over. I know you're gonna get excited with the . . ."

"Max."

He kept his face averted while he decided whether or not to let her get it out her own way. But his instinct was to seize the initiative; he turned abruptly toward her.

"Okay, sweetheart. Let's have it. So you're in love. So what? I'm in litigation with the IRS." He turned up his palms. "Stormy weather. But we'll both come out okay. We'll get over it."

"I don't want to get over it."

"Bones, the only constant in life is that given a little time, you get over everything."

"Maybe. I'm over *you*, Max."

"What's that supposed to mean? You're 'over me'? What's to get over? What? A successful career? An exciting way of life? I made you an offer. A very good offer. You took it. You've done okay. Do you think you would have done as well without me?"

She shook her head.

"Do you think I've asked too much in return?"

"Maybe not enough . . ."

He chose to ignore this.

"What do you want you don't have? You want to bang the boy on a steady basis?" Max threw up his hands. "What am I? A house detective?"

She just looked at him. He shook his head. "I don't see your problem. Listen to me, sweetheart. I'm not standing in your way. He's an attractive guy. I don't blame you. You're overdue, I guess. So go on, let 'er rip. I can live with the embarrassment. It'll hand a few people a laugh . . . it'll hand *Connie* a laugh. What the hell? She can use one. So be in love. Shack up, if that's what you want."

Without warning, tears ached in her throat. She could neither swallow nor speak.

Max moved in fast. He came swiftly around the desk to her, leaned down, and took her face in his hands.

"Sweetheart . . . just tell me what you want. It's yours. Anything you want. *Tell* me."

"I want to be something else," she blurted. "Something *more*." Knowing that everything she could say was going to sound stupid, she began to get angry.

Max was infinitely tender. "What *more*, honey? You're already the whole megillah. You're everything they're out there dreaming about . . . you're *unreal*, for chrissake. Sweetheart, you're already a fucking *fantasy!*"

He said this with such conviction, with such an innocent commitment to *his* fantasy, that a tickle of laughter fluttered in the depths of her throat. Pinned between laughter and loss, she had never, she thought, come so close to loving him. But anger at herself, the inability to sound the right words, overrode the emotion. She despised the banality of her accusation: "If I'd ever known where I stood. With you."

A liar begging to be believed: "You stood with your little foot on my neck, sweetheart. From the first day."

Finally she found one right word. "Balls."

He was offended.

"Oh Max, let's don't lie any more."

"When did I lie to you? *When?*"

She had to smile. "Max . . . just for the record, now that it doesn't matter, you can tell me the truth. How many of us are there? I don't mean over the whole fourteen years. Just . . . how many of us are there now?"

There was no anti-aphrodisiac like a woman demanding the truth.

Max straightened up and moved back around the desk.

"For chrissake, Bones, you sound like Connie."

She shook her head. "No. What I want to know is . . . how many lives do you need? How many?"

"There's only one of *you*, sweetheart. Look—" He shrugged. "—who wouldn't take more than one life if he could get it? But you're *part* of me, Bones. To lose you would be a goddam amputation. And *that* is the truth."

"I got married this morning."

Max sat frozen. No expression crossed his face. She read no shock or hurt or rage there, but it was an endless, airless minute before he spoke. His voice, when it came, was gentle, reasonable.

"Don't worry, sweetheart. We'll get it annulled. Nothing to it."

In Max's phrase, she had to hand him. "*Max.* I don't want an annulment. I want to be married to Steven."

His manner was that of an experienced psychologist submitting proposition after proposition to a child of disordered temperament. "You don't know what you want. You never have. And you still don't. That's why you've been with me all this time. Also from me you get the idea you're in charge. The boy won't give you that, sweetheart. He'll *expect* things."

"Yes, he will. What he'll expect is for me to love him. That's all. It's as uncomplicated as that. Max . . ." She leaned toward him, determined to make him understand. "Max, I *want* to love him. Just to let go and love him. And that's what *he* wants. He's not like you, Max. He's very *different* from you. And from *me.* He's different and . . . better."

Max's lip curled. "Better?"

"Yes, he is. He's better than us."

"So tell me how."

"He wants different things . . . for himself. And for me, too."

"What things?" He crowded her.

Bones' teeth ached from embarrassment, but she said it. "He wants me to have children."

Max snorted. "Oh, shit. And that's the big Win Window, is it?"

"Why not?"

"Any alleycat can have kittens."

"Then why can't I?"

"Bones, listen to me. Always leave the track before the last race. Don't try to win them all, you know?"

"But I feel lucky, Max."

"That's a loser's feeling, sweetheart."

He pushed his chair back a bit and stared at her in cold appraisal. "What are you going to live on? You and all the kiddies. Routledge hasn't got a pot."

"I've got a pot."

"That's exactly what you've got. A pot. You're used to living like a very rich woman."

"I'll manage." She stood up.

He made a powerful effort to repress the great swell of his outrage. "Let me know if you don't."

Bones could feel her skin prickle in warning. She faltered. Every instinct told her to go around the desk and kiss him, beg for his understanding. But she stood rooted, defiant.

His mouth gave her a pleasant, impersonal smile. His voice gave her nothing.

"You better run along now, darling. I've got a guy waiting."

Bones felt a lurch of loss and a sudden dizzying chill.

"I'll talk to you in a few days, Max. When you . . ." When he what? She didn't know. "When you feel better . . . about it."

"I'm all right, sweetheart. It's you I'm worried about."

The self-destructive words spilled out: "But you don't have to worry about me. Not anymore."

Their eyes locked briefly, then Max's disengaged, and he swiveled his chair around to face the window.

His gaze set stubbornly on the oxblood vase by the north window, he listened to the door being opened and closed. He knew, from the brevity of the pause between the two sounds, that she had not lingered. She had probably not even looked back.

Max removed his contact lenses. First the left, then with more trouble, as usual, the right. He placed them carefully inside the little leather case with his initials gold-embossed on its lanolin-rich surface. He put the box in his desk and softly closed the drawer.

Then he lowered his head onto his arm and wept convulsively.

His febrile, disordered thoughts accused her wildly . . . it would be too late . . . mouth-to-mouth resuscitation . . . crowds held back . . . open-heart surgery . . . how long would it take before she heard the news? His sobs tore through him with such savage power that Stella, from the other side of the door, panicked. She entered his office.

Looking down at him, Stella was appalled by the inchoate animal noise.

"*Max.*"

He raised his head, tears streaming. He tried to wipe them away with his wrists, but they kept coming. The hot springs overflowed, flash-flooding down the arroyos of his wrinkled cheeks.

"Jesus, Max . . ."

His face was red and swollen.

"Stella." His voice was hoarse.

"I'm a dead Jew."

She went into the bathroom, ran cold water on a towel, and brought it back to him. When he made no move to take it, she walked around the desk and gently wiped his face, his eyes, even his wet, berserk hair. He accepted her attentions as passively as a sick spaniel, shivering, mutely grateful. Once she had wiped him free of the floodtide of tears, Stella dropped the towel in a wastebasket.

"Comb your hair, Max."

"I don't have a comb," he complained fretfully.

Stella went back into the bathroom, got a comb, then stood quietly by while he ran it unsteadily through the scarecrow strands.

"If you have dark glasses up here, you'd better put them on. Your eyes look terrible."

Max put down the comb and peered dimly at Stella.

"Sit down."

She sat, but he only blinked emptily at her for a moment before turning his eyes back to the vase.

"Max . . ." Stella decided to go off the high board. "What in the name of God did she do?"

He was still peering sightlessly through the wet and foggy windshield of his eyes, but his voice was almost steady.

"She got married. She married that punk." Max paused. "He's different."

His eyes suddenly focused and he fired at the vase a look of such concentrated malevolence that Stella expected the delicate porcelain to fracture and disintegrate. When he finally turned the murderous glare back toward her, Stella lowered her own eyes in quick, reflexive prayer. Don't let him do it! . . . whatever he's going to do . . .

"Okay. So fuck her. *Okay.* First, the gallery. I'm dissolving the partnership. The company was set up with a thousand shares. Bones and I took fifty each. That leaves nine hundred authorized but unissued. I've got a ninety-thousand-dollar loan outstanding which I never called in . . . I figured it was better for her to keep it invested in inventory . . . so, now it's better for me. That loan is convertible into nine hundred shares at current value . . . roughly a million-two, forget the goodwill since I don't intend to sell. Send a Day, Meyer truck around immediately. I want the gallery emptied and everything taken and put in a new storeroom in my name. Make out a check to that hummingbird she's got in charge—two weeks' salary. I want him out of there by four and a padlock on the door by five. But get the phone cut off *now.*"

"You're not leaving her *anything?*"

"I'm leaving her what she's entitled to on paper. Five per cent of book value. But it's going to take the lawyers a *long, long* time to get it cleared."

He scarcely paused. "Two. I'm buying her out of Burton Productions . . ."

"Oh, Max . . ."

"Shut up and listen. I hold fifty-one percent of the stock and if she doesn't like my offer, I'll close up shop . . . call Bernie and tell him he just attended a Burton directors' meeting and he voted with me."

Stella forced herself to ask, "What are you going to offer her?"

"Fifty thousand. I think that's fair."

"Fair! Fifty thousand?! For a business bringing in over half a million a year!"

"*This* year. It could all disappear in one season. That business is a crap game. Who knows what will happen when you're forced to change shooters?"

"Change shooters how?"

"Bones out, Warner in. Bones is going to be too preoccupied to run a business. Those kids are in love, Stella. They're young. Let 'em have a chance to be together, right?"

Every answer that sprang to Stella's mind, and they were many

[194]

and varied, was suppressed in the interest of her own survival.

Max regarded her with approval. "So. When you've got all that in the works—and I'll give you forty minutes—I want you to contact Elder and Green. They manage Bones' building . . ."

Softly: "I know that."

"You just fucking shut up and listen, Stella. *I'll* tell you what you know, all right?"

Stella nodded.

"*All right.* I will buy any two apartments in that building. *At any price.* The only requisite being immediate sale. The present owners can stay on at their convenience, but I want title. *Fast.*"

"I don't get it."

"If I own apartments in that building I can blackball anybody she tries to unload hers onto. She's stuck with three-thousand-a-month maintenance."

"Max . . ." Stella's voice failed her and her eyes darted from side to side like a pair of trapped birds. "You can't—"

"I can't *what?* What the hell's the matter with you? I *can't?*"

"The apartment . . . it's the *building* . . . you know . . ." she stumbled frantically. He stared at her with visibly escalating ire, then, grasping her meaning, remembered how the building's ethnic purity had always tickled Bones. No Jews.

He laughed. Stella breathed.

"Tell you what you do, Stella. You call Mr. Prentice Tilford Farquhar the Third at Morgan Price. Tell him you hate like hell to take him away from his backgammon game, but he'll have to get his ass over to my lawyers to sign papers. He's buying a little real estate."

Max showed his teeth. "Let's see Elder and Green try to shoulder out Prentice Tilford Farquhar the Third . . ." Max was now in full swing, becoming playful. "And tell Farquhar he can have one of the apartments for his own use. He can keep those two little spades of his in it. Let's see how Elder and Green handle that set-up."

Stella listened in dumb awe.

"And I'll tell you something else. Those Italian paintings of Bones'. . . she'll try to dump them at auction, and the whole lot won't bring what one Post-Impressionist would. You know how many times I begged her to go Post-Impressionist?" He shook his head sadly.

"She got that Italian junk to bug me. You know that? That's all it was. Something to bug me. So she wound up screwing herself. Just another half-smart broad. What a waste."

He straightened up, his color high, his eyes, though still red-rimmed, now clear of tears, impenitent and shiny as oil slicks.

"Get moving. Close down all store and restaurant accounts. Cut off the garage. And call in that office decorator. Tell her to get to work fixing up the office for Warner." A smile. "Personally, I see Warner in beige and brown."

"And sweetheart . . ." Max stood up, Stella followed suit, and he walked around the desk to give her arm a friendly pat. "Sweetheart, when I come in tomorrow, I'm going to get off on the thirty-fifth floor. I'm going to walk down the hall, and when I do, I don't want to see that cunt's name on the door."

He headed for the bathroom, then stopped short, turned back, and chuckled.

"Like they say, kiddo. What's a day without fluctuations?"

Max turned on the cold-water tap full force and put his head under it. If he had been able, he would have opened up his skull and let the hard spray wash her out. Her and all the rest of them. There was something wrong with them. All of them. All his girls were . . . bent . . . damaged . . . worn out . . .

Max carefully dried his face and head. He wanted a new girl. He *needed* a new girl. He was overdue, he told himself, toweling his hair. He wanted a new girl now. Tonight.

Max seldom used seasoned pros. He did not like set-ups with fixed fees. His entrepreneurial nature needed to feel each time that he might make a monumental contribution to the girl's life and future.

Tonight, though, he knew he was going to have to settle for whatever was available. His thoughts turned, as they had several times lately, to Cathy Kronig, and although he was tempted, he reluctantly dismissed the notion because during this mess with Bones, he could not afford to incur Stella's further displeasure.

What he wanted for tonight was something new and fast, and for that there were always guys like Norman who buddied around with fashion photographers and could come up with a . . . Brucie!

In four long strides Max was at the phone, dialing. While he waited for an answer, he recited, with rising spirits: " 'Snow or mud, shit or blood, Ginsburg rides tonight!'. . . Hello? . . . Hello, honey. This is Max Herschel. Put Norman on."

Brucie had sounded only mildly pleased to hear from Max again, and had refused to come out, but if he wanted to, she had told him, he could bring some groceries over to her place.

"Sure, sweetheart. I'll cater us from La Grenouille."

"From what?"

"La Grenouille. Very good French cooking."

A pause. "Couldn't you bring something kind of spicier? Chili? Or Szechuan?" She giggled. "Spice makes you sexy."

"What'll it be? Chili or Szechuan?"

"Bring Szechuan. We all like Szechuan."

Now it was Max who hesitated. "You *all* like Szechuan? How many of you is that?"

"Three."

Another pause, then, "Great."

Ginsburg galloped on.

Max arrived at the door of Brucie's West Side walkup burdened with forty dollars' worth of damply cartoned Szechuan and three bottles of wine. He had to press her buzzer with his elbow.

A voice squeaked through the grill. "Yeah?"

"It's me. Max."

Suspiciously: "Who?"

"Max. Max Herschel."

Silence. After a long moment he buzzed again and, finally, the querulous voice came through once more. "Who *is* it?"

"Brucie, will you for chrissake push the button? It's *Max*. I've got the *Szechuan*."

After a brief pause, the voice said, "Oh. Yeah. Max."

And the buzzer controlling the front door sounded. Max made a desperate leap. He had no confidence in getting a second buzz from upstairs.

He bounded up two flights and knocked, as best he could, on 3G. A while later, the door opened somewhat less than the six inches the chain allowed.

"Hi, honey. Here I am," Max offered brightly to the dark crack between the door and the wall.

A portion of Brucie's little imp face appeared in the shadow; one eye stared at him.

"Oh. Yeah. Excuse the security—" The chain fell and the door opened slightly. "—but we get all these rapes."

Max and the Szechuan squeezed through.

But once inside, Max recoiled. He felt as if he had been plunged into a tub of blood. The walls, floor, ceiling, were all painted a throbbing burgundy, and there was just enough light for Max to perceive, across the room, the hairy and savage face of a massive black man. Christ, he thought, no wonder she gets all these rapes. The demonic-looking black was sitting on a profusion of floor pillows while a young black girl teased and shaped his Afro. The girl's own coiffure was the general size and shape of a Busby Berkeley beach ball.

Brucie waved a vaguely introductory hand at the couple. "Billy Joe and Tanya. Tanya's from Barbados."

"Everybody hungry?" Max offered. Tanya responded not at all, but Billy Joe nodded and smiled shyly. Max turned to Brucie, gestured the cartons. "Where can I put this stuff?"

Brucie led Max to the kitchen, pointed out the pertinent cupboards, and suggested that he serve the food to suit himself.

"You can clear that off if you want to," she indicated a cluttered desk in the main room which, together with the kitchen, seemed to make up the entire apartment. "I've got to finish my exercises . . ." She stuck her pert face close to his. "You wouldn't want my couze to clutch up, would you? I mean, you got here sooner than I expected and I was in the middle of my exercises. Okay?"

She left Max in the kitchen with his forty dollars' worth of damp Szechuan.

He stood very still, working out options. What were the odds against any girl recommended by Norman setting him up for robbery and/or murder? Negligible. Still, this Brucie was the one who had made a pass at his picture. What else? Nothing. He did not remember much of what had happened at the house. Considering the amount and quality of the hash they'd smoked, it was amazing he remembered anything at all. Brucie had been a little acrobatic, he dimly recalled. But that was it. She hadn't demanded anything or stolen anything.

What the fuck were those two Zulus doing in there? Did they *live* here? Did they *all* live in that one goddam room? Was he supposed to make it with Brucie while the Zulus set their hair? Or were they expecting to be part of the act?

And what the hell was that about Brucie's couze clutching up? Max took a couple of cautious steps on tiptoe to the kitchen door and peeked into the other room. Still deeply involved with their hairdos, the black couple paid no more attention to Brucie, who was now lying on the floor, than they had to Max. Brucie lay on her back, her knees bent but spread out from her body at an alarmingly wide angle, her hands behind her head. In the dim, reddish light, her piquant little face was expectant, eyes closed and eyebrows raised, nostrils dilated, lips half-parted, to reveal small but aggressive teeth. Little rabbitty teeth.

Max cleared his throat and stepped back into the room. No head turned. After waiting a few seconds, he did the only thing he could think of. He started clearing off the desk. Then he returned to the kitchen. While the food heated on the stove, Max located plates and forks and brought them out to the desk.

"Where are the napkins, Brucie?"

Brucie, speaking from the floor, addressed the ceiling. "I think there's some paper towels."

Max went back to the kitchen. He unearthed, from under the sink, a roll of paper towels printed in blue fleurs de lys. He repressed a shudder as he tore off four double squares of toweling and neatly folded them into napkin shape. Then he went back into the other room and conscientiously set the "table" with an attention to symmetry more normally expressed by brides and caterers.

From time to time he would cast a furtive look at the trio on the other side of the room. Brucie lay unmoving in her obscene but apparently gratifying position. The couple had exchanged roles, and Billy Joe, now kneeling, tended Tanya's hair. Max figured the black man must be about six foot five. Even on his knees, Billy Joe towered over Tanya, who was now engrossed in an Archie comic book. As he moved back and forth from desk to kitchen, Max could hear them talking to each other. Billy Joe's voice was pleasantly modulated, his speech rather upper-class, clipped, and pedantic.

". . . waste your time reading *rubbish!*"

Tanya's response was cool. "*You* say it rubbish, don' make it rubbish."

"I have nothing whatever against your reading comic books, Tanya. But there are comic books and comic books. That one is rubbish."

"*You* say it rubbish, don' make it rubbish."

"Listen, Tanya, have you ever seen a Spiderman Comic?"

"Huh. Spidahmon. *Sheet.*"

"Well, you couldn't be more wrong. Spiderman is the apotheosis of pop."

"Of *sheet.*"

Aggrieved: "Now just tell me why you say that, Tanya."

She turned her head around and looked up at him disdainfully, her beautiful eyes moving whitely in her broad, black face.

"Spidahmon," she stated flatly. "He full of it. He *say* he got de powah. But *he ain't got de powah.*"

She smiled cynically as she turned back to her study of the high-school adventures of Archie and Betty and Veronica.

When at last the Szechuan and the wine got them all together, it was revealed to Max that Billy Joe was the son of a professor at Ohio State. Brucie's father was head of the department, and Brucie and Billy Joe old friends who were once again neighbors. Billy Joe taught American History at Horace Mann, but he was restless and was beginning to feel he was in the wrong profession. He was taking night courses in business administration and economics at the New School and he tried to sound out Max about his chances in Wall Street.

"I know that I'd have to change my image, Mr. Herschel."

"Max."

Shyly, seductively, he flashed his ivories, and Max realized with a start that Billy Joe was gay. He shot a curious glance at Tanya, whose unshakable hauteur gave away nothing.

Max's risibilities were suddenly tickled by the idea of sicking Billy Joe onto Mr. Prentice Tilford Farquhar III and all the fellows down at good old Morgan Price.

"Sure, Billy Joe. I'll give you the name of a great guy."

Max dictated Prentice Tilford Farquhar's name and the Morgan Price number to Billy Joe.

Max would have liked to determine the beautiful Tanya's sexual proclivities, but there was no time. Immediately after they finished eating, Billy Joe rose to his full black-velvet glory and told Max he was delighted to have met him. He thanked Max for the phone number, then pulled Tanya to her feet. Brucie waved good-bye without rising from her nest of cushions. Max felt constrained to play host. He got up and accompanied Billy Joe and Tanya to the door.

"Good night, Billy Joe. Good night, Tanya."

Tanya, for the first time, smiled. It was a smile that took in Max and the supine Brucie in the background. It was a sly and wicked smile.

Billy Joe held on to Max's hand. "Mr. Herschel . . ."

"Max."

"Well, sir . . ." Billy Joe lowered his voice to a whisper. "Brucie's a friend of my family, you see . . . She never goes back to Ohio."

Max empathetically lowered his own voice. "How's that?"

"She's out of her tree. You understand?" Billy Joe shook his head sadly. "Or you wouldn't be here, sir." He looked Max straight in the eye. "I just wanted you to know she's from a good family."

Max spoke firmly and finally. "Thank you, Billy Joe. And good night."

When Tanya's full, ripe mouth opened and expelled a peal of rich, rolling laughter, Billy Joe grabbed her upper arm and pulled her into the hall. As he was closing the door behind them, Max overheard Tanya's taunt.

"He don' got to *say* he got de powah. He *got* de powah!"

Moving slowly back toward Brucie, Max looked down at her androgynous little face. Her eyes glittered up at him, as innocently corrupt as a magpie's. He hesitated, wondered what the hell he was doing in this horrible apartment with this nutty kid and all those dirty dishes. "Lie down," she ordered.

Max lay gingerly back in his own nest of pillows.

"Billy Joe's gay," Brucie announced. "Tanya's a hooker. She's my best friend. Billy Joe just met her a few nights ago. He's trying to see if he can make it with a girl."

Brucie's eyes sloed at him while Max digested this, then she took one of his hands and examined it.

"You have beautiful hands . . . nails. Do you get a manicure every week?"

Max nodded.

"Do you want to snort?"

"You mean cocaine?"

"Do you?" she demanded.

"I don't need it. You don't either, sweetheart. That's hard stuff."

She stared at him. With the heavy curve of her overbite thrusting the upper lip provocatively forward, he thought that she looked like a baby rabbit. The baby rabbit spoke. "Do you want to put your hand in my cunt?"

Max flushed scarlet.

Brucie's mouth curled in derision. "Want to reconsider the coke?"

He would cheerfully have belted her. "*Listen*, Brucie. Did you stick a white string on my picture?"

"Uh-huh," Brucie nodded. "The coke is good stuff. Seventy-five dollars a gram." Max shook his head.

"No thanks."

He wished he were out of this crummy place. What if he just got to his feet and . . . again he thought about the dishes.

"Hadn't we ought to clean up the kitchen?"

Brucie knelt and began unbuttoning her jeans, sliding them slowly down her hips until they bunched around her knees. Then she plopped over on her back with her legs in the air, pulling the jeans completely off and flipping them away. Without changing positions, she cast a sidelong glance at Max.

"There are no involuntary muscles. Not really. Every muscle in your body can be trained to respond to a conscious command. Even places you don't think of as having muscle. Look . . ."

She grabbed Max by the arm and pulled him over her. "Look at my left earlobe. *Look*."

Max looked at her left earlobe. It twitched.

"If I can do that with my earlobe, what do you think I can do with my . . ."

Max didn't want to hear it and cut her short. "Where did you go to college?"

"I didn't. I quit school when I was seventeen. And I wish I'd quit sooner." She smiled and, taking Max's hand, placed it firmly between her legs.

It was like putting his hand on a very lively, bristly animal. The crisp, mysteriously animate pelt pushed through and around the ineffectual strip of nylon. Black tendrils escaped to coil and spring around its borders. What possible purpose was that little triangle of panty supposed to serve? It was like putting a hairnet on the head of Medusa. Max felt an instant, not irrational, concern for his hand, but when he made a tentative move to withdraw it, Brucie closed her thighs. Thighs like . . . Jesus!

"Hey . . . Brucie, be nice . . . come on . . ." he laughed uneasily. He really couldn't get his hand free. Somehow, Brucie managed to divest herself of the wisp of underwear while keeping Max's hand hostage. He wanted it back. He wanted to go home. He didn't even give a damn about the dishes. After all, *he'd* fixed the dinner.

"I'm going to show you, Max . . ." She slipped her own two hands between her legs and grabbed Max's fingers, then slowly she opened her thighs. "I'm going to show you what exercise can do . . ." Her voice was throaty, *threatening*. "I can take your whole hand inside me and I can *hold* it and . . ."

Max panicked. He tried to clench his hand into a fist, but she had a finger lock on him and bent his index finger back until he cried out. Embarrassed, he attempted to turn the yelp into a laugh.

"Hey, Brucie, don't—listen, kid, listen—I'm not—I'm not *ready*. Listen. I *would* like the coke."

She raised her head and looked him in the eye. "What's the matter with you?"

"Nothing. Just let go my hand for a minute, honey. *Please?* I think I hurt my finger . . ."

She smiled icily. "Then *fuck* me. If that's all you want."

Christ! Put his *cock* in that!?

"Don't you want to?" she teased. "Huh? Huh?"

"Yeah, that's what I had in mind," he insisted gamely. "But how about the dope?"

She lifted her short upper lip in a sneer. "You don't want the coke, you old fart. You're just waiting for me to let go so you can make a run for it."

It was true. "Why the hell would I want to run out?" he demanded indignantly.

"Because you're afraid of my cunt."

True. Max's head spun with unspeakable images of the serrated mouths of conch shells, of meat-eating orchids, of unknowable holes and the horrors of black entrapment that awaited unwary sexual speleologists. He forced himself to speak calmly, even kindly.

"You're a darling girl, Brucie. Adorable. And terribly sexy . . ." If she didn't let go of his hand he was going to use his other one to knock the shit out of her. ". . . and I've thought about you a thousand times since I saw you. Darling . . ." He knew he ought to show his sincerity by putting just *one* finger in that—he couldn't even *name* it, much less penetrate it—*Christ!* His whole *hand?* ". . . Darling, you're the kind of kid an old joker like me dreams about, you know that, sweetheart? You make me want to do things for you, take care of you . . ."

Her eyes sparked.

"Then *take* care of me. *Now*." She pulled him on top of her with a strength that surprised him not at all, and in one motion, released his hand and locked his body between thighs tight enough to cut his breath short. At least his hands were free and he could, he rejoiced, choke the crazy bitch until he made her let him go. But suddenly, he felt his sex stir.

Even as he began, almost without volition, to make love to the mad child, he was disgusted. It was ugly, *ugly,* his heart cried. The violent red room, the kitchen piled with soggy cartons and dirty pots, Brucie's nasty obsession, worse, possibly, than his own? At least, he thought sadly, he would try to get her teeth fixed, correct the overbite. Maybe if she were *prettier* . . . oh shit, orthodonture *again?* What was he *doing* here! Damn Bones. Goddam her. He felt his eyes go hot with tears, and he was seized with a vengeful rage so powerful that even Brucie's appetite was very nearly appeased.

Chapter 16

Bones tried everything.

On the thirty-sixth floor, she swept into Max's office, which was, as Stella had called after her, empty. Stella had shaken her head helplessly. Max was "away."

The next morning at seven a.m., Bones confronted Teddy at the front door of the Beekman Place house, and he confirmed his employer's absence.

"Then what is Miss Liberti doing here?" And Bones, pushing past Teddy, headed for the elevator. Teddy hurried after her and made the mistake of laying a restraining hand on her shoulder. Bones swung around and aimed straight for Teddy's nose. She was already in the elevator headed for the fifth floor as Teddy, using a handkerchief to staunch the flow of blood, bravely pressed the intercom button in warning.

Bones got out on the fifth floor, stalked past Stella and Ruth without a glance, and walked through to Max's bedroom. It was empty. Empty and made up. She checked the bathroom. Ah. Empty, but *not* made up. She pulled open closet doors, flung back curtains, even looked under the bed, then she went back to Stella.

"I know Teddy called up and Max is hiding. Get the prick out. I'm not leaving until I see him."

"He took the stairs, Bones. He's gone." Stella shook her head sadly. "He's not going to see you. You'd better make up your mind to that."

Bones sought the older woman's eyes. "He's stolen everything, Stella. *You* know what he's done."

"Honey, will you take a word of advice?"

Bones was silent.

"Give it a little time. Let it all settle down. Give him a chance to reconsider."

"He's stolen my gallery and my company, Stella. He had my *name* scraped off the glass. At both places."

Stella nodded. "I know. I know. But give it time."

Bones straightened up. "When I find him, Stella, I'm going to kill him."

"Sure, honey. But first you've got to find him."

The two women looked at each other for a protracted second, then Bones turned and left.

Next, she tried Bernie, Baby, Dolores, Pat Langdon, Jill, Betsy Pennypacker, Annamarie Venturi, and Annamarie's orthodontist. She paid an unexpected call on Bart at La Guardia. She checked Connie's current clinic. She did a systematic rundown on hotels in London, Paris, Zurich and Geneva, Rome, the Palace in Monte Carlo, the Ritz in Madrid. She drove to Bedford and interrogated the Swedes.

When she had done everything she could think to do, when she had called every place she could think to call, she sat silently in the library of her apartment for over an hour, staring at a spot on the wall between the new Severini and a Marinetti she had always particularly disliked.

Steven decided it was time to step in. "Bones?"

Bones screamed. She threw back her head and screamed and

screamed. After a while, Steven began to understand that she could not stop, and he took her in his arms, holding the small body which shook uncontrollably as the shrieks ripped through it.

She screamed for almost half an hour, then lay in Steven's arms, sobbing hoarsely and trembling like a malaria victim. Eventually, he undressed her and put her to bed, then got in next to her, and held her until she fell asleep.

She slept for several hours. Steven dozed intermittently, but never let go of her. She started trembling again, and he spoke softly to her, but when she did not answer, he realized she was trembling in her sleep. She had a fever.

Steven found Dr. Rossman's name in Bones' address book. Dr. Rossman came, but Bones, shaking under the piled-up covers, would neither look at him nor speak. Dr. Rossman told Steven that she either had the flu or was in some kind of fit. If it was flu, Steven was to keep her quiet, give her aspirin, see that she had plenty of liquid, and if her fever went above a hundred and one, fill the prescription for the antibiotic and follow the directions. But if, in Steven's judgment, it was a fit and continued for more than another twenty-four hours, Steven was to call him back and he'd come over and shoot her full of some damn tranquilizer or other. In the meantime, whatever she had, it probably wouldn't hurt if she swallowed a Valium every six hours. Steven nodded. Rossman gave him a searching look.

"When did you two get married?"

"Four days ago."

"Does Max know about it yet?"

Steven nodded.

Rossman nodded. "Give her the Valium."

She shivered silently for three days.

In the course of those three days, Steven did a lot of thinking. He would make Bones sell the apartment and spend a year in Vermont. A *minimum* of a year. He would knock her up. He would finish the new book. He would break his ass to make it commercial. He would take care of her.

And if that rotten sonofabitch Herschel so much as dropped her a postcard from Disneyland, Steven would take after him with a baseball bat. And *he* would find the cocksucker.

Steven nursed Bones with patience and tenderness. Between

holding a cool cloth to her head and rubbing her back and trying to get her to swallow some soup and checking her temperature, he would sit near her bed with his notebook and write. She seemed to like this. Although she never spoke or smiled, she would watch him fixedly and seemed not to shake quite so badly when he sat beside her. At night, he would climb into the bed and go to sleep holding her limp, damp little body in his arms.

Steven was deep in sleep when she woke him up about five o'clock on the third morning.

"Steven . . ."

Instantly alert, he opened his eyes. "What is it? Are you all right?"

"I had a terrible dream."

She told him that she dreamed she was in the Middle East. In the desert. And alone. Surrounded by Arabs, armed with rifles, firing at her. She was lying behind a sand dune, trying to keep out of line of the bullets. The Arabs kept shooting at her from all sides. Bones had a gun too and was trying to shoot back. But it wasn't any good, because while her rifle had a perfectly normal stock which fitted reassuringly into her shoulder, the gun's barrel was made of lavender-colored calico, printed in little sprigs of flowers. In order for the bullet to go through the calico barrel, she had to hold it up. Hold up the limp and useless passage through which the bullet phlumphed and lost force and stuck.

"I couldn't get it up . . . *out*. The barrel. It was just . . . flimsy cotton . . ." She began to cry.

Steven did not laugh, he did not even let her see him smile. He shushed and patted her and told her she was all right. After a while, she wiped her eyes on his arm and said she thought she was hungry.

"Of course you're hungry. You haven't eaten anything in almost three days. What do you want?"

"I want pizza. I'd give anything in the world for a pizza."

"Pizza?" Steven jumped out of bed. "Stay still. It's going to take a little time." He flipped on the bedside radio for her, and dialed in an FM station. "Have some Sibelius while you wait."

Then he walked barefoot to the kitchen, puzzling over how to manufacture a pizza.

Bones struggled out of bed to the bathroom. She looked at herself in the mirror with disgust. She had let Max do this to her. Grimly she acknowledged that she had invited Max's attack. Now all she wanted was to forget him.

She washed her face and brushed her teeth and combed her hair. She even put on a touch of blusher. Shakily, she managed to change her nightgown, then went to the kitchen, looking for Steven.

He was not there. He was in the laundry room, ironing out a loaf of unsliced bread. Bent over the ironing board, he was intently flattening the loaf, attempting to shape it into a circle.

She had been watching him for quite a while before he realized she was there, and when he finally looked up, he was surprised but pleased to see her combed and showing a trace of color.

"Hey!"

His eyes followed hers to the bread on the ironing board.

"What do you think?" he asked. "I think it's going to work. I mean I can get it *flat*, it's getting it *round* that's tough. But I can trim it with a knife and then when I put on the cheese and tomatoes and stuff . . ."

"I love you, Steven."

Two days later they drove to Vermont.

Bones had left the apartment in the hands of Elder and Green with an asking price of three hundred and fifty thousand. Mr. Cutler, who would be handling the transaction, told her that he had not the slightest doubt that she would get three hundred. Did she by any chance want to sell any of the furnishings? Bones unhesitatingly pointed out every piece which had been a choice of Max's, and told Mr. Cutler to see what he could do.

In ten days Max had negotiated a quiet take-over. Without involving the corporate identity of Herschel Industries, he had put Steven's publishers, Darby Press, in his pocket.

He had also run a check on Steven's financial background and moved in on the small Vermont bank which carried the mortgage on the farm. Max could not get at the annual pittance which came to Steven out of Boston from a grandmother's trust, but it was, in any case, beneath contempt. It would not keep Bones in bath oil. Max had also looked into the financial standing of the Routledge aunts and uncles, all solid but no longer living off the income of income. Not one was in a position to resist certain pressures, if Max saw fit to exert them.

Max sat in his office, reviewing the newlyweds' situation. No income other than the trust—every time Max thought of Steven's trust, he smiled—and whatever Steven could earn from writing. *Windrift* you could forget. And Max controlled the new book, since he now controlled Darby Press. So that was it for Routledge.

Bernie would see to it that Bones' equity in Burton Productions would be a long time coming. She could and probably would sell furnishings and paintings from the apartment. Fucking peanuts. She would soon learn she could not unload the apartment itself, and the maintenance would be a fatal drain on her own finances. She had exactly six thousand and eighty-one dollars in a checking account and ninety thousand in bearer bonds, which Max held in one of his own safety deposits in Zurich.

She had the jewelry. Like a villain in a Victorian melodrama, Max literally ground his teeth at the thought of it. He batted around the notion of having it stolen. It would be a cinch and he could raise suspicions with the insurance people. He would see she shouldn't collect. His frustration raged a brief moment, then dissolved as his intuition took over.

He did not have to snag back the jewelry because Bones would not sell it. Max *knew* that. He did not know how he knew, but he wasted neither time nor energy probing his instincts. He followed blindly where they led. Bones would not sell the jewelry. She would hang on to it somehow. Max *knew*.

So. There they were. The proud and penniless young author, and that rotten, spoiled, ungrateful cunt. Max leaned back and gleefully reviewed in his mind all the things he knew Bones hated.

Thinking about money.

Handling money.

Taking advice.

Taking orders.

Filling out forms.

Waiting in lines.

United States Post Offices.

Mailmen.
Bank clerks.
Store clerks.
Store elevators.
Being kept waiting.
Being crowded or touched.

All the people in the world who were, by Bones' definition: Non-productive. Lazy. Curious about Bones. Incurious about Bones. Unfriendly to Bones. Too friendly to Bones. Ignorant. Naive. Smartass. Anyone who wore or admired the color purple. Or was incompetent. Or too competent. Overweight. Overdressed. Loud. Boozers. Dopers. People who took too much time at coffee breaks. Who used the telephone as a social instrument. People who played radios outside the confines of their bedrooms. Women who played cards. Women who played tennis or skied. Women who had never worked. Women between the ages of eighteen and forty-five who *did* work in any field approximating that of Bones.

Bones hated dirty taxis. Max recalled the time she had spotted a used condom on a taxi seat and had picked it up before she realized what it was. She had screamed and flung it at the driver.

Bones loved movies, but not in movie houses. She hated movie audiences. Audiences eating candy and popcorn and getting up and down and carrying umbrellas and packages and wearing coats which they took off and put on. Audiences that laughed at the wrong places and did not laugh at the right places.

Bones' hairdresser always came to her apartment or office. Because Bones hated beauty salons. She was repelled by all those women under dryers who looked as if they were being scientifically *hatched*.

Max, the hotel man, had taught Bones to demand a change of linens every day, twice a day if she napped. And he had taught her to demand hospital corners and artfully arranged pillows.

Bones hated unmade or improperly made beds.
Bones hated making beds.
Ordering groceries.
Putting away groceries.
Planning menus.

Executing menus.

She disliked stockings or pantyhose which had not been carefully pressed. Or finding her flesh-colored lingerie mixed up with her pale pink lingerie. She did not like her nightgowns folded in drawers.

She did not like any prescription drug left in its pharmacy container.

Now Max came to the list that gave him a full, satisfied feeling, like a meal rich in carbohydrates.

Bones did not like: gardens, gardening.

Worms, caterpillars.

Ants, grasshoppers, crickets, bugs, bees, wasps, flies.

But she hated insecticides.

She loathed: toads, lizards, snakes, owls, bats, racoons, mice, rats.

But she hated traps.

Mud.

Chickens, cows. Goats, sheep.

Weeds.

Moss.

Swamps.

Wind.

The dark.

Cold.

This last list was especially pleasing to Max in its relation to Vermont. Let's just see how long the bitch sticks Vermont. And she can't *afford* New York.

All he had to do was wait. And make a bargain with God she shouldn't get what she wanted. She shouldn't get pregnant. He tendered an offer. God wouldn't let Bones get pregnant and Max would spend a week on a boat with Connie. Wasn't that fair? Max felt confident. It was more than fair. He buzzed for Stella.

"Call Dolores. Tell her to charter us a very nice boat and spring Connie . . . we'll cruise up and down the Coast a few days . . . give Connie a treat . . ." he hesitated. Maybe he ought to lock God in a little tighter? "Ask Jill and Pat and the kids too. Get a *big* boat. And a snorkeling teacher and a water-ski teacher for the kids." He had a thought, brightened. "Get us a marine-life guy, too, who knows all about dolphins and stuff like that. Maybe even a doctor, you know? But young."

He was doing his part. God would do his.

Contented with the day's progress, he remembered that he had not been on a tennis court for days. He decided to rout Jock out of the club and play a couple of sets. Tennis reminded him of Cathy Kronig, and that he had done absolutely nothing to rescue her from that prick, Jock. Now he devoted two minutes to the problem while he washed up. Simple.

El Jocko was looking pale, run-down. What El Jocko needed was sun. He would take Jock Kelly to California and dump him on Gloria Sutro in Palm Springs. Gloria was forty-two. She was very rich. She played tennis three hours a day, seven days a week. Gloria would eat old Jocko up. Yeah. Max would put Kelly on loan-out. Indefinitely.

When he left the office, Max made a point of locating Cathy and maneuvering her out of Stella's sight.

"Cathy, I've been meaning to speak to you ever since the party. You made a big hit with my wife."

Cathy's eyes widened with uncertainty.

"She thought you were the prettiest girl there. And the nicest."

Cathy couldn't believe it. To the best of her memory, Mrs. Herschel had never once glanced in her direction after they had been introduced. Was Mr. Herschel teasing her? She blushed, and stammered her gratitude.

"Jock tells me you're a great little tennis player, that right?"

"Oh. No, sir. I *used* to play . . . in school . . ."

"You've been out a couple of times with Jock though, haven't you?"

Cathy knew her face was turning scarlet. "Y—yes, sir . . . I mean . . ."

Max grinned. "*I* mean. On the *tennis* court, Cathy."

Cathy ducked her head. "Yes, sir. He's been trying to improve my overhead. I have a very weak overhead."

"Well, that can be corrected. Ever play on a grass court, Cathy?"

"Oh, no, sir. No, I haven't. I always wanted . . . it seemed so *awful* when they tore up the grass at Forest Hills . . ."

"I've got a grass court in Bedford. Another month, six weeks, as soon as the turf is in shape, you'll have to come out and try it. Would you like that, Cathy?"

The words tumbled out of her. "Did you ever know what the Duke of Norfolk said to Queen Elizabeth—the *first* Queen Elizabeth?—once when she accused him of trying to marry Mary Queen of Scots and make himself a king? He said, 'Nay, madame. I need it not. For when I am in my own tennis court at Norwich, I think myself as great as any king.'"

Max was delighted to hear it.

"Where did you learn about that, darling?"

"Darling"! He had called her "darling"!

"I read it," she gulped, "in a biography of Queen Elizabeth."

"You like to read?"

"Yes sir. I do. I read a lot."

"What do you like to read especially?"

She found her voice again and spoke up boldly. "I read everything I can, Mr. Herschel. But I especially like biographies."

"Yeah? Tell me one you've read recently you liked."

Her mind went blank, and she blinked foolishly at him. He prompted her in kindly tones.

"Modern biographies or historical? About men or women?"

"*Women,*" she declared forcefully, then blushed extravagantly once more.

"You a libber, sweetheart?" he asked seriously.

"Oh *no!* I mean . . . not exactly . . . I mean . . . sure, in a way. But what I meant I guess . . ." She smiled shyly. ". . . *You* know. I like to identify with them. With women who were important enough to get biographies written about them"

Max studied the girl with growing interest. Not such a dumb bunny, maybe? Just young and scared? He patted her arm and left the office.

Cathy was paralyzed, quite literally unable to navigate from the spot on which she stood. Since the ousting of Miss Burton, Cathy was frightened almost witless by Max Herschel. By now she had ferreted out virtually every detail of what Mr. Herschel had done to Miss Burton. He had had Miss Burton's name *scratched off of everything*. Like Nefertiti's. Just a few weeks ago

Miss Burton was rich and powerful; today she was a nonperson. And Miss Burton had been with Mr. Herschel fourteen years. She *knew* him. Knew him well. She had been smart. She had been rich. She had been beautiful and clever. He had adored her. She had been *in there*. But Mr. Herschel had mashed her like a doodle bug. If he could do that to Miss Burton, what could he do to *Cathy?* If he got the chance?

But it was interesting, she thought, as she eventually redis-covered the reflexes to carry her back to her desk. It was certainly interesting. It was particularly interesting that since Mr. Herschel had stomped out Miss Burton, Cathy's panties stayed very, very dry. Nor did she have to hunch her shoulders to hide her traitor-ous nipples. Just now Mr. Herschel had patted her arm and called her darling and invited her to play tennis on his grass, and Cathy had blushed and stuttered, but she had not creamed. On reflection, Cathy's fear of Mr. Herschel might be a good thing. A *practical* thing. Every time she saw him, she would remind herself of poor Miss Burton. That ought to do it.

When Cathy arrived home after work, she found a hand-delivered envelope waiting for her. Inside were some cards. They were membership tickets to The Society Library and the Metro-politan Museum Picture Series, a charge plate for Doubleday's "Special Customers," and a year's membership to the Grand Central Tennis Academy, with one hundred hours prepaid. There was also a card from Max. It read, "I love your thin wrists and your thin ankles and your fat mind." It was signed "Max."

"*Max?*"

Cathy nearly fainted.

Chapter 17

Bones stepped outside and shivered violently, but forced her shrinking flesh to meet the vicious wind head-on. The mailbox was a quarter of a mile from the house, but desperation for news from Mr. Cutler about the apartment outweighed her hatred of the walk.

In Central Park it was real spring. It was probably summer in Beverly Hills. Although the snow and ice had disappeared from the undersides of stones, and the farmer had begun to cut dreadful wounds in the earth, in Vermont it was still wet and gray. Bones hated seeing Mr. Schmirski's tractor slash the fields. She hated the tractor. She also hated Mr. Schmirski. And she hated Mrs. Schmirski, who had permanently lost her tongue when Bones had chummily informed her that Roberta Jeunesse, the pale and put-upon young heroine of *Generations*, was a tough dyke who wore jockey shorts under her junior-miss dresses. Bones had honestly thought Mrs. Schmirski would be interested.

It was not the only honest mistake Bones had made in Vermont. She was in awe of Steven's house, deeply admiring its mysterious integrity, and she had wanted to offer it something of herself, to have it accept and welcome her. She wanted to belong to it and have it, even marginally, belong to her.

So she had brought to Vermont monogrammed sheets, a fur spread for the bed, stacks of heavy linen bath towels, and a pair of eighteenth-century faux tortoise hanging shelves. The shelves were for displaying the eccentrically exquisite French bottles which Bones had collected over the years and which she cherished.

The shelves and the bottles looked ridiculous in the spartan little bathroom with its linoleum floor and ancient, footed tub. The tub's porcelain finish was old and pitted and almost impossible to keep clean-looking, although Bones scrubbed it furiously. There was no proper closet space for the linens. There was no proper closet space for anything. Only dinky, dark little interstices between rooms. No built-in shelves, nor drawers, nor cupboards.

The house was always cold. If Bones moved more than ten feet away from an open fire, she began to shiver. Once she got cold, the only way she could get warm again was by soaking in a hot tub; but here, one could never draw more than eight inches of hot water before the hot water gave out. If the tub had been longer, the meagre eight inches might, if one were thin enough, have covered the whole body. But the tub was so short that even Bones had to sit erect in it. The hot water barely rose to her hips, and the rest of her body blossomed with goose bumps.

No, Steven declared firmly, there was not enough electricity for a larger water heater. Why did she want to spend so much time in the tub anyway? Kissing her bare bottom, Steven told her she was quite clean enough for him. She flopped angrily over on her back and yanked her nightgown down around her knees.

"I take baths because I get *cold*."

"Your blood's thin. You need exercise. You should eat more." He repositioned the level of her nightgown.

For some crabbed, masochistic, Dedham-Massachusetts reason, Steven had not built a fireplace in his bedroom. Bones went to bed cold every night, and she got up cold every morning. So the next time she traveled to New York, ostensibly to hear Mr. Cutler's explanation of why the board had found all five prospects unacceptable, she went to Jackson's and surveyed antique Austrian stoves. One, of plain white tile with only a touch of brass, was particularly beautiful and the perfect size. Big enough to throw out serious heat, small enough not to dominate the narrow confines of the Vermont bedroom. She would buy the tile stove, and it would serve them elegantly until they could afford to restructure the upper story of the house.

The stove cost thirty-seven hundred dollars, and to pay for it Bones sold the birthday Severini to a dealer she knew. He did not give her a good price. In fact, she was fortunate to get *any* offer, he told her. Take the money and run, he advised.

"Italian Futurists are the I-don't-give-a-shit of your dreams, darling," he said.

Bones accepted the offer because she passionately wanted the tile stove.

Installed in the Vermont bedroom, the stove looked as ridiculous as the tortoise shelves and Gallé glass did in the bath. Although it gave off a bit of heat, aesthetically it was a dud. Which, for reasons Bones could not grasp, endeared it to Steven.

"It's wrong, wrong," she mourned. "I thought it would be absolutely perfect."

"Absolutely perfect's a bore, Bones," he asserted.

It was a new idea to her.

Still, she was not comforted. Steven's house, Bones brooded on the death-march to the mailbox, rejected her. It would not compromise. She felt that it looked down its disdainful New England nose at her, and at all her outlander's clumsy attempts to soften it up. The tile stove was like a sacher torte at a Girl Scout cookie sale. It shamed her.

She had only been in Vermont seven weeks, but it seemed a very long time. Not a bad time, but a long one. Time made up of monotonously dark days, beginning with eerie ashen dawns and, even in midday, never lightening enough for her to read without electricity.

Bones never went outside except for the death-march. Not unless Steven quit work and drove her over the fields, beating at her boot heels with a stick and making her laugh breathlessly as she stumbled up hills. She did not *want* to laugh, but his ebullience, his disregard of the elements, excited and stimulated her. She loved him and bore with any action that focused his attention on her.

For his part, Steven accepted, without censure, Bones' resentment of domestic chores. He was sublimely indifferent to comfort or discomfort, heat or cold, good food or bad. That the meals provided by Bones were generally elaborate and bad had no significance to him.

Bones believed there was a local cabal against her; she could not, at any price, get a woman to come in for regular domestic work. Mrs. Schmirski had cautiously offered, before her shocked retreat after the Roberta Jeunesse slander, to do occasional cooking for the Routledges in her own kitchen, a baked hen, a macaroni casserole, whatever she was doing for her own family. But Mrs. Schmirski had quickly withdrawn and now there was not a woman or teenage girl available. These people were poor. They needed the goddam money, yet no one would come to the house to *work*. It was a conspiracy and nothing Steven could say would convince her otherwise. So she cleaned and cooked and ironed and loathed every minute of it.

Still, she cleaned compulsively, particularly when she discovered that Steven was not just untidy; he was actually dirty. He kicked dirty shirts and underwear under the bed. He never cleaned out the washbasin or tub. He left *hairs*, which reduced her to a state of quivering disgust.

Steven was utterly stunned by what he considered Bones' middle-class fetish for sanitation. It had certainly never occurred to him that she would elect to occupy her own time with such tedious pursuits. Why did she let a little mess bother her so? Surely brushing up once every week or so would do it? What was the matter with the two of them *together* cleaning the house and doing the laundry, say once a week? Forget ironing. Take the stuff to the laundromat in Stowe, bring it home and wear it. Who *saw* them, he asked. Who was policing the tucks and cuffs? The Schmirskis?

"*Me. I'm* policing the tucks," she wept. "I can't wear wrinkled *underwear*, much less shirts and slacks!"

Steven forebore to ask what she had grown up wearing in Gum Springs, North Carolina. Instead, he had kissed her and said, okay, they'd try to find somebody, somewhere, who would iron. If they couldn't well, hell, any man who had ironed a pizza could certainly iron ladies' drawers.

Bones then wept bitterly and delivered, between sobs of frustration, a lecture on the value of Steven's time and the expenditure of energy that should go, not into idiot ironing, but into creating.

"How about you? How about *your* creating?"

"I'm going to start any day now," she assured him.

She guessed she was probably pregnant already, but she wouldn't be absolutely certain for about eight or nine days. That must be the reason she was weeping so much. And using the point of a pin to clean maniacally around the edges of the stove burners.

Every week Bones tallyed up exactly how many times in the preceding seven days she and Steven had made love. How satisfactory the numbers were. How dizzying! And so, when she wasn't crying or brooding, she was smugly smiling. She lay awake nights in her sleeping husband's arms, fantasizing that Max had planted infrared cameras in the house, that all the hours and hours of her and Steven's passion were being photographed. Indelibly recorded for Max to *see*. Let him. Let him see, finally, what love was. What it was supposed to be. What it was for her. *Now.*

The one condition of her marriage she could not accept was that she forfeit her power over Max.

As for other lost powers, Bones tried not to watch *Generations* every day or Nick's show at night. When she did, she always ended up by turning off the set, sick with rage at the slightest change. To see Warner's name where her own should be, to know that the shows she had created and conducted were functioning perfectly without her, to visualize Warner sitting in her office, giving the orders and taking the credit, cramped her stomach and constricted her throat, and once had actually caused her to lose her dinner.

Plus the bitter fact that when she had left Burton Productions, not one person out of the staff of twenty-eight had so much as telephoned her, let alone written a note. Not even Mark. Mark, who, she knew in the dark of her marrow, was now batting his eyelashes at Warner Magill.

Bones at last explicitly understood what she had only intuited before: when a gambler leaves the table, he moves alone and unregarded into the void while the other players shift reflexively into his space. In that one moment the other players meet shoulder to shoulder, and the drop-out, winner or loser, is worse than forgotten; he ceased to exist. The only life is the life of the game and, however unwillingly, Bones had left the table.

Her battle now was to make herself believe that in Vermont she had simply moved on to a different game. But the problem with this new one was that its rules eluded her. She could not figure out the stakes. The only chips she had ever used were power and money, and she had believed them to be acceptable at any table, in any room. What were the stakes on this farm? With Steven? She didn't know and, worse, couldn't even guess.

She brooded about all this as she laboriously washed the supper dishes, first soaking them in soapy suds, then with a sponge on the end of a stick, mopping them individually plate by plate, glass by glass, then rinsing them with water from the tap, then putting them to drain before pouring boiling water from the stove over them.

As soon as the apartment was sold, fuck the ecology. If Steven would not deal with the utility company, she herself would install a generator, then a dishwasher, a disposal, and, as a symbol of self-assertion, a goddam *trash-masher*. There would be a proper laundry room, and she would convert the barn into living quarters and make them irresistible. If she couldn't find any local labor, she would go to New York and get herself a couple of nice faggots who wanted to ruralize. She wasn't about to handle diapers and bottles with no generator or faggots. *Forget it.*

She poured boiling water from the kettle over the dishes, got herself a fresh cup of coffee, and wandered aimlessly out of the kitchen. Steven always worked for two hours following the evening meal, after which he carried the wet garbage out to his unspeakable pit, then put away the dishes.

Those two hours when Steven worked were Bones' bleakest

time of day. She missed the jangly, nervous fatigue of her city evenings, the luxury of soaking in deep, hot, oiled, and perfumed water, reviewing the day's trials and errors and plotting tomorrow's moves. She would check the strings, figuratively flexing her fingers. Lift the index finger, Warner danced; lower it, Warner sagged. Twist her wrist to the left, Max would sweat. What the hell, give him a break, twist it to the *right*. Let the bastard do a jig, let him lift up his head and shout!

That's how it had been. Wasn't that how it had been? Of course it was. She had loved it, and she was confident that someday she would have it all again, except better. She would have the sweet reality of Steven instead of the bitter illusion of Max. She would have it *all*. And there wouldn't be a woman alive anywhere in the Western world who wouldn't kill to change places with her.

Bones settled down in the living room with her coffee and a novel she judged good enough for a TV special, if not for theatrical release. She was considering taking an option on it, because as soon as she sold the apartment . . .

Steven had stopped typing. Bones, unaware that she was holding her breath, waited for the sound to begin again. When it did, she exhaled and stared unseeing at the page of the book she was holding.

This time, with her to muscle it through, Steven's novel would be a best-seller. There would be no nonsense about publishing it with genteel hopes, gentlemanly expectations. She did not know what kind of second-echelon quasi-amateurs he had been dealing with at Darby, but all that was *finished*. This time the book would be sold straight to Hollywood from the *typed page*. It would be *sold*, not *peddled*. The movie deal would include money for promoting the book. The paperback deal would be sensational and have beautiful escalator clauses and a huge movie bonus.

Smiling dreamily, she did not hear Steven come into the room. He saw the rapt expression on her face and thought she looked like a Reinhardt madonna.

Some nights, Bones would make sure Steven was engrossed at the typewriter, then move quietly upstairs and get the crocodile box from under the bed. She would open it and put on bracelets, pins, especially the hook earrings. If the typing stopped, she would hastily remove the jewelry, throw it into the case, and thrust the case back under the bed.

After that very first night, Steven had never again commented on the jewelry's symbolism. He had appeared not to notice when, preparing for her three New York trips, she had got out a few pieces and had worn or carried them with her.

The only jewelry Bones wore in Vermont was two rings. Aunt Cora's diamond had been mounted in a simple Tiffany setting, and Bones wore it alongside the narrow wedding band which she had not removed since Steven had put it on her finger. She often studied the rings, twisting and admiring them, taking childish pleasure in them. Her obsession invariably made Steven smile and kiss her hand, then her mouth.

On the seventeenth of May, they drove down to New York together. In a sudden manic burst of energy, Steven had completed a draft of the book and was eager to deliver it personally to Jerry at Darby Press.

Mrs. Patterson had agreed to return for a few days so that Bones could enjoy a few days of luxury. She would make them comfortable while Steven waited for a report from Jerry. Bones had been eager to spend a few consecutive days in the city. She was anxious to see Mr. Cutler and find out why none of the people solvent enough to make offers on the apartment were acceptable to the cooperative's board of governors. She also intended to see about putting the Futurists up at Parke-Bernet. She never wanted to look at one of the ugly things again. They were painfully hateful to her now. She had left them on the walls solely for the benefit of prospective buyers.

She had also made an appointment with Dr. Benechek. She was not pregnant and she wanted to know why she was not.

First, the apartment. When she went over Mr. Cutler's head and talked with Mrs. Elder, she got the distinct impression that the woman was not being candid about the nature of the board's rejections.

Mrs. Elder knew that Mrs. Routledge was prepared to sell, at a bargain price, one of the best apartments of its size that Elder and Green handled, and they handled top apartments. Even in a depressed market, a buyer's market, the Burton apartment was a steal.

Mrs. Elder estimated that Miss Burton had spent easily two hundred thousand on top of the original purchase price, and was not even trying to get her money out, going instead for a quick sale. There had been plenty of takers. Two of them impeccable. Three acceptable by any reasonable accounting. But the board had turned them all down. Unequivocably.

Mrs. Elder was a woman who had done well in New York real estate by virtue of her compulsive curiosity, and she had nosed around the Burton situation. What she knew but didn't tell Boncs was that the man with the blackball was Mr. Prentice Tilford Farquhar III, who did not live in either of the two apartments he had so recently purchased. These apartments were still occupied, on a rental basis, by the people who had sold to Mr. Farquhar. In the most unprecedented manner, Mr. Farquhar had become a member of the governing board of a cooperative in which he did not reside. It was all quite smelly, but it was no skin off Elder and Green. Mrs. Elder felt no obligation to give the details. Very queer, but hardly a story to pass on to Miss Burton . . . Mrs. Routledge.

Mrs. Routledge did not press Mrs. Elder, except to ask for a listing of the board members which, of course, Mrs. Elder was obliged to give her. Mrs. Routledge looked over the list, and noticed that since she had last seen it, a new name had been added: Mr. Prentice Tilford Farquhar. The name seemed familiar.

"Then I remembered. Farquhar is a guy on Wall Street who owes Max. Max has queered the building," she said flatly. "He's not going to let me sell." Pacing rapidly from one end of the rug to the other, she would turn and retrace her steps, over and over, as she told Steven what she knew for sure and what she surmised.

"He's sticking me with this fucking apartment and three thousand a month maintenance, and if I know him, it won't be long before his stooge starts complaining about the service and submiting motions that the building is understaffed and falling into disrepair and that the maintenance should be upped. Only a reasonable amount, of course. 'Say five hundred?' "

Steven did not believe her "You're paranoid. Why should Max go to that kind of trouble? It's absurd. What can it gain him?"

"He's angry."

"But that's not something an angry man would do, Bones. It's something a *nut* would do. Max Herschel's pretty frisky, but I don't think he's ready for the net.

Bones slapped the palms of her hands together with a popping noise. She couldn't explain. Steven's definition of "nut" was not hers. Or Max's. She understood exactly what Max was doing.

Steven reminded her of their first talk about Max. "You once told me that if people didn't go along with Max, he just cut them loose."

"That's what he's doing. He's cutting me loose. On an ice-floe."

"If it's what you say it is—and I don't believe for a minute that it is—then it's vindictive to the point of lunacy. It's petty and mean and vicious. It's *pointless*."

The next day Bones saw Benechek, who explained that a woman coming off the pill could sometimes be sterile for months.

"Then why did I get pregnant before? When I skipped the pill a week or even a couple of days?"

He shrugged. "It happens. Often because the woman wants it to happen. Consciously or unconsciously."

"I want it to happen now. Very, very consciously."

"Then it probably will." He also remarked that she seemed tense and nervous and that anxiety didn't make it any easier to get pregnant.

"You think I wasn't tense and nervous with Max?"

Benechek smiled. "Well, that was the normal way to be with Max." Patting Bones' cheek, he told her to go home and relax and be happy. It was nice being married, wasn't it?

Bones hated Dr. Benechek. She hated gynecologists generally, but she hated Benechek in particular because he was a memento of strange losses.

Getting dressed, angrily wiping the lubricant from between her legs, Bones experienced the same turbulence that followed every visit to a gynecologist. The table enraged her, the instruments enraged her, her helpless need to invite the invasion enraged her. The doctor's patronizing good humor enraged her.

She strode out of Benechek's office and began walking. She walked almost twenty blocks before her composure was somewhat restored. She had walked, without thinking, toward Rockefeller Center, and when she realized where she was, she went into the coffee shop.

She sat down at the counter in the cleanest area she could find, ordered, and waited, forcing her mind away from the scene in Benechek's office. If she reacted like this to a routine check-up— and she *always* reacted like this—how could she contemplate having a baby and enduring everything that implied?

Because after she had endured it, she would have the baby. She would have something totally her own, something *she* had made.

Her coffee came and the waitress carelessly slopped some of it into the saucer, making no move to clean it up, to bring a new saucer, even to tender regrets. Bones' anger flared again, and it was all she could do not to sweep the cup and saucer off the counter. What she did do was slap a dollar bill into the small brown puddle between the cup and the saucer. Then she stood up and took her twenty-five-cent check to the cashier.

As she was putting a quarter on the rubber mat, Bones' peripheral vision caught a deep aquamarine stare from the nearest booth. It had to be Mark. She turned her head, but before she could catch his eyes with hers, he dropped the richly fringed curtain of his lids. And Bones knew that Warner must be sitting across from him, hidden from Bones by the booth. Mark kept his lids lowered against her. She felt herself flush, and made a frantic, cowardly dash out of the shop, leaving her coin purse on the counter.

Shame and grief for herself, homicidal hatred for the two men, propelled Bones blindly into the street and almost under the wheels of a taxi. Shaken, she stumbled back onto the curb and hurried down the block, away from the network building. At a safe remove from Mark and Warner, she spent ten minutes waving impotently at taxis that would not stop.

The one that finally did, afforded her only the briefest sanctuary. The jagged edge of a tear in the plastic seat-cover caught and rent her left stocking. Muttering, "Shit! Shit!" she slid over to the other side of the cab, then became sickeningly aware of the assaultive stink of a cigar. She looked at the driver, a small, fat man with an enormous nose, a piebald stubble on his chin, and two inches of soggy White Owl protruding like a hideous growth from the corner of his mouth.

"Would you mind awfully . . ." Bones asked, loathing him but attempting to keep her tone conciliatory, ". . . would you mind *awfully* not smoking your cigar while . . ."

He twisted his head back and gave her a look of crazed hatred.

"Would I mind '*awfully*'? You get in my taxi and start in obscene language and then you start would I mind '*awfully*'! . . ."

He had jerked forward again and, addressing himself to the accelerator, propelled the polluted vehicle around a double-parked delivery van. He was aiming for a clot of pedestrians at the corner. "Goddam whoor gets in *my* car and starts in shit this, shit that, and then *I* shouldn't smoke a cigar in my own car! 'Awfully'! Yuh don't like the ride yuh can walk, yuh whoor, yuh!"

"Stop this car! Stop this car immediately!" Bones demanded.

He obeyed with more immediacy than she would have wished and she was thrown forward against the back of the driver's seat, then jolted onto her knees. Before she could scramble up from the filthy floor, the dreadful fat maniac was out of the car, wrenching open the back door.

"Out! Get out of my car! In my car I don't take orders from sewer-mouth whoors!"

He was yelling at the top of his considerable lung power. By now, terrified that he would lay violent hands on her, Bones fought her way out of the taxi.

"One dollar-thirty-five you owe me read the meter! Get it up you think I won't call a cop you try to stiff me you whoor! Pay up and shut up . . ."

She struggled with trembling fingers to extract a bill from her purse and at last managed to pull one free. It was a ten. She threw it toward the madman's face, then turned and fled, only dimly conscious of people casually watching the beautiful, well-dressed, deranged young woman tearing up Park Avenue, her stockings ripped, one knee bleeding.

When Bones finally reached the apartment, she took two Valium tablets and soaked groggily in the tub, letting the knee bleed out of sight under a thick fleece of foam. She was still in the tub when Steven returned.

Bones was placidly, dopily pleased to be told that Jerry had finished reading the book and had been delighted with it. And so was another, more senior editor, a Mr. Brandon. Bones listened to Steven's voice, coming to her through the fog she had put between herself and the world. It was Brandon, said Steven, who suggested that a slight renegotiation of the advance might be in order.

"It's fantastic!" Steven exclaimed, helping her from the tub and throwing her a terry robe. "You *know* that means they think they've got a hot one. When they start escalating numbers, you know somebody up there has read it and liked it. Somebody *way* up."

Steven grabbed Bones and whirled her around. She smiled dreamily, limply, letting him handle her. He asked her what she thought about their staying on in New York while he did rewrites. He thought he could work in the apartment now that he had cracked the book. He knew that Bones could use a respite from Vermont weather and dishwashing. How about it? How about a month in town?

Bones murmured it would be lovely. She could sell some things to see them through.

Steven said not to worry. Their days of penury were almost over. Mr. Brandon had told Steven that if he did his rewrite with all due speed, Darby Press could get the book out in December. "That means Christmas sales!" Steven crowed. And furthermore, he told Bones, Darby planned a first printing of twenty to twenty-five thousand copies. They felt certain of a movie sale, "and when the temperature's right, the paperback rights will be auctioned." Although the senior editor had spoken cautiously, not making any guarantees, Steven knew from the publisher's voluntary upping of his advance, that Darby expected every subsidiary benefit from *The Nephew*.

For the next three days, Steven was in and out of the apartment, reporting exultantly on editorial meetings, contractual points, and lunches filled with publishing gossip.

During it all, Bones was cocooned in the comforting Valium fuzz. Steven, who had known instantly that she was taking something, asked what it was.

"Valium. Don't worry. I'm not taking many. I just feel too lousy to cope for a couple of days." She had told him about Mark and Warner. "I'll be all right in another day or two. Then I'll go out and get a job."

"We'll talk about the job when you're sober." When Steven checked the Valium bottle he saw she was taking just enough to keep her pleasantly high. Enough to keep her from thinking about Burton Productions and the sonsofbitches who had usurped it.

Bones passed her days listening to music and dozing and trying on clothes from the great silk bags of spring and summer dresses in the storage closets. Even potted, she was obviously enjoying the luxuries of the apartment, her escape from the death-march. Steven felt sure she would soon simmer down and sober up. Then she could make the systematic inventory of the apartment furnishings and sell what she no longer wanted.

He was not worried. He was going to bring out a bloody bestseller and cream off some Hollywood money and take care of his wife. On his way to a lunch date, he fantasized briefly going up to her old offices and beating the shit out of Warner Magill and Mark Whatsis. Stand-ins. Beat up the stand-ins on the thirty-fifth floor. Steven smiled, knowing that he was not going to storm the thirty-fifth floor, let alone the thirty-sixth floor. He was not going to mop up on Max.

Steven was not bitter about Max. As long as Max let Bones alone. Steven's concern was with Bones. She had been a gangster's moll so long, Steven worried, that she thought in terms of betrayals, vengeance, scores, power-plays, muscle, leverage, hits. She had tried to score off Max; Max had revenged himself and made her pay, but beyond a reasonable price. Now she owed Max one. If Steven were on her team, he would want, would need to move in and even the score.

She never said it, never suggested it, maybe never consciously thought it, but Steven knew that on some level she was raging against him for not taking on Max Herschel. However, he would proceed with Bones according to the principle that she was not too old to learn.

By Thursday, Bones had gone off Valium. She knew that unless she got some immediate cash, the apartment and their New York expenses would wipe them out. She told Steven she was going to Parke-Bernet. She went, instead, to see Sam Teich at CBS. When she left Teich's office, she left with a job. Teich had hired her to produce a ninety-minute network special.

Sam Teich knew, as everyone in television knew, what Max Herschel had done to Bones, and had hesitated to hire her. Nobody was eager to schwitz out an attack by Max Herschel and because, as good as Bones was, she had never worked for anybody but herself. She had never been a hired hand. She was arrogant and egocentric. He had heard plenty of stories. Then, too, it was embarrassing to offer her only the money he *could* offer her. He was aware to the dollar what she had made every week off Burton Productions, but when he had muttered the sum CBS was willing to pay for the one-shot, she had spoken right up.

"That's fine, Sam. For *this* one. If it's a success, you'll give me more next time."

He had an instinct, then, to tell her to kiss off, but she defused him with a soft "and thanks, I really am grateful for the job, Sam. I'll remember you gave it to me."

Steven accepted her news with equanimity. The CBS job would only last for three months, and it would take about that long to complete his rewrites. He felt confident of being able to work in the apartment and was experiencing a powerful conviction that he had written not only a good book, but a commercial one. He felt free and loose and *warranted*.

Over dinner they decided that Steven would return to Vermont for however long it took him to close up the house, while Bones stayed in town to deal with the apartment problems, to sort things for sale, and get underway at CBS.

"Steven, bring back my jewel case. I want to put everything in a safe-deposit box."

"Everything? Why everything?"

"Because I don't want Max hiring some bentnose to steal it, that's why."

"You're raving!"

"You think so?" She said no more, but that night in bed, after twice reading through the fifteen page outline from which her show was to be developed, she thoughtfully rolled up the pages and tapped at her knees with them.

Steven lay beside her, happily at work, making vigorous, ruthless marks on the pages of his manuscript. Bones' knee-tapping distracted him.

"What's the matter, darling? Isn't it good enough? Don't you think you can make anything out of it?"

"Sure. Why not?" She regarded him curiously. "It is absolutely beyond your wildest imaginings that Max would steal my jewelry, isn't it?"

"Yes, it is," he smiled.

"Because he's such an honorable guy, right?"

"No, he's not an honorable guy. But on the other hand, you're pretty romantic." Steven smiled.

"You don't hate him, do you?"

"Why should I hate him? He's no rose. But he's not what you think he is either. He's just a man who's spent his life hustling. That's all he knows. Hustling and hustlers."

"He's a monster."

"No, he's not. He's only kind of a shit. He's not a monster. He's . . ." Steven sighed, ". . . he's just a man on a wheel."

A man on a wheel. Bones considered the image. Then restructured it. Max *was* the wheel. The *fixed* wheel. She reached out and touched Steven's arm.

"You know what?"

"What?"

"When I first met you I thought *you* were a shit. A first-class shit. Did you know that?"

"Sure, I knew that."

"But you're the nicest man I've ever known."

He gave her a comical, woeful look. "A highly qualified endorsement."

"And I mean more than just nice. I mean *good*. Do you know how much nicer, how much better you are than other people?"

"Yes," he nodded solemnly. "Yes, I do."

She smiled. "Have you always known you were nicer?"

"Yes, I have."

"When you first realized how much nicer you were than other people, how did it make you feel?"

He reflected a moment before answering.

"Sad. It made me sad. It seemed sad that other people weren't as nice as me."

"Does it make you feel sad that *I'm* not nice?"

"No. Not particularly."

She wriggled her feet and watched the covers move. "That's not the right answer. You should have said, 'But you *are* nice, honey.'"

Steven obligingly mimicked her intonation. "But you *are* nice, honey."

She persisted. " 'In fact, you're very nice.'"

"In fact, you're *very* nice."

" 'Actually,' " she continued the drill, " 'actually, you're the nicest person I know.'"

"Actually, you're the nicest person I know."

" 'In fact, Bones, you're even nicer than *me*.' "

"Now you've gone too far."

She laughed and hit him with the rolled-up pages. He grabbed her. She went limp and pushed her face up against his arm. "Steven," she whispered, "I *want* to be nice. Teach me how."

Chapter 18

Cathy Kronig had used up sixteen hours of court time before Max approached her again. When he had brusquely waved away her attempts to thank him for everything, Cathy had correctly guessed that he did not want Stella's curiosity aroused.

Time passed. Max came and went between New York and California, New York and Europe, New York and Canada. Whenever he appeared at the office, he greeted all the girls with cheerful impartiality. Cathy was no longer singled out. It was as if she had never been to his house, seen his bedroom, never gone to his party and danced with him in clothes he had paid for, never received a card indicating his approval of her wrists and her ankles and her mind. A card signed "Max."

Cathy was bewildered. She was also embarrassed. She shared her two-room flat with a girl named Sally who came from Richmond, Virginia, and worked as a receptionist at Young & Rubicam and put on irritating airs about being from the Tidewater region of the Old Dominion.

Cathy had regrettably confided in Sally about Max and Max's "letch" for her. As time passed and there were no new developments, Sally, tired of waiting for the next chapter, had begun to tease.

"Looks like your old fat cat's off chasin' pussy up some other alley."

Sally was always going on about her gentle origins, but in Cathy's private opinion, Sally was a little common and could be, at times, downright crude.

When Cathy, on an impulse one Saturday morning, had her hair streaked blond, Sally's response was devastating.

"Kind of albino skunk!"

Cathy had cried for the rest of the weekend. And when she dragged in to the office on Monday, Stella's shocked eyes told her that Sally had probably understated the effect. The other office girls tried to be nice, but Cathy's attempt to be what gentlemen were said to prefer was a demoralizing failure. And it had cost her fifty dollars.

The first time Max saw her striped head, he smiled and nodded but withheld comment. His reaction baffled Cathy. Max was, in fact, appalled by the bad job that had been done on the kid's hair, but he was touched that she had made the effort. Max was always touched by women's efforts to be attractive to men. Even a lousy dye job was better than dull brown. What counted was that she had *tried*.

When Max made his move, Cathy was caught totally off guard. She was walking to the bus stop one Friday night after work when Mr. Herschel's limousine drew up by the curb and the back door opened.

"Get in, sweetheart. I'll drive you home," the voice said.

Scarcely daring to look at him, Cathy had settled herself primly on the forward edge of the seat and addressed Ben.

"I live at Twenty-two East Thirty-Sixth, please."

The chauffeur headed downtown.

"What have you read lately?" Max asked. "That you liked?"

"I just finished the Glenway Wescott collection of Colette

novels and now I'm reading *Out of Africa,* by Isak Dinesen, who was really a Danish countess, you know."

"Colette. She was a dyke or something, wasn't she? Or what?"

"Well . . . she was kind of bisexual at one time in her life. But she was mostly a woman. A really wonderful woman. She was the only French woman ever accorded a state funeral. She was a legend in her time." Cathy, feeling as if she were giving an oral book report, blushed but went on. "So was Isak Dinesen. A legend. Her home in Denmark is a museum now."

"So's my house in Bedford," Max sighed. "But closed to the public. How's your tennis?"

"I've been playing four hours a week."

"Who with? Now that Kelly's not around?"

For the first time since entering the car, Cathy turned to Max and smiled.

"Well, it's not hard, you know, to find somebody to play with when you belong to a club and you've got court time already paid for."

"Then you're in shape, right? We'll play tomorrow at Bedford. See how you like grass. Ben will pick you up at nine. Of course, if the weather turns bad, we'll have to use the indoor court. We'll eat lunch at the house and get back to town by the middle of the afternoon. Okay?"

Cathy, her heart pounding, sternly reminded herself of the late Miss Burton. "Mr. Herschel . . . would it be all right . . . would you mind if I brought my roommate along? She'd *love* to come." Cathy rushed on before Max could say no. "Her name is Sally Ferguson. She's nineteen and from Virginia. She's blond and a lot prettier than me."

Max patted Cathy's hand.

"Bring anybody you like. Just as long as they're nineteen and prettier than you."

The rest of the ride to 36th Street passed without comment. Max, preoccupied in his own corner, whistled tunelessly through his teeth. Cathy, sitting well away from him, tensed to repel the pounce which never came. At Number 22, the car stopped and Max, jumping out first, handed Cathy from the car as if she were a legend in her time, a Danish countess or a famous French bisexual.

Once inside her building, Cathy charged up the stairs to puzzle out what she would wear for tennis and lunch at a Westchester, New York, estate. And there was the problem of Sally. Cathy knew that wild horses couldn't keep Sally from coming. *If* Cathy were, in fact, to invite her.

It was a delicate problem which required cautious deliberation. To go alone with Mr. Herschel to his country house with *nobody in it* and suffer the consequences, or to put up a fight and make him mad or maybe just make a fool of herself. *Or,* to take along Sally, who *was* prettier than Cathy except for heavy ankles. Sally had never failed to exhibit avid curiosity about Max Herschel, no matter how much she wrinkled her nose and made gagging bleghkk sounds at the very idea of a dirty old man even touching *her.*

Inside the car headed back uptown, Max continued his tuneless whistle. The whistle did not translate well. Inside Max's head was not only rhythm and melody but the copyrighted lyrics. "When they beginnnnnn the Beguinnnnn . . . It brings back the sound of music so ten-*dor* . . . It brings back those niiiights of tropical splen-*dor* . . . It brings back my yooooouth, evergreen . . ."

After the most judicious weighing of pros and cons, Cathy had invited Sally to chaperone the Bedford expedition.

Max had them flown out in the helicopter, and the damn-the-expense display set Sally off into convulsions of writhing, lip-wetting, and Tidewater-type teasing. It was enough to turn your stomach, Cathy thought, disgusted and embarrassed. She tried to offset Sally's performance by sitting up very straight, keeping her knees pressed together, answering only when spoken to, and always addressing Max as "sir." On the tennis court, as soon as she warmed up and got the feel of the grass, she played to win.

Watching from the sidelines, Sally scornfully reflected that Cathy was even dumber about men than she had supposed.

When Cathy won a point, she didn't even have the sense to claim it was just luck or accuse Mr. Herschel of *letting* her win . . . and Sally knew that when Cathy came off the court, after playing hard like that, she was going to be all covered with *sweat*. And her hair would be draggly and her face would be red and there would probably even be *lines* on her dumb forehead. While Sally would just be there waiting, sweet and clean and cool and telling Mr. Herschel what a *fantastic* game he played.

On the court, Max was shocked to realize that if he wanted to beat the little girl, he was going to have to put some effort into it. When Cathy broke his service, he stopped kidding around and began to watch her.

Cathy's game was erratic, but her ground strokes were hard and businesslike. She was not afraid of the net and she was *fast*. Those sexy little ankles curved upward into long, strong, smoothly muscled legs, which knew how to move.

Time after time, Cathy made gets on balls Max had felt sure were out of her range. She never stopped to consider whether a shot was possible, she *went* for it. But the main thing was, she was smart. It had taken her only two quick games to size him up and decide to hit to mid-court whenever he would have to use a backhand unexpectedly, and use it on the come. Then, when she had worked him center-court, she lured him to net, the position he loved. Then she lobbed. And she lobbed. And she lobbed. It takes more energy to move backward than to move forward, and Cathy's game was a classical demonstration in cold reality. In any match between a nineteen-year-old girl and a sixty-two-year-old man, energy and endurance, if the man can't cap it, will carry the day.

She was a smart little Charlie, and she did not make the slightest effort to patronize him. She wanted to win. Nor did she seem to worry about giving him a heart attack if that's what it took. The little mouse had a tough streak he hadn't figured on.

Max would have laughed if he could have spared the wind. They played three sets. Max won, but only just: 5–7, 6–4, 6–4. When they came off the court, Max was spavined and spent. Cathy was breathing easily, sweating freely. She had enjoyed the game and was in high spirits.

"Hey! I *love* the grass. It's so *fast*. I love it *fast* . . ." She looked at the exhausted man. "Did I run you too hard, sir?"

Max grunted. "Not hard enough to win, sweetheart." He gasped mightily for air. "But hard enough to maybe kill me."

Sally bubbled over. "But you play a *fantastic* game, Mr. Herschel! It was like watching one of those players on the television!"

Max eyed Sally's beautiful, bouncing, braless boobs. Bouncing for him, he knew. What a cunt. He gave her bottom a fatherly little pat. Maybe someday when he had a minute, he'd pop her one. In the meantime, he'd give her name and number to Norman. He owed Norman.

He turned back to Cathy. "Sweetheart," he beamed, "you and I are going to play a lot of tennis."

That evening, Max took Cathy to dinner at Twenty-One. They sat at Max's usual table, Number 9 downstairs. Cathy wore the chiffon dress that Max had given her for Baby's party, and not until they were inside the restaurant did she realize what a gaffe the long gown was. All the other women were dressed with a kind of elegant indifference that shocked Cathy. She knew next to nothing about clothes. Bloomingdale's was where you went if you had real money to throw around. She couldn't believe that Bendel's actually existed outside of her Cinderella spree.

When Max and Cathy were seated, she said softly, "I'm sorry I'm so overdressed, Mr. Herschel. I didn't know it would be this casual."

"You look beautiful, sweetheart. You're the best-looking woman in the place. What will you have to drink?"

Cathy hesitated. She was dying to ask for champagne, but since she was already overdressed she did not want to overorder.

"What do you think I should have, Mr. Herschel?"

"How about some champagne?" Max had never known a midwestern teenager who did not crave champagne.

"Oh, that would be lovely," she beamed.

Max ordered champagne for Cathy and white wine for himself.

When the menus came, Cathy examined hers uneasily. With

the exception of steaks and chops, she did not know what any-thing was, as she candidly confessed to Max. Not only was she unable to read any French—in high school she had elected to take Spanish—she wouldn't know what the dishes were anyway.

"Why don't you order for me, Mr. Herschel?"

She sipped the champagne.

"Okay. What do you like? Chicken? Fish? Veal?"

"Is there something with mushrooms? I love mushrooms."

Max nodded. "Sure. There's a nice veal dish with mushrooms."

Max ordered. The filet de veau en cocotte bordelaise for the lady and a steak bleu for himself. They would begin with céleri-rave . . . he stopped, questioned Cathy. "Or would you like caviar?"

Cathy held herself firmly in check. "Oh, no. I'd much rather have what *you* say. Much rather."

She was so adorable that Max felt the warm, sweet possibility of tears. Gratified at this evidence of his sensitivity, Max patted Cathy's hand. She was *adorable*.

Over the céleri-rave he got her to talk about herself. She told him she was the middle of three girls. The eldest was married and living in St. Louis. The youngest was only sixteen and still at home. She could be a real good tennis player if she worked at it, but she was lazy. Cathy also worried about the younger sister's grades, and no one in the family liked the boy she ran around with. He was just plain common.

Cathy's father had worked for many years as a chief expeditor for Railway Express, but the REA office in Flatcar had closed down when Cathy was fourteen, and for a while, they had had a pretty rough time financially. But her daddy had a good job again now, although it was one which meant driving the forty miles both ways to the outskirts of Kansas City where there was a big new UniRoyal plant. What was upsetting everybody was that Daddy was talking about moving to Kansas City. Everybody had been *born* in Flatcar. Cathy's mother's *mother* had been born in Flatcar.

Max listened to all of this with an expression of rapt concern. "Wasn't there enough money to send you to college?"

"It wasn't just the money, Mr. Herschel. I could have gone to a junior college in Kansas City and commuted with Daddy. But . . . you . . . see . . ." she blushed and halted.

"But what?"

"Well, you see . . . people all said . . . they thought I was the prettiest girl in Flatcar. *Everybody* thought I ought to be a model." She smiled sheepishly. "For *Vogue* magazine," she mocked herself. "Even my mother thought so. And she's *very* level-headed. So . . ." Cathy shrugged, "I just *did* it. I took all the money I had saved and what Daddy could give me, and I came to New York." She made a wry face. "I knew in two weeks I'd never make it on *Vogue*. But I felt ashamed to go back to Flatcar just like . . . *bingo* . . . So I got a job." She smiled. "With *you*."

"And that's the life story, is it?"

"It's not very interesting, I guess."

"Tell me about your New York life, sweetheart." You dated Jock a few times. What else? You and Sally in tight together?" Max's tone was faintly accusatory. "Same boy friends? That kind of thing?" Max prompted.

Cathy shook her head vehemently. "No, sir. I mean Sally *has* a lot of boy friends, of course. And I . . . oh, good heavens, Mr. Herschel . . ." She laughed. She was on her third glass of champagne and suddenly the idea of Mr. Herschel's stern catechism struck her funny. "I've had three boys friends since I've been in New York, but they were all very callow kids." She peered at him over the edge of her glass. "I'm not a child. I'm not a virgin."

Max smiled. "I never thought you were."

Cathy did not know whether or not to be offended. She finished her third glass of champagne and decided she had better eat a roll. She felt light-headed.

"Do you ever wish you could go back to school?"

"Yes, sir, I do. It makes me ashamed to be so ignorant. And anyway," she declared, "I want to *be* somebody."

"What kind of somebody?"

"Well," she hesitated, then plunged. "What I'd like to be, I think, is a banker."

Max found himself without a suitable reply.

The entrees arrived and Cathy tucked right in. She liked the veal, which had a thick, heavy brown sauce. She beamed at Max.

"Ummm! About being a banker . . . you see, for one thing, I'm very good at math."

"Good at math."

"Yes, sir. Did Miss Liberti tell you I've been working an hour, sometimes two hours, every day in accounting? Your accounting department is *very* interesting."

"Even the unindictable parts?"

"Oh, Mr. Herschel . . ." Cathy laid down her knife and fork. Her blush was intense. "I didn't mean interesting in *that* way. My God, Mr. Herschel!"

"Eat your veal, sweetheart."

Max ate, but now Cathy could only pick at her food, worried that she had unintentionally suggested something about the Herschel Industries' accounting department.

"A banker beats me, sweetheart," Max said at last. "That's a new one on me. Aren't you interested in the arts? The theater or painting? Books? I thought you were kind of literary."

"I'm *interested* in the arts, Mr. Herschel, but I'm not any *good* at them. I mean I don't have any talent. I mean not *any*. At *all*."

"But you're very good at math," he teased.

"Yes," she said stubbornly. "Yes, I am."

"But that doesn't mean you have to be a banker, sweetheart. I mean a *banker?*" Max's imagination refused the jump.

"But bankers have a lot of . . ." she could not contain her enthusiasm. "They are kind of in the middle of everything, aren't they? I mean sooner or later practically *everybody* has to go to bankers. I mean, I saw in the books, why even you . . ." she stopped herself, appalled at the things she seemed to be saying. Was she *drunk?*

Max grinned. "What did you have in mind, sweetheart? You sitting behind a desk in a big, wood-paneled office and poor broken-down old Max Herschel comes shuffling in whining about remember when you used to work for him? . . . how he gave you your first break back there in his very interesting accounting departme . . ."

"Oh, Mr. Herschel!" At last he had made her laugh.

"Why don't you break down and call me Max?"

She was slow in answering. "Because . . ." She must say this *just right.* "Because I don't think I *should.* Because like if I play tennis with you and I start in calling you by your first name all the time and get in the habit, then I might slip up and do it in the office and I know Miss Liberti . . ."

"I don't think you'd better go back to the office, Cathy."

His face was grave.

Did he mean she was fired? Oh God. He didn't even look friendly. Not just fired but . . . *finished?* Her head began to spin. She was not thinking clearly. She had not eaten enough bread. She had eaten it too late. She realized with horror that she was probably going to throw up.

Max saw the girl's skin go white. Just when he had got used to the nice pink blush, she had suddenly turned white. Greenish white.

"You all right, darling? You want to go to the ladies'?"

She sat very, very still. All her life, Cathy had enjoyed the rudest of health. She had not thrown up since she was twelve, when she had eaten an entire crock of whipping cream that her mother had intended for a picnic-sized strawberry shortcake. With strict self-discipline, Cathy pushed the memory of the whipped cream from her mind. She felt certain that if she did not move or speak . . . and thought about . . . *daisies* . . . if she thought about daisies, the nastiness would go away.

It did.

"I'm all right, Mr. Herschel."

"You went dead white." He accused her roughly, because she had frightened him. He didn't want to be thrown up on at Twenty-One's downstairs' table Number 9.

"Am I fired?"

He was taken aback. "Fired? Of course you're not fired. What made you think that?"

"You said I couldn't go back to the office."

"No, I said I didn't think you'd *better* go back to the office. Because of Stella, sweetheart. Stella's set in her ways, but I couldn't do without her. If you stay in the office I can't see you. Understand? Stella draws the line."

"Then what am I supposed to do?"

"Go back to school. We're going to make a deal. You and me."

"What kind of a deal, Mr. Herschel?"

"A deal where you get to go to school and I get the pleasure of it."

"What else?"

He smiled. "Everything else."

Cathy was shy; she was even a little timid. She had sweet manners, and she was often shocked. But Cathy's great-grandfather had singlehandedly taken on a band of eleven Kiowa Indians and lived to tell about it. Cathy was brave. She turned and faced Max squarely. She would lay her cards on the table, explain her worries and doubts. She would get his reassurance.

"Mr. Herschel . . ."

"Max. Come on, try it. Just *try* it. *Max.*"

"All right. Max. The thing is . . . about making a deal with you, Mr. Her—Max. The thing is, it's not that I might not *want* to . . . but . . ." Max's face lost its smile. Cathy felt tremors of uneasiness and a stinging suspicion that she might be fouling everything up. *Everything.* She fumed at herself for being inarticulate, for not being able to make him understand, in a way that was not ruinous, that she wasn't *dumb.*

"So if you don't *not* want to . . . what's the problem?" Max prodded.

"The problem is *me.*"

Max's gaze was now coolly measuring. "Don't give me any bullshit about you couldn't go to bed with me, Cathy. Because you already have. In that little head . . ." He reached over and put a finger against her left temple. ". . . in *there* you have. I'm not one of your real callow kids. You think I don't notice what happens to you every time I'm around?"

Her face had turned bright pink again, but her voice was steady. "It hasn't happened lately. When you're around."

"That a fact? No sinky feeling?" he teased. "Nothing happening up there between your . . ."

"No, sir. Nothing."

He had to laugh. Her reply was as succinct and disciplined as a private reporting in the clap shack: "No, sir. No discharge. *No, sir.*"

Max was inexplicably touched. He patted her cheek comfortingly.

"Why not, sweetheart? What turned off the heat?"

Since she had gone this far, she might as well finish it.

"Because of Miss Burton."

The smile drained from Max's face.

"What about Miss Burton?"

Cathy soldiered on.

"About what happened to her. It was scary. It scared me."

"So what did happen to her? She got married. To a handsome, talented young man she's in love with. That's scary?"

With bowed head, Cathy whispered, "You had her name scraped off of everything." Now she was truly terrified of the dark, forbidden closets she was daring to open.

Max sighed. What explanation did he owe this little bint? He didn't owe *anybody* an explanation. He ought to get up and leave her sitting there with that fecockta veal and its disgusting brown sauce. That was supposed to be *mushrooms?*

Two great tears splashed from Cathy's mournful eyes into the brown sauce.

"I'm sorry," she murmured. "I'm so *sorry* . . ."

"What about?" Max demanded angrily. "What the hell do you have to be sorry about?"

"I shouldn't have reminded you . . ."

Max tried to make up his mind. *Kids.* A pain in the ass. Every time out. But on the other hand . . . he heaved a great sigh.

"Wipe your eyes, sweetheart. You'll upset the waiter. What do you want for dessert? Listen, I'll tell you what. I'll get the apple pie and you get the cheesecake and we'll divide it all up between us. How about that? Okay?"

She sniffed. "Okay."

Over dessert, he aired his side of the case. He hadn't walked out on Miss Burton. Miss Burton had walked out on him. With no warning. No warning at all. After fourteen years. It had hurt him very badly. And his first reaction had maybe been a little heavy . . . he'd gone a little too far. Now that some time had passed, now that he thought it over . . . now that Cathy had pointed it out . . . now he could see that he shouldn't have had Miss Burton's name scraped off everything. He had over-reacted. He admitted it. He'd been very childish. But he'd been deeply hurt. Fourteen years was a long time.

"Did you love her very much?"

"You stay with somebody fourteen years, Cathy, you're bound to love them. In one way or another."

"Like you're bound to love Mrs. Herschel, too?"

"That's right. Thirty-three years married. A lifetime, sweetheart."

"I like the cheesecake better than the apple pie."

He smiled. "I like girls who know what they like."

He hand-fed her a bite of cheesecake from his own plate.

"You're adorable, Cathy. You're honest and you're sweet, and you're intelligent. You're a fantastic kid. Plus you're good at math."

He skipped a couple of moves. "So when you get back into school, Cathy, what courses are you going to take? Besides math?"

She sighed, greatly relieved that everything seemed to be settled. Thank *God*. She perked up and answered with enthusiasm.

"Well, economics and psychology and I guess whatever you *have* to take when you're a freshman. But I'm very interested in taking an outside course in corporation and contract law."

Cathy attacked the rest of her dessert with gusto. If Miss Burton had known anything about corporation law, she couldn't possibly have let herself get kicked out of her own company. Not *possibly*.

Max chewed slowly, thoughtfully, covertly eyeing the girl. She was, he thought with considerable amusement and a touch of awe, a fucking little Frankenstein. Corporation law. Where did she think a dumb little kid from Flatcar High was going to get in? Barnard? Followed by Harvard Business School?

"Where would you like to go, sweetheart? Any idea where you might be able to get in?"

"Barnard. I have a four-year straight-A average. And I didn't have to grind to get it either. I had a lot of extra-curricular activities that will count for something. Of course, public high isn't like a good preparatory school. But with my academic and personal record plus I know all admission boards have to go for *some* regional representation, plus I'm a *girl* interested in *business* and they've got to at least take tokens, and I've had a year of actual experience in the field. So to speak."

She gave him the radiantly pearly teeth. Only the faintest flush now tinted her throat and face.

"I don't think I'll have any trouble getting in Barnard."

He signaled for coffee. There was not much more to be said, but Max felt that it was incumbent on him to put the seal on their bargain. He took one of her hands in his, for the first time claiming a physical part of her. Taking her hand was planting the flag. This hand was now Herschel territory. Understood. He looked down at the hand to see what he was getting.

The hands were strong, square, the fingers blunt. The nails were short and clean and neat. There were two hard callouses on the right palm. That firm tennis grip. She was, he thought, a girl with a generally firm grip.

Beneath the table his free hand tried to stake another claim. But it was instantly rebuffed, caught and frustrated by the long drifts of chiffon. Never hesitating, Max sent his other hand into battle.

"Lift your hips," he ordered.

Wide-eyed, she obeyed his command, and as one of his hands ruthlessly ruffled the chiffon up around her waist, the other spread her knees and thrust high between her legs.

He looked quizzically into her eyes, and for his trouble, got precisely what he wanted. Her pupils were dilating and her face, neck, and what he could see of her chest were burning scarlet. Between her legs, he felt the flooding invitation.

Her voice was faint, breathless. But her words were considered.

"And another thing about Barnard, Max. It's in New York. Where *you* are."

Whether that was good or bad, Max thought, remained to be seen.

Chapter 19

Bones got the show in on schedule, almost on budget. It would make the lists of the year's best. It would get an Emmy nomination. But Bones would never work for Sam Teich again.

Teich had hired Bones against weighty advice, and he was wired to her success or to her failure. Nothing but a mutual drive for survival kept the two of them functioning together until the show was finished. Their battles became legend.

"Can't you get it though that chicken head that everything you do, *everything*, is subject to network approval? And network approval means *me!* Have you read the lettering on my goddam door? 'Vice President in Charge of Programming.' The operative words are *In-Charge-Of!* Where the hell do *you* get off guaranteeing Leo Widner—*Leo Widner?!*—twenty thousand dollars! Do you realize that the maniac who represents Widner also represents the stars of three of our biggest-grossing *series?* So there is no bargaining once he's heard a name and number? And *you* named

Leo Widner *and* the number twenty thousand in one girlish breath! Have you *no* sense of responsibility? Of obligation even? You clear budget with *me! Me!* Can you get that through your head? *Me!*"

Bones sat as cool as lemon sherbet, gazing distantly out of Teich's executive window, her gray eyes polluted pools of disdain. She waited for Sam to run down.

Teich yelled and sweated and yelled. He was fifty-seven years old, forty pounds overweight, and unaccustomed to the strain of shouting at female underlings. At last, wheezing noisily, he stopped for breath. Bones let Sam's heavy breathing hang between them for a long moment before she spoke; she spoke quietly, her eyes still turned fastidiously away from Teich's red, wet, bald head.

"Widner is the best actor for the part and twenty thousand is his price. He's *worth* twenty thousand. He's first-rate and his face is fresh. In my judgment twenty thousand is not an unreasonable price to pay for the face alone. For a face that is not associated with Drāno ads or one of your schlock . . ."

"*Your* judgment is irrelevant! What counts around here is *my* judgment!"

"Really?" Bones nipped. "That explains so much."

And then again: "The *budget* is four hundred five but that does not count the network's *airtime.* So the figure you are dealing with, *Miss Burton,* is four hundred five plus the three hundred thousand which the airtime is worth. *So.* When you divide *seven hundred and fifty thousand dollars* by nine little commercial breaks you come up with eighty thousand dollars a minute and there ain't nobody, baby, is gonna pay you eighty thousand bucks for a one-minute commercial! You are now playing with CBS money and CBS *patronage.* CBS is *trusting* you . . . trusting *you* with the equivalent of three hundred thousand extra dollars. And you do not make unilateral decisions with *that* kind of money!"

"*You* don't, Sam. But *I* do."

Teich took another deep breath and let it out, then spoke with lethal deliberation.

"Bones . . . *CBS-is-not-Max-Herschel.* CBS is not in the Sugar Daddy business."

Bones stood up and smoothed her skirt. "Tell CBS to bugger off."

"You'll never work on this network again, you bloody bitch!"

"Sam, I'm going to tell everybody connected with the show . . ." She smiled softly, a little Fragonard on a blossom-garlanded swing. ". . . that to get you to honor the Widner commitment I had to go down on you. Right here in this office. But that it could have been worse because you clocked out at only twenty seconds."

And that was exactly what she told everybody.

The saga of the Teich-Burton wars was not confined to the corridors and watercoolers of one network. Bones knew that she would not get another job soon. Anywhere. If the show won an Emmy, there might possibly be a general epidemic of amnesia about Bones Burton's temperament and refractory fiscal practices. In the meantime, Bones accepted reality. She would not get work, not work she wanted.

She slept badly for the next several nights. During one of them, she lay awake, wondering exactly how much she could get for her jewelry. Enough to finance a new independent company? An office, and a secretary, typing services? Enough money to option properties, hire good writers, court stars, directors? She toyed with ideas of new ways to sell, short cuts through the ruinous costs of pilot shows. Without Max, she was totally at the mercy of network support.

The CBS production had taught her that she did not know how to cut corners. Max had not only neglected to teach her, he had discouraged her from learning. Expensive was the only way of working that she knew. Then why not go, she thought, in for a penny, in for a pound? Why not abandon television and move head-on into feature film production? It could not cost any more in initial outlay, maybe even less. Perhaps she could approach a new medium unhobbled by the habits of the old one.

She decided to have the jewelry reappraised. Just a new appraisal, that's all.

She drifted into an ugly, troubled sleep, and wakened suddenly to see a naked man walking away from her bed in the dark. Terror struck her so swiftly, so brutally that she lay paralyzed.

She did not know who the man was . . . she did not know . . . *what?* . . . where she was? The true source of the horror came over her like a mud-slide . . . she did not know . . . *who* she was.

She could not move her sweat-chilled, weighted body.

Her unblinking eyes focused on the light coming from the bathroom. She heard the toilet flush, then saw a shadow . . . the man's shadow, then his black outline in the door's light . . . the light went out.

As Bones' pupils dilated with unnatural speed, she kept the approaching menace in her sights, trying to ready herself for whatever was to come. The man was less than ten feet from the bed when she was seized by a depthless despair. She realized she would not struggle, that she would let him kill her without protest, that she would die passively, never knowing who his victim was.

"Hey . . . did I wake you? I'm sorry." Steven crawled in beside her and pulled her damp and rigid body close. "Jesus . . . what's the matter? Are you sick?"

She gasped out the lie: "A nightmare . . . I had a nightmare . . . and I didn't know who . . . who you were . . ."

What she could not say was that wide awake she had lost herself.

She lay limp in Steven's embrace, but her nerve-endings could not tolerate the memory of what they had experienced. She turned on Steven and made fierce, aggressive love, denying her partner . . . feverishly denying him . . . any active role.

Steven lay back, bestraddled by his small, frenzied rider, somewhat astonished, but with lazy, sensual pleasure, accepting the novelty.

During the time her show was in production, Bones had been too preoccupied to consult closely with Steven on his new contract, which had been signed in the days of Bones' Valium drunk.

The check for twenty-five thousand, minus the agent's commission, had come through with unusual promptitude and Steven had spent the subsequent forty-eight hours in a state of euphoria.

Bones had been pleased, but much less sanguine than Steven. Twenty-two thousand, five hundred dollars would cover less than two-thirds of the apartment maintenance for a year.

Their money problems could only be solved by a substantial film sale of Steven's book. Bones knew *The Nephew* would make a good movie. It was romantic, funny, sexy, and the characters were attractive and dramatically drawn. More important, the book was a vehicle for a male star.

Two days after her bad night, Bones told Steven they should call a conference.

"Get started now on the movie sale. Let's make some lists and decide exactly where and to whom we should take it."

"*We* should take it?"

"For the movie sale."

"But Darby is handling the movie sale."

Bones was dumbstruck to hear that the twenty-five thousand dollar largesse was the quid pro quo for signing the film sale rights over to the publishers. *The Nephew* would be peddled at Darby's discretion. To a studio or an independent of Darby's choosing.

"*Why?*"

"Why not?" Steven understood neither her indignation nor her alarm. "They know a hell of a lot more about marketing a book than I do."

"They don't know more than *I* do, goddam it!"

"Really? How many novels have you sold to the movies in your time?"

"I know how it's *done!*"

"So do they."

"You've been screwed!"

"You're out of your box! Why shouldn't the publisher want the best sale possible?"

Steven was taken aback by the tempest of recrimination. He was bewildered by her reaction, but finally, angrily, put it down to meddlesome possessiveness. He refused to discuss the subject any further.

Steven knew that the most constructive thing he could do,

professionally and psychologically, was to return to Vermont and start writing again, writing anything.

But he could not remove himself from Darby Press. Bones had succeeded in shaking his confidence in the new contract, and his compulsion to be on the publisher's premises, to feed his formless suspicions, kept him going back to those offices day after day.

He got tired listening to Jerry. And he was impatient with Brandon, the senior editor assigned to oversee Jerry on *The Nephew*. Steven wanted to know why they were not submitting the book to film studios *now*. The senior editor advised him that submission of film rights was going to be done correctly, and correctly meant slowly. They intended to go to one carefully chosen prospect at a time.

"We've been gang-banged too many times by the studios. You submit a property to a studio, and if one semiliterate UCLA reader doesn't like it, the word goes out from Culver City to Burbank. No sale. No sale on a grand scale, dear boy. Studio submissions are absolutely out as far as Darby is concerned."

That meant, the editor elucidated, one director, one star at a time. A tedious process, perhaps, but the correct one.

The senior editor was a man who wore three-piece suits. He seemed knowledgeable; he seemed sincere and Steven could not identify the source of his own unease.

A week later, Jerry told him that Darby Press had decided to submit *The Nephew* to Richard Bradford. Steven asked Jerry if he knew that blond male stars had short careers. When Steven told Bones about Bradford, she said, great, he should get a firm yes or no from Bradford within two years. *Easy.*

Bones had had her jewelry reappraised. She had gone to Harry Winston's because Max never bought at Winston's, and she was not known there. Her collection, the Winston man had told her, was charming. No major stones, of course. The pieces were highly personal, original, even . . . eccentric. An enchanting, *personal* collection. Not easy to sell, however. The problem was getting a fair or even respectable price.

"One hundred thousand. With luck one hundred and twenty-five," he stated.

Bones knew that the relative value of her jewelry was easily three times what the Winston man had suggested.

"Will you buy the collection?" she asked him.

"I'm so sorry, Mrs. Routledge. We couldn't possibly give you what it's worth. And I reiterate, it is not a question of the quality. The quality is excellent. Excellent. But what could Winston's do with these pieces? We have our own style, you see. And most of our pieces are custom designed. Now, the best thing for you to do, I should think, is to take your chances at auction. Always a gamble, of course, unless you have exceptional stones, but you *could* do very well indeed. With a little luck. With a little luck you might realize far in excess of what you could ever expect from a private buyer."

Bones thanked him and left.

She had known almost from the moment she entered the Winston premises, even before he had given her the ridiculous evaluation, that she would not sell the jewelry. She did not *want* to sell the jewelry. It was *hers*. It was hers in a way that nothing else was. She would sell off the things in the apartment down to the silver swizzle stick Connie had once given her, but she would not sell the jewelry.

She needed to think, and she needed to read. To read until she found some passed-over novel or story that she could option or buy cheap. She would gamble everything on a feature movie if she found a property. She worried fleetingly about getting pregnant, but decided, just as fleetingly, that the preliminaries of independent film production would provide an ideal pastime for the long months of pregnancy.

She had to read, and Vermont seemed the perfect place to do it. In the country, with nothing to distract her, she could read twelve, fourteen hours a day. And *Windrift* was the first book she would tackle. She did not believe in its film potential, but she wanted another look. It would be beyond stupidity to pass over a property which was not only available, but which would be, for all practical purposes, free.

Steven was surprised that she wanted to go back to Vermont.

"Couldn't you hold out in New York another week or two?" he objected. "I've got a feeling I should stick around town a little longer, Bones."

"What for? Since you have such blind confidence in all those show-business giants at Darby . . ."

Steven restrained himself. "They want a fairly significant change in the arrangement of the last hundred pages. The editors' suggestions will be ready on the sixth and I want to do the work here. They're giving me an office at Darby."

"Why?"

"I asked for it."

"Why?"

"I don't know . . . it's more convenient."

"Convenient for what?"

"*Work*, for Christ sake! It's a tough job. It's going to be tough for me to rethink those pages so soon after writing them. I need to concentrate."

"You can't concentrate in Vermont?"

"I don't *want* to concentrate in Vermont!"

Steven wanted, in fact, to concentrate at Darby Press *on* Darby Press. He wanted to concentrate on that weird feeling which intensified and became more inexplicable every time he entered the premises.

There was nothing specific, nothing he could put his finger on. Steven liked the design for the book jacket. The one detail to which he had objected was obligingly corrected. When he had asked to sit in on any promotional meetings that might be coming up, it was suggested that the first meeting be held now, while he was in New York. Everybody at the meeting agreed with every suggestion he made. Following Steven's reiterated stand against television appearances, there were no arguments, no attempts to persuade, no pouting, as there had been at the *Windrift* meetings.

This time, Steven was assured that most publishing houses and certainly Darby were coming to regard television as a mixed blessing. Few authors were effective as television salesmen; some were fatal. Why force the issue? There were other ways to promote books. Steven listened while the sales people kicked around ideas, some of which sounded original, even creative.

Steven should have come out of that meeting in high spirits. He had not. He wondered why.

Bones gave in about Vermont. She understood that Steven was nervous about his book, restless and unfocused.

She settled down to begin her reading job in the New York apartment.

Making certain that Steven would not interrupt her, Bones took her copy of *Windrift* from a shelf in her library. She had been both touched and impressed that Steven, knowing she was searching for a film property, had never once hinted about *Windrift*. The dispensation was so gracious that it clutched her heart, and she damned Max to eternity for teasing Steven into believing in the book's cinematic potential.

In less than fifty pages, Bones knew she had been right the first time. She finished the book because it was good and because she was enjoying reading it again. But there was no movie in *Windrift*. Regretfully, she put it back on the shelf, then tackled the piles of old paperbacks and library books she had been collecting.

Steven's restless comings and goings, his interruptions, his moods during the next few days distracted her badly, but she was patient and gentle, looking ahead to the sixth when he would move, with his partially edited manuscript, into an office at Darby Press. She kept her face straight when he complained that there had been no word from Bradford.

"Who's next on the list if you get a negative?"

"If Bradford says no, then they'll go after a director."

"Who?"

"They've got a list as long as my arm."

"A list of directors worth *having* is as long as your thumb. *My* thumb."

They agreed to drop the subject.

"I'll make tea," Bones suggested.

"No, I'll do it. Go on reading." He started from the room. She called to him.

"Steven . . . Steven, listen. If I find something I like and that interests you, would you want to try doing a treatment on it?"

"How do you do a treatment?"

"Break down the book into the elements that will dramatize.

You tell the story in the most dramatic way you can manage . . . straight narrative interspersed with highlights of dialogue from the key scenes. Fifteen to twenty pages."

He considered it. "Not easy."

"I didn't say it was easy. I asked you if you wanted to try."

He gave her his best smile, the one that reached the eyes. "I'll make cinnamon toast, too."

For a while after that, things were sweeter between them. Steven grew calmer after the sixth, when he settled down to work at Darby.

Alone in the apartment, Bones read for long hours. When she became impatient or discouraged, she made appointments with antique dealers who came to view whatever she had a notion to sell. Selling antiques, like selling jewelry, was not, Bones discovered, like buying. But occasionally she would give in and take the proffered price. The dealer would leave Bones with a check and a light-headed feeling. "Tough shit, Max. You really liked that one," Bones would console herself.

She sold the Nelson mirror, two rugs, a painted French desk, a pair of Louis XV bergères, all things that Max had particularly admired. Parke-Bernet had agreed to sell the Futurists, but arrangements for the sale would take months, and would provide no immediate funds.

Compulsively, Bones would always return to the stacks of books. In two weeks, she found three possibilities, none of them strong enough to consider without the added weight of a top screenwriter. She kept reading.

Their evenings consisted of scratch dinners illumined by candles in half a dozen old crystal candlesticks. They ate spaghetti with various quick sauces, pepper steak made from hamburger and, once, Mexican TV dinners. But they ate off fine china. Neither of them seemed aware of the incongruity. They chattered about their days, gobbled down the dreadful fare, and went cheerfully to bed, pleased to be together again after the long day apart.

Steven had been spooking around Darby Press for two weeks when he found out about the printing.

He had not gone to lunch that day because he was working well and did not want to take a long break. He had ordered in a sandwich. But when it came, the bread was dry and the sliced chicken was tasteless. It needed salt and butter, or mayonnaise. Then he remembered the big blond down the hall in Production. Steven had met her when Jerry gave him a tour of all the desks occupied by what he called "table pussy." Steven remembered that in one of the drawers of the blond's desk, he had seen a regular PX store of provisions.

It was ten of one and the offices were virtually empty. Steven got up and strolled over toward Production, where he had no trouble locating the right desk. And in the drawer, as he remembered, he found Sweet 'n Low and salt and pepper and tubed mayonnaise, a package of Gauloises, a compact of Ovulen, and, face up, a note in what he instantly recognized as Jerry's script.

Up yours, Baby. Anytime and anyway.
Jere

Jerry's pathetic bravado made Steven smile. He helped himself to salt and mayo, and closed the drawer. He had stepped away from the desk before he realized that on a form sheet, piled with a stack of other papers on the desk, he had seen his own name. He turned back.

The form was a Manufacturing Estimate. Steven read with interest that the text paper for his new novel was 55# Antique Cream and that the binding was "Perfect." Then his eyes moved down the paper to look at the listings under EDITION COST. The first item in that column was Quantity. In the space left beside Quantity, the number 20,000 had been typed in, then crossed out, and 5,000 had been substituted. *Five thousand?*

Steven felt like a hospital patient who steals a peek at his own chart and reads "prognosis negative."

Carrying the sheet with him, Steven walked slowly back to Jerry's office to wait.

Confronted with the hard evidence of the sheet, Jerry paled and denied everything.

"You're a goddam liar, Jerry."

Jerry went running for the senior editor. In a short time, Brandon came to Jerry's office accompanied by another older man, who was introduced as Mr. Carruthers. Jerry did not return.

Steven's verbal assault on the two senior men was compounded of accusations, calumny, demands for explanation, and one threat of physical injury. But no tactic unearthed a valid reason for what was happening to him. The editors stood pat on their hand. Paper shortage, trouble with printers, distributors, shippers. Five thousand was a most respectable runoff in this terrible fiction market when every book, regardless of its promise, needed reviews to get the publishing ball really rolling, to confirm editorial judgment. . . .

Steven stared at the men with cold loathing.

"You're fucking liars. Fucking liars and fucking frauds. You're deliberately killing my book. And I want to know why."

"You're being very wrong-headed about this, Steven. As your publishers you must allow us to judge what . . ."

Steven cut him off. "You're not publishers . . . you're gofers. Who are you two running coffee and Danish for? Who's given the order to kill my book? It's not *you*. You haven't got the muscle, you sonofabitch."

"Mr. Routledge, this is a publishing house, not an Eighth Avenue bar!" flared Brandon, Brandon who had once talked about being gang-banged.

"Listen, Brandon. I've just been mugged and rolled. It's not so different here from Eighth Avenue."

The man turned and walked from the office.

But Mr. Carruthers, a thin, gray man in his late fifties, stayed, although he would not meet Steven's eyes. He spoke sadly.

"Go on home, son. This isn't getting you anywhere." Then he added with a vehemence that seemed to surprise even himself, "And it isn't getting me anywhere. Anywhere that I want to *go*." Carruthers walked out the door, leaving Steven alone.

From Darby Press, Steven went looking for his cousin Jess, and finally found him at the Links. They drank there for a long time, then at a bar in the neighborhood. They got drunk and before they lost complete track of their moves, they took in Elaine's, Maxwell's Plum, Casey's, and the Spring Street Bar.

It was almost eight a.m. when Steven woke up in Jess' apartment in bed with a long, lovely redhead. Who did not know his name either.

Steven did not stay for breakfast.

Bones had lain awake all night, alternately trying to read, then checking emergency rooms, then going back to a printed page, upon which she could not focus. When she finally heard Steven's key in the lock, her relief was mixed with such fury that she dashed into the bathroom and got under the shower before he could reach the bathroom.

"Bones? . . . Are you in the shower, honey?"

Bones knew guilt in a man's voice when she heard it. She turned on the cold water and let it chill her through before she stepped out of the stall. She pulled a robe tight around her and walked into the bedroom, stopping just short of the hangdog Steven.

"Well. What was that all about?" she asked nicely. "A night out with the boys?"

"Something like that."

She smiled evenly, waiting for him to continue.

For the first time since they had met, she unnerved him. He had a strong impulse to flee, but resisted.

"Want to tell me about it?"

He told her about it. And as she listened to what had happened at Darby, her fury against him faded. She was incredulous and as outraged for him as he had been for himself.

They breakfasted together. And when Steven described the night's debauch, all he had to edit was the redhead. He asked Bones' forgiveness for making her worry. She nodded, less concerned with the bender than with what had prompted it. Neither of them could come up with any explanation that made sense.

Then at nine-thirty the phone rang and a Mr. Carruthers asked to speak with Steven.

On the phone Carruthers told Steven that he had just handed in his resignation from Darby.

"No, Mr. Routledge, to be perfectly honest, I am not leaving for your sake. I am leaving for mine. When elements of the business world—elements never before associated with publishing—come in and are allowed to hand down final word on the artistic aspects of *my* work, I cannot, in good conscience, or in fairness to myself, stay on. You are young and talented and will write many more books. I am not young, and I will not edit many more. When I have relocated, I will let you know where I am. And please believe that I am sorry, but in *no* way responsible, for what is happening to *The Nephew*."

Steven repeated to Bones, almost verbatim, what Carruthers had said.

She sat down on the bed and looked with eery serenity at absolutely nothing.

"Max," she said. "He's going to hound us to death."

What followed was their first real fight. It was a peculiar sort of altercation, with no raised voices, no accusations or counter-accusations. Instead, it took the form of a dialogue which began after Bones had convinced Steven that Max was indeed behind the sabotage. Her conviction was so total, so instinctive and without reserve, that he had to believe her. She told him that nothing was ever going to stop Max until he got what he wanted.

"Which is what?"

"For me to belly-crawl. He wants me to call his office, ask for an appointment, be told that he can't see me for a month or so. But that if I'm free somewhere around . . . say, the first of October, he can give me half an hour . . ."

Neither of them was aware of it when the quarrel, deep as a bear pit and eventually as bloody, actually began.

"And when I get there, I must tell him that I finally realize how much he did for me, that I was crazy to think I had made the gallery and the production company on my own. That all I want now is for him to know that I finally understand. And that . . . I need his help again. Desperately need his help."

Steven's profile, it occurred to Bones, was as stylized and sealed as an Egyptian frieze.

"You're married to me, but it's *his* help you need."

She shrugged, silent.

"Need his help how?"

"How do you think?" she asked. "He'll let the book go if I ask him to."

"Oh, I see. And that's what you propose to do?" His voice was so blurred with ambivalence that she had trouble understanding his words.

"Of course!"

"*Of course.*" He echoed.

Bones laughed angrily. "If I'd understood how far he was going to carry this ludicrous vendetta, I'd have gone weeks ago. Listen. It's not worth it. I'll drag-ass back up to the old thirty-sixth floor and eat shit for half an hour, and then we can go on with our goddam life."

"I'm not sure, Bones, that would be a life I'd want to go on with."

She reached out to touch him, but his reflexive move away from her hand was too fast for her to misread. She pulled back, startled.

"What else can we do?" she demanded, "He's holding your book hostage! He's taken all my money and left me burdened with this bloody apartment. Do you believe for one moment he can't think of anything else to do to us?"

Steven walked across the room, sat down on the bed and lighted a cigarette. He took a couple of thoughtful drags before he spoke. "Bones . . . he just keeps hitting us in the pocketbook. That's all. Only the pocketbook. Look, he has no intention of keeping *The Nephew* completely out of publication. That could mean a lawsuit with publicity and trouble he might not be able to control. So the book *will* come out. It will be published. And reviewed, if it deserves to be. There's nothing on God's earth Max can do to alter the fact that I've written a good book." There was a white line around Steven's mouth and Bones knew that he was angrier than she had ever seen him. What she did not understand was that a large part of the anger was directed at her.

"That is, you will excuse the high-flown expression, a *verity*. Nor can Max affect . . . what we are . . . not unless we let him. Another verity."

"What do you mean—'what we are'?" she asked.

"It is inconceivable that you go to that pig and make piggy noises for him."

With a rising resentment, Bones damned his youth. But she

kept her voice soft. "Steven, it won't hurt me. *Truly*. Believe me. It won't hurt."

"If I believed that, I wouldn't give any variety of damn whether I ever saw you again!"

His vehemence impressed her more than his words; she tried to be reasonable, to find some way around his moral intransigence.

"All he wants are the *words*, Steven. He's not looking for 'verities,' for God's sake. He wouldn't even know what you're talking about. I'm not even sure I do. How can it hurt me to . . ."

"What caused those three days of silence and fever when he first started in on us . . . on you?"

"Shock. Shock and surprise that he would do it to *me*. A bruised ego. And I don't kid myself . . ." She gave the wall a bitter smile. ". . . the loss of over a million dollars. *That* hurt. It hurt like hell, because I did earn that million, and the prick knows I did. But if he's determined to hear me say I didn't . . . If I have to say it . . . I'll say it."

"You'll say *nothing*. Not now. Not ever."

Bones vaguely understood Steven's attitude, but she did not agree with it. He was a spoiled upper-class brat who had never had to shovel his way out of the shit-pile. She had done a lot of shoveling. All that mattered was getting out. What kind of shovel you used was not important. Bones stared at her young husband, despising him for all he had never experienced. Steven caught her look and knew, in detail, everything she was thinking. He was saddened beyond measure that she did not know, perhaps *could* not know, the slow but fatal wounds such labors as she proposed inflicted.

Methodically, Steven began undressing, taking off the clothes soiled in his evening's travels. "Max Herschel is a dead issue, Bones. The million bucks is a dead issue. Control of *The Nephew* is a dead issue."

"Steven . . ." she tried, but he turned his hanging-judge face at her. Her head spun with wild combinations of words that might crack the wall of his principles . . . the stupid, self-defeating, infantile principles . . . she tried to stop herself from taking *that* train . . . concentrate on . . .

"Listen to me, Bones. I'm going to give you two choices. And whichever one you make, I'll go along with."

She hated his face when he looked so closed and cold. She started, once again, to speak, but he put his hand over her mouth.

"Listen to me." Then he took her head between his hands and held it cruelly tight, forcing her to look up into his face.

"The choices are: one, forget Max Herschel. Whatever else he does, or tries to do, ignore it. Sit down and *think*, and make yourself understand that he cannot, in any real sense, affect *us*. Try, please try to do that. But if you can't, I give you the other choice." Steven let go her head, and began unbuttoning his shirt. His voice lost its violent undertone, and became again just Steven's normal, we're-out-of-eggs voice. "The other choice is, I kill him."

Bones started to laugh, then thought better of it and quietly, watched him take off his shirt. Before he could drop it on the floor, she made a grab for it. He sat down on the edge of the bed and began untying his shoes.

"I will figure out a way to kill him which, hopefully, I'll stand a chance of getting away with. You can help. You know his habits."

Bones stood with Steven's soiled shirt in her hands watching him remove his shoes. She believed, beyond any doubt whatever, that he was making her a genuine offer, and that if she accepted, he would work out a way to get to Max and kill him. Or try to.

She went into the dressing room and put Steven's shirt in the laundry basket. He walked past her into the bathroom. She followed.

"God, I need a shower," he complained.

Bones put her arms around him and laid her head against his chest.

"I'll forget him, Steven. I'll try not to hate him or think about what . . . or *anything*. I'll *try*. I swear."

"Okay. I'm going to clean up and go back to Darby. I want to know precisely what they are going to allow me."

What Darby Press was going to allow Steven was a first and probably final printing of five thousand; they would be allowing five hundred dollars for promotion. If by the wildest of chances Richard Bradford or anybody else wanted to make the movie, the Darby Press terms would be beyond reasonable negotiation.

"What's the publication date?" he asked.

"The same—December."

Steven found out later that day why December was the very worst month in which to publish a book. That bookstores are so busy in December with selling that they don't even bother to unpack incoming shipments of books. That to have a book in the stores for Christmas, it must be out by mid-November. He also heard, for the first time, the expression to "privish" a book. He did not have to be told what it meant. *The Nephew* was being "privished."

That night Bones swallowed a double dose of Valium and slept heavily, but Steven lay awake in the dark. His mind worked diligently on the case of Maximilian Herschel. It was interesting, Steven considered, that he felt no hatred for Max. Rather he was consumed by curiosity, and his curiosity, Steven knew from experience, was a thing with its own life. There was more than one way to kite a capitalist.

Steven appreciated that Max was not one-of-a-kind. Men like Max Herschel were in somewhat long supply, on the spot when needed, as they so often were by people sensible of their own human vulnerability. People needed men like Max to enfold them in a greater power, to give them the illusion that *somewhere*, in *someone*, the center held.

Max's life provided the stuff of fantasy. Max never hesitated, nor stopped to ponder, to worry, to vacillate. He moved. He did it. He did it first. And look! He *did* it! He *got* it! He got *away* with it! There he is. Alive and well and living on Beekman Place. Max gave sanction to dark deeds. He even gave sanction to his own destruction. "Catch me if you can."

Steven turned over, closed his eyes. His breathing deepened, and he was almost asleep when the cruel fingers of a bad memory pinched him awake.

He rolled over carefully, turned on the bedside lamp, and inspected Bones' sleeping face. Yes. That had been it. He saw it now, fully surfaced, clearly defined. During their quarrel, when, right after the call from Carruthers, she had said, "*Max.* He's going to hound us to death," Steven had only sensed the subtext. Now it had surfaced. Now, in her sleep, her response to Max's threat was nakedly exposed.

She was *smug.*

Max would "hound them (her) to death."

She was thrilled.

Steven turned off the light and, surprisingly, went straight off to sleep.

Chapter 20

The next morning, after Steven had left the apartment, Bones telephoned Stella.

"Listen, Bones, I don't want to talk to you on this phone."

"Then meet me for lunch someplace. Meet me at that Schrafft's on Fifty-Ninth and Madison. In the back. One o'clock."

Bones and Stella, hidden in the tomato and tunafish depths of Schrafft's back room, felt safe from Max Herschel, their security impenetrable. It had been seven months since the two women had seen each other.

"You look wonderful, Stella."

"Well, I'm *not* wonderful."

Stella examined Bones' face as suspiciously as if it were a piece of auction art with no provenance. "Well. You look good, Bones. But older."

Bones sighed. "If aging me is what Max is shooting for, you can tell him he's on target."

"Him I tell *nothing*."

Stella signaled for a waitress. "What do you want to eat?"

Bones said she would have a baked ham and tomato on toasted

cheese bread with no lettuce and Russian dressing on the side. Stella's eyebrows shot up.

Bones smiled. "Didn't you know I used to be a waitress at the old Schrafft's Seventy-Ninth Street?"

"No, I didn't."

"Well, I was. Let me recommend the toasted cheese bread with Russian dressing on the side."

Stella laughed and said why not. There was a moment of silence, then Stella put her hand square on the table.

"I've tried everything I know to stop him, Bones. Everything but quit. I even tried that when he took the kid out of the office."

"What kid?"

Stella had known Bones for a long time; she was not used to pulling punches, nor had it occurred to her that Bones' intelligence sources would not have informed her about Cathy Kronig.

"I thought you knew . . . hell, it's nothing. Just one more little girl. But he really pissed me off, taking one of *my* girls. Out of *my* office. If I'm going to run a cathouse I want a lot more money."

"Which girl? A new one?"

"Not so new. She's the one who got sent over to that party for Baby . . . the last one you'd expect. Little Miss White Mouse." Stella's sense of betrayal bubbled up irrepressibly. "Miss White-Mouse-Good-at-Math," she sniffed.

"Is she bright?"

Stella was grudging but honest. "Brighter than I figured. She fooled *me*." Stella sighed. "Yes. She's bright."

"Where'd he get her in?"

"Barnard. She got herself in. And taking a sixth course at Columbia."

"Oh. *Very* bright." Bones felt the sick stirring of antique anguish. Only a reflex, she thought, and quashed the motion. Out of order.

"Stella, I didn't drag you to Schrafft's to talk about new additions to the harem. The harem doesn't concern me anymore." She caught the long-suffering look in Stella's eyes.

"Oh, Stella. I know it's your own personal Dismal Swamp. I'm sorry. I really am. He ought to be slapped down hard for raiding your herd."

"I told you I quit. I said, 'Max, that's it. *Fini.*' And I put on my coat and took my purse and walked out."

"Really walked out?"

Bones was impressed. Stella had been threatening to leave Max for as long as she had been with him, but she had never, to the best of Bones' knowledge, gone through the actual moves.

"You bet I did," Stella declared with pride, then shrugged, "all the way to the elevator. Max came running after me and shoved me away from the elevator door and grabbed my *purse* and ran back into the office with it . . ."

Bones could not help laughing. "*Echt* Herschel."

Stella smiled wearily. "Naturally, by the time I got it away from him again, he'd spritzed me back to my desk." She looked shyly at Bones. "The next day, he sent me a mink coat."

"High time." Bones thought a moment, then asked, "Where did it come from?"

"Bergdorf's."

Bones smiled. "Is it gorgeous?"

"Yes, it is. Black Emba. Female skins. Enormous collar. Not that I wear it much. Only to mass and special occasions. *He'll* never see it on me."

The sandwiches arrived and a short silence fell between them before Bones told Stella what she wanted.

"But, Bones," Stella was distressed. "It's not a question of his seeing you and giving you a hard time, and then relenting. He won't see you. He won't see you at all."

"I don't believe it. I know him. I know what he wants. All he wants is me on my knees. Well, okay. Just tell him . . . tell him . . . oh shit, say you saw me and I was terribly shaken up and crying and that you won't take the responsibility for what I might do if he won't see me."

"You think Max doesn't know you better than that? He'll never believe you'd try to hurt yourself."

"So let him put his own interpretation on it. Let him think I might be planning to take a shot at *him*."

"Are you kidding? That he'd love! I can't think of anything in the world he'd like better than the idea of the big scene with you . . . pistol in your trembling little hand . . . oh, come on. *Bones*, he is *not going to see you*."

"Try, Stella. I think he will. Just try. Try this afternoon or early tomorrow, whichever you think is best. But don't call me. I don't want Steven to know I've been in touch. I'll call you. I'll call you tomorrow at two."

At exactly two p.m. the following day, Bones called the Herschel office and asked Stella what Max had said.

"What he said . . . exactly, if you insist on knowing . . . was, 'Tell the plucky little woman to go pluck.' . . . No, that was *it*. In *toto*. That's every word he said . . . *Of course* I told him you were crying. I also said you'd lost weight and needed a manicure. He loved that. In fact, his spirits rose in direct proportion to details of your distress."

There was silence from the other end of the line.

"Bones? Are you there? Bones?"

"I'm here, Stella."

"I'm sorry. I don't know anything else to do. I'll run across to St. Pat's and make an effing novena next time he sends me to Saks . . ."

"Thanks, Stella. I'm sorry I bothered you."

Stella's stern sense of justice churned. "Listen, honey," Stella promised, "if there's any way to sabotage the bastard's purge . . . I mean from the *office*, anything *I* can do . . . I *will*. Believe me, Bones."

"I do. And thank you, Stella."

"You keep in touch. Okay? And so will I."

Bones went back to the apartment and ran a tub full of hot water into which she poured a half-bottle of bath oil, then she got in and lay down, her hands folded across her breasts. The marble tub, the horizontal woman, lying white and still with closed veinless lids, the crossed hands . . . a picture portentously, vulgarly symbolic of death.

But not the death of the woman. Bones lay in the soothing hot water, her mind coolly considering the second choice Steven had offered her.

Bones had been in the tub over a quarter of an hour when the call came for Steven.

For the rest of her life Bones would wonder if the call had not come when it did, whether she would actually have asked Steven to kill Max.

The call was from a Jules Raskin who said he was anxious to talk with "Stevie" and would she be sure "Stevie" got this number. He would wait for "Stevie's" call.

Bones did not give Mr. Raskin the Darby Press number. That morning, when she saw that Steven was leaving the apartment, Bones had asked where he was going.

"To work. I've got to do more work on the last three chapters."

Bones had been awed by his composure. "You're going back there and just calmly sit down and . . ."

He shrugged. ". . . I want those five thousand copies to come out as perfect as I can make them."

Bones protested passionately. "But that's like . . . it's like . . ."

"I'll tell you what it's like. It's like practicing conscientious dentistry, doing fine inlays, at Auschwitz."

At six o'clock, when Steven came home, Bones nearly forgot to give him the message from Mr. Raskin. Her head was still filled with scenarios for the death of Max Herschel.

Bones had believed . . . had wanted to believe . . . Steven's offer to kill Max. She played with the scene, wrote and rewrote the lines. "Yes. I want him *dead*. That's what I want!" Pregnant pause, then: "Okay, that's what you want . . . that's what you get." But she did not like the tone in Steven's phantom voice. What did he plan to do? Take the contract, do the job, then walk away from *her*? Away from the bloody bitch who . . .

What was wrong with all this, she had to tell herself, was that she was not fantasizing. She was really thinking about it.

"Oh, yes," she remembered. "A Jules Raskin called you. He left a number and said for 'Stevie' to call him right away."

Steven frowned, shook his head. "Raskin? Jules Raskin's all I need."

"Who is he?"

"I told you about him, he's the . . ."

The phone rang. It was Jules Raskin. Steven made a resigned

[271]

gesture—he would take the call; Bones handed him the phone and went into the kitchen.

It was a full five minutes before Steven joined her there, a rather silly expression on his face.

"We're going to make a movie out of *Windrift*."

Bones let a sigh escape. Oh God. *Please*. Not that sheep-dip *too*. Not on top of . . .

"Listen, Steven, don't let yourself get all . . ."

"Don't interrupt. Just listen . . ." Steven consulted a scrap of paper on which he had scribbled. "While I can still read this stuff . . . and remember it . . . It's what Raskin calls a step-deal—"

"That means somebody is willing to put up a part—"

"Don't *interrupt*. It's a major studio. They're putting up . . . he called it 'development' money. They will buy the book and pay for a screenplay. Raskin says that if I will take a token payment for the book rights and defer principal payment, he knows he can get me the screenplay job plus, *plus* I will coproduce. With him. With Raskin. He can get me twenty-five thousand for the screenplay. Ten when I start, five more when I turn in the second set of revisions, the last ten on the start of principal photography . . ."

Steven reeled off the terms as if they were nonsense syllables he had memorized for fun. "Then . . ." catching the look of total disbelief in Bones' eyes, he delivered the lines straight at her. "*Then* I would *also* split the producer's fee with Raskin. That's another fifty thousand. Thou . . ." Steven almost giggled. "Twenty-five thou for good old Julie and twenty-five thou for Stevie. 'The fee is so *mingy*, really chicken-shit, Stevie, because you see the picture has got to be budgeted as tight as a First Lady's twat. A million-two *tops*.' Of course, Raskin and I will also share points, ten percent of a hundred percent of the profits, defined as profits above two-point-six of the negative. Whatever the hell that is. Then . . . did I mention that the token payment for the book is five thousand? With fifteen thousand deferred, escalating to a total of forty thousand plus, according to the profit position. That is, I get twenty thousand more when the

[272]

picture goes into profit, plus a *bonus* of twenty-five thousand *more* if it grosses above fifteen million."

He paused, then picked up again before Bones could comment.

"The other thing is, I leave for California tomorrow on American flight three out of Kennedy at one p.m. First class round trip. I will stay at the Beverly Hills Hotel and should be able to get everything cleared with a go-ahead on the project and be back here by Friday."

"What's the studio?"

"Artists International."

"But that's the studio that Max . . ."

"Don't say it. Because it *isn't*," Steven said fiercely. "If he were pulling something, that's the *one* studio he wouldn't use. And what, for God's sake, would be the idea anyway? Knocking one book out from under me and setting up a movie sale of the other one twenty-four hours later? Bones . . . *Max Herschel* had *nothing* to do with this. Raskin has been trying to get *Windrift* going as a movie since a week after it hit the stands! He's a little cheapy, but he loves that damn book and believes in it as a movie. And if he's made a deal I don't give a shit where he's made it!"

"What has he produced before this?"

"Four beach-and-bikini flicks a long time ago, and some way or other he got co-billing on an old Elizabeth Taylor movie. A *bad* one. What else can I tell you?"

"What you want packed."

Bones went to Kennedy with Steven to see him and Raskin off.

Jules Raskin was a classic meatball, short, round, greasy. He had a little pencil-line mustache. His clothes were not only bad, they were dirty. And Bones knew instantly that he was gay. She remembered that Michael Berger was gay. Not that she thought it reasonable that Berger would be attracted to Raskin but they had possibly crossed paths in Hollywood.

That Michael Berger and Jules Raskin were both homosexual reassured Bones. It made a tenuous but logical tie between them.

[273]

To Bones, Michael's and Jules' shared ineptitude in judging screen material had seemed a suspiciously weak connection. To find the sausages more securely linked encouraged Bones to think that the meat was not, perhaps, being ground out by Max.

When Bones was introduced to Jules at the American check-in counter, she shook his hand and let him do the talking. The meatball talked fast. She knew the argot. She knew Jules Raskin. She knew he was an outer-fringe, two-buck theatrical hustler who was quick-witted enough to stay out of jail. She also knew that Hollywood was full of former outer-fringe, two-buck theatrical hustlers who were now living big in Bel Air. She wished Raskin luck. She wished Steven even more.

As Bones watched the odd couple go through the security arch, she waved good-bye and wondered suddenly if she had ever told Steven . . . if he knew that Michael Berger was gay. She'd have to call him in California tonight.

When they were out of sight, Bones went to a phone and dialed Stella.

"Stella, have you ever heard, even in passing, of a man named Jules Raskin?"

"Rings no bell. What does he do?"

"Movie producer?"

"Never heard of him."

Bones hated to ask more, but felt compelled, for Steven's sake if not her own. "Stella, is Max . . . I know I'm asking this out of school, and if you feel you shouldn't answer, don't. But what I want to know is, is Max mixed up again, or still, in any way, with Artists International?"

"Uh-uh. He got rinky-dinked bad by Seymour Berger. Got left holding virtually worthless stock in one hand and a limp member in the other." Stella chuckled meanly. Stella was, Bones thought, on the other end of the line, still feeling vengeful because Max had fouled the office nest. Stella went on, pleased to relate Max's come-uppance from Artists International.

"On that deal Max even got smeared by that walking, talking-ing Old School Tie, Mr. T. Tilford Smith. He's getting his own back with Smith, and I guess in the fullness of time he'll follow old Seymour's casket with a suitably solemn expression on his face. But as far as the studio's concerned, everything's on the hold button for Max. Old Berger's in the back room calling the shots and Queen Michael gets to keep his fairy wand." Stella laughed outright. "As you may have gathered, Max is not here. He flew to the Coast last night to try to shovel out poor old Pat."

"Pat Langdon? Out of what?"

"You didn't read the papers today?"

"I don't know what you're talking about."

"The Son-in-Law has been indicted for fraud. Section one, page five, column two, the *Times*. You'll love it."

Bones was incredulous. "Pat *Langdon?* Indicted?"

"The Golden Goy himself. Jill is on twenty-four-hour hysterics."

"Stella . . . was it the freeway thing? Max's scam? He didn't let Pat get caught in *that!*"

"No, no. This was all Pat's. *All* Pat's. Max is livid. He says back in February Pat asked him all about how a particular kind of land development thing worked and Max told him, but then Max got worried and thought maybe some smart operator might be pulling Pat in for a front, so Max had the set-up investigated and didn't like the smell. Told Pat to stay out. Told him in no uncertain terms. Told him not to go within three counties of it. But apparently old Pat didn't listen."

Bones thanked Stella and told her she would appreciate hearing if Raskin's name ever came up. Then she hurried to a newsstand and bought a copy of the *Times*. She turned to page five and saw the headline and leader.

PROMINENT CALIFORNIA LEGISLATOR INDICTED
Fraudulent Use of Federal Funds
Claimed in Indictment of Gubernatorial Hopeful

Bones read swiftly through the three short paragraphs. Max Herschel's name was not mentioned. Bones wondered, as she walked out of the terminal, the name of the AP rewrite man who had owed Max.

Max arrived in Pasadena to find Jill, not hysterical, as Stella had suggested to Bones, but in full battle dress, holding the hapless Pat prisoner in empty servants' quarters over what had once been stables. His meals were sent to him on a tray. The children had been taken far behind the lines, to Hawaii in fact, with their delighted nanny.

Jill, with steely Sunderson eyes, informed Max that she had no intention of being socially tarred by Pat's situation. That she had already filed for separation.

Max was aghast. "He gets slapped with one lousy little indictment and in twenty-four hours his wife files for separation? *Sweetheart!*"

"I will not be dragged down in his mud, Daddy."

"But, Jesus, sweetheart. Who says there's got to be any mud? It's all a mistake. I'll straighten it out. He just got the tip of his big toe in . . ."

"He is *under indictment!*"

"So what? We'll get it quashed."

"It's been in the papers!"

"It won't be anymore. Show a little confidence in me, sweetheart."

Max had gone from Jill to the stables to confer with Pat and Pat's lawyer. Pat's lawyer did not impress Max, so Max gave him a couple of suggestions which required him to busy back to the office.

Alone with Pat, Max asked for only one thing. Names. The name of the state's attorney who had filed the papers, and the names of that gentleman's superior and his immediate subordinate. Then he told Pat to sit tight, look at TV. How about *Rhoda?* Did Pat like *Rhoda?*

"I don't have a TV set, Dad."

The stockade was not provided with a TV? Max sadly shook his head at Jill's hardnosed behavior, and assured Pat that he would get a nice big color set within the hour. He prepared to leave.

"But, Dad . . . sir, what are you going to *do?* What *can* you do?" groaned the shaken young man.

"Spend a little money," answered Max poignantly.

As it turned out, he had to spend more than a little. He had to take in a partner on the freeway enterprise.

Within forty-eight hours, Pat was out of the stable and back in the house. Not back in Jill's peach-and-green bedroom, but in the house. When, if ever, he got back in the bedroom would depend on how much damage his political career had suffered. It would take time to tell. Pat's position in Pasadena was provisional.

Before he left California, Max had got Jill's petition for separation put on ice. When he thought he had done all he could, Max flew back to New York in the Gulfstream.

Chapter 21

With her academic load, her new life style, her obsession with Max, Cathy had bitten off a lot. But she chewed hard and swallowed fast. There was not one minute of her day in which she did not revel, from the moment she opened her eyes in her small but airy, prettily appointed apartment on East 86th to the moment (never before two a.m.) when she finally put down her books and turned off her bedside lamp.

She loved her classes, her textbooks, her teachers. She loved her down sofa (not foam rubber, *real down*), her set of silver (*not* stainless steel but Gorham's Chantilly, her *mother's* pattern, service for *eight*). She loved the delicate Brunschwig (new frame of reference; Cathy loved a new frame of reference) print that covered her bed and chaise. She loved the chaise.

She loved her beautiful blond head. It had cost three hundred dollars. First the streaks had to be stripped out and dyed brown.

Then her whole head had to be bleached almost gray. Then the hair was *painted!* The process took two whole days and was personally overseen by the salon's owner.

Cathy loved her new clothes, all the school things, the pants and shirts and leather jackets. The wolf coat, with the hood. She loved the underwear—lingerie—that the school clothes hid. Lingerie à Bendel's. And when her weight settled down to exactly one hundred and twelve pounds and stayed there, Max was going to get *real* lingerie *made* for her in Milan. Milan, Italy.

Cathy loved the robes. There were *seven* robes. For when Max came. And tennis dresses and *two* new rackets. Aluminum. Arthur Ashe. And her *car.* A BMW. It was compact, got good mileage, and was built so strong that you had great odds in case of a crash. And the *garage.* A hundred and seventy-five dollars a month for the garage because it was dumb to leave a good car out on the street.

Cathy loved corporation law. She loved her little microwave oven that cooked bacon in three minutes with no pan to wash. She loved Max.

She cried when he told her about the trouble his son-in-law was in. Cried bitterly for poor Max and the burdens he had to carry. She wanted to go out to California with him . . . just *be* with him. He had said she was adorable but that she should stay put and keep up with her work. He'd call her every night.

He did call her every night, and it was almost better than his actually being in New York. When he was in New York he sometimes didn't call her for days, much less see her. When he was in California he reported in like clockwork. He was *thinking of her* in spite of all he had on his mind. He was thinking of *her.*

Cathy had a lot on her mind too, but always, on some level, all day long, she was thinking of Max.

Cathy loved Max. As she told him over and over. And it bothered Cathy that he never said *he* loved *her.* She knew he *did,* but he wouldn't say it. He would only say that he adored her.

Cathy adored Max, too. But she also loved him.

While Steven was away, Bones read most every day. She had

found one good possibility. It was only a novella, not a natural for filming, but it had one marvelous character and it had a spine. The book was several years old and she had trouble tracking down the writer, who, Bones was surprised and discouraged to discover, was represented by a tough and singularly venal female agent.

The asking price was ten thousand dollars for a year's option and forty thousand for an outright sale.

Bones laughed and said, "Sadie, you're full of it." And hung up. Then she lay on her sofa, tortured by her impotence. Only a few months ago she would simply have signed a check and taken immediate possession of the book, granting no further concessions whatever to the agent.

But she would have no money until the Futurists sold. She could . . . what? Gut the drawing room? Oh Christ if she could only sell the apartment. Could she bring an action against Max or the cooperative's board or the realtors or Prentice Farquhar III? They were acting . . . in restraint of trade? She spoke the phrase. "In restraint of trade. Your honor." She smiled scornfully at herself and shut off the silly fantasy. How else could she get money? Sell the jewelry.

At the thought of selling the jewelry, her head began to ache and she headed for the bathtub and a hot soak. Where could she get her hands on ten thousand dollars fast? Borrow it? Who from? Who the hell did she know that Max hadn't fritzed for her? Baby. She knew Baby.

Bones lay in the tub pondering the likelihood of getting money from Baby. Baby was rich. Bones knew exactly what Max had settled on both girls. Baby would give her the money. The question was—should she take the money from Baby? Ask Baby to betray Max? Bones was amazed at the nicety of her reasoning. Why the hell shouldn't she ask Baby? Why should she tie her own hands for reasons Max would be incapable of understanding? Max would *admire* her if she squeezed what she needed out of his daughter. Max would never understand that she would not use Baby, because . . .

Because of Steven? "Where did you get the money, Bones?" "From Baby." "You went to *Baby?* For money *he* gave Baby?"

"Look at it like this, Steven. It's a fraction of what he *stole* from me."

She lay in the tub fuming with indignation at Steven and his scruples.

But in the end she knew that he would regard her petitioning Baby for help precisely as he would regard her bending the knee to Max.

All right. So forget Baby. If asking Baby would make Steven go all New England Puritan, the hell with it. Let *him* put up the money.

Feeling suddenly better, Bones got out of the tub. She would demand that Steven take out a second mortgage on the farm and loan her whatever he could get. Ten thousand for the option, plus enough to cover a treatment.

Bones called Sadie Cox to say she would pay no more than five thousand for a year's option, and even that five thousand was generous, as Sadie knew better than anyone. They settled for seven thousand with the right to pick up a second year at the same price. Bones arranged to see Sadie in about ten days because, she told the agent, she would be in Rome until then. Let the bitch sweat for ten days. But Bones knew that Sadie Cox wouldn't sweat over seven thousand dollars. It was Bones who was sweating.

After she hung up, Bones went back to reading, hoping to find a second story she could buy for the three thousand she had left from the ten. Which she was getting from that dumb-neck Vermont bank. When Steven came back.

Steven got off the plane at Kennedy and talked for two straight days.

You couldn't believe it till you'd been there, he told her and when she smiled and said well, she had been there . . . he said No, no, I mean been there for the *treatment*. What was all that snow about the "New Hollywood?" It was, as far as Steven could see, still one hundred percent pure Gloria Swanson. Michael Berger lived in a house made out of Lucite.

"He buggers boys in broad Lucite?" Bones laughed.

"There are discreet, opaque Lucite-no-color curtains that can be drawn on Mike's most private and precious hours . . ."

"You call him Mike?"

Steven grinned. "Oh, all of us call him Mike."

"Who's all of us?"

"Just the regular crowd," he mocked. "Liza, Warren, Nicholson, *me* . . . all the kids. You know, the *young, fun* crowd. No Hollywood bullshit. Nobody cares what kind of car you drive, you know? Nobody sucking up because I mean what the hell, in our crowd everybody's got their own projectionist. You know? So what's to prove? Right?"

Bones grinned, encouraged the act.

"What are you smirking at?" He challenged her, managing to profile a pelvis thrust alarmingly forward. "God, when you get away from the Coast everybody looks so *white* and *flabby*. Mike says that as soon as I come back out he can get me on Laszlo's schedule. He says Laszlo's about to give up on Dustin and when he does, I can have Dustin's time."

"Who's Laszlo?" she laughed.

He looked at her as if she had just admitted she'd never slept with any of the Kennedys. "*Laszlo* is only the *top* Tai-chi instructor in B.H." He regarded her sadly, remotely. "You're really out of it, you know. You poor dumb cunt."

Later, in bed, she begged, "Do me some more. Do me some more Beverly Hills."

"What's so crazy, and this is no joke . . . that studio's supposed to be in such trouble . . . you know what their bank debts amount to?"

She nodded.

"Fantastic. But Julie and I were given *suites* at the Beverly Hills. You know what room-service breakfast—small orange juice, three strips of bacon, one egg, no toast, coffee—costs at that place? Nine dollars and forty cents. Without tip. And, oh yes, the flowers. One modest arrangement of carnations from the management plus a basket of fruit, but two insane funeral sprays three feet high— *roses*—from the studio! To *guys!* Bones, I blushed . . ." He grinned. "And my God, the girls in that lobby! It's wall-to-wall couze! And gorgeous. *Unreal! Unreal!*"

Bones listened and laughed and enjoyed the pleasure he took in recounting the old, old stories. Old until they happened to you.

He told her his versions. Swimming pools, for instance, were out, he said. And all the gardens were being bulldozed. Tulips out, tennis in. She should see, he declared, Julie Raskin in tennis whites.

"Is Julie digging up tulips too?" she asked.

No. Julie, Steven related, good old Julie hadn't lost his head. Julie was looking for a very modest place. He didn't need either a pool or a tennis court because he had the entree to Mike's. Anyway, Julie didn't actually *play* tennis. He had only bought a dozen sets of whites in which to call shots. Julie called all balls in.

Julie and Mike were trying to get Steven to do the script in California. Down by the courts.

"What did you say?" she asked.

"I said no *way*."

She smiled at him, and shook her head in wonder. "You really loathed it, didn't you?"

"Loathed it? Who do you think you married? Cotton Mather? I *loved* it. I loved every gaudy, gorgeous, grungy minute of it. I can't wait to go back."

"Oh. When will that be?"

"I don't know. I'll just see how the work comes." He kissed her lightly. "I see myself more in the role of commuter. A month to six weeks in Vermont, roots you know, then five to ten days in B.H. That should do it." He teased, then spoke more seriously. "It's too rich for the blood. I don't see how anyone can take it for more than a week at a time."

"What will you do when you have to go into production? You can't do that one week on, six weeks off."

"I'll slowly acclimatize. Build up my red corpuscles. You know. Like they do when they try for the Eiger." He took a deep breath and pulled her to him.

"Let's go *home*, Bones. Let's go to Vermont in the morning. What do you say?" he asked.

"I say yes."

She had cooked a real dinner for him. He acknowledged it as the celebration it was.

Over dessert, she told him about the novella and said she had to have twenty thousand dollars . . . doubling the amount on impulse. The only person she could get the money from was

Baby, and she didn't feel quite right about going to Baby. But she needed the twenty quick. Would he mortgage the farm? She knew how he felt about keeping it clear, but . . .

Steven never hesitated. Whatever a mortgage would bring, she could have.

Bones burst into tears.

Steven took her to bed and made love to her. Before they slept he said, "Whatever happened to our baby?"

From drowsy contentment and a feeling of once again being on the win, Bones crashed.

"I've been too tense, that's all. It'll be all right now."

"You think so?"

"Yes." She tried to joke. "Let's aim for a spring production."

"That seems like a lot of spring productions. Sure you can handle multiples?"

"I can handle anything." She squeezed tight against him. She would love him and take care of him and not let those dumb fucks in California break his heart when the movie went sour. She would get him back to real writing. She would give him a baby and pay back the mortgage and produce a brilliant movie and get them out of this goddam trap Max thought he had her in . . .

Just before she fell asleep, it occurred to her he had never mentioned selling her jewelry instead of mortgaging his farm. She would make it up to him. She swore she would.

They left for Vermont the next day. Forty-eight hours later, Steven was turned down for a second mortgage on the farm. The bank was giving no second mortgages at this time. None at all. Nor did the bank's manager-president wish to renegotiate Steven's existing loan. Steven was incredulous. He had constructed a fine house on what had been a ruin. In the three years he had owned the farm, the price of his land, so near the best skiing areas, had sharply escalated. There was no question that Steven's farm was worth considerably more now than when he had bought it. And the mortgage that it already carried was negligible.

The bank's refusal to give a second mortgage or to enlarge the existing one was incomprehensible. Steven told Bones that he would call Boston and consult Uncle Arthur, Jess' father.

Uncle Arthur readily agreed with Steven that the farm was a perfectly sound risk for another mortgage, but that money was tight. Terribly tight. Everywhere. Steven could hear in Uncle Arthur's voice the plea that Steven not ask *him* for money. Steven did not.

Steven had no way of knowing, since Uncle Arthur did not want to worry the boy further, that a long strip of land bordering the Routledge section of the Dedham cemetery was being threatened in a way that was causing Uncle Arthur sick anxiety. An extraordinary offer had been made to the long-time owners by a buyer who proposed to construct an aerosol can factory on that stretch of land. A factory. Right up against the sacred mounds of the Routledge dead. The owners of the strip did not *want* to sell, but the offer was spectacular. Uncle Arthur was working seven days a week to harness the finances of the elder Routledges and counteract the ruinous proposal.

"He sounded distinctly . . ." Steven was not certain of the word. He made an attempt. ". . . distressed. I didn't want to press him. I'll call Aunt Cora and see if she has any cash lying around."

Bones would not hear of asking Aunt Cora for money. She was astonished at herself, but there it was. "Nice" could cripple.

The next day, she flew back to New York and sold the fishhook earrings. The man at Winston's had admired the emeralds from which the jeweled lures swung. But when the earrings were whisked away and the check for them placed in her hand, she knew that she had sold them to wound Max. Except he would never know he'd been wounded. She went to the ladies' room at Saks and threw up.

She took a cab to the apartment and threw up again. She was sick all night. Around two a.m. she did not care if she died. But when she read the bottom line, she knew that she did not want to die. She wanted Max to die.

Max was sixty-two, she comforted herself. He soon would be sixty-three. His life style was suicidal. He had himself shot out of a cannon seven days a week. His heart would give out. He could

eat yogurt till it came out of his hairy ears, but sooner or later
that overtaxed muscle inside his ribcage would give out, and Max
would die.

But not, please God, *please* God, not soon and not too fast.
Let him live long enough to see Bones rich and successful and
happy . . . a wife, a mother, an Academy Award winner, a gentle *hospital visitor*. A hospital visitor wearing *jewelry*. Doing everything to make Max's last days memorable. Telling him about the
fantastic eighteen-year-old blond beauty who was starring in
Bones' new film . . . and had he got a look at that little desk
nurse on his own floor? Breathtakingly beautiful! Looked about
fifteen! But, oh dear, of course he hadn't seen her . . . he wasn't
ambulatory.

Oh, God, Bones prayed, kill him for me, but not too fast . . .

Back in Vermont, she began reading again, this time screen-
plays and a few prize-winning TV scripts. Since there was no
longer any question of Steven's attempting a treatment, she had
to find a screenwriter. Steven was closeted in his workroom,
agonizing over his own project.

She could have told him how very difficult it was to write any
sort of film-script, but that to adapt one's own novel took the icy
perversion of a child-killer.

As Steven struggled day after day, skipping lunch, as he
emerged in the evening, white-lipped with frustration and dis-
couragement, Bones longed to tell him to give it up, but knew
she could not.

Julie would call every three or four days, filled with words of
good cheer, startling gossip from Emerald City, and always, a
plea to Stevie to pick up the old Remington and fly to California
where he would have pretty people to consult with and experienced hands to give him support. Stevie should be talking to
directors. Just wait till Stevie *listened* to some of these guys . . .
kids right out of college film courses. *Eleven*-year-olds! Incredible.
Hey, Stevie, what do you say? Mike thinks you should *definitely*
be working out here. He's worried, if you want the truth. Can we
afford to worry Michael Berger? . . .

It often took a little time and a lot of somebody's money before

Julie made Steven laugh, but he always succeeded. It was about the only time Steven did laugh.

Bones' script-reading produced four young writers whose work made her want to meet and talk with them. Only one lived in New York. The other three were in California.

Bones thought it all over carefully, then proposed to Steven that they go to California. She felt *she* had to. She thought it would do him good too. He had been locked in on the book for three weeks.

What did he have to show for it? He had seven separate outlines and five scenes. Bones asked if she could read them. He backed off.

"It's all crap."

"Let *me* say that."

"I don't want to hear *you* say it."

"*Please*," she insisted. He gave her the pages.

All seven outlines were bad, too complicated, too intellectualized, too static, all wedded to the book. Of the five scenes, three were garbage, but two were exciting. Alive and kicking. Her heart turned over. He could write a scene! Bones looked up at Steven, her face a cartoon of delight.

"Two good scenes. Two wonderful scenes. *Steven*. Two wonderful scenes!"

His relief was short-lived.

"Just two?"

She was not going to bullshit him. "Just two."

"What about the outlines?"

"No."

They closed up the house and left for California as soon as Bones had met the New York writer. The man was older than she had expected and seemed ponderous. He had been *somewhere* a long time. If he had been *anywhere* as long as that, she should have known his name. Since she did not, there had to be good, or, more likely, appalling reasons. She promised to let him hear from her. She and Steven flew on to California that night.

At Kennedy, Bones sat seething on a plastic contour chair in the public waiting room. They had to wait an hour and a half for their plane which gave her plenty of time to examine her fellow passengers and to react to them with individual and collective loathing. She mourned for the Gulfstream—luxurious, convenient, *private.*

They were booked into the Beverly Hills. When Steven had called Michael Berger's secretary to say he was coming to the Coast and his wife would be with him, the secretary had assured him that Mister Berger would be delighted to put Mrs. Routledge up at the Beverly Hills along with Mr. Routledge. Exactly how long would Mrs. Routledge be staying?

After they checked into the room, Bones suggested Steven use the bathroom first. She told him she had to go down to the drugstore to replace some stuff she'd forgotten.

Safely away from him, she headed straight to the house phones in the lobby.

"Operator, will you ring Bungalow Four? Mr. Herschel. This is Mrs. Munshin calling."

The operator told her that Mr. Herschel had checked out two days ago.

Bones went next to the drugstore and bought all of the Los Angeles papers, then walked across to the coffee shop and ordered a cup of tea. She scanned the papers carefully for any mention of Pat Langdon or Max. There was nothing. She sat quietly for a moment, then went back up to the lobby and called Pasadena. A houseman answered and told her that Mrs. Langdon and the children were on holiday in Hawaii. Mr. Langdon was in Sacramento. Bones called the gerbil-keeper. No, Mr. Herschel had not been at the lab for several days.

There was no point in contacting Dolores.

Bones threw away the papers and went back to Steven, who had finished with the bathroom. She mopped up after him, then ran a tub for herself.

That evening they had dinner with Julie at his small rented house in the Hollywood Hills—too tiny to accommodate a couple, he apologized. The guest room had a single bed and its bath was in the hall. Of course, after Bones left, if Steven wanted to stay there until he got himself settled . . .

"Won't the studio keep me at the hotel?" Steven asked.

"Your contract gives you a fifty dollar per diem, sweetums. You can't hack the B.H. on fifty a day," Julie explained. "They'll pick up your tab there for a week, maybe ten days, till you find a place. I mean they wouldn't do *that* except Michael's so glad to have you back and relieved you're going to do your little tap-dance out *here*."

Steven's nose, to Bones' surprise, did not go all knife-thin. He continued to be amused by Julie and showed only a kind of benevolent Great Dane tolerance for Julie's obese-but-perky pug dog routines.

Back at the hotel they put off discussing how they would arrange themselves when their ten days' grace was up. Bones said she would play it by ear, and urged Steven to concern himself with getting a death-grip on some old hack who could help him chop an outline from the book. Let Michael Berger pay for it. He was such a big-hearted boy.

When they went through the lobby the next morning at ten-thirty, the beauties were already out. Steven asked Bones if she didn't think this was the world's greatest hotel.

"Only if you've got terminal satyriasis."

They went their separate ways.

On the third day Steven found his writer and Bones found hers. Michael Berger set the old Hollywood veteran before the young novelist's feet, like a still serviceable mink thrown over mud so the princess needn't dirty her shoes.

Berger presented Steven with his hack, but no one was going to give Bones her writer. His name was Clegg Pruder, he was thirty-two and he had two feature credits under his belt. He was full of beans and sure of himself and he wanted fifty thousand dollars. He liked the novella. He had, he said, "gone Dracula" for it. It was really his neck meat. But he had to have fifty thousand.

Bones knew he would take thirty, maybe twenty-five, but she did not have even that. She told him not to get mixed up with anything else before checking back with her, assuring him she wanted him and that it was only a question of pulling one other ingredient into the production. Young Clegg Pruder gave her a tired old man's smile. He knew all about pulling in those other ingredients and said, "Sure thing." She picked up the lunch check. It was thirty-six dollars.

That night they were invited to a dinner party at Michael Berger's. They were encouraged, somehow, to believe the party was for them. Or for Steven.

As she dressed, Bones wondered why Michael Berger, production head of Artists International, would be giving a dinner party for Steven?

She was almost dressed when Steven came up behind her and bent his knees so he could see in the mirror to brush his hair.

He was beautiful. Oh well, if that was what led Michael Berger to give dinner parties and pay hacks to do outlines . . .

Eat your heart out, Michael, she smiled to herself.

"Ready?"

"Do you really think this dress will go with the Lucite?"

They were admitted to Berger's house by a handsome young black butler.

The house was virtually all glass, early Philip Johnson, Bones reckoned, sitting high on a ledge that overlooked the city. Nothing overlooked the house. There were no neighbors on a geographic level with Michael Berger, so there were no eyes to throw stony looks at his glass walls.

The foyer, drawing room, library, and dining room were, indeed furnished largely in Lucite. There was a bit of chrome, some antique steel, but everything else was glass or Lucite. Even the two ten-foot sofas were Lucite bases with a great profusion of leafy green cushions. The few ornaments, other than pieces of art, were of dazzlingly polished silver.

Michael Berger's decor showcased only one artist, Ernest Trova. Bones spotted three Trova paintings and four sculptures which looked, she suddenly realized, like slightly abstracted silver versions of the Oscar. All seven Trovas were masterpieces of antisepsis, representations of machined men, striding or falling through clean space, smoothly machined legs transporting silver, science-fiction bodies . . . not-quite-men going not-quite-any-where.

The floors were covered with a rich grass-green carpet, and Bones' eye, practiced at pricing house plants, estimated that the public part of Michael Berger's house supported about twenty thousand dollars' worth of foliage. Artists International aside, Michael Berger was Seymour's grandson. A rich young man. On closer examination Bones noted that none of the rare and luxuriant plants were flowering. Lushly, even threateningly green, but they would never blossom. In this stunning greenhouse, Michael Berger was the single precious bud.

The bud greeted Steven with enough warmth to spill over and include Bones. He was an extraordinarily handsome young man who strongly resembled his grandfather except for his coloring. Tall and dark, he had long, almond-shaped, fudge-colored eyes which sought affirmation from whomever they focused on. Michael was handsomer than any male star in Hollywood. His chin sported a cleft you could lose your way in, his natural hairline was like that wonderous peak manufactured years ago for Rita Hayworth, and—the cherry on the charlotte russe—his cheeks were dimpled.

Michael warmed Bones' hand in both of his.

"How wonderful! Steven's *wife!*" He made it sound like "Steven's *unicorn!*" Michael's Almond Hershey eyes begged her to like him, to find him acceptable, *nice*.

She did. Bones recalled Steven's first flip description of Michael —"A really sweet guy . . ." And so he was, Bones decided. Too sweet to run a studio.

Among the guests who had arrived before the Routledges was Julie Raskin, dressed in hand-tailored denim pants and safari jacket, but wearing black lisle socks and old New York Florsheims. Viewing Julie, wrong anywhere, but fatally wrong against the inhuman perfection of Michael's glass and silver, Bones gave young Berger even further credit for sweetness of nature.

Julie had escorted to the party a smartly dressed, good-looking woman whom Bones judged to be in her early thirties until she saw the woman's hands. Closer to fifty-five. Or *worse*. But the face was unlined, serene. The moment before they were introduced, Bones recognized her. She was the first wife of an aging star who recently had made off with his third wife's brother, a great European industrialist with no previous history as a cut-up. The first wife shook Steven's hand with evident enthusiasm, Bones' with absent civility.

There were two other couples present. One was a short, neat young man who hovered with smoldering intensity over the most beautiful girl Bones had ever seen. The girl's face was as animated as an oyster; her eyes were glazed. She responded to introductions with a slow blink, the kind of blink Bones associated with the brain-damaged victim desperately trying to communicate to the detective who it was who pushed her over the cliff. The damaged beauty's keeper spoke and shook hands for her.

The second beautiful woman was called Gloria. Gloria was deeply tanned and smooth-muscled. She was with Jock Kelly.

"Hullo, Bones," Kelly greeted her lazily. "How's Max? He comes in and out all the time, but *we* never see him." Kelly either hadn't made the mental effort to separate Bones and Max or else he assumed her situation was the same as his. He was on loan-out to Gloria Sutro; she was on loan-out to somebody named Routledge.

Bones sat down and made an effort to chat with Kelly and his beautiful lady jock. He told Bones all about the new air-conditioning in their indoor court at Palm Springs. The air-conditioning was not coming up to expectations.

Gloria Sutro had met Bones with Max, but Bones was no longer *with* Max. Gloria clicked Bones' assets off in short order. She covered Bones' tan, her tone, her haircut, her jewels. She saw no threat whatever and turned to Steven.

Within ten minutes of the Routledges' arrival, the remainder of the party was assembled. They were sixteen for dinner. Bones never got the others sorted out except for one older woman in a monstrous wig and full Follies make-up. The woman was with a boy almost as beautiful as Michael Berger. The woman was a fabled gossip columnist, and she paid no attention whatever to either Bones or Steven.

The last person to arrive was a breathless and beautiful girl called Tilly. She appeared to be Michael Berger's date for the evening. Bones gave Michael another point. He was not intimidated by female beauty. Nor did he, Bones surmised, require Tilly to wear the house colors. The gorgeous girl was not decked out in silver or green. She wore dirty blue jeans and seemed to have come straight from a stable. She was a stunt rider, she said, and doubled for practically all the female stars. Barbara Stanwyck, she confided, was the only one Tilly had ever heard of who would go the distance with a horse. Having made this startling pronouncement, Tilly led off into the dining room.

The male partners of the other two couples were both actors, stars in fact, and even better looking in person than on the screen. It was the skin. The skin was *powerful*. One of them came with his very young wife. She was beautiful. The other brought a girl friend. She was about nineteen. She was beautiful.

Among the beautiful women present—the beautiful *young* women among whom Bones stubbornly placed herself—Bones was the least beautiful. At the Lucite dinner table, between Michael Berger and the older and more devastatingly handsome of the two male stars, Bones felt herself outshone not only by the other women present, but by most of the men. *Everybody* was beautiful. Everybody but the gossip columnist and you couldn't tell what she was, underneath the wig and the lashes and the make-up and the plastic work underneath the make-up. Maybe underneath everything, she too was beautiful. Maybe, Bones thought dully, the columnist perversely wore a disguise of age to make herself *different*. Maybe her dark secret was that under the disguise, she was beautiful. Just like everybody else. Anonymously beautiful.

Bones felt worse than anonymous. She felt invisible. Michael Berger made it his hostly duty to see her, but no one else did. Eyes wandered, turned away, turned inward when they chanced upon her. The male star on her right offered a few words about his next film, but did not bother to see who was receiving the word.

This was the first Hollywood gathering Bones had ever attended where she was not under the banner and preceded by the military band of Herschel Industries. Then she had always felt herself a kind of star. Much court was paid her, much attention given. Under the auspices of Herschel Industries she had never noticed that other women were more beautiful than she. Tonight, Bones was maddeningly aware, in spite of Michael Berger's graciousness, that she had been demoted to supporting player. She ate a great deal of food because she was anxious and angry.

They had reached the second course before all at once Bones understood. Beauty was basic. It could get you in the game, but only for the first pot. After that, what counted was simply muscle. The amount of weight behind your punch. And fame counted, any kind of fame. As production head of a major studio, Michael Berger was a light-heavyweight. He counted. The two male stars, the columnist counted. Even the ex-champion, Jock Kelly, counted. Bones noted with interest that the aging star's first wife also got her share of fluttery, flattery attention, more this month than last, Bones guessed, because of the recent scandal attached to her husband thrice-removed.

Oh, Max, you bastard, Bones thought. You *liar*. I *could* have got laid out here. If I had had my foot on a studio's neck. *Man*, could I have got laid!

Over dessert Bones inquired discreetly if Michael Berger had heard the latest developments in Pat Langdon's troubles.

"Troubles? What troubles?" asked Michael.

"Who's Pat Langdon?" demanded the male star on Bones' other side. He did not seem to be able to see her, Bones thought bitterly, but he could intercept a whisper intended for Michael Berger.

Michael knew who Pat Langdon was, but knew nothing about the land fraud. The male star lost interest when it became clear that Langdon and his troubles were not in the Business. Bones gave up attempting to make conversation with the actor. She finished her dessert in silence, glad when dinner was over and she could have Steven back at her side.

Coffee was served in the library so that the movie could begin. Bones and Steven forcefully claimed positions side by side on the great sofa, beating out a number of after-dinner guests who stormed into the house at the last moment, giggling and making grabs for the best seats.

When the lights went down, the largest Trova levitated, a gigantic screen descended from some mysterious recess, and the movie began.

It was worse than dull. It was a heavy narcotic. Heavy enough to pull its weight against others being passed among the audience. Bones accepted, briefly examined, and passed along intact a small silver bowl full of cocaine. Then came a properly cedar-lined silver humidor filled with professionally rolled cigarettes containing, Steven whispered to her, grass treated with ether. She also passed up a box of the richest looking chocolate she had ever seen, as rich, Bones thought drowsily, as Michael Berger's eyes.

Bones had eaten too much food, drunk too much wine. She felt herself dozing off, fought briefly to stay awake, then blissfully escaped from the tedium of the film into the satisfactions of digestion and deep sleep.

She did not wake up until the lights went on and the Trova squeaked back down into place. Sitting up and looking groggily around, Bones' first waking thought was that the track for the Trova needed oiling. Then she saw that except for herself, the room was completely empty. Not one beautiful boy or girl was left. Even the beautiful young girl hiding under the ugly disguise of the aging gossip columnist was gone.

Everybody had obviously waited for Bones to fall asleep, she thought with fuzzy hostility, and then tiptoed out to go somewhere and be beautiful together.

Where was Steven? She stood up and made her way toward the closeted area where the projectionist must be, but before she found him, Berger's beautiful black butler found her.

"Mr. Berger drove Mr. Routledge out to the studio to see some night shooting. He said they would be back before the film was finished. Can I get you anything, madame?"

"Where is everyone else?"

The butler looked properly apologetic. "No one seemed to care for the film, madame. They just slipped away." He offered a small conspiratorial smile . . . two adults among children . . . "You know how they are . . ."

Bones thought, "I don't mean to brag, Sam, but you know

them better than *I* do." Aloud, she said, "I see. Well, I'll just wait. I'll find something to read."

"Can't I get you a brandy?"

She shook her head.

"Nothing at all?"

She smiled at him. Poor devil. You've come to the one place in this country where your *looks,* not your color, make you invisible.

"Nothing at all, thanks."

He told her to ring if she changed her mind, then left. She looked at her watch. It was only eleven-fifteen. She was waking up. She felt better. She began to stroll around, examining details of the house. It was awesomely dreadful, Bones thought, but striking.

Bones wandered from the library into the living room, then out to the vast expanse of cantilevered deck that went around two sides of the house. The lights below glittered like . . . oh, shit, they glittered like the lights of Los Angeles.

Just a million or so split-levels and California Cape Cods and the freeways that threaded through them.

Turning away from the lights, she walked along the deck, looking into Michael Berger's house. Seen from outside, it was like looking at those maniacally decorated display rooms at Bloomingdale's, side by side by side by side behind velvet ropes, like stately halls in England . . . for the tourist in Britain, for the tourist in Bloomingdale's, for the tourist in Bergerland . . .

Bones crossed into new territory. She was now walking past a room where opaque but gossamer curtains shut off her view. A bedroom, she supposed, moving on. The next room was uncurtained and lighted. It was a sitting room, not a rain forest, just a normal sitting room. It had an oriental rug on the floor and comfortable suede-covered furniture. A man's room. Who used it? Suddenly, she stopped. And stared.

Moving toward the glass wall that separated her from the room, she tried its metal catch. The catch gave. Bones opened the wall and entered the room. She walked over to the table and stood, unbelieving, in front of the vase. It *was.* There was no question at all. It was Max's Gulbenkian. She put out a finger and tentatively caressed the urn's creamy surface.

"The only beautiful thing in the whole house, for my money . . ." the voice declared. Bones turned around.

". . . Except for my grandson," concluded the frail old man in pajamas and dressing gown.

"Mr. Berger?"

"That's me. Don't I know you, dear? *Sure!* Sure I do. You're Max Herschel's little friend. Have I got it?"

"Yes, you have." She smiled at him. "I'm Mrs. Routledge now."

The watery blue eyes gave her an unexpectedly sharp look. "I think I heard. Something. Sure. Routledge. I know the name. Writer?"

"Yes. The writer. We came for dinner tonight with Michael."

"Sure. Lots of people do. Personally, I can't eat the food. Too fibrous," his voice trembled plaintively. "What do kids care about fibrous?"

Bones was shocked at how old, how shrunken Seymour Berger was. How long since she had seen him? Several years, but Max had told her in . . . February? . . . how great old Seymour looked, how vigorous he was. This was not a vigorous old man. This was clearly a feeble old man.

"I haven't seen you in years, Mr. Berger. You're marvelous to recognize me . . . I hope I didn't give you a start. I know I had no business coming in here but . . ."

"You spotted the vase, right?"

"I was never so surprised to see anything in my life."

Seymour cheered up. "Life's full of surprises."

Bones turned back to the vase.

"I never thought Max would let it go. Never. How long have you had it?"

"Six weeks? Two months? We made a deal."

Seymour Berger shuffled over to one of the suede chairs; he lowered himself carefully into it, motioning Bones to sit opposite him.

"I don't sleep so great any more. Nice to have company."

Bones risked the question: "Have you been sick?"

"Sick you couldn't imagine. *Kidneys,* very bad. Also bad hip, bad colon, bad temper. Old age you can have it, dear." His eyes returned to the vase, and he fell silent. Bones kept silence with him.

"My wife died, did you hear? My Marsha?"

"No, sir. I didn't know. I've been living in Vermont . . . I don't . . . see Max. I'm terribly sorry . . ." Bones wondered how long ago Berger had lost his wife, but was afraid to ask.

He read her mind. "A month ago."

"I'm really sorry, Mr. Berger."

"Not as sorry as me, dear," his frail old body shook under the weight of his sigh. "Fifty-six years together and not one unkind word or deed from my Marsha."

He eyed Bones challengingly.

"You should do so good to your husband."

Fifty-six years of total kindness. Bones shriveled.

"Ladies aren't *brought up* to it these days." Berger seemed to know everything she was thinking. "Of course, only part of it is how they're brought up. A lot of it is pure heart. Marsha's in the vase."

"What?"

"In the vase. My Marsha. I got it just in time. Marsha died sudden. Very sudden. Out here in California. She would never in her life dream to die in California. But life's full of surprises, like we agreed. Marsha died and the shock . . . they had to cart me off to the Cedars, kidney failure, they claimed. Broken heart's the truth. You can't travel they said. Here you are and here you'll stay. Then I want my Marsha with me, I said. And I had them do it. Against the religion, you know. But I had it done. You have to move with the times. Nuns gun-running and marrying priests. God couldn't understand I needed her with me? Sure he could. I did it." The old man nodded affectionately at the vase. "And there she is. Marsha's in Max's Gulbenkian." Berger's voice took on more snap. "*My* Gulbenkian. And nobody deserved it better than Marsha."

As he talked, Seymour watched Bones' lovely face with its gentle curves, its soft mouth, its sweet, childish forehead. Its cold gray eyes. Seymour thanked God he had never shared Max's perverted appetite for icy-eyed, icy-hearted shiksehs.

He remembered Bones more clearly now. She was the *one*. Sure. So it was *her husband*. Monkey business. *Max* business. Seymour remembered how instinctively he had disliked this girlie when he first met her. What? Ten years ago? As good as. Too bad that momzer Max didn't still have the dubious pleasure not to mention expense. Seymour did not understand Max's game. It was expensive. *Very* expensive. Aside from that, all Seymour felt sure about was that Max's game was not *nice*. In some meshugganeh way, not nice for the *boy*. Of that Seymour was absolutely certain.

Max had insisted it should all be secret. The boy shouldn't know. His pride shouldn't be hurt, Max said. If the boy shouldn't know, should the girl? Seymour looked at Bones with five thousand years of patience.

"Your husband's sold his book to my Michael."

"That's right," Bones nodded.

"I read it. The book. Nice book. Good writing." His face was worried. "Who knows these days what makes movies?"

The implied doubt about *Windrift* as a movie potential brought Bones to smart attention.

"Michael seems to have a lot of confidence in it."

Seymour's mouth smiled with a grandfather's indulgence.

"Well, sure. *The boy*. We all have to learn."

Bones knew she was being played. Her belief in Seymour Berger's failing power was put on immediate suspension.

"But *you* don't think *Windrift* will make a good movie, do you?"

Seymour's bony shoulders shrugged all the way up to his ears.

"What do I know, dear?"

"I don't know what you *know*," she came at him head-on. "But I know that you can veto any of Michael's projects budgeted over a million."

Seymour shook his head fondly. "Max, Max. He couldn't keep it to himself. He shouldn't have told you that, dear."

"But it's true," her statement demanded an answer.

"It's true."

"Then if you don't think *Windrift* will make a good movie, why didn't you veto it?"

Seymour hesitated as he made up his mind. Max obviously didn't want his girlie to know about the deal. Max was giving her husband some kind of fritz. That meant some kind of fritz for the girlie too. Didn't it? Or was it a fritz *just* for her? Seymour couldn't figure the play. It must be pretty fancy. To throw away so much money . . . still, it was not beyond Max, Seymour thought, if she'd hurt his pride bad . . . and now he had a *new* one, Seymour had heard. One he was crazy about. Poor Max. A feeling of compassion trickled through Seymour. But thinly.

It would be nice to play Max one last trick. How many tricks, Seymour plaintively rationalized, did he have left in him? How many more chances would come his way?

His head nodded absently as he thought about all this. Bones sat quietly waiting. Finally Seymour looked up at her.

"You know, young lady, I understand Max he'd talk out of school to you. You're a good listener. Old men don't get a girl every day like you, would listen to business." He chuckled. "Max Herschel can talk out of school. Seymour Berger can talk out of school. Right?"

She sat very still, regarding him with unwavering concentration. Seymour's mind was made up.

"Your fellow's book, it's a very fine *book*. But what you'd definitely have to call special. Not sure-fire for a movie. Not even sure-smoke." His chuckle turned into a shattering cough which he had trouble bringing under control. Bones waited.

"Still . . ." He resumed, his voice weaker, unlike the glint in his eyes. "Still. You know Max." Seymour's eyes seemed to warm with wry affection for the absent Max. "Max is a very generous man. Right? Very generous."

"Very generous," Bones' firm voice did not belie the words.

"When Max wants something, price is no object. We both know that. Nothing stops Max. He goes all the way."

Like Barbara Stanwyck, Bones errantly recalled.

"So Max is determined to do something good for Steven Routledge, he doesn't mind the cost."

"You're saying Max put up the money for the picture? All of the money?"

"Sure all the money. But still . . . even free, an arty picture about the Six-Day War with an *Arab hero?* Does Artists International need the name?" Seymour shook his head. "Even Max puts up all the money, I have to object to the project. Can you understand that, dear? You're in the television business, right? You know even free some shows aren't worth it, I'm not insulting your *husband*, dear. He's a fine writer. A *book* writer."

Bones would not be side-tracked. "So why is the company making *Windrift?*"

"I'm only human, dear," the old man sighed. "I'm a very human fellow. You show me a man that doesn't have his price I'll show you a man that never got the offer."

"Are you telling me Max gave you his *vase* to make this movie? I don't believe it."

"He didn't *give* it. We made a deal. The vase was part of the deal. When Max threw in the vase . . . what could I do, my arm twisted behind me . . . Max always knew how bad I wanted that vase."

Bones' intelligence refused to accept this account. Max was hounding her, yes. He would spend some money for spite. Yes. But Max never, never carried vengeance to the point of hurting *himself.* He would not give Seymour Berger his Gulbenkian vase to spite anybody. Not even Bones.

Seymour read Bones' face.

"Maybe, dear," Seymour suggested gently, "maybe for *you* . . ."

She stared at him, making no further attempt to disguise the disbelief and suspicion that narrowed her eyes and turned down the corners of her mouth. Seymour once again gave his thanks to God for fifty-six years with his Marsha. This one . . . oh, did that momzer deserve this one.

"He wants you to be happy, dear. He wants your young husband to make a good living . . ."

"He wants my young husband to fall on his ass!"

[301]

"For that Max would give up the Gulbenkian? I couldn't believe it!" Seymour denied piously. "No, dear. It was he wanted good things for *you*."

The door to the room opened and Michael Berger stuck his head in, smiled nervously at finding his grandfather in Bones' company.

"Here you are! I should have known," he came in and put an arm around Seymour. "Okay, Big Dad?"

"Okay, Mikey. We've had a nice visit, haven't we, little lady?"

"Gee, I'm sorry we took so long," Michael apologized to Bones. He told her Steven was waiting in the library. He escorted her to the door.

"Good night, Mr. Berger. I enjoyed our talk."

"Good night, dear." Seymour held up a bony finger. "Our little secret, nu? You wouldn't want to turn loose a terror like Max on a poor sick old man . . ."

She shook her head. "I won't be seeing Max, Mr. Berger. Or talking to him. Don't worry."

She and Michael left the old man alone.

"You and Big Dad have a secret?" he inquired anxiously.

"Not really. We were just talking over old times."

Bones and Steven didn't talk much as they were driven back to the hotel in Berger's car. The movie was dreadful, they agreed. Steven apologized to Bones. When Michael got a call saying he was needed on the lot, he had asked Steven to accompany him. Bones had been sleeping so peacefully it seemed a shame to . . .

It was all right. Bones hadn't minded. She had got to see old Mr. Berger.

They fell silent again. Then Steven said quietly, "Bones, I've got a feeling . . . hell, more than a feeling . . . he as much as came out and said it . . ."

"Said what?"

Steven lowered his voice to a level the chauffeur could not overhear. "That I can dump Julie. Take over the production myself. You know?"

"Why should you want to dump Julie?" she asked cautiously. "I mean, he's schlock, but at least he knows a shooting schedule when he sees one, a budget sheet . . ."

"Michael says any one of a half dozen production managers on

[302]

the lot can do the same thing as well or better than Julie. And the project would then be all mine . . . no listening to Julie's idiot casting ideas . . . having to go for a director who pretends to go for Julie . . . *you* know what I mean . . . God, can you picture Julie in session with an *art* director?"

"But Julie's the one who got the project started."

"That's what Julie said. But Michael said he had read the book on his own. He was interested in it a long time ago. Before Julie."

Max. Max. Max. Max . . .

She knew now precisely what Max was about. He had beggared her, made her dependent on Steven. Then he had killed Steven's new book, the one that promised to be big, to get out of control . . . to make her and Steven free. Max had killed it. And he had then set Steven up with *Windrift* . . . her mind suddenly bolted back to Vermont. Why hadn't that bank given Steven a mortgage? She would think that one out later. *Windrift* would be a disaster, but that was not enough. What Max wanted . . . what he wanted . . . Bones' feet and hands were cold. Her nose was cold. It wasn't just Steven's failure Max wanted. He was spending a fantastic amount of money. And imagination. He was really setting Steven up.

"You want to see what the high-hats are made of, sweetheart? It's easy. Set 'em up. Offer them something they never dreamed of. Give 'em the old entrepreneurial itch." She recalled his laugh. "You'll see very quick what they're made of. The same thing we're mad of. Scratch a Lochinvar, find a lendler."

Max's shibboleth: the infinite mendacity of man.

She remembered her farewell words to Max. "He's different from us, Max. He's different and he's better."

Bones turned now in the dark of the moving car to look at Steven's sharp profile.

"You wouldn't feel bad about dumping Julie?"

"Michael thinks he can find something else for him."

Bones did not speak again until they were back in their room. She tried to concentrate on the puzzle of the vase.

"*All right*. This time he's put a gun in *my* hand. And I'm not

going to turn it in to the authorities, Bones. I'm going to use it."
Steven stood naked in the middle of the room while Bones huddled in a chair, dully picking at the loops of the bathtowel in which she was draped. She had determined to keep Berger's story to herself until she could think it completely through. But when she came out of the bath to find Steven in bed and smiling a lazy invitation, something in her had balked. She did not want to go to bed with Steven while her head churned with Max. She had sat down on the chair furthest from the bed, and told him the entire story. His first reaction had infuriated her. He had studied her, then quietly suggested she was flattering herself.

"It must be pretty gratifying to believe that when you walk out on a man it tears him up to such an extent that he . . ." Steven laughed, and the sound was not attractive. ". . . one, ruins you financially, two, buys into or completely takes over a major publishing house just to screw up the new boy friend . . . Bones, I took your word for that, as insane and unlikely as it was that Max Herschel would or even could move in on an old firm like Darby. I took your word because *something* happened there. So, let's say it *was* Max. Do you have any idea what a maneuver like that would cost?"

"What difference would it matter to Max what it cost? It's a good house isn't it? It's not bankrupt. What did he have to lose?" she demanded.

"He had damned little or nothing to gain for a large investment. Which means that the money he put in Darby is out of play. Hardback houses just squeeze by these days. They aren't printing *money*. But for the sake of argument, let's say maybe he did it. Herschel Industries took over Darby Press. And no word leaked out about the take-over? In a business where if you can't flush the john at Knopf, they call the plumber at Viking? Anyway. Let's say we buy it. Say he pulled it off. Now we come to number three. He digs up Julie Raskin as well as subverting the Bergers? Remember it was Julie who came with the offer. Not Michael Berger . . ."

"But you yourself told Max about Julie . . ."

"Okay. Skip Julie for the moment. Let's go to Artists International. You are claiming that not only did Max give Artists International over a million dollars to make a movie he thinks will be a flop, but to show his good faith and seal the bargain, he turned over to his oldest enemy the one possession that he treasures beyond all others? All this not just to make me take a dive which may or *may not* happen. *Windrift* might be a freak. It might be a hit. Or at worst, make back its money. I might come out smelling like frangipani. So the odds aren't good enough for a sure-thing bettor like Max. So. What he's after is to *corrupt* me so that *you* will see that I'm no better than Max? *That* is the aim of this three? five? eight? million-dollar Rube Goldberg concoction of chicanery?" He let out his breath. "Bones, you're a-fucking sick."

She had flared at him. "I'm sick all right. I'm sick that he's making it all work! '. . . dump Julie!' Julie's suddenly a millstone. As suddenly as you get the word you *can* dump him. But Julie's the one who came to you the week *Windrift* was published. He's the only one who had any real faith in it. But now you smell a little power so *let's dump Julie*. 'Scratch a Lochinvar, find a lendler.'"

"What's a lendler?"

"Literally? Landlord, I think. Someone who's out for nobody but himself. The guy who says 'Fuck you, Jack. I'm all right.'"

Steven considered himself in the role of lendler. He almost laughed, but stopped himself when he saw how deadly serious Bones remained.

"Bones, look, I wouldn't kick out old Julie unless he had something else to go to. Michael said he would."

"That's not the point. I think Julie has had the real script from the beginning. I think he was paid to come in, suck you into the situation, then move out, the betrayed whore, as soon as you got a taste of blood. So it doesn't matter about Julie. What matters is that you're following the script too."

"Bones," Steven told her coldly, "it's a wet dream. You're so valuable—either as a possession, or failing that, as the object of vengeance—that The Great Dictator goes bananas and spends millions of dollars and every waking hour—"

"Every waking hour? Max? He's probably spent half a day altogether on the whole megillah. And he hasn't lost the money. He's just invested it. *Windrift* he'll write off as a tax loss. You don't understand *how he operates!*"

"You're scared to death of him," Steven said softly. "That's what I've never understood."

She screamed at him then. "I *know* him!"

"Look at it this way, love. He's what—sixty-two?—"

"Three. He'll be sixty-three this month," she said.

"We must remember to send flowers. Anyway, sixty-three. I'm thirty. If nothing else, I'll outlive him."

"Don't bank on it," she advised grimly. "Anybody can die anytime. It's not something you line up for according to age. Sixty-three-year-old men live to be a hundred and three. Thirty-year-old men eat polluted clams and that's all she wrote."

Steven sat down on the end of the bed, faced her squarely, his hands on his knees.

"All right. What do you want me to do?"

"I want you to . . ."

But that was the problem. She did not *know* what she wanted him to do, only that it should be something wonderful. Something magic and unexpected. Above all, it should be something that Max would never have dreamed of doing.

"What?" he pressed. "What shall I do? Turn back my advance, tell Berger that Julie is the man for the job and Harry the Hack is the new Hemingway? Old as Harry but new as Hemingway? Then what? Write a letter to Max . . . 'Take back your mink!'"

Bones knew the rest of the old Frank Loesser lines: "Take back your poils . . . What made you think . . . I was one of those goils!" In spite of herself, she smiled. Steven came to her, squatted down, and claimed her hands.

"Isn't this all pretty silly?"

But it wasn't silly. She knew it wasn't. Max had bought Steven, and when the market was right, Max would sell him. And what was going to happen to *her?* She began to weep softly. Only one small tear to a cheek, a slow, steady leak. Steven tried to pull her into his arms, but she drew back in the chair, resisting every comfort.

He stood up, walked away from her, then whirled around.

"You claim he wants me to fall on my ass. Expects me to. But by God, so do you. Admit it."

She did not look up when she spoke, almost a whisper.

"I have never thought *Windrift* would make a good movie."

"Seven to ten says you're wrong. I'm going to write a good script. And I *am* going to get rid of Julie. He knows nothing about producing this kind of movie. I'm going to ask Michael for the best on-the-line producer Max's money can buy. And I'm going to *learn.* And if we don't make a hit movie, we sure as hell will make a respectable one. And fuck Max. I'm not afraid of him. If he wants to play so damn bad, then I'll get in the game."

Bones turned moist gray eyes up to him. "You believe it all, anyway. Don't you?"

"What's the difference if I believe it? *You* believe it."

"But it kind of excites you, doesn't it? You want to go after him, don't you?"

"I want to make a good movie."

"And then what?"

"And then, goddam it, I want to make a blockbuster . . ." he looked into the mirror, caught sight of the naked man in the combative hands-on-hips stance. He laughed. "A real blockbuster. Like *The Godfather.* I want to get rich like Francis Ford Coppola, and fuck Max Herschel from Brentano's to Doubleday's. And when I finish with him, I'll address myself to those swine at Darby . . ."

"You look like a crazy long wax bean," she whispered.

He broke off, walked over to Bones, and pulled her up.

"Come to bed. With the bean."

Bones let Steven lead, responding with silky intuition to his moves. She initiated nothing, but put every part of herself where he wanted it, almost before he wanted it. He was greatly excited, and exigent, but neither as sensuous nor gentle as she had always known him. He was not considerate, he was not careful. He satisfied himself, letting her needs feed from the leavings of his own excesses. She was bruised and bent and rudely penetrated, bitten and burned. When, at last, he fell away from her and went instantly to sleep, she was profoundly shaken. Was this, she wondered, after all, a reason for picking cotton?

At five-fifteen in the morning, she awoke from a nightmare which she remembered vividly. Most of it. There had been a rat dressed in a kind of smock and a tall hat. And she and the rat were together in a stone room . . . a basement? . . . a cellar? . . . and they were going to drown . . .

She was frightened by the dream. She got out of bed and walked out to the little terrace. The rat . . . the drowning rat in the tall hat . . . he was a . . . a *sauce* cook in an apron . . . not a smock . . . an apron. Bones dropped down onto the terrace chaise and laughed in relief to be awake and out of the nonsensical but terrifying dream. It wasn't as if the rat had threatened her. He was drowning too, the crazy sauce-cook rat. She knew, at that moment, without a conscious thought leading up to it, that today she would go back to New York.

When he waked up she told Steven there was nothing for her to do in California until she had money to pay a writer. It was hopeless going to a studio with the book until she had a proper treatment of it. Neither she nor the book had enough weight to inspire a studio to hand out development money.

Over breakfast, she said she was going back to New York to see what she could do about shaking loose from Bernie the fifty thousand dollars Herschel Industries still owed her for Burton Productions. Failing that, she would think about selling her jewelry.

Steven bit into a piece of soggy room-service toast and patiently chewed on it. His eyes were quizzical.

"Are you sure you want to do that? Sell all that stuff?"

She shook her head. "No, I'm not sure. But I want to think about it."

His thin smile was not only enigmatic, it was somehow ominous.

"What does that look mean?" she asked uneasily.

"If you sell it . . . you're letting go of the last rung."

Steven had always understood about the jewelry. Had understood more than Bones had. "Letting go the last rung." Bones stared at him. If they were to go on together, she finally grasped, she would have to get rid of the jewelry. Not for the money, but because it was Max she was hanging onto.

Steven held her tight as she wept brokenly, her throat retching up agonizingly choked cries. Her mind rattled around like a loose head in a drawer. She had never known, she thought, such sadness. It was a sadness that would not light anywhere but fluttered and flickered on everything, touching and soiling every corner of her life.

For the first time since the trouble with Max began, Bones consulted a lawyer. She demanded to know what could be done to expedite payment of the money Herschel Industries owed her from the take-over of Burton Productions. Fifty thousand dollars had been the amount Bernie Seiden had agreed to pay. Eight months had passed.

Bones also informed the lawyer of Max's various acts of harrassment against her and Steven. The lawyer, Mr. Otis, listened sympathetically to Bones' recital.

He took a few notes. When she had finished, he told her that he would look into everything. He did not feel that she had evidence of harrassment, but certainly something could be done to get her the fifty thousand. Mr. Otis asked Bones what law firm had handled the transaction.

"Mr. Herschel's personal lawyer is Bernard Seiden. Mr. Seiden was also a member of the board of Burton Productions."

Mr. Otis shook his head. "I know Mr. Seiden by reputation. A difficult man."

"Yes."

The lawyer stood up. Bones stood up. They shook hands. He said he would call her as soon as he had anything to report.

Bones went out into the freezing February wind that whipped Park Avenue. It was after four, almost dark, and there were no taxis. She walked the thirty-six blocks home.

When she was finally safe inside, she stood in the middle of her denuded living room, looking at the gray silk walls pocked with paler squares and rectangles where pictures had formerly hung. The room was dusty. The windows needed washing. She drew the curtains across them, shivering, then went to draw a hot, consoling bath.

She lay in the tub, giving herself gratefully to the heat and the fragrance. "I am only thirty-one," she thought. "And my feet hurt."

The next day Mr. Otis called. He had talked to Bernard Seiden, he reported. "Mr. Seiden was most reasonable," Mr. Otis said with some surprise. "He says he can't imagine why you have not received your money. He will look into it immediately."

Bones did not respond.

"Are you there, Mrs. Routledge?"

"Yes, I'm here. I think we will have to sue to get the money, Mr. Otis."

Mr. Otis objected. "I think Mr. Seiden was speaking in good faith, Mrs. Routledge. Let's give him a little time."

"I've given him eight months, Mr. Otis."

"Let me have a couple of weeks. All right?"

"All right, Mr. Otis. Thank you."

She hung up knowing full well that she would not see the fifty thousand unless she sued and that Bernie would drag out the suit until it cost her the entirety of the settlement, if not more.

A deep lassitude overwhelmed her. She stayed in the apartment, never dressing or making up. She slept a great deal and dreamed a lot but had no nightmares. In fact, she enjoyed her dreams. They were not particularly interesting, but she liked them. She never dreamed again about the sauce rat. She did not even think of him again.

When she was driven by hunger she fixed expedient, unappetizing snacks. She drank a little wine, but not much. She did not need Valium. She read or watched television, but usually dozed off before the program was over or the chapter concluded. She bathed every morning and put on a fresh nightgown in which she spent the rest of the day. At one point it occurred to her that she might be sick. She took her temperature. It was normal.

She went back to her routine. Every other night she talked to Steven in Beverly Hills. She asked him a lot of questions about the script, about his days, his nights. He told her he was looking for a little house or even an apartment. He had a couple of good leads. Harry the Hack was quite useful, he was learning from Harry the Hack. But mostly Steven was writing. He always said how much he missed her but he seemed busy and content. She wondered, dully, which of the lobby girls he was fucking.

Steven never inquired about the jewelry.

Almost three weeks passed.

On the eighteenth day, Bones woke up with the problem solved. She would sell the jewelry to Baby. Baby would, Bones knew, loan her the money without the jewelry, but Bones would not ask. She would give Baby the jewelry. Bones brushed her teeth and dialed Boston. When Baby answered, Bones only said she wanted to see her. She did not say why.

Baby sounded delighted and asked no questions. They agreed that since Baby was working and Bones was not, it was better for Bones to come to Boston.

That night Bones emptied out the crocodile case. She picked up every piece, one at a time, and held each one in her hand for just a moment. Then she packed them all back into the case, which she closed and locked.

The next day she waited until 3 p.m. to fly to Boston. There was no point in arriving before Baby came home from the university.

Bones was met at Baby's by Jeffrey, who held the door for her but neither spoke nor met her eyes when she greeted him. She was barely in the front hall when a wild-haired Baby came plunging down the stairs dressed in a suit, carrying a purse and an overnight bag.

"Oh, God. *Bones!* I forgot you!"

Bones knew it was serious. *"What?* What is it?"

"Mother. She's dead. She died. At *home!* Daddy was with her . . . he was going to take her to a new place up in New Hampshire . . . where the patients go cross-country skiing . . ." Baby's voice faltered.

Bones grabbed Baby's suitcase and shepherded her out the door.

"I'll take you to New York. Where is Stan?"

"I haven't been able to reach him. Jeffrey's going to go looking for him and get him packed . . ."

Baby was not crying, but she was distraught almost to the point of incoherence.

They got to the airport in time to go to the bar and get a big slug of brandy into Baby before they boarded the five-o'clock plane back to New York.

Strapped in, under restraint, sedated by the brandy, Baby was able to tell Bones what had happened. Her mother had choked to death. At the luncheon table. With Max sitting there. At first vaguely annoyed, Baby surmised, as he always was with Connie's chronic but minor physical convulsions, then alarmed, pounding on her and trying to put his hand down her throat and even, he had stuttered over the phone to Baby, trying to make himself use a knife on her throat, to perform a tracheotomy. But she was already dead. She had died in minutes. Minutes . . . two, three minutes. How was it possible! Oh God, poor Daddy . . . frantic and helpless to stop it and watching her turn blue and . . .

Baby went white and began to retch. Bones found a vomit bag and held Baby's head.

When they arrived in New York, Bones got them both into a cab and dropped Baby at Beekman Place. Bones was clearly not expected to accompany her into the house.

"Thank you, darling," Baby gave Bones' hand a squeeze. "Thank you, Bones . . . I'll call you . . ." She turned and ran toward the door.

Bones drove off, the jewel case intact. Baby had never noticed it.

Chapter 22

Baby found Max in his study, sitting behind his desk, in the middle of a phone call.

". . . and six, the make-up man is to use only a blusher. No foundation creams, no eye-make-up, no lipstick. A little gloss, okay, but no high *color. None* . . . No. You heard me. No pencil, no shadow, no mascara. I've seen your 'cosmetic work,' you son-ofabitch. You people take a six-year-old boy and make him look like Belle Watling. You leave my wife's face alone. It's a beautiful face. *Just the way it is.* I'll be in to check." He banged down the receiver.

"Daddy . . ."

Max would not look up at her. He sat ramrod straight, glaring down at the phone.

"Oh, Daddy . . ." Baby ran around the desk to him and knelt to throw her arms around his waist. At her touch, he crumpled. He grabbed her and held on hard. He babbled.

". . . Connie . . . my fault, Baby . . . I was scared to use the knife on her . . . her little throat . . . face all blue . . . hated me, Baby, hated me all these years . . . my fault . . . everything, everything . . . help me . . . help me . . . help me . . ."

Baby managed to ring for Teddy, and between them they got Max into bed where Baby lay alongside the shaking, sobbing man, holding him as if he were her child, until Dr. Rossman arrived and gave him a knock-out shot.

Three days later, when Max was still in the same condition, and they had all agreed, Baby and Stan and Jill, that they would hold off the funeral until he was fit to attend, Baby remembered Bones. She telephoned.

Baby told her she wanted to get out of the house and they agreed to meet for a drink at the Carlyle.

"He even blames himself for the . . . what she choked on. He was going to take her up to New Hampshire that afternoon and he was afraid she would be nervous in a new place and wouldn't eat any dinner, so he ordered a big lunch. Beef Wellington."

"Beef Wellington for *lunch?*"

"Mother liked it. And Daddy wanted her to have it because she didn't just eat the beef and pick off the pastry. She always ate the crust too." Baby paused. "That's what she choked on. Beef Wellington." Baby took a deep pull on her vodka.

"It's horrible, Bones. You couldn't believe that Daddy . . ." Baby gulped down the rest of the drink and ordered another. She told Bones that Max's collapse was the worst thing she had ever witnessed.

"He begins crying the minute a shot starts to wear off. He won't eat and he won't get dressed or anything. He's like a *baby*. Dr. Rossman sent a nurse and when she tried to give him pills, he spit them out. Right at her. He just keeps saying Mother's name over and over . . . even when he's asleep." Baby turned

[314]

wondering eyes on Bones. "I never thought he even *liked* her."

"He liked taking care of her," Bones said. "And he depended on her."

"Depended on Mother? What on earth *for?*"

The corners of Bones' sweet mouth turned up ever so slightly. "For protection."

Baby mulled this over. "*Oh.* Yes. Of course. Of course he did."

"When Max pulls himself together he will face the world a beleaguered man. Threatened on every side by armies of women . . . and without Connie . . . " Bones couldn't help it. She laughed. "I'm sorry, Baby. Really. It's just . . ." She didn't finish.

Bones fed herself peanuts while Baby talked.

Daddy was calmer when she or Stan sat with him. They kept separate watches. He wouldn't have Jill or Pat. Jill, Baby said, was so busy snubbing Pat and overseeing the flower arrangements that she never seemed to notice.

"Shall I go to the funeral, Baby?" Bones finally asked.

Baby hesitated before she spoke. "I just don't know what to say, Bones."

"Then I won't. But I would like to go to see Connie. Would that be all right?"

"Oh, Bones . . ." Baby began to cry softly. "Mother never seemed to mind about *you* . . . I guess she must have, but she never said anything *against* you. Ever. All she'd ever say was how pretty you were or how well you dressed or how clever you were. One time . . . years ago, you came to the house for some kind of a dinner . . . you had just done over the gallery . . . put up the linen walls, remember? And that night after everyone left . . . she and I were alone, and I remember Mother saying what a clever girl you were. Then she said. . . she laughed, and she said, 'I think she gives Max a hard time, Baby.' And then she didn't say anything for a minute. Then she said the only hard thing I ever heard her say. She said, 'Wouldn't it serve him right if he loved her? But that's asking too much, I suppose.'"

Bones shivered. "Did she really say that?"

Baby nodded.

When Bones and Baby separated outside the Carlyle, Bones walked uptown to the funeral chapel. She asked a dark-suited young man if she could see Mrs. Herschel and was escorted into a dove-gray room with folding chairs, a guest book, and a casket. The casket was surrounded by masses of lavender- and peach-colored flowers. Ah, Jill.

Bones hesitated briefly, then walked slowly to the open casket and looked down onto the lovely, still-youthful face of Constance Parkins Sunderson Herschel, born 1919, deceased 1975. Fifty-six. Connie had been fifty-six. Bones reflected on the emptiness of those years. And what it had cost to maintain Connie comfortably in emotional antisepsis. Bones figured, roughly, that it must have cost, over the years, in the neighborhood of fifteen million dollars.

"Well, Connie, you died the way you lived," Bones whispered. "En croute."

Bones turned and marched out of the room, refusing to sign the book the man urged on her.

She walked a few blocks south before she realized that she was feeling faint. She caught a cab and went home. The next morning, she had what she recognized instantly as morning sickness.

On the fifth day after Connie's death, Max was forced by a relentless Stan to get out of bed and shave and dress and eat at a table.

On the seventh day they held the funeral.

Max bore up through the ceremony, but broke down at the graveside. He knew Connie would not have wanted to be buried in New York State. He thought she would want to be with the Parkinses in California. He vowed that as soon as he was himself again, he would dig her up and take her west. He felt that by burying her in this hostile foreign soil, even temporarily, he was once again betraying her. He began to sob. Baby and Stan assisted him to the limousine, where he huddled, abandoning himself to guilt. Once the rock of confrontation was lifted, Max faced a conscience danker, darker, wormier, than the ground into which the remains of Connie Sunderson Herschel were being lowered. Max stuffed his handkerchief in his mouth to muffle the scream he felt coming.

Baby and Stan looked at one another, Baby horrified and helpless, Stan outraged and helpless.

Two days later, on the morning that Benechek agreed with Bones that she was probably pregnant, Max had his attack.

Something in his chest "stopped, then just turned right over," Max told Dr. Rossman. He had choked and almost passed out. He couldn't feel his heart beating! . . . don't tell *him!* He knew as much about cardiac arrhythmia as Rossman!

Dr. Rossman agreed that was entirely possible. Max might know even more. Max was, Rossman assured him, certainly the greatest authority on the *anticipation* of the coronary Rossman had ever consulted. Calmly, Rossman suggested they might want to call on a third opinion. Perhaps he and Max might consult with Claude Jowdy? Head of cardiovascular research at the Heart Institute?

Max fucking well would. He'd consult with Jowdy at the hospital, so call the goddam coronary-care ambulance, then call Jowdy.

Max was rolled on a stretcher to the waiting ambulance. As Baby walked along beside him, and Stan and Jill watched from the doorway, Max sat up and yelled back at Stan.

"Get Stella to the hospital. Then call Boston. Get Jeffrey on the shuttle to New York. I'll need him at the hospital too." Then he squawked back at Jill. "Sweetheart . . . run through the house . . . pick out five or six pictures . . . small but good. Send them over."

"To the hospital?" Jill seemed bewildered.

"The last thing I look at in this fucking life is *not* going to be a blank shit-green hospital wall! Get me some pictures, kid!"

Max was lifted into the ambulance. Baby and the attendant crawled in with him, and the driver shut the door.

They had gone no more than four blocks when Max demanded a siren. There ensued a battle between Max, the young attendant, Baby, and the driver, which was settled only when the attendant gave Max an injection.

The ambulance proceeded to Mt. Gilead without a siren. Max lost that round.

Two hours later Max was examined by Dr. Claude Jowdy, who worked him over with the flattering intensity of a diamond cutter.

After a portentous half hour in which Dr. Jowdy repeated Dr. Rossman's diagnostic moves—palpating the thyroid, auscultation, and pressure-pointing the carotid sinuses—Dr. Jowdy let out a deep breath, stepped back, and smiled at Max. Dr. Jowdy agreed, he said, with Dr. Rossman's diagnosis. Dr. Jowdy did not just smile as he made this benign pronouncement, he beamed.

Max went off in his face like an unloaded gun on a drunken Saturday night.

"Fuck Rossman's diagnosis!"

Dr. Jowdy blinked in disbelief. Dr. Rossman sighed deeply. What Max had suffered, in Rossman's *private* opinion, was a fit of bad conscience. But he had suggested to Max that he had reacted to severe emotional tension, fatigue, and grief. The spasms in Max's chest were, at worst, multiple premature contractions. Dr. Rossman had prescribed a week in bed, *alone*, and ten mg of Valium three times a day. That was the sum of Dr. Rossman's prescription. Max had been his patient for eighteen years.

Max's diagnosis differed radically from that of the doctors. Max had suffered, he informed them, an episode of *heart block!* A slowing of rate just short of a Stokes-Adam attack! With the SA nodal rhythm whacked out and taken over by an ectopic focus in one of the ventricles! It could happen *again!* It could be *fatal!* He needed a pacemaker implantation and he needed it *immediately!*

Dr. Rossman told Max that with no arteriosclerotic damage or block visible on the electrocardiogram, no nausea, no anginal pain, no significant fall of blood pressure, he, Alan Rossman, could not, certainly for the present, unless further and more alarming symptoms asserted themselves, recommend the surgical implantation of a pacemaker. Max did not *need* a pacemaker.

"Balls! And you don't have to be Jewish to like Levy's! Also you don't have to have anginal pain or nausea with heart block! You sure as hell don't have to have a period of asystole for the cardiac output to be compromised. Severely compromised! Don't you read the fucking literature?"

Dr. Jowdy interposed. "Mr. Herschel. Actually, Dr. Rossman has *written* some of the literature. He was present at the very first operation in this country to implant an artificial pacemaker. He wrote a paper on it."

"Yeah? When was that? Nineteen-oh-three? They've made a couple of improvements since then and reached a couple of more sophisticated conclusions. *I want a pacemaker.* I want it put in tomorrow. And I want a General Electric Sentry 75 Demand generator. A *G.E.* Don't try to palm off a Medtronic on me. The company that makes Medtronics is in Minnesota," Max paused significantly. "My *father-in-law* came from Minnesota."

Rossman seemed to be nodding in agreement with Max's demands. He was, in fact, signaling the nurse to give Max another injection.

Over coffee and prune Danish, Dr. Rossman and Dr. Jowdy discussed the case. Dr. Jowdy agreed completely with Dr. Rossman's reading of the EKG and with his assessment of the etiology of Maximilian Herschel's condition. But Dr. Jowdy was interested in Max's diagnosis.

"Irregular runs of a paroxysmal ventricular tachycardia in the presence of a blockage are, of course, a possibility. It imitates multiple premature contractions." Jowdy smiled at the expression on Rossman's face. All the ancient sorrows of the race had surfaced on that countenance.

"We've all had our Herschels, Doctor," Jowdy tried to comfort him.

"I doubt it."

"Well, a buck's a buck," said the distinguished consultant.

"Oh no. It's much worse than that," mourned Rossman. "I *like* him. He's a nut and he's impossible, but I've been his doctor for almost twenty years. He's a friend. In his way. I hope we can go for another twenty years. But I want to tell you something, Dr. Jowdy, if I don't give him his pacemaker—his *G.E.* pacemaker— he's going to check out of this hospital tonight and start telephoning. He'll let his fingers do the walking. He'll get the yellow book and turn to Physicians and Surgeons and start with A. And he'll telephone till he finds some quack, somewhere, who'll put in a pacemaker."

Jowdy considered this. "Where did he get all his information—

all the technical terms? They were accurate and feasible . . .
Did someone in his family suffer from . . ."

Rossman shook his head. "No. He gets his dope out of *Merck's Manual*. When I'm lucky. But sometimes it's *Vogue* or *Family Circle*." Jowdy had a bemused look on his face as he swallowed the last of his Danish. "I'm only the consultant. You have to live with the man. But I'm being handsomely paid for my advice. Here it is. Put in the pacemaker. He's like a child with a low-grade fever who's hysterical because he's going to miss being in a parade. I say better let him go. If it runs up his fever a degree or so . . . what the hell. Holding him down on the bed and frustrating him will run it up too. Mr. Herschel has experienced some kind of arrhythmia and certainly has a bradycardia. He's sixty-three and according to his history, he's overdue for something. If he doesn't need the pacemaker now, he may need it six months from now. Or next year. The operation is simple, as you know. Mr. Herschel seems to evidence a touching faith in General Electric. Sometimes faith works wonders."

Rossman stared with great sadness at the passing bottom of a pretty nurse. Finally he turned back to Dr. Jowdy and gave a defeated nod.

"Max has a saying, Dr. Jowdy. I think it applies. If Max were me, what he'd say is . . . 'It vouldn't help, it vouldn't hoit.'"

Jowdy laughed. "Doctor, we both make a living because of the natural tendency of the human body to heal itself."

The pacemaker was to be placed in Max's chest Thursday morning, which meant that he had all day Wednesday in which to take over.

Jill had come by and hung pictures in his room. The bed now faced a small but dramatic Vlaminck of which Max was particularly fond. On the wall next to the bathroom door were a sunny Pissaro and a bright little Matisse collage. Jill had had the foresight to bring a collection of antique dhurrie throws to cover the plastic chairs. When she had finished hanging the pictures, she had kissed Max and asked if there was anything else she could do. He had said no, that he'd better be left to Stella.

Stella had come to the hospital with an overnight case full of tens, twenties, and fifties. One of Jill's Indian throws was draped over the case and Jeffrey sat guard over it. When he wasn't darting up and down the halls dispensing the contents of the case into pockets where it would do the most good, he perched, cross-legged, atop the case. Max, who was unable to cover the floor staff from his bed, relied on Jeffrey's judgment.

Jeffrey made cash deliveries to the switchboard, to the kitchen where Max's food from home was reheated and put on hospital trays; he tucked bills into the pockets of astonished black and Puerto Rican menials who were instructed to mop and clean at times dictated by the patient and never at times scheduled by the hospital. The better-looking nurses were favored on principle. The homely ones because you never could tell.

On Wednesday, from Room 294, Max and Stella did a good day's business. The assurance that he would get the pacemaker dispelled Max's anxiety about himself. Dispelled as well, it seemed, his excessive grief for Connie. Max was too busy for grief. He not only had business to attend to, he had the extra burden of subverting the hospital staff.

Dr. Rossman explained Max's MO to the authorities and asked their indulgence. Mr. Herschel would be out in less than a week. Mr. Herschel was, they were reminded, donating a large and extravagantly appointed new wing to the hospital. Dr. Rossman hoped they would all be patient. What could it hurt, a little baksheesh passed out among hard-working, underpaid employees? The authorities magnanimously agreed to overlook the eccentricities of Dr. Rossman's patient, silently hoping that some of his largesse might overtake themselves.

Stan and Baby visited Max briefly, but since life was once again under his control, he didn't need them. He advised them to take in a good movie or two. However, Jeffrey was to stay put.

From his perch on the money-box, Jeffrey's dark eyes regarded his adoptive mother and father. Stan, meeting Jeffrey's eyes, could plainly read in them the boy's allegiance to Max. He gave the child a solemn nod and escorted Baby out.

In the elevator going down, Stan turned to Baby and burst out laughing. "It's Volpone and Mosca!"

Baby ignored him. "I wonder . . ." she mused. "Stan, I want to call Bones."

"*No.* You stay out of that." Stan guided her off the elevator on to the main floor. As they crossed the lobby, he resolved to get Baby back to Boston as soon after the operation as he could.

It was Stella who brought up the subject of Bones.

"I told her you're in here," she stated defiantly.

Max was riveted. "You did? What did she say?"

"She wanted to know how bad it was, and I told her it wasn't bad at all . . ."

"You're fired!"

". . . at the *moment,* but that it might *develop* into something. So they were taking no chances. That you were going to be operated on."

Max leaned back luxuriously. He was going to feel wonderful. When the pacemaker was in, he'd be a new man.

"Did she want to come to the hospital?"

"Yes."

"How did she sound?"

"Worried about you . . ." Stella hesitated, decided to go ahead and say what she was thinking. "She sounded funny, Max. Very down. I think something's wrong."

Max snorted.

"See her, Max."

"I'm going to, Stella. I'm going to see her soon." His voice was contented. "It's almost time."

"It's past time," Stella retorted. "You should have seen her months ago."

"Well, kiddo, if that's all you know about timing."

The door flew open, and a wild-eyed Cathy burst into the room.

"Oh, my God! I just found out from a girl I used to know at the office! My God, Max!"

Stella squinted dangerously. Max talked fast.

"Stella, I want you back at the office. Get things moving on all those notes. Talk to Bernie. Tell him to call me here within the hour. I want to go over my will. *Move.*"

Stella passed Cathy without a word or a glance, but Cathy did not notice.

The girl was in wild disarray. Her skirt was twisted. Her sweater had been selected at random and pulled down as she ran. It did not go well with her skirt. Outside the snow was deep and cold, but Cathy was not wearing boots. Her shoes were ruined. Her legs and feet were wet. She had nothing on her head, and her hair, always so neat, so *naturally* neat, circled her head in crazy flight patterns. Her eyes filled with tears as she flung herself across the room toward Max's bed.

"You'll be all right! You'll be all right. Oh, Max! Why didn't anybody call me?" She relaxed her death grip on his bedcovers and raised her tear-streaked face to his, to put her cold little hand—Max could feel the strength of that hand even in a gesture of infinite tenderness—against his face.

"You'll be *all right!*" she implored.

"Listen, sweetheart. *Listen.* I'm *fine.* What they're going to do . . . it's nothing. Local anesthesia. In and out, fifty minutes. They just stick a little gadget right under the skin here . . ." Max touched his chest on a level with his right shoulder, but about five inches toward the center of his rib cage. ". . . right here. And that's all there is to it. It's like a new pump regulator. Precision engineering. Regular as a clock. I won't have to depend on the old arrangement anymore. I never trusted it." He grinned. "Take my advice, sweetheart, when your pants hang loose, use a belt *and* suspenders."

Cathy sniffed. She felt Jeffrey's eyes on her, and cast an uneasy glance in his direction.

"Cathy, this is Jeffrey Munshin." Max introduced them. "Baby's kid. I've told you about him. He's here helping me keep the place oiled."

Jeffrey's direct stare, his oddly knowing eyes, made Cathy blush and duck her head.

"Hi," was all she got out.

Jeffrey stood up in front of the money-case and gave her a bow. "How-do-you-do." Then he sat back down. Cathy was disconcerted by the child's presence. She wanted to ask Max a lot of personal questions. She wanted to tell him how much she loved him and how frightened she had been. How frightened she *was.* Max understood, but he did not dismiss Jeffrey.

"You can talk in front of Jeffrey. He's on my side."

"Oh, Max!" she moaned. "I haven't seen you for so long and then to find you here! Like this!"

"Come on, sweetheart. It's not a big deal. I'm telling you. Go wash your face. And blow your nose."

Cathy fished in her coat pocket for Kleenex, found one, and gave her nose a stentorian honk. It made Max smile.

"Oh, Max . . ."

"Come on. Try a whole sentence. One that doesn't begin with 'Oh, Max.'"

"After you get the . . . the *thing* put in . . . will you still be . . . you know . . ." Max had not seen her in this splendid a flush for a long time. From her chest, where her chin had sunk, her words, muffled, but audible to Max, stuttered forth. ". . . the *same?* I mean . . . the *same?*"

He laughed. "Absolutely, sweetheart. Maybe even better. Rossman claims there's no blockage, but if there's not, then why the hell did I ever get tired? Not enough oxygen pumping through, that's why. Sweetheart, once I've got the gadget in there, I'll be able to climb Everest in patent-leather pumps and fuck every thousand feet. Going up, coming down."

Jeffrey sat. Cathy squirmed. Max was regally unconcerned with propriety.

Cathy whispered so softly that Max, only inches from her mouth, could scarcely hear her words. "I love you, Max. I love you *so*. I wouldn't want to live without you."

She meant it. Max's heart skipped a beat . . . Jesus! Not that again! He slapped an admonishing hand over his heart and used his other palm to push the girl away from him.

"Sweetheart . . . not here . . . give me a break . . . you're going to have to hang in there . . . just for a week . . ."

The door opened and a young black nurse came in, pushing a tray containing an assortment of chrome and enamel vessels and instruments. Max sat up. Alert as an animal at bay, he glared at the tray.

"Good evening, Mr. Herschel," the nurse said cheerfully. "I'm going to get you ready for tomorrow morning . . ."

The hell she was! Max swung around toward Jeffrey and rubbed his four fingers back and forth rapidly against his thumb, a gesture which, east or west, implied *money*. Jeffrey trotted over, extracting a large roll of bills from his pocket.

The nurse smiled down at Cathy. "I'm afraid it's all over for visiting . . ."

"Oh, Max!" Cathy wailed.

"You go on back home now, sweetheart. I'll call you as soon as I come out of the operating room, okay?" He kissed his forefinger and waggled it at her. He was hard put to give her the attention she deserved because he had to keep both eyes on the treacherous nurse.

"I'll sleep here at the hospital, Max! I'll sleep in the waiting room!"

"I want you to go *home*," Max said. "Now do what I tell you and don't give me any trouble, sweetheart. You go on out and *go home*. I'll call you tomorrow."

Cathy gave Max a long, anguished look, then turned and fled. He caught the sound of a muffled sob as the door closed behind her.

Max wanted to call the poor little thing back, to comfort her, but he had this nurse on his hands.

The nurse turned to Jeffrey. "You too, young man. You'll have to go too."

"The kid stays," Max said. "It's all taken care of."

"Who says?" the nurse challenged, good-humored but tough.

"Dr. Rossman, Dr. Jowdy, Dr. Collins, and the head nurse on this floor . . ." Max looked to Jeffrey for the name.

"Miss Delano," Jeffrey said.

"Yeah. Miss Delano. Read the chart, sweetheart."

The nurse eyed Max, then Jeffrey, then picked up the chart and read it carefully. She looked up at the undersized Arab urchin.

"Your name Jeffrey Munshin?"

"Jeffrey Munshin," the boy affirmed.

The nurse shrugged. "No skin off mine." She turned back to her tray. "Okay, Mr. Herschel. Now I'll have to ask you to take off your . . ."

Max snapped his fingers, Jeffrey handed Max the roll of bills. Max peeled off two fifties, and stuck them into the nurse's uniform pocket. She looked suspiciously at Max, then Jeffrey, then she reached into her pocket and pulled out the bills. Her eyes widened and she gave a little whistle.

"A hundred dollars? What for?"

"For *no enema.*"

"No enema?"

"*No enema,*" Max repeated.

Max Herschel and the twenty-four-year-old black girl from southeast Texas stared at each other for a long, drawn-out moment. Then, the girl raised one shoulder in a half shrug.

"Okay, Mr. Herschel. Money talks. No enema."

Max let out a gigantic sigh of relief.

"But I'm gonna have to shave your chest."

"That's okay, sweetheart, Have at it." Cheerfully, Max began unbuttoning his pajama top.

Half an hour later, the nurse was gone, leaving Max and Jeffrey at peace for the night. They were reading *Playboy* and the *National Enquirer.*

In the nurses' center, the black girl had moaned with pleasure and laughed until her ribs ached. "A hundred bucks for not giving an enema I wasn't gonna give in the first place! That Mr. Herschel's my kind of man!"

The operation was performed at seven the next morning. Dr. Collins, the surgeon, assisted by Dr. Rossman, inserted the pacemaker in the region of Max's right pectoral. The operation was completed in fifty-five minutes, during which time Max lectured steadily on the technique of the endocardial approach. Dr. Collins moved surely through each step as Max coached him, encouraged him, made every effort to build the surgeon's confidence.

When the operation was over and Max was being wheeled out of the operating room, he smiled at Dr. Collins with approval.

"We make a good team," he complimented the surgeon.

A great sigh was caught and held behind Dr. Rossman's surgical mask.

Chapter 23

When Max was out of surgery, Stella called Bones again.

"He's great. Directed the whole operation. He's back in his room sipping a lemonade. He's going to have a sore chest for a few days and he can't use the microwave oven anymore, and he's out several thousand bucks but he's delighted with himself and the new tick-tock."

"Stella, he really didn't have a heart attack? Please be honest with me."

"He really didn't, Bones."

"Then I don't understand why . . ."

"What's to understand? He *wanted* it."

"Connie? Because of Connie?"

Stella's sigh wafted over the wire. "What difference does it make?"

"How long will he be in the hospital?" Bones asked.

"Five or six days. And you know what?" Stella laughed. "When he gets out, he's going to be worse than ever."

"Fun for everyone."

Once again Stella was unable to interpret the off-note in Bones' voice.

"Are *you* okay, Bones?"

"Sure, why wouldn't I be?"

Liar, Stella thought. But what she said was, "Bones, he's going to want to see you pretty soon. He told me."

"Tell him to fuck off," Bones said mildly, without energy. "When he gets out of the hospital."

"Don't cut off your nose, honey," Stella advised. She was uneasy about Bones. Something was very wrong. "How's the hubby?"

Bones laughed a little at that. "The hubby's great. He's still out there. Working very hard."

Stella did not know what else to say, so she said good-bye, and promised to keep Bones posted.

When Bones did not hear from Baby, she decided she would wait on the jewelry until things were back to normal with the Herschel family.

After seeing Benechek, she had had a urine test. She was pregnant. It had happened, she felt sure, that last night with Steven. Something in her had given up, had given up and given in. So now she had what she had wanted. What she had waited for and worried about. Christ. She had, she figured, seven months, maybe less, to get money, to hire Clegg Pruder, to squeeze a good script out of him, to sell the result to a studio or a distributor . . . she could make it. There was enough time.

So why was she crying?

She waked abruptly and sat up in bed. It hadn't been a rat. It had been a mouse. It was . . . Mickey Mouse.

Bones turned on the light.

Mickey Mouse a *sauce cook?* In a tall hat and an apron? But if he was a cook why wasn't the tall hat rounded like a chef's? It wasn't. It was pointed and had a brim.

Bones worried with the dream as if her life depended on it.

Mickey's hat was pointed. Like a witch's hat . . . like the hat he wore in *Fantasia* . . . as the . . . what? She began to sweat. Cold, sick sweat. *Apprentice!* The *apron* . . . then she caught the visual pun . . . the *approntice*. Mickey Mouse was the Sorcerer's Apprentice. *Sauce—Sorce—Sorcerer*. The apprentice . . . only a novice. He hadn't learned all the spells yet, the right incantations. He couldn't control the cauldron's mix, and when it overflowed, Bones had been caught in the deadly flood along with him. Caught with the *apprentice* sorcerer . . .

The meaning of the dream became perfectly clear. She shivered, too frightened to weep.

"You want to see what high-hats are made of, sweetheart? . . . They're made of the same thing *we're* made of," Max had said. So Steven was not different. He was not magic. He was just a man. Max's religious conviction in the cosmic corruptibility of all men was the true religion? Steven was only . . . Max's apprentice? The sorcerer's apprentice. She had forsaken the security of the wizard's world to take her chances with . . . just another man? Just another man. In that moment, knowing the child was in her, and that she was adrift with it, cut off and helplessly adrift, she found her own frontier of fear. For the first time in thirty-one years, Bones looked life squarely in the face, and saw it as a ringer for death. One or the other, life or death, both were terrible . . . terrible . . .

It was the third day after the operation, and Cathy still refused to go home except to bathe and change clothes. Whenever she was allowed, she sat in Max's room chattering cheerfully and touching him often. When she was dismissed, she sat in the visitors' lounge with her school books. She also slept in the visitors' lounge. Which upset Max. But she would not leave the building and there were no empty hospital rooms to rent for her. It was all very dramatic and flattering and Max relished it, but at the same time, on a deeper level, the girl's tenacity and devotion made him profoundly uneasy.

Jeffrey watched and listened and the impression he got was mysterious.

Max was afraid of the young girl. Jeffrey began to watch and listen with the intensity of a hunting dog on the point.

He froze, became one with the background, as Baby talked to Max about the girl.

"Well, sweetheart," Max chuckled nervously, "the kid loves me."

"It's worse than that, Daddy. She's *in love* with you. Going through that lounge is like running a gauntlet for the rest of us. She sits out there waiting to pounce, just for the chance to *talk* about you."

Max's "Yeah" was noncommittal. Baby squeezed up her eyes and tried to see Max as Cathy must. Baby understood the tidal pull of Max's sex appeal. She had felt it herself. All her life. The magnet of that terrible seductive energy. The mesmerizing effect of his attention . . . always brief, but devastating in its effect. Plus the practiced, theatrical exercise of power. Baby had no trouble understanding the sexual dynamics. Even for a girl Cathy's age. What Baby had trouble grasping was the violently *romantic* nature of the girl's affliction. Baby had never seen any of Max's other girls in that condition. It did not seem . . . reasonable.

"How do you feel about *her*, Daddy? I mean I know you . . ."

"I adore her, sweetheart. I adore her."

But he adored them all, thought Baby. She felt ashamed for someone . . . for him or Cathy or herself . . .

"She seems very bright," she tried.

"Bright as paint. You know I think she's smarter than Bones? I mean than Bones was at that age."

"Daddy, aren't you ever going to see Bones again? Be friends?"

"I'm thinking about it."

"Let her come to the hospital. I know she'd like to." She gave him a hard look. "What's the matter? Are you afraid to let her see you in a weakened condition?"

He laughed, then sighed. "Shit." He gave a bark of angry laughter. "You know something, Baby? There isn't much I wouldn't give to have Connie back."

Baby swallowed hard and leaned over Max and kissed him, then she made ready to leave. She asked Max if Cathy should come in, but Max said no, not yet, he had at least twenty phone calls to make. Max had had two private lines installed and had laid a fortune on the switchboard. He was again in *contact*, the scar on his chest had begun to itch reassuringly; he was almost back to business as usual. Almost ready for Bones business. Max patted Baby's hand and told her to see if she couldn't get Cathy to go *out*, take in a movie, or go shopping. Buy something pretty. Buy *anything*. Baby said she'd try.

"She doesn't have a real knack for spending," Max confided to Baby, his voice edged with misgiving.

Jeffrey, sitting on the money-case, peeled the wrapper off his third Mars Bar of the day. He had listened not only to Max's words, he had listened to the melody. And the dominant note that he had heard was fear. Max was afraid. He was afraid of the girl. Jeffrey knew it.

After Baby left, Jeffrey spoke.

"Where do the family of Miss Kronig live, sir? Are they far away?"

Max turned suddenly combative eyes onto the boy. Jeffrey met the look and shrugged his bony little shoulders.

"I only asked, sir. I meant nothing."

Max continued to glare at the boy, who lowered his own eyes and nibbled at the Mars Bar.

"Jeffrey."

"Sir?"

"I want you to make a phone call for me."

"Certainly, sir. Who must I call?"

Max lay his head back against the pillows and sighed.

"I don't want you to say I told you to call. You just call up and say that . . ." He amused himself in the concoction of the speech Jeffrey was to deliver.

"You say that Mr. Herschel *needs* her. At the hospital. Don't say anything more than that. Tell her to come straight to the room without speaking to anybody. Then you say good-bye like you're in a hurry. And hang up quick."

Jeffrey knew beyond a doubt that he was being asked to call in

Miss Burton. The *old* whore. Jeffrey understood expedience. There was a fire in the young girl that the Father sensed was getting out of control. Fire you fight with fire. Jeffrey understood everything, but when Max asked, "Have you got it straight, kid?", Jeffrey kept his eyes blank and asked in turn, "Who is it that I speak to, sir?"

Max picked up the phone and began dialing.

"You speak to Miss Burton, Jeffrey." He handed the receiver to the boy.

When Bones heard Jeffrey's soft, foreign voice on the line, she was instantly alerted. And when Max's creature announced that she was needed, needed by Mr. Herschel, her thrill of vengeful triumph was intense as a jolt of electricity. He *needed* her! He could *rot!* But in the moment before she spoke, the image of the Gulbenkian vase, sitting in timeless beauty on a table in Bel Air, flashed before her in flawless detail. Why had Max given up the vase?

When Max gave something up, he expected something in return. Something real, an asset. Not the empty negation of revenge. Then for what? To . . . get her back? *To get her back.* Everything he had done . . . had been done to get her back? She closed her eyes against the sweet dizzying drug of her pleasure.

Jeffrey, his eyes wide with worry at the prolonged silence on the other end of the line, looked to Max for a cue. Max snapped his fingers at the boy, signaling him to press on, and Jeffrey spoke again.

"Miss . . . why do you not answer?"

Bones expelled all the stale air from her lungs. Greedily, she sucked in a fast, fresh breath and told Jeffrey she would get to Mt. Gilead as soon as she dressed.

Jeffrey murmured "Thank you, Miss," and hung up, nodding affirmatively at Max. Max sighed deeply and lay back, his eyes on the Matisse. After a moment's thought, he turned to the boy and gave him instructions. And then rehearsed him.

When he had performed twice to Max's satisfaction, Jeffrey went out for another candy bar. He was excited and nervous. He craved the sugar. On his way to the vending machine in the visitors' lounge, he passed Cathy. Jeffrey smiled. He liked Cathy. His black eyes slid in her direction and noted that the girl, curled up in an uncomfortable chair, was immersed in a textbook.

Jeffrey dropped a quarter in the machine and punched the Mars Bar button. The candy fell free. Then, thoughtfully, he put a second coin into the candy machine. He walked back by Cathy, stopped in front of her, held out a Mars Bar. She looked up and accepted the offering with gratitude. Gratitude not just for the candy, but for Jeffrey's acknowledgment of her existence.

"Why, thank you, Jeffrey."

"That's okay," he said, silken lids and thick black lashes lowering discreetly over his eyes. He wondered what it must be like to use this clean, pretty girl for pleasure. He wondered why Max feared her so. She was very nice, but only a girl, like any other. He, Jeffrey, was already twelve. Almost a man. The girl was only seven years older. He hoped that by the time he was thirteen she would still be as pretty and as clean-looking as she was now. Jeffrey desired Cathy. He bestowed on her a promissory smile, then went back to Max's room, and sat down upon the money to wait for the other one.

Chapter 24

As her taxi approached the corner which formed the apex of Mt. Gilead's gigantic ell, the word HERSCHEL leapt out at her. She saw that it was boldly painted on a sign attached to the front of a commercial building which adjoined one end of the ell.

She tapped on the plastic screen behind the driver's head. "I'll get out here."

Bones paid and walked over to the sign.

To Be Constructed on this Site,
A NEW HOSPITAL WING, DONATED TO
Mt. Gilead Hospital by MAXIMILIAN HERSCHEL.
This wing will be devoted to the study
and treatment of special diseases.

Oh, Max, Bones thought. *You* are a very special disease.

Jeffrey had told Bones the room number, told her to take the stairs and come through the visitors' lounge, down the hall to the left and straight to Room 294. She was not to knock, just slip in.

Bones entered the lounge, giving a passing glance to the only person in it, a young girl bent over a book.

Something familiar about the girl caused Bones to falter, look closer. The girl glanced up. Bones and Cathy stared at one another. The woman from Gum Springs, North Carolina, and the girl from Flatcar, Missouri. They did not speak. Cathy sat, with her hands frozen around her book; Bones stood rooted, her face protectively empty of expression until her mind began to work again. When it did, she broke the tableau, nodded gently at Cathy, and walked on.

When Bones opened the door, moving discreetly into 294, Max was on the telephone, listening to Bernie scream. All the way across the room, Bones could hear the echoes of Bernie's tantrum . . . something about Max's will . . . "got all they fucking deserve! Let it stand! Not another fucking penny you out of your mind? You in the psycho ward over there or what? . . ."

Max looked up, saw Bones.

"Talk to you later, Bernie. I seem to have a visitor." He hung up, his look of surprise changing to one of ominous exasperation.

"Who the hell let you in?" he demanded.

Involuntarily, Bones' eyes swept toward Jeffrey, who jumped to his feet. Shooting a guilty look at Max, the boy made a bee-line for the door. He did not run, but he reached the exit in record time.

"Come back here you fucking little wog! Did you have something to do with *her?*"

But Jeffrey was gone.

Outside in the hall, he stopped short, grinning. He had performed well. He put his ear up to the closed door, but it was metal and heavy and he could not hear through it. Then he remembered Cathy. In a flash, he was off to the lounge. He would use this time to comfort the girl. Reassure her.

Bones had Max alone, but she was off-base. Max had not sent

for her. But the boy . . . she couldn't think. She could not take her eyes off Max, that seemingly ordinary old man in rumpled pajamas, slumped in a hospital bed, needing a shave, and looking at her with something less than warmth. A spasm of longing tore through her, twisting at the very linchpin of her structure.

She surrendered. "I'm back, Max. Here I am."

"Is that a fact?" he snapped. "Where's your husband?"

"Where you sent him."

Even as she walked to the bed and brushed his lips dryly with her own, she warned herself how much she still had to lose. How cautious she must be.

"You don't look sick, Max," she said. "How do you feel?"

"Never felt better." He gave her a slightly more tolerant look as he scratched his scar. "Okay, Bones, since you've traipsed all the way up here, you might as well sit down for a minute." He indicated a chair placed at a nice distance from him. She sat, silently, obediently.

"You come through the visitors' room?"

Bones swallowed painfully. She nodded. "If you mean did I see Cathy, the answer is yes, I did."

"That's a great little girl," he scowled. "Very loyal. And *bright*."

Bones kept the bitterness she felt out of her voice. "Stella told me she got herself into Barnard." Bones even disciplined her mouth into a smile. "She's out there in the lounge studying calculus."

The word "calculus" raised Max's simmering anxiety. The anxiety proved greater than his instinct for self-preservation. He let the words spill out.

"She's going to marry me."

Bones stared at him. Not "I'm going to marry her" but "She's going to marry me."

Max was scared.

Ah. He *had* sent for her. The scene with Jeffrey had been an act. He was scared and he needed her. She started to speak, stopped short. Once again the image of the vase came to her. But . . . he had given up the vase before Connie died. So he not only needed her, he *wanted* her. *The war was still on.*

Leaning back in the chair, she counted slowly to five, then spoke.

"I'm sorry about Connie, Max."

"I couldn't help her, Bones . . ." Max mourned sincerely. Then, anger bubbling up along with the frustration: "I couldn't do a goddam thing. I was *helpless*." He fell heavily silent.

She sat just as silent, waiting for his next move. After a few moments, he looked up, gave her face a hard once-over.

"You don't look bad, Bones. For a thirty-one-year-old broad."

"I'll be thirty-two soon."

Max grinned malevolently. "What do you want for your birthday?"

"What would you like to give me?"

"I'd like to give you a kick in the ass." He shrugged. "Well, where's the litter? I thought by now you'd have one by the hand and another in the pouch."

She felt sweat pop out on her neck and under her arms. How did he . . . *Stop that*, she cautioned herself. He knew nothing. Nothing.

Bones knew that if she wanted to keep this baby, she was going to have to get Max out of that bed and into hers. Within days. Because if there was one thing Max could do, it was count. The big thing she had going for her was that he would be anxious to try out the pacemaker, and he would probably prefer the trial run in old, familiar waters.

Bones managed to present Max with a rueful little face.

"No litter."

"No? How come?"

"It just didn't work out. Nothing worked out."

Max softened visibly.

"Why not? I thought everything was going to be so 'different.' I mean with such a 'different' type of guy."

"He isn't all that different."

"That a fact? Not so much 'better'?"

"Not really."

"Then what?"

"He's . . . nicer. That's all. Just a little nicer."

"Any of it rub off on you?"

"Maybe a little. Not much. But a little."

Max snorted. "The poet's so nice, then what are you doing here?"

"I was told you needed me, but," she risked the bluff, "I don't believe you do. It was a mistake. I'd better go." She started to stand up, he gestured her back down.

"Sit down. You're here, you're here." Maliciously, he echoed her first words to him: "I'm back, Max . . . *here I am!*'"

She sat silent, not answering, letting him rag her, maintaining a distantly affectionate smile.

He lay back, again scratched his scar pleasurably with his left hand, as he carefully stretched the right one behind his head.

"Tell me all about the movie business."

"I was only out there once. I ran into Seymour Berger."

Max's shiny black eyes never wavered. "You saw Seymour? How was he? His wife died, too, you know."

"He looked terrible. Very old . . . frail."

Now his eyes narrowed in quick interest. Bones leaned slightly forward.

"Max . . . darling . . . I'm sorry about your vase."

"What vase?"

"The Gulbenkian. I saw it. Mr. Berger's got his wife's ashes in it."

Max froze. "Ashes? Seymour had Marsha *cremated?* A good Jew like Seymour? I don't believe it."

"He said you had to move with the times. Anyway, he did it, and his Marsha's in the vase."

"Jesus Christ."

She repeated, slowly, testing the water. "I'm sorry about the vase, Max. I know you loved it."

"What are *you* sorry about? I had some business with Seymour and couldn't move him without a little schmeer. The vase is only on loan. I get it back when he dies."

Bones should have known. Should have known Max would hold the string. He nodded, comfortable in the conviction of where the vase would finally end up. "You say he looks bad?"

"Yes, he does."

Max frowned. "What if when I get the vase back . . . what the hell am I supposed to do with Marsha's ashes?"

Bones couldn't help it, he was so preposterous. She laughed.

Max remembered he was the host.

"Want a drink?"

"No, nothing, thanks."

Bones had pulled her hair back and tied it in a ponytail. That was how she had been wearing it that day at Abercrombie's. Had she consciously done it that way again, Max wondered? Did she have the fishhooks concealed somewhere? Sure she did.

"You made me pretty mad when you took off the way you did, you know that?"

"You made it quite clear."

"How are you fixed for cash?"

"You owe me fifty thousand from Burton Productions and you're holding out ninety thousand dollars in bonds that belong to me. That's how I'm fixed."

"You mean you haven't collected your dough? Christ, I don't know what happened," Max scowled. "Some problem with Bernie, I guess. But he only tries to do what's best for me. You know that, sweetheart. He just gets overzealous sometimes."

"Sure."

"Still have the apartment?"

She nodded.

"Hung on to your jewelry, I hope."

"Not easy to sell. No major stones."

Max laughed. "You never would listen to me. You were always going on and on about 'style' and things that were '*you*.' So much for *you*, kid." Her face remained serene, granting nothing to his cruelty.

She smiled, delivered her own blow. "I sold the fishhooks. I needed cash to get an option on a property. So I sold the hooks."

Max couldn't believe it. He felt the flush hit his face. She'd sold *those?*

He was conscious of a stinging pull in the raw new scar. He wanted to touch it to reassure himself. But he did not.

"What did you get for them?"

"Nine thousand."

"I paid thirty!"

"I knew they were worth a lot more than nine, but I took what I could get. I wanted that option."

She *wanted!* The cunt *wanted!* He studied that little-girl face, looking for some sign that she was trying to rinky-dink him. But, no—he believed her. She had really sold his lures . . . One thing about Bones. She had always been good for a surprise. She hadn't changed.

"Tell me where you sold them. I'll get them back."

Only his eyes showed his fatigue. Bones longed to give vent to her pity, her love. But she curbed the dangerous rush of emotion, drove it safely back. And was rewarded almost immediately.

"Bones, that little kid . . . Cathy." The look of fatigue spread from his eyes. It moved into the lines of his forehead, his mouth. "She loves me. This is not bullshit. I mean the kid is in *love* with me. And she's a very special little girl. Bright and nice and *good*. She's going to be a banker."

Bones bit the inside of her cheeks. "My word."

Max squinted suspiciously. "I'm telling you the fucking truth."

"I believe you."

"I tell you she *loves me*."

All right, Bones decided. Throw the die now. She leaned toward him, spoke slowly, softly, but with great intensity, her words carefully spaced and enunciated. "Max, I'm going to tell you something. I'm only going to say it once, so listen closely, because I won't ever say it again."

His eyes glittered; he leaned toward her.

"*What?* What is it?"

"I love you too."

Bones counted slowly. She got to five before Max began to laugh. He collapsed on his pillow, howling with laughter. He laughed till he hurt. Until he had to put both hands protectively over his scar.

Bones sat and watched him, satisfied with his reaction to her sentimental declaration.

At last he brought himself under control. He wiped his eyes with his wrists, peered nervously inside his pajama top to be sure he had not split his stitches. Then, he blew his nose and lay back

[340]

with a deeply contented sigh. Neither of them spoke for a while.

"Bones," he said finally. "I'd rather marry *you*."

It was the last thing in the world she had expected to hear. Reactions . . . answers . . . ideas . . formed and re-formed in crazy patterns, but the thought that held sway over all the others was that if she married Max she could positively keep the baby. And not have to give a damn about *anything* ever again. Not even that the baby wasn't his. Because by the time he found out, if they were married, Max wouldn't care. If he *owned* the baby, had stamped it with his name, Bones knew Max would figure he had rolled Steven for a bonus.

She made a tentative move toward opening the negotiations.

"If I ever did marry you, Max . . . and I'm pretty sure I never would . . ."

"Why not?"

"You'd be a pain in the ass as a husband." She lifted her shoulders gently. "And I don't believe marriage is exactly *my* thing, either."

"Sweetheart, you've got to look at marriage like a *deal* . . ."

She nodded. Her nod said, yes, yes, she could appreciate that way of looking at it . . . nevertheless . . .

"A deal with both parties agreeing to certain principles. You've got to work out the terms. Get the quid pro quos all nice and tidy. Know what I mean, sweetheart? You can't just run off blind like you did with . . ." He stopped himself. "But what were you trying to say . . . if you ever did marry me? *What?* You were getting ready to name a condition. Right? What was it?"

"That if the occasion arose, you wouldn't get Stella to make me an appointment with Benechek."

As Max considered this, Bones realized that she was in jeopardy. Benechek knew the dates. Max shouldn't hear them too soon. She would have to square Benechek. The pulse in her temples hammered. She began the mental exercise of relaxing her muscles, one by one by one, starting with the scalp but skipping the face, because she had to keep her smile steady.

"Okay. God forbid, but agreed. If the occasion arises. But listen, sweetheart," he snapped his fingers at her. "Don't get big ideas. The occasion probably won't arise. Because let's get it straight right now." He grinned. "I won't be home a lot. On a regular basis, sweetheart, you won't be getting much."

She had never supposed she would.

"What do you want to do about Cathy?" she asked gently.

"*Keep* her. I'm going to keep her. I don't want to marry her. But I want to keep her."

"All right." Bones went to the heart of the matter. "I won't let her marry you." She paused. "And I couldn't care less if you keep her," she lied, her smile steady.

They now moved into principal clauses and conditions.

"I know you, Bones. You're a greedy girl. You're going to try to gouge me, sweetheart. I know that. So speak right up. Just tell me what you want. Then I'll tell you what's possible. I'll tell you *my* terms. And we'll hammer it all out together, sweetheart."

"Max, I'm not even going to *consider* marrying you or talking about terms or anything until you show a little good faith. You took me over the coals and that's okay. But you had no reason or right to try to pulverize Steven. You did some pretty shitty things."

Max's eyebrows raised incredulously. "*What?*"

"Darby Press. I want you to let his book come out the way it should."

Max agreed without hesitation.

"Okay. I read the book. *Myself*," he said proudly. "It's pretty good. Make a good movie. We handle it right, it'll be a winner for us."

Bones asked, "By 'us' you mean the publishing house?"

Max nodded.

"Do you mind telling me how you got in there? With no noise?"

"Paper. For their paperback line. They needed Canadian paper and they needed it *bad*. Derek made the deal with Darby. Canadian paper at a price they couldn't turn down. Derek handled it. Very nice."

Bones laughed. "Max, stop it. Stop calling Morris by that ridiculous name!"

Max was indignant.

"What's ridiculous about 'Derek'? It's a great name. It's a great *Canadian* name."

She sighed, relieved and happy to be home. "You'll bring the book out right, the way it deserves, and you'll let Steven go. Leave him alone. He hasn't anything to do with us anymore. He's out of it."

"Okay. You want Routledge out. He's out. Personally, sweetheart," Max beamed, "I never wanted him in." He paused, considered. "However, he and I have some unsettled business. We had an agreement. I carried out my end of the bargain, but he owes."

"What?"

"We agreed I would get his first book to somebody in Hollywood, and he would get that goddam vase dug up and schlepped out of Aleppo for me. He's never done a damn thing about that vase."

"Just remind him. In the same memo that advises him of a twenty-five thousand first printing on *The Nephew*."

Bones knew that sooner or later, Steven would write about Max. About Max and her. And that what he wrote could hurt. But she would not tell Max this. Let it happen. Max had it coming. So did she. They would just have to take their knocks.

Figuring he was finished with Steven, Max nodded. So much for the poet. Max wanted to get down to the real business. He knew perfectly well that despite Bones' protestations, she had come here expecting to deal. What she had not expected was that when she sat down at the table, she was going to be tendered an offer infinitely bigger and juicier than she had dreamed of getting. She was *creaming* to parley. He reckoned that he had better begin by giving her a couple of shots . . . not too damaging, but hard enough to open up old scars, let her bleed a little.

"Let's hear what it is you want, darling. I wouldn't like to get in over my head if you're going to make it too tough for me. I'd rather pull back right now . . . I'm making you a big offer. Big enough so I don't feel you're due many concessions. Nevertheless, I'm willing to listen. If you've got terms, I'll hear you out. But let's be honest, sweetheart. Let's put our cards on the table. You tried to shit me. Right? So, we've got a couple of little problems going in. One, *trust*. You shook my trust in you. Two, you don't have the same assets you had a year ago. A year ago you were riding high. You had money, you had a business going for you." He gave her face and body a critical up-and-down. "You were a year younger."

She never hesitated. "So were you, Max. And you had a wife for protection. Now you're alone with that lovelorn little teenager snapping at your ass. And you've got a dicy heart. That's *really* something to consider. Who knows? You could wind up an invalid, with me having to take care of you." She leaned back, crossed her ankles and pointed her toes, which now floated above the floor. "I wouldn't like that, you know."

Max's eyes glittered combatively. He admired the ferocity of her attack. If he had taught her nothing else, he had taught her to go for the jugular. This year hadn't weakened her. She was strong and tough and he was proud of her. She was *his*.

"So call your little shots."

"I want Warner's head," she opened.

"You've got it."

"And Mark's."

"Don't be mean, sweetheart."

"And Mark's."

"We'll discuss it."

"I want that studio."

"No dice."

She felt a shot of pure adrenalin. *"I want that studio."*

Max lay back and took both the private lines off their hooks. He smiled beatifically as he picked up the hospital phone, waited for the switchboard to answer.

"Hullo, honey. This is Max. Don't put any calls through here till I ring you back . . ." He was still talking as he returned the phone to its cradle. " . . . I'm negotiating."